The Long Lost Future

Ian Cattell

To Mom and Dad. Wherever they are now.

For anyone who's ever looked at the state of the world
and thought... 'Seriously? Are you kidding me?'

Thanks to enthusiasm provider and online joke-tester Mary-Ann Kent -
Mat Taylor, who utilised his entire highlighter pen
collection on the draft manuscript -
and Yeti, who just wanted to get her name in a book.

Special thanks to Phil Brownlow for the fantastic cover art
(http://www.philbrownlow.co.uk/) -
Frank Zappa for the word 'deflicted' -
and Lyons Ltd, for Viscount minty biscuits.

Find out more at -
www.iancattell.online

Any similarity to persons living or
dead is probably synchronistic.
Perhaps...

About the author

Ian Cattell is a software developer who wanted a change from staring blankly at a computer screen all day. So he decided to write a book.

Yeah, I know...

Over the next six months he learned that there are many advantages to writing a book compared to writing software, the main one being that he doesn't have to re-write it whenever Microsoft decides it's "time".

He enjoys astronomy, baking organic bread, and trying to figure out why some people insist on using Macs - but when his neighbour is out he likes to play his drums. He's got a Roland TD-11KV with the extra CY-12 Crash cymbal and double kick pedals, he runs it through a 150W Mosfet PA amp via a BOSS...

Oh... your eyes have glazed over... never mind.

...

Time is notoriously tricky stuff.

It's a pretty slippery concept for even the brightest of brainsteins. One of the most difficult concepts there is, in fact. Very hard to grasp indeed - in quite a number of ways.

Where does it come from? Where is it going? Why is it there? What, actually, is it?

Some of the tippy-toppest of top thinkers have even suggested that it doesn't actually exist; that time is an illusion caused by... er, well... they're not quite sure what it's caused by - let's just call it "energy" of some sort, that should cover it. Moving on...

It flows - though we don't know how, or why it chooses to flow in the direction it does; it can be stretched and warped - if luminaries like Roddenberry or Asimov are to be believed; it's very probably infinitely long - not that anybody's ever likely to measure it; it stops when you're in love - which is nice; it slows down when you're moving, and it speeds up when you're not - which is daft, surely.

It also slows down when you're *bored* and speeds up when you're not. And that simply has to be the wrong way round.

Someone should complain.

You can make it, you can save it, you can buy it, you can spend it, you can waste it, you can serve it, you can tell it, and you can run out of it.

But one thing you can't do is escape it.

Or so they say...

Chapter 1.

Randall James lay back on his bed staring absent-mindedly through the window at the sky. He couldn't actually see the sky - the rain was in the way - but he didn't mind; the steady drumming on his roof and gurgle of the gutter was relaxing, and had put him in a nostalgic mood. Happy memories of his school days were playing out in his mind.

Lying in a small boulder-field of self-inflicted biscuit crumbs, on his comfortable but worn out mattress, in the sock-strewn bedroom of his small but acceptably serviceable house on the outskirts of the averagely well-off district he lived in, he was relaxing at the end of a longish day, cheerfully remembering his reasonably happy time at the slightly above average school he'd attended.

He smiled as he remembered the certificates he'd been awarded on his last day. He'd got pretty good grades in the essentials - Panglish, Citizenship, and Media Studies - but as he walked across the stage to collect his recommended vocation from the careerbot, he knew he wouldn't be following its advice. The exciting life in advertising he was destined for didn't appeal to him very much.

Randall had other plans...

He was lucky enough to be a relatively wealthy man, that is to say, his relatives were quite wealthy and he was now a man, and he enjoyed the modest benefits of the moderately affluent - such as being able to avoid having his mind turned to mince working at GloboCo Media, for example.

The family money came largely from his long deceased grandfather, and to some extent his probably deceased father, who had both been successful inventors. In fact, as far as Randall could tell, his ancestral family line was scattered with intellectuals, scientists, and inventors, and he was quietly proud of the fact.

As he rolled over in bed, memories of the time he'd first studied his ancestry, as a gangly, acne ridden, twelve-year-old drifted across his mind. It was a rather odd project he had thought at the time; genealogy was something anyone could do if they had a terminal, and he didn't see much educational benefit in it, but he worked at it diligently anyway, as he always usually sometimes did. Perhaps his teacher, Mr. Han, inspired by Randall's illustrious recent ancestors, thought it would be useful to the class somehow.

Trawling through nearly six hundred years of computer records showed that until fairly recently his family were quite ordinary, but also quite ludicrously lucky over the generations...

According to the databases he'd managed to access, the luck appeared to start five hundred and twenty-seven years ago, when his ancestor had escaped the utter devastation of the Earth Shifts by choosing that month to go to the newly established Starlight Hotel on the Moon. Had he been at home in California he would most certainly have died - along with the two billion or so others lost in the cataclysm.

It took a hundred and fifty years for the world to recover, and information about the period was unreliable to say the least, but the next notable record of his ancestors' exploits was every bit as fortunate.

Peter Stuart James had been living very happily with his latest wife in an expensive part of Rome for five years when a massive earthquake destroyed most of the city. He and his family would have been killed outright - had it not been for the fact that, once again, they weren't there at the time.

Peter had been something of an amateur historian, and had spent extensive periods in the Vatican Archive studying the history and catastrophic decline of the Catholic Church following the Earth Shifts. Strangely, however, just as he was about to publish his first historical paper (entitled, rather pompously, "The death of religion: Why Pope Bonoface [1] was assassinated") he suddenly upped sticks and went to live with family in New Los Angeles.

In fact, when Randall looked into it, he discovered that they'd left Rome only the day before the quake. "Lucky" isn't the word...

---

[1] The Church desperately tried to update its image towards the end. Boniface was just *so* fourteenth century. And there'd already been eleven of them for Christ's sake.

The fifty-odd years that followed Peter's miraculous escape, were filled with stories of bankruptcy magically being turned into fortunes, and vice versa - mostly vice. Allegations were rife. Nothing was ever proven, but that was only because the people involved were subtly persuaded not to look very hard. The sudden and unaccountable increases in the investigators' personal wealth at the time attested to that.

But then, a hundred and seventy years later, the world famous Zachary James developed the first version of what was to become Temporal Vortex Theory; further refined fifty years later by his grandson Jon Z. James, using the new mathematics of Prof. Hochinara. The Hochinara/James effect, of course, being the basis of Randall's grandfather's invention, the Temporal Splitter; a device that enables the viewer to get hazy images of actual events from the past - if the viewer is an authorised, appointed, government sanctioned historian, of course.

The only real anomaly in this long line of illustrious luminaries, limited lawbreaking, and lucky layabouts was his late - or at least no longer on time for anything - father, George James Junior, the actual inventor of the time-travel machine itself; who in most people's eyes was neither illustrious nor lucky. The jury was still out on the lawbreaking too.

George Jr's father - Randall's grandfather - George Z. James, was a mathematics genius who had intimately studied the works of his ancestral namesakes for decades, before finally coming up with his Temporal Splitter and opening up the past for inquisitive (but not too inquisitive) historians. It was only then, at the age of sixty, that he married his long time lab-assistant and subsequently fathered George James Junior.

He died eleven years later aged seventy-one, after his third stress induced heart attack.

George Jr, contrastingly, grew up to be "a bit of a fly-by-night" as Randall's mother called him (or "dodgy little bastard", as everyone else called him). Drinking, gambling, womanising, fighting, drugs, shady business deals... the list goes on. If he hadn't actually invented the time machine in a "stroke of genius" at the age of twenty-five he would have been a nobody. And so would Randall. Literally. His mother would never have married his father had it not been for the fame and the money, so Randall wouldn't even exist. Probably.

His dad, like Randall himself, had received a good education, and was no intellectual slouch, but - as is often the case with children of the rich and famous - he lacked ambition. He was cocky and he was arrogant, but he was famous; or, more accurately, infamous. His life was an endless litany of less than flattering news reports about his various nefarious exploits and shameless shenanigans.

Until the "revelation" that suddenly enabled him to build the first time-travel machine in human history, of course. Then everything changed.

How he did it was anybody's guess. He never told anyone while he was alive, and now that he was almost certainly dead he was even quieter on the subject.

The world went completely mental upon the announcement that he had "cracked it" and would produce a working time machine within six months. The press release was met in equal amounts with amazement, bafflement, ridicule, and scorn - but he worked them all like a pro.

Milking the media is a skill few are blessed with, but George Jr seemed to have been touched by angels in this respect. He was on air almost every night for weeks, squeezing the golden teat of celebrity for every last drop. He even appeared on Davdroid Dimblebot's rather appropriately named panel show, Question Time.

His natural charm oozed out of the vid-screens and into the collective mind of the world, and he even became the media's new darling to some extent - but however much he was questioned by the pundits, he tenaciously kept the secret to himself, and would only reveal the science behind his discovery *after* he had built the machine.

Which, surprisingly, he did.

Twenty-seven weeks and a new bride later, he announced that he and his undisclosed contractors had succeeded and were testing the machine. Further announcements would be forthcoming.

If the world went mental last time, this time it went totally fruitcake. The network was full of it. Every ad-board, net-feed, terminal and VidCast in the world featured pictures of George Jr - often accompanied by a suitably alliterative headline like: "Genius or Joke? Is George James Junior Genuine?"

Unfortunately, George then spent a few days getting quite recklessly out of his mind on certain rather expensive illicit compounds his new friends in the media had introduced him to, and after a celebratory drunken binge one evening he jumped into his new time machine, with a mad laugh and a cry of "I'll fuckin' show 'em", before disappearing forever in a blinding flash of light.

He had at least had the foresight to record "The Departure", as it became known, on NetCam for all the world to see, but the date he departed *to* was lost forever due to the chrono-computer blowing a whiskey infused fuse the instant he disappeared.

Fortunately - for Randall at least - this all happened about two months after his father's wedding to his mother, so Randall was well on the way to existence when his father "Departed".

That old school genealogy project was now open on Randall's terminal as he lay in bed at the end of the day feeling nostalgic for his childhood. He scrolled through the pages slowly, with a smile on his face, recollecting the exploits of his early ancestors. It felt good to take his mind off things occasionally, now he was so busy researching all the time.

Time. The one thing he theoretically had in abundance thanks to the dad he'd never met, and the one thing he was forbidden to meddle with.

The whole "Time-travel thing", as Randall dismissively referred to it, was mopped up by the World Police as soon as it happened. The remaining transceiver section of the machine was rather clumsily confiscated almost immediately; leaving severed cables, shattered components, and broken noses strewn all around the contractor's facility.

The technology was then heavily discredited. A disinformation campaign was set up to show that the NetCam video was a hoax, and that George Jr had fled the country to escape his debts to the notorious drugs baron known as "Emperor" Sorosa. Temporal Vortex Theory was subsequently attacked in the popular science journals and it was "proven" shortly afterwards that time-travel was totally impossible. The only people who knew the reality of time-travel from that day forward were his long departed dad, the WP, and possibly some of the very hastily silenced contractors - if they were still alive.

But he was going to change all that...

As far as anyone who'd met him could tell, Randall was a bit of an oddball; understandable given his father's disappearance and the subsequent notoriety, and it was an image he was all too happy to portray. He was polite and respectful, but he came across as a slightly shy kind of guy who was living frugally off family money, and who mostly kept himself to himself.

Caring nothing for fashion, or trends, or sports, or any of the other irrelevances thrown up by his world, he lived a quiet little life in his quiet little house, carefully keeping his secret research hidden from the WP.

What nobody knew - because he made sure they didn't - is that he studied hard on the quiet. He read all his progenitors' works, published and private. Even though most of them had been banned he eventually managed to obtain a complete set. He got good at maths and electronics. He loved physics. He ate it and breathed it and he was going to recreate his father's greatest (and only) invention.

If only his dad had kept some records...

It was as if he'd simply clicked his fingers one day and schematics for the time machine magically appeared before him in a puff of fairy dust. There were no detailed theoretical descriptions, no notebooks, no rough diagrams on the backs of napkins, no invoices or receipts, and nothing in his diary apart from an entry on the day of the discovery which simply read: "Well that was interesting".

The only other record, apart from the video, was a note written about two hours before the Departure that Randall's mother kept from the World Police by the simple expedient of hiding it in her knickers. He was slightly less drunk and a bit more coherent when he wrote it, but it still didn't make much sense. It was a lot of barely decipherable scribbling about his "amazing revelation", and how the whole thing came to him one afternoon while he was smoking cannabis with an unnamed friend. No details about what actually came to him though, just hyperbole and bluster, but there was an interesting line towards the end of the note that read: "If I'm right, my son will know in twenty-five years".

This cryptic remark had always interested Randall. Firstly, because at the time of the Departure not even his mother knew she was pregnant, and secondly because twenty-five was the age of his father when he Departed.

With a couple of blinks, he closed the old school project down and switched his terminal to Emergency Communications Only mode, or "Ecom", the closest equivalent to "Off" that it would allow. It was his twenty-fifth birthday tomorrow - correction, today, it was already past midnight - so he would perhaps get some answers soon enough.

He awoke briefly only once in the night, when his terminal flashed him the emergency message that his credibility and standing in society would be in serious jeopardy unless he bought GloboCo's new nano-carbon infused socks and boxers set immediately.

It was a justified emergency because the 10% offer was only available until 8.30 am.

Chapter 2.

In the most luxurious hole in the ground in the world, in a perfectly clean, perfectly warm, perfectly adorned bedroom, in a bed that was softer and cooler and more sumptuously comfortable than any other double divan anywhere on the planet, the secretly richest man in the world finally slept the sleep of the righteous.

Almost.

It had been a big day, and it took some time for him to get to sleep because tomorrow was going to be an even bigger day - the penultimate point in the start of the culmination of the end of his life's work, in fact - and the adrenaline had only recently finished coursing through his veins.

Lying there for more than an hour on his majestic mattress, he hadn't, like Randall, been staring out of the window. But only because holes in the ground don't have windows. He had instead been staring at an ancient and now highly illegal device with a faintly glowing screen; a window of a different sort.

Eventually, he laid the device carefully on his bedside table, rolled over in bed, and began dreaming of the ancient past...

... and of his place in it.

It's a good job you can't hear the snoring. Jeez...

Chapter 3.

The next day, Randall woke up a year older.

He showered, shaved, and the other thing beginning with "sh" carefully, rather than his usual half-arsed morning scramble. He was having the day off, and nothing was going to get him thinking about the time machine, or his father, or any of that stuff.

After briefly switching on his terminal to thank the few of his friends who had bothered for their kind words on his birthday - all of them very thoughtfully generated automatically by their own terminals - he switched it to ECom, and prepared to go shopping.

His clothes were getting a bit threadbare, as is often the way with obsessed people, and his house was in need of some new furniture. A visit to The Store [2] was in order. Normally he would have made all his purchases through his terminal, but today he was determined to get out and meet people for a change, so he smartened himself up as much as was possible with the limited wardrobe available to him and prepared to go shopping. Even so, he still ended up looking like his clothes had been glued on by a blind monkey in boxing gloves. In a hurricane.

Sticking down the annoying clump of morning-hair that always stuck out at a right angle from his head with spit (even *after* showering,

---

[2] 'The Store' now being the only retail chain store available on Earth. Five centuries of piratical corporate mergers had resulted in a behemothic world-girdling retail mega-corporation with a compound name so unwieldy, with so many hyphens and little bits of the original names of the corporations all jumbled together like a random Scrabble game, that they could no longer fit it onto the letter heads. Rebranding as 'The Store' was the result of a two-year series of focus group consultations and marketing think-tank brain-storming sessions.

The Store was swallowed whole by GloboCo the following year, but they wisely chose not to spend another twenty million credits thinking up a new name.

somehow), he put on his tatty jacket and left the house. Almost immediately the hair sprang back into its more customary perpendicular position.

The plan was to have a nice lunch at one of The Store's restaurants and be back home for the early afternoon, when he could install his furniture and try on his new clothes. Then, later on, he would invite his few friends over for a pleasant evening, drinks, and maybe some sex.

It was at the restaurant that his day, and indeed the rest of his life, changed. Well, he wanted to meet people...

With his clothes and trinket purchases tempting him from under the table, he sipped his Water+ (wetter than water - from GloboCo) and waited for his food to arrive. Ordering Water+, rather than a GloboCola or a Gloopy-Shake, was an unusual choice, and garnered the occasional snooty look from the small gaggle of waiterbots gathered by the bar, but Randall wasn't a fan of overly sweet drinks, preferring the subtler taste of Water+ which had only a miniscule two grams of Aspartosweet in it.

He had chosen the old fashioned restaurant of the four available, and would have to wait for up to five minutes before his genuine hand microwaved meal was brought to his table. He didn't mind, he was prepared to wait an otherwise unacceptable five minutes for the historical theme of the decor.

Old artefacts from the last few hundred years of Earth's history were tastefully displayed all over the walls and ceiling. They even had an authentic pre-shift device from the twenty-first century on the wall by the kitchen entrance. It was a gadget he was somewhat familiar with, called a "Smart Phone", which was a sort of primitive early terminal, although not implanted like today's; you couldn't implant something that size. He wondered, and not for the first time, how they managed back then with all the bulky devices they had to carry around.

An interest in history was another offshoot of that old school project he so fondly remembered. The middle-early period - from the late twentieth through the mid twenty-first centuries - was his speciality, and he was quite knowledgeable about the technology of the time. It fascinated him with its embryonic versions of the devices that had now become integrated and implanted.

Unfortunately, knowledge of the period was a bit sketchy. Not a lot of the digital information from that era had survived because it was before the invention of permanent quantum drives, but he had himself managed to unearth some old data from something of that time called, rather strangely, "Facebook". Although it was illegal, it was still possible to buy ancient devices recovered from Earth Shift excavations when they came up at underground auctions, and if you were devoted and had the time, it was sometimes possible to recover data from them.

Randall had done exactly that, and discovered some "posts" on "Facebook". There were three of them in all. Two were in the form of the Japanese (remember them?) Haiku; still a popular poetry form today. He had the full text of the first poem, but it annoyed him that he was missing the end of the last word from the second. They read:

Sleep is elusive.
Haiku poems fill my mind,
but not very good ones.

... and...

The apples are small.
The bananas, not yet ripe,
are pricey. Waitros…

The third post, recovered from the same device, read:

You know you're getting old when shaving takes longer because you have to do your ears :)

If only he could find the name of the owner of the device, he could perhaps do some research and discover more about the context of the posts, because they seemed rather dour and depressing to Randall. Perhaps they were comments by a sad old man nearing the end of his life, lamenting the degeneration of his body and the passing of his intellect. The strange punctuation at the end of the third post seemed to corroborate his theory, but he would probably never know.

As he was mulling over these thoughts, his baked potato with Cheez (now with added Preservamite - from GloboCo) arrived at his table. It took six minutes rather than the advertised five, and he was within his rights to complain, but he was in a good mood and decided to let it go. He cleansed his palate with a sip of Water+ and was about to tuck in, when he was politely but insistently disturbed by a tall elderly gentleman with rather shockingly long grey hair.

He wore old fashioned but obviously well-made clothing, rather refined looking actually, but the long hair in a pony-tail was letting him down badly. Men didn't wear their hair long anywhere other than in historical photographs. He looked like a fool, and an old fool at that.

'Randall James?' enquired the man, pulling out the chair opposite Randall and making motions to sit down. 'I'm Marcus Han,' he said, waving away a stray hair from his face. 'It's a pleasure to meet you. I believe you're acquainted with my brother.' He sat down.

Randall nearly spat his Water+ all over the intruder, but the facial similarity to his old schoolteacher was quite striking now that he looked; and although it was a huge breach of etiquette to pull out a chair and sit down at a stranger's table, he managed to swallow his drink and shake the proffered hand.

'We need to talk,' said Han urgently, before Randall even had time to construct an opening sentence. 'I've been looking forward to this for over thirty years.'

'What? Meeting me? You must be misinformed, Mr Han,' replied Randall. 'Today is my twenty-fifth birthday; you couldn't possibly have been looking forward to meeting me for thirty years.'

'Over thirty years,' said Han. 'Thirty-one to be precise. Ever since I was assigned to your dad in fact.'

Randall was instantly suspicious. He leaned back in his chair. 'What are you? WP? Secret Service?'

'No, no, nothing like that,' replied Han, holding up his hands and looking around nervously. 'And I'll thank you to keep your voice down. The last thing we want is the World Police onto us.'

'Us? We? What do you mean, we? I've only just met you and you're making no sense at all. I don't think there's any call to be using words like "we". I don't even know you.'

'You will. And quite well. And by tonight *we* will have embarked on a journey together that you couldn't possibly imagine in your wildest dreams.'

Randall leaned forward, relaxing slightly. 'Is this something to do with time-travel?' he asked quietly, as some of the pieces began dropping into place in his mind.

'Yes, Randall. It's something to do with time-travel,' said Han with a huge grin on his face.

A short while later, after repeatedly and rather embarrassingly calling him "Mr Han" on the journey home, Randall felt more at ease and had started to call him Marcus.

They entered Randall's home. Han looked around briefly.

'You could do with some new furniture,' he said, matter-of-factly.

'Yes, well, that was kind of the plan for today, Marcus.'

'Yes I know,' he said, also matter-of-factly.

Randall resisted the urge to raise his hand in the air before asking the next question, something he'd already done twice on the way home. 'What do you mean you know? How could you possibly know my plans for today?' he demanded.

'The same way I knew you'd be at the restaurant. It's all in The Book.'

This time Han was not matter-of-fact. He looked like he was tiptoeing on lit-up lightbulbs, and had a worried, inquisitive look on his face; like this could go one of two ways.

Randall looked him in the eye for a second. The brow above it raised slightly.

'Okay. I'm not rising to your cryptic melodramas any more,' he said. 'Why don't I pour us both a drink and you can tell me all about it?'

Han relaxed, it had gone the way he wanted.

Randall didn't normally drink alcohol during the day, even on his birthday, but this wasn't an ordinary day, or even an ordinary birthday. He grabbed a bottle of Gin, some tonic, two glasses, and directed Han to the threadbare sofa in his cramped and untidy lounge.

'Can I see your shed?' enquired Han, excitedly, as Randall passed him a glass, made a space on the table barely big enough for a bottle, and put the bottle in it.

'Do you want any ice in that? And what's my shed got to do with it?' asked Randall.

'You probably won't have any ice, and everything,' said Han, back to matter-of-fact mode.

Randall went to the kitchen to look in his fridge. 'Okay. Talk,' he said, after confirming that he did indeed have no ice.

Marcus took a deep breath and looked Randall straight in the eye. 'You're not the original Randall James,' he said, bluntly. 'You are in fact the second iteration of Randall James, just as I am the second iteration of Marcus Han and most people are the second iterations of themselves.'

'Iteration,' said Randall.

'That's right. You're familiar with the term "grandfather paradox"?'

Randall nodded.

'Well you can think of our situation as a great-great-great-grandfather paradox. Or something similar. Much worse than a simple grandfather paradox anyway. The mother of all grandfather paradoxes you might say. The fate of the world rests on our shoulders.'

'Grandfather,' said Randall.

'Yes. We have to travel back in time and alter the future, which is of course our past, and we will do it because we've already done it in the other timeline.'

'Future,' managed Randall.

'No, the past. Are you okay?' asked Han. 'You sound like a defective echo.'

'Oh I'm fine,' replied Randall, snapping out of it. 'Peachy. I've just been told I'm not actually myself and that I am, in fact, a sort of copy of an original time-travelling hero version of me whose fate it is to save the world. Why wouldn't I be okay? And anyway, what's wrong with the world? It doesn't seem like it needs any saving to me.'

'No, it doesn't *seem* that way, but to be honest your thoughts are not your own, and never really have been. You've been trained, just as everyone else has, to think in a certain way that has forever blinded you to the...' he trailed off. Now wasn't the time and he could see Randall wasn't buying it. 'Just believe me when I say you'll understand when you read The Book,' he said.

Randall was doubtful. 'What book? You keep going on about this book like it's sacred or something.'

'This book,' said Han, producing a slim device from his jacket pocket.

'I know that. That's a... a Kandle isn't it?'

'Kindle,' said Han. 'And yes, it is. I'm glad my brother managed to get you interested in history. You're going to need it where we're going.'

Two hours later Randall still hadn't read The Book. They were standing in the shed at the end of the garden, and Han was excited.

'To think this is where it all happened,' he said for the seventeenth time, enthusiasm exuding from every pore.

'Happened?' said Randall, who had caught up with the overall scheme of things but was still quite vague on most of the details.

'You know what I mean,' replied Han. 'Going to be happened, or used to be happened, or something. I never was very good at temporal linguistics.'

'Apparently,' said Randall, who had been reduced back down to single word answers when confronted by Han's exuberance.

So far, Randall had worked out the following things:

1. In an alternate and no longer existent timeline, a family of inventors and scientists, the James family, took it upon themselves to develop a means to time-travel into the past to undo some catastrophic errors made by the people of that era. This destroyed their own timeline and created the alternate one Randall was now living in. This didn't surprise him as much as he thought it should.

2. He would be the one who, along with Marcus Han, would actually travel back to the twenty-first century. He knew this because his counterpart from the lost timeline had done so, and to "ensure the time loop doesn't collapse" (Han's phrase) they must do so too. He had a lot of questions about this. Worrying ones. An infinite number of increasingly furious looking Randall's were shouting at him in his imagination.

3. Marcus Han, although clearly quite elderly, had almost limitless energy. And it was starting to get annoying.

'Let's go back to the house,' said Randall eventually, after watching Han walk around touching things and exclaiming, "Well, well" and, "Who'd have thought it" for the last ten minutes.

Back in the lounge Randall asked one of the questions he'd been meaning to ask for most of the evening, though he strongly suspected he knew the answer already. And it wasn't a good one.

'So what happens if we don't go back?' he said.

Han glared at him. 'That,' he said, emphatically, 'is something I wouldn't care to speculate about.'

'You don't know?' Randall almost shouted. *He* had a pretty good idea of the consequences, so Marcus must surely know *something* about it.

'Not for certain no. The theory isn't entirely clear on this point, but according to the mathematics we've figured out so far there are three possibilities,' he said. 'One - and this is a very low probability, hardly worth mentioning in fact - nothing happens and we live out our lives as we would have done before. The time loop heals over and the world keeps turning. Two - higher probability - everything we know disappears and the world instantly snaps back to the original timeline. And you wouldn't want that to happen, let me tell you.'

'Why? What's wrong with it?' Randall interrupted.

'Why do you think the original you wanted to go back and change history?' Han replied. 'They were living in some kind of squalid hell hole bunker in their timeline. Do you see much evidence of squalor, hell, holes, or bunkers around you now?'

Randall paused for a moment, thinking. 'But that must mean that they, I mean we, fixed it. Dawkins knows [3] this world isn't perfect, but it works okay. Why should we go back in time and risk messing things up? This world isn't so bad.'

'Because the world isn't fixed, it's just different. And because of the third and by far the most probable outcome if we don't.'

'Which is?' Randall thought he knew the answer but wanted to hear it from Han.

'The instant and total annihilation of the entire Milky Way Galaxy!' he said, managing somehow to pronounce the exclamation mark as he did so.

That wasn't the answer Randall had been expecting at all. The

---

[3] Like "God knows" but more up to date.

sudden shocked expression on his face gradually gave way to an increasingly furrowed brow. 'The whole Galaxy? I thought maybe the planet, or possibly the solar system... but the Galaxy? Why? How can a localised effect alter reality so much?'

'Time paradoxes are tricky things, Randall. They start off localised to the immediate vicinity of the paradox, but the subsequent paradoxes caused by that location's sudden non-existence starts a cascade effect in the Thornhill field [4] that ends up short circuiting the intergalactic plasma medium.'

Randall's blank stare spoke eloquently about how much of the last sentence he had understood. Marcus pretended not to notice and ploughed on regardless.

'The maths is complicated, but I assure you it's the most probable outcome. Think of it as a huge computer circuit that suddenly blows a capacitor in one small section. It may only be a tiny defect amongst a billion components, but the computer as a whole will fail. Rather than repair it, we would probably throw the computer away, and it seems the universe does something similar. At least that's what the numbers say.'

Han left a few moments for this to sink in and then said, 'It's all in The Book.'

'Which I haven't had time to read yet,' said Randall, pointedly.

'I know,' Han replied, reaching for his jacket. 'It's time for me to go. We have a busy day tomorrow and you need to rest. Happy birthday by the way.'

'Thanks,' said Randall. What else could he say?

---

[4] Named after 21st century physicist Wal Thornhill, who received a posthumous Nobel prize in 2064 - after all the orthodox opponents to the electric universe theory had finally died.

Chapter 4.

Elsewhere - if that's the correct word to describe a field of potential that exists beyond the material universe, where "where" has no real meaning - a mind slowly stirred into awareness. If you could apply the word "slowly" to an event taking place outside of the constraints of time, of course.

From a state of total blankness, utter oblivion, the mind gradually became aware of something. What it was, the mind couldn't tell. It was very bright, and very big, and awareness of it was definitely happening in some form or another, but it struggled with the recognition of the thing it was becoming aware of, and of how it was that it was aware of that thing in the first place. It was something it couldn't comprehend yet, but it was trying.

The realisation that it could sense itself trying, feel the awareness developing, was a revelation to the mind. It could only mean that there were now two things it was aware of: the thing that was there before, and now its own awareness of that thing. The difference between those two things, the mind now realised, could even constitute a third thing, and it paused to consider that conundrum. The considering of the conundrum was the fourth thing it became aware of, and that's when it started to get complicated.

The fact that it was now able to count the things it was aware of became the fifth thing it was aware of, but then, as the numbers grew ever larger, they started to interact with each other, flying off in all sorts of directions, and the mind became lost in them.

Numbers, seemingly, were everywhere.

It was puzzled.

The mind realised that it was using something called "words" to do the puzzling with, and it puzzled over that too. Very quickly, it noticed that the words were occurring one after another, in a sort or sequence that evolved in a linear fashion, and it puzzled even further about that.

Eventually - if that word has any real meaning in this context - a new word popped into its awareness. It was the word "time", and the mind recognised instantly that that was what was now suddenly happening to it; "time" had started to "flow". The next question was, where from? And more importantly, where to? Also, how did it know that? And why was it happening "now"?

Immediately, the mind became aware that it had a memory; a store of its previous experiences. It recalled again the instant of waking, when there was only one thing it was aware of, and it replayed the whole unfolding of its experience from that moment, analysing each new revelation again.

The analysis quickly doubled, and then tripled, the number of things it was aware of, and it started to get terribly confused. The number of things, and the number of relationships between those things, became too enormous.

As more and more concepts, and questions, and scraps of awareness impinged upon the mind, it quickly became overwhelmed and began again from the beginning.

'What was the thing I was originally aware of?' asked the mind, of itself.

... ('**I**? What does **that** mean?') ...

'It was everything that isn't me,' it replied, again to itself.

'What do I call everything else? Does it have a name?' came the next question, almost unbidden from the depths of the mind's... mind.

... ('Come to think of it, do **I** have a name?') ...

'The Universe,' came the answer, from yet another part of the mind; presumably somewhere in the memory, which seemed to be a lot bigger than it should be, given the limited length of its awareness so far.

He began to poke around in its depths...

... ('He? I'm **Male**?') ...

More questions, but fewer answers, followed. Only one thing was certain - he was outside the universe!

The panic of realisation that he must immediately get back into the universe rose unbidden from the depths of his psyche, completely overwhelming him, and he began to move as fast as he could towards it.

Which was pretty damn fast.

... (*'I **think** I begin with a **G.***') ...

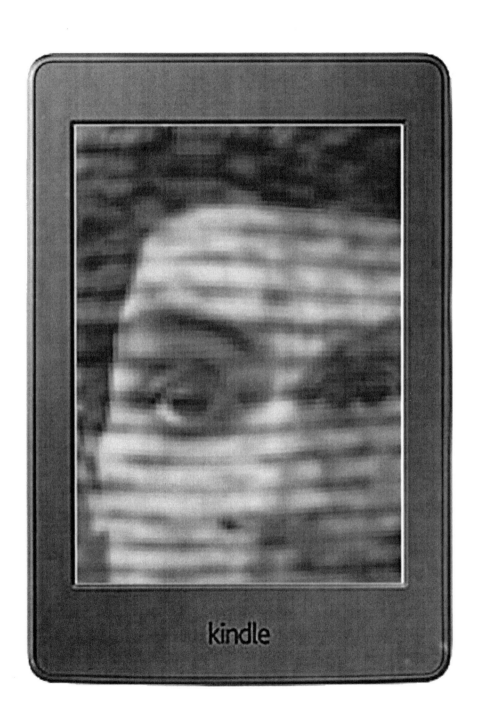

Chapter 5.

This book is for the eyes of Randall James II.

'A promising start,' thought Randall, 'already I'm Randall James II. Not the original. Not the first. Not the one that was supposed to be. No, I'm just one of a number of Randall James's. Which, if I'm right, could eventually turn into an infinite supply.'

The anticipation made his hands tremble. He steadied himself with a sip of Gin and read on...

I am Randall James, the re-inventor of the time machine. Believe me, I know how you must feel. It must have been a very strange day for you. Happy birthday by the way.

Randall began to wish complete strangers would stop wishing him a happy birthday. Even if one of them was himself.

If I'm right and the changes we made to the twenty-first century pan out as we hoped, then you should be living in a reasonably calm and stable world. If you're not, then we tried our best, I'm sorry. It can't be any worse than the planet we lived on.

I have no idea about your personal circumstances, but if our plan comes to fruition, you should have a strong interest in history and be well versed in Temporal Dynamics, Vortex Theory, Chrono-matrices and the rest. In fact, if you're reading this then you must be well acquainted with those disciplines. Excuse me, it's hard for me to get my head around sometimes, you know?

Of course you do. You're me. Or rather, I'm you.

Sorry. I'll start again.

'This needs a drink,' said Randall to himself. With shaky hands he poured himself another from the half empty Gin bottle on the table. His ECom messages had been ignored. He would explain to his friends another day. Tonight he was keeping his terminal as Off as he could get it...

The world we lived on was a man-made hell. For twenty-five years I lived in one of only seven giant bunker-cities, dotted around the globe, that were the remains of our once great civilization. Ours was called Oceania, and we were three hundred miles from the nearest open water. The surface was virtually uninhabitable. The oceans were dead. The rivers, dried up. The forests were all but gone. The air was virtually unbreathable, and life wasn't worth living. Hope was long since dead.

Wars, over consumption, conspiracies, pollution, and natural disasters had brought humanity's numbers down to under a billion, and we lived like cockroaches squabbling over the meagre resources remaining. Some of us aspired to live like cockroaches. That's how bad it was.

There were a hundred and fifty million of us crammed into Oceania. There was no privacy. There was not enough food. There was disease, there was crime, and there was death.

Except for the elites. They lived like gods in their fortified palaces.

Our ancestors screwed up, badly. Beginning sometime in the late twentieth century, the governments and corporations of the world were gradually taken over by a super-rich, criminal-elite, who raped the planet for profit and cared nothing for the biosphere. They poisoned the populace with artificial food and brainwashed them with insidious propaganda until they were too weak and too stupid to do anything about it. They tore down mountains and dried up oceans in their ridiculous quest for profit. Nothing was sacred.

They took control of everything. The criminals at the top owned the whole world and everyone on it. A Global Police force kept us subservient and afraid of our neighbours. Pointing out corruption became a crime. Protesting became a crime. Growing your own food became a crime. Even collecting rainwater became a crime. Eventually, having children became a crime - unless you passed the test.

Except for the elites. They bred like rabbits. And they fought like rats…

Randall was entranced and horrified in equal measure. He read on, even though it was late and he was half drunk. His eyes were affronted by page after page of horror stories about this hellish other world that chilled him to the core. More so because the descriptions of their Global Police were spookily similar to the system currently running the show on Earth. The WP weren't as demoniacally corrupt or brutal, not by a long way, but they were similar nonetheless.

He read of his "other" father's disappearance during the testing of their first machine, and how the original Randall had devoted his life to perfecting his work.

Yes. Eerily similar.

He poured himself another drink, most of which actually did end up in the glass somehow, and read on.

… and then, on my twenty-fifth birthday, I was introduced to Marcus - my old teacher's brother, my soon-to-be travelling companion, and friend.

My commander picked him for a number of reasons, not least of which was his incredible historical knowledge; the man is a walking library. He and his ancestors would be our way out of the paradox that would ensnare us if we went ahead with our plan.

Don't worry, you'll understand soon. Your Marcus will explain tomorrow.

So we decided to change the world. Erase it. Wipe that misery out of existence. It was a difficult and dangerous thing to do, for sure, but we were desperate.

Working in total secrecy it took six generations to complete our task. But our family's sacrifice will never be recognised; only the commanders of the resistance knew about our work, and they don't exist anymore. They knowingly ended their own existence and that of all of humanity to escape that hell.

I don't know what kind of world you live in, Randall; I don't even know for sure that you will ever read this, I can only hope. The Han family will be a great help, but even they might not be able to steer events with as much precision as we will need, and their own paradox might come back to haunt us. Again, I can only hope.

You have much work to do. In just six months you must join us here in the twenty-first century and begin the task of altering the future. All the theory and plans for the time machine are contained in the hidden library. Study them well.

If you're anything like me, which I think you must be, then you will be full of questions and probably quite afraid. Don't worry, your questions will be answered, and your fears allayed. But you must know this: you have no future in your current timeline. Your destiny is to live out your life in the twenty-first century and I'm afraid there's nothing you can do about it.

It's not so bad here. Once you get used to the smell.

I'm sorry to have to do this to you, Randall, I really am. But there is no other way. You and Marcus are the two most important people in the world. You must learn to trust him as I have learned to over the last few years.

You cannot fail. The world, and the future, depends upon it.

Randall James - November 5th 2017.

Randall had never really been in a proper state of shock before. It was most unpleasant. He drained his glass, filled it again, and tried to get his thoughts straight.

So many questions. So many variables. So many ways this could go really badly wrong. What if they got caught? The WP would feed them into the algae tanks if they found out what they were up to. Sliced and diced. What would happen to this timeline when they go back? Will it just disappear, like the last time?

"The last time". Strange how a simple phrase can change its meaning so much in just a few hours.

Who was the mysterious Marcus Han really? How did his ancestry fit into all this? Will they be able to build the time machine in time? What will they do when they get to the past? What will happen when he meets his other self? Will he even like himself?

He realised openly what he had known subconsciously for the past few hours: he was resigned to going into the past. He had no choice if he wanted the Milky Way to continue existing. It would be churlish in the extreme to destroy an entire galaxy out of spite.

Switching off the light, he lay back on his bed and knew, half-drunk as he was, that he wouldn't be able to sleep.

Two hours later his terminal flashed an ECom message to him informing him of the relaxing benefits of GloboCo's new Zombinol easy to swallow sleeping aid tablets. He blinked on the "Order Now" button. It looked like he might need them in the coming weeks.

Half an hour after that he was sent an advert for a psychotherapist for some reason.

The next day, at the crack of 11:37, Marcus Han showed up at the house. Randall had finally roused himself just after eleven am, gone through bleary-eyed ablutions, and was clearing a space in his kitchen to make coffee.

To test a theory, one of many he had formulated during a restless night, he made two cups of coffee. As soon as he'd poured the second cup, his terminal lit up and showed a picture of a smug looking Marcus Han outside his front door.

He blinked on "Open door" and shouted, 'Do you take whitener or sweetener?' He could be smug too.

'No thanks, Randall. I like my coffee as it comes. I see you're beginning to put some of the pieces together. Well done.'

'I have a lot of questions, Marcus. But I suspect you know what they are already,' said Randall, trying to tease some details out of him.

'To some extent yes,' said Han, taking his coffee and raising an eyebrow at the smell. 'The six months our counterparts spent together was documented in great detail, and although we are different people living in a different timeline, we will share many of those experiences with them to differing degrees. It seems the similarity in events is especially great when it comes to those intimately concerned with the potential paradox, so you and I are thoroughly entangled in both timelines. My great-great-grandfather called it Verticular Timeline Synchronicity, but then he always did like high-falutin' terminology. I call it Slippage.'

'Slippage?'

'Yes. It seems there's a connection on the sub-quark level between ourselves and our other selves. This causes significant life events to "slip" between timelines. Yesterday was significant for you, that's how I knew you would be in the restaurant and that you would have no ice in your fridge, because that's how it transpired in the other timeline.'

'Quark,' managed Randall. *Damn*, he thought. It was happening again.

'The details are different of course. In their timeline the restaurant was a café used by the resistance, but it was in the exact physical location that our restaurant is today. In their timeline they went back to "your" quarters and "you" had no ice for the home brewed hooch they drank. Their shed was actually a walled off and hidden section of Oceania that the resistance used as a laboratory, but it was where your shed is now.'

'And they spent six months recreating the time machine together,' said Randall, finally breaking the monosyllabic spell. 'So we have to do the same?'

'That's about the shape of it.'

Randall's brow furrowed as another query formed in his head. Marcus could see the thoughts coalescing but waited until he was about to speak before pre-empting him.

'I know you're worrying about there eventually becoming an infinite number of you, but that isn't how it works,' he began.

'When we go back, we'll give details of our history to our other selves and tell them how our timeline turned out. They incorporate that data into their plans, and with our help a new timeline will evolve from that point, hopefully a better one. Each loop, the equivalent Randall and Marcus of that timeline should live in increasingly better societies.'

Randall's face was a mask of incredulity. Marcus judged the probability of the next question containing either the word "paradox" or "infinities" to be a certainty, so he ploughed on before he could ask it.

'It may take a few loops before we create the society humanity deserves, but at that point, when our last counterparts travel back from a perfect world for the last time, there will be no need for any extra intervention and so the loop can be gradually broken over time. The other "me" won't pass on any information to my ancestors and so our families will continue as they would have done without intervention. The likelihood of us interacting, or even existing, six hundred years later is infinitesimal. The slippage will cease, time-travel won't be invented, and the paradoxes will resolve naturally.'

'It all sounds terribly risky.' Randall really wasn't sure about any of this. "Terribly risky" was his polite way of saying "Totally bonkers".

'More so if we break the loop now, that would be disastrous.' Which was Marcus's polite way of saying "Utterly catastrophic for the future of humanity and the entire Galaxy".

Randall was deep in thought. *Time for some good news*, thought Marcus.

'This time round, of course, we have the plans for the machine, so it'll be easier for us,' he said.

Randall's thoughts rose from the depths and broke the choppy surface. 'But when you taught my father how to build his machine you knew he'd die in the Departure six months later, didn't you?'

'He's not dead, Randall,' replied Han. 'He's just not here anymore.'

'You know what I mean. You knew he'd disappear never to be seen again.'

'Yes, I knew. But it's not my place to be changing the course of events. He disappeared in the other timeline, so he had to disappear in this one too. Time has a sort of momentum, it was inevitable. Although this time around he did rather shout his mouth off to the world, unfortunately. Caused a few problems for me that did.'

'So tell me about your family, Marcus,' said Randall, after a short, tense, pause. 'How have they interfered in my family history? I presume the miraculous escapes of my ancestors are something to do with your ancestors, correct?'

'Yes, Randall. Our families have been intertwined for over six hundred years. Your very existence in this timeline is down to my family and ultimately to me. Right from the moment when my ancestor persuaded yours to go to the Moon to avoid the Earth Shifts, up to when I introduced your father to your mother and inspired him to build his machine. My granddad taught yours how to build the Temporal Splitter. My six times great granddad worked with Zachary James to develop Temporal Vortex Theory.'

'But that's a paradox,' cried Randall. 'That isn't how it happened in the original timeline. They worked out those things for themselves in a desperate attempt to end their suffering.'

'Yes it's a paradox. But apparently not a serious one. Originally, my family's only contribution was my other self, who travelled back with "you" to the twenty-first century. "My" contribution was to instigate the changes that needed to be made to society and then to pass on all of my information about the future to my ancestor. "I" made sure they were wealthy enough to look after the passage of your family through time.

'We intervened as little as possible in the beginning, only saving your ancestors from crises that might otherwise have resulted in the extinction of your family line. But then we realised that our Zachary James was never going to discover Temporal Vortex Theory on his own. Though he was a genius in his own right, he wasn't focused on the problem of time in our reality. My forbear, Enoch Han, coaxed Zachary, and little-by-little he got him thinking about the problem.

'Eventually, they formulated the theory together. Only then did Enoch tell Zachary of his real identity. Enoch insisted that his name be removed from the authorship of the paper and Zachary got all the credit. He was sworn to silence of course. As was your father and grandfather.'

'And your family has intervened ever since,' said Randall, 'nudging the development of time-travel in the right direction so that we could eventually repeat our journey.'

'Not repeat, Randall. Remember, that other timeline winked out of existence as soon as they changed their past and created our present. It doesn't exist except as a quantum possibility in the Vortex.'

'Again, a paradox…' Randall interjected.

Marcus cut him off with a gesture. 'Paradox is a word you'll hear a lot over the coming months. You'd better get used to it. Come on, drink up, we have to go.'

'Go where?'

'To my place. I have something to show you,' said Marcus. He didn't drink his coffee.

Twenty minutes later they arrived at Marcus's place, although "place" was probably the wrong word. "State" or "shambles" were more appropriate words to describe the derelict, ramshackle, mess that confronted Randall. "I'm not fucking going in there" would be on the tip of your tongue too.

'Don't be fooled by the shabby building in front of you, Randall,' said Han. 'My place is around the back. It's quite safe.' Randall didn't hold out much hope.

They walked along a dank corridor on the ground floor past half a dozen doors in various states of disrepair. The scent of decay was prominent, but didn't completely dispel the odour of stale urine which predominated. One door advertised a discreet massage service. Randall chose not to speculate about what kind of massage one might receive there; or how likely one was to survive it without being infected with a difficult to explain and embarrassing ailment; or ending up in a number of iced boxes ready for the organ transplant black market; or at least three other things he was desperately trying to stop his imagination from going into in too much detail about.

It was a huge old building, converted at some point in the past (maybe two hundred years ago, thought Randall) into flats. The stonework looked sound but was thoroughly dilapidated, fitting in well with the rest of the neighbourhood, which was also fairly low rent. As they reached the end of the corridor Han took out a bunch of keys and opened the grubby door of the flat they had stopped in front of.

'I have to maintain the illusion of poverty to allay suspicion,' he said as they entered the flat.

'You're doing a very good job,' replied Randall, looking around. 'The mould on the ceiling is a particularly nice touch. As are the discarded pizza boxes and the dead rat in the corner. At least I hope it's a rat.'

'Thank you, Randall,' said Han, ignoring the sarcasm. 'Despite appearances I live in some luxury as you are about to find out. Would you move away from the window please? Thank you.'

He pressed a button disguised as a knot of wood on the door frame they'd just come through and quickly walked towards the fireplace, where he kicked a tile in the tacky facade surrounding the ancient, lethal looking, gas fire. Suddenly there was a muted clunk and the whir of barely audible machinery. The floor by the window began to slide away to reveal a staircase below.

'My family built this house over three hundred years ago,' said Han, over the faint rumble of gears. 'Very few outside my family in all that time have known of the existence of what I am about to show you. Your father was the last. You will speak of this to no one. Do you understand?'

Randall spotted the note of seriousness that had crept into Han's voice. 'Of course, Marcus,' he said, solemnly.

Lights spontaneously brightened as they descended the stairs, which went down quite a long way under the garden at the back of Han's house and eventually ended after two ninety-degree turns at a thick and obviously very secure door. It had a sign on it saying "HOUSTON".

'Just my little joke,' said Han as he keyed in his entry code to open the door.

Randall didn't get it. 'What's so funny about Houston?' he asked. 'You mean the little town in Texas?'

'Mission Control,' said Han. 'That's where our ancestors threw chemical rockets at the sky in their first attempts to get into space.'

'Of course!' exclaimed Randall. 'I remember now. One Short Leap and all that. What was his name... Buzz Lightyear? Something like that.'

Marcus corrected him as the door swung open. 'Neil Armstrong and Buzz Aldrin,' he said. 'And it's "One Small Step for a Man".'

'Oh ye...' said Randall. He didn't finish the sentence, because that's when his jaw flopped open.

Chapter 6.

Randall gathered his meandering mandible and looked around in wonder as he walked into the underground building. He'd never seen a home like this one before. From the curve of the floor to the tilt of the ceiling this was an entirely original work of architecture, totally unlike anything else on Earth as far as he could tell.

The comfort and ease of living were obvious, as was the stylish elegance. Sunlight flooded in from skylights in the ceiling to illuminate a variety of plants in a kind of indoor garden. There were no windows, tasteful art filled the walls and beautiful statuary abounded.

Then Randall noticed the tech. It was all around him in subtle, hidden ways. From the dodecaphonic system, that was playing music completely unlike anything he'd ever heard before, to the ancient 3D multi-printer in the corner, this place was like a shrine to banned technologies. There were even ancient personal computers and holographic devices that probably had their own internal hard drives. They didn't store their data on anonymous servers in The Space [5]. The users of this tech did their own computing. At home and in private.

A shocking thought struck Randall; he turned slowly to face Marcus.

'You're not wired in. Are you?'

Han shrugged. 'No, Randall. I'm not,' he replied. 'I'm off grid.'

'You don't have a terminal at all?' he asked, incredulously. 'How do you shop, or get medical attention, or travel... or do anything?'

---

[5] The progression, over the centuries, went like this: The Cloud - The Sky - The Space. GloboCo had recently been working on the latest upgrade - The Universe. The advertising campaign relied very heavily on semi-naked models seductively repeating the catchphrase 'Big Bang' - and intimating how many more of them you would be having with the similarly scantily clad sexpots that would flock to you when you upgraded.

'I have my means,' said Han, cryptically. 'Being guardians to your family is not without its benefits. Remember that I'm an anomaly, a paradox. The other me in that other timeline altered our reality so much that I'm surprised I even exist. I'm very different to the original me, I don't really fit into this timeline and so I interact with it as little as possible. The trouble we had getting my brother employed at your school is testament to that - but that's a discussion for another time. Let me show you The Book Room.'

They walked a short distance down a curved corridor with eight large rooms leading off it. It certainly was a spacious and well-appointed, hidden, illegal, underground bunker complex.

'So your family have a lot of investments I should imagine,' said Randall, teasing again. 'They knew the future so they could invest confidently with the ultimate insider knowledge. They'd never lose. They'd be there at the beginning of every new technology, every new discovery. Holy Dawkins, you must be richer than Emperor Trump the fourth.'

'Considerably more so in fact, but all that means nothing. I can't take it with me to the twenty-first century. I have no children to pass it on to; I'm the end of the line. It will remain forever a secret.'

There was a pause just long enough to allow the tension to rise to an unbearable degree.

'But we could live very well during our last six months,' said Randall, at last.

Marcus smiled, 'Oh we will, my friend,' he said. 'We're gonna live like kings.'

In the Book Room Randall's jaw dropped again. It was a sort of library, but not of electrotainment chips, or even ezereed books.

It was full of ancient devices of different types and was split into two sections. The first part was filled with Kindles in what appeared to be chilled lead sleeves; all hooked up to an old off grid computer that looked like it was monitoring their batteries and functioning. The other section was composed of a variety of devices old and new, and even some ancient paper volumes. An alcove in one corner served as a workbench and maintenance station.

Han pointed to the Kindles. 'The books in that section were written by our other selves, and mostly contain the details of their history from 2001 to the day they left in February 2608,' he said. 'They not only contain historical details from their timeline, but instructions on how to avoid certain natural disasters, political movements, dangerous technologies, and the like. Their ancestors had survived their versions of those very experiences, but there was no guarantee that their alternate progeny would, so they tried to make sure. They also contain all the maths, theory and engineering disciplines needed to create a functioning time machine.'

'Wow! And the other section?' asked Randall, in awe.

'Those were written by my ancestors from 2008 to the present day. They're a sort of generational diary of the interactions between our families over the centuries, and a detailed description of exactly how they interfered with the society of the time. They also contain our collected discoveries on time-travel theory and practice. Through the ages we've amassed quite a lot of knowledge that not even your great ancestors or our other selves knew. Slippage theory for example.'

'So you're saying that between us we have more knowledge of time-travel than they did in the other reality. But that's a...'

'Paradox. I know,' interrupted Han. 'That's one of the things we know more about than they did. Some paradoxes can happen. Small ones. Bigger ones tend to make the universe sit up and take notice, and that means the erasure of the paradox, or, if it's big enough, the erasure of the galaxy it occurs in. We happen to be the biggest paradox in this galaxy - that we know of - so we have to complete the loop.'

'I know, I'm convinced. You can stop trying to persuade me, I'm going to do it. But I need more time and more information before I get my head round this. What other paradoxes are there? Have any been so big that they erased themselves?'

'We have no idea,' said Han, plainly.

Randall considered this for a moment. 'Because they erased themselves. Stupid question,' he said. He wasn't thinking straight, and was starting to get a bit edgy. He knew he would do a lot of reading and have a lot of frustrating conversations before all this was over. A pragmatic approach was required.

'Well let's get on with it then,' he said. 'Where do I start?'

Han turned to look straight at Randall.

'I start,' he said. 'By hacking your terminal.'

'Are you out of your mind? You're not touching my terminal. What do you mean by hacking? Are you a surgeon?'

Randall was horrified and started to back away from Han. He had mental images of surgical lasers slicing through his head.

Marcus held up his hands. 'Relax, Randall,' he soothed, as calmly as he could. 'Hacking is terminology from your period of expertise. I thought you would be familiar with it. I'm sorry. It refers to the practice of altering a device's functionality or gathering data from it, usually through changes in the software. It is painless, there will be no surgery, and you will be quite safe.'

Randall began to calm down. He sat in one of the exquisite, exceptionally comfortable, automatically adjusting, massaging chairs, set at the reading table in the centre of the room - and he instantly calmed down some more.

'Wow! That's amazing. Where did you get this chair? I want one.' Randall felt the tension lifting from his shoulders as the chair adjusted to his body shape, sensed where he was storing his stress, and began to ease it away with a combination of infra-sound, infra-red, and massage. Quietly relaxing tones flowed soothingly from the speakers set in the headrest.

Han was happy to change the subject. 'Just one of a number of nice toys my family has acquired over the centuries,' he said. 'These were a gift from the Emperor of America to the newly appointed President of Europia just over fifty years ago. My dad knew they would be going spare shortly afterwards so we were in a position to acquire them when the time was right.'

'You're kidding! These are *those* chairs?' said Randall. 'But didn't President Saxe-Coburg get caught with his trousers down on one of these chairs?'

'The one you're sitting in.'

Randall laughed. 'This gets better and better. The chair that Sex-Cockburg got gobbled on. I hope you cleaned it.'

'We had them re-covered. And had the bugs taken out.'

Half an hour later Han was ready to hack Randall's terminal - who was still in the chair and almost asleep. His restless night and hangover, combined with the soothing effects of the remarkable chair, had got the better of him.

And that was fine with Marcus, from his perspective everything was going well. He was "off script" now, the books couldn't help him here because this wasn't at all how it transpired in the previous iteration. In the other timeline the implants were much more pervasive and intrusive, they could not be hacked. Their only choice was to time-travel with their implants intact but blocked, which was a very dangerous tactic that almost resulted in their capture. This time they would have a bit more of an edge, and wouldn't have to wear tin-foil hats or anything similar.

He wondered whether to tell Randall that he was about to press the button that would initiate the hack, but decided against it. He was about as calm and relaxed as Han could have hoped for, telling him would simply alarm him.

He pressed the button. The hack would take about thirty seconds to complete.

It was a simple process that would achieve great results. From now on, any time Randall was in this building, his terminal would transmit a copy of the brainwave patterns that he was producing now. Most wired in people - which was everybody apart from Han and a very few others - had no idea how much data was being transmitted about their physiological responses and their brain states. From that data the WP could reconstruct the sort of thoughts you were having at any time, and intervene if you were up to something nefarious. Even if you weren't.

But not anymore. In future they would only receive calm relaxedness from Randall's terminal, modulated slightly by Han's computers so it never quite repeated exactly.

'Okay, it's done,' said Han.

'Hmmm? What is?'

'Your hack. It's done.'

'But I didn't feel a thing,' said Randall, yawning.

'I told you it would be painless. Now remember, if you're ever questioned about this place you come here regularly for a massage, okay? Your terminal will transmit nothing but calm as long as you're in this building.'

'What about when I'm at home?'

36

'I'll deal with that in a few days. I want you to take this recorder home with you today.' He handed Randall a small metallic device the size of a boiled sweet. 'It will record the transmissions from your terminal, and with that data I'll be able to construct an average pattern for when you're at home. I'll upload it back to your terminal in a few days. Try to do normal things until the next time we meet, okay? Try not to get too excited or anxious, just be yourself.'

'That might be easier said than done, Marcus.'

'I know, but you must try. Your Zombinol will arrive soon, use them until next time we meet, they should help.'

'How do you know I ordered Zombinol last night?'

'Because I read your cache while I was running the hack,' said Han. 'Your terminal stores the last twelve hours as a backup in case of interference on the transmission. You were quite anxious last night and your terminal noticed that. It constructed the scenario that you couldn't sleep because you were concerned about not getting many messages on your birthday, so it gave you an advert for sleeping pills. It then realised that you hadn't contacted your friends that evening as you were planning to do, but had stayed home and got drunk instead. So it sent you the advert for the psycho-babble guru.'

'I never knew it was so sophisticated,' said Randall. 'I thought it had noticed my tossing and turning in bed or something.'

'You'd be surprised how clever it is. Not so clever that we can't fool it though.'

'Luckily for us.'

'No luck involved, Randall. This is technology I invented for this very purpose.'

'You mean it was invented just for me?' Randall was slightly worried now.

'That's right.'

'And I'm the only person you've done this to?'

'Er, yes.'

'Don't you think it might have been better to tell me that beforehand?'

'No, Randall. It would have made you anxious, and that's the last thing I wanted if the hack was going to be successful.'

'What if it had gone wrong?'

'It didn't.'

'I know that. But just supposing?'

'The best outcome? It would have messed up your terminal's OS and you would have had to go to GloboCo to get it fixed.'

'And the worst?'

'Let's just say you wouldn't be worried about it now.'

'You mean it could have killed me?' Randall was disturbed, and had started shouting.

'Not quite, Randall,' said Han. 'It's best not to think about it. Please calm down. It's done now and all went well, as I knew it would.'

'With how much certainty?' Randall was getting hysterical.

'Better than 99.9%. Look, Randall, if it was a serious risk I wouldn't have done it. You are the most important person in the world. I wouldn't do anything to risk you. I weighed the options and decided it was worth doing, our chances of success have improved considerably because of it.'

'Just keep me informed in future will you? I want to know before you go messing around in my head and risking my life.'

'After I upload your average pattern back to your terminal in a few days I won't have to mess around in your head any more. Now please, just relax, you're undoing all the chair's good work.'

Randall noticed that Han had not said "I won't have to mess around in your head *and risk your life* any more", but decided it was best not to make too much of a fuss. He relaxed back into the chair and took a few deep breaths. 'So what's next?' he said.

'Now I start ordering the parts and materials we need to get started. I have to get them because they can track all your purchases. I've already built up the machine shop and started on some of the components, but it'll take a few days to get all the parts we need and you won't hear from me until then. I can't risk using sub-contractors this time, so we'll build the components of the machine here in my workshop, but we'll have to actually put it all together in your shed and travel to the past from there. That'll be the most risky period. If the WP are on to us, that's when they'll strike. Your shed isn't exactly an ideal place to leave from, it's not very secure.'

'Can't we risk it? Do it all from here?'

'Best not to. The theory stresses the point of departure should be the same as the original, there's too much risk of a paradox otherwise, the universe will notice. The closer we are to the original way it was done the better. You leave all that stuff to me, and stop worrying, okay?'

A deep breath, and then... 'Okay,' said Randall.

What else could he say?

Chapter 7.

The mind that thought he began with a 'G' engulfed the universe; which wasn't quite what he had been expecting. Although why he had been expecting anything in the first place was puzzling him. Again.

He felt like he should have been engulfed *by* the universe, not the other way around - at least, that's what his newly found but rather hazy memory had told him should probably have happened.

Instead, he found himself spread over the entirety of space-time. Not that he knew that yet, his grasp on his own mysteriously large memory was only tentative, and concepts like space-time were still a long way off. All he knew was that he was suddenly aware of everything that had ever existed, right back to the beginning of things themselves; and that's an awful lot to be unexpectedly made aware of.

He counted them in an instant, and was surprised by the answer. Not by the answer itself - which was a staggeringly huge number, and didn't really mean much - but by the fact that he actually got an answer at all.

Numbers, it seemed, were his thing.

(...'Got it! **George**! That's my name.' ...)

And then it all started flooding back... memories, feelings, concepts, knowledge ... all began pouring into his awareness as if from an enormous cosmic mind jug. Strangely, he started to feel as if he was hideously drunk.

At the same time, with consternation and biliousness rising, he felt himself beginning to merge with the universe; it seemed as if he and it were gradually becoming one thing, a single entity, and he began to panic wildly. He felt his individuality fading as his giddy awareness of the universe grew exponentially...

Before long, he hiccupped and blacked out.

Coincidentally, as George blacked out, another universe spanning consciousness - one with a bit more experience of it than George, and who also began with a 'G' - smiled. And watched...

Chapter 8.

When Randall returned home later that day, he placed the recorder Marcus had given him on his table, as instructed, and tentatively looked into getting the security of his shed upgraded.

Nothing spectacular. Nothing out of the ordinary. Nothing any other citizen wouldn't do. Nothing that would bring the WP crashing through his door to drag him off for interrogation and eventual feeding to a vat of Yeest (digests 99% of all organic matter - now also in soylent green flavour - from GloboCo).

Realisation that he was getting a bit paranoid dawned on him slowly, and he tried to calm down. He should carry on as normal, as Marcus had said. He should buy his furniture, spend the rest of the day putting up shelves, and maybe get rid of the horrible wicker chair that his part-time girlfriend had "renovated" and persuaded him to install in the corner. He was fond of Cindi, but there wouldn't be much time for her and her views about Randall's lack of style from now on.

He tried, with varying degrees of success, to focus on the mundane.

After ordering some furniture with immediate delivery - no point in saving the credits now - he prepared a large meal to make up for his skipped breakfast and waited for his sofa to arrive. It was just as he was piling the dishes by the sink and realising he would only get to use his new furniture for six months, when his terminal lit up.

It had arrived, too late to cancel now.

The delivery men were typical of delivery men everywhere. They were efficient, courteous, polite, and cheerful. They efficiently helped Randall move his old furniture out of the house. They courteously accepted a cup of coffee and a biscuit. They politely moved his new furniture into position. And they cheerfully helped themselves to a bottle of whiskey from his drinks cabinet on the way out.

It doesn't matter, thought Randall as he discovered the theft sometime later. GloboCo's men were notorious for minor acts of thievery, but there was nothing you could do about it, complaining was just as likely to get you a brick through your window. Maybe Marcus was right and the world wasn't as fixed as he had supposed.

He unpacked his new shelves, discarded the instruction leaflet [6] - which seemed to have been written originally in Sanskrit and translated into Panglish via Klingon - and thought about it some more.

From what he had discovered during his bedtime reading, the other Randall and Marcus had intervened in the twenty-first century by telling the world about the secret cabal that was taking over the planet. They revealed them as the criminals that they were with absolute proof. Secret documents, hidden bank account details, proof of false flag events... the lot. The system was shown to be massively corrupt. The bankster families and their psychopathic sycophants were exposed, and the population began to react.

Others from that time had suspected as much of course, but they were mostly silenced or terminally ridiculed. Randall and Marcus had given them the proof they needed. The people did the rest.

It went down in history as the First World Revolution, and it was one of the most difficult periods ever recorded. The powers in control fought back mercilessly as their integrity was scrutinised, but in increasing numbers the people stopped complying with their bills and tax demands when they learned the horrible truth. Hundreds of thousands died as the ruling powers stopped complying too, and dried up the food and energy supplies; mostly from cold and starvation during the bitter winter that followed.

Randall was suddenly acutely conscious of a sort of second-hand guilt for being the cause of a series of small wars that had happened nearly six hundred years ago, but he just as quickly dismissed the feeling as being ridiculous. He hadn't actually been the cause. Yet. Er...

------

[6] Because he was a man, and therefore had an instinctual understanding of how these things worked. He knew how the parts fitted together, but, like most men, he was always trying to get Peg D to fit into Slot C.

Eventually, by sheer force of numbers, the people won. From that day on, the world should have flowered in art and culture and been free from tyranny. Various technologies that had been suppressed by the vested interests of the time should have become common knowledge, and a new egalitarian economic model should have arisen. So what went wrong? Was it Slippage? Certainly some of it was, but that was mostly concerned with himself and Marcus; events in the outside world were only tangentially similar. Did the old powers gradually infiltrate the newly emerging free governments? Very probably, perhaps he could do some checking on that point. Was there any way to prevent the world from becoming a tyranny, albeit a reasonably-pleasant-if-you-ignore-the-screaming-and-keep-your-head-down kind of tyranny? Perhaps. Perhaps not.

It was all getting rather complex, and not a little depressing. Maybe The Book would answer some of his questions, though it was just as likely to leave him with a hundred more.

It was early evening now and he decided it was time to lie to his friends about his absence last night. He'd constructed a plausible enough story about how the shelf unit had dropped on his foot and broken his toe. He would have to be sure to limp for a while when he was out and about, just in case, but he reckoned it would dig him out of the hole.

He recorded the message and sent it to his friends. A little discourteous maybe, but he pretended to be groggy from the influence of the pain killers, so that should do the trick. Then he thought about his mother. What the hell was he going to say to her?

'Hello, Mom. You remember when Dad disappeared?' No.

'Mom, I'm going travelling for a few years.' No.

'Hi, Mom I met a man who shouldn't really exist and we're going into the past to maybe wipe out the present timeline and replace it with something better.' No.

'Hey, Mom, you remember Marcus Han don't you?'...

Of course! Marcus had introduced his mom to his dad! She must have known him. Perhaps Marcus had already said something to her and she knew all about it. Maybe he should just tell her the truth. She would understand that her only son from her marriage to her long missing husband was going to suddenly disappear just like he did. Wouldn't she? No, on second thoughts, probably not.

He decided to postpone the call and retire early to read his book. He ran a bath. A luxury perhaps, but seeing as he wouldn't be paying the bill it was a luxury to be indulged in. After a long soak, he dried himself and went straight to bed. With a bottle of Water+ by his bedside he relaxed and picked up The Book, determined to get some answers.

Ten minutes later he was fast asleep.

He woke early, refreshed and relaxed. Then he remembered the events of the past two days and the tension began to set in again. If only he could get one of those chairs here. He made a mental note to ask Han in a few days' time.

After breakfast, he settled down in the lounge with a coffee and The Book. Even after nearly six hundred years it was still in perfect working order. Randall had no doubt that the Han family had replaced parts over the centuries, possibly even copied the data to another device entirely, but it was still nice to have the feel of the thing in his hands. A genuine artefact from the twenty-first century, still functioning and about to perform that function.

He switched on the Kindle. There were two sections to The Book; he'd read the first already, and was now prepared for the second...

Hello again, Randall. I hope you've managed to acclimatise yourself to your new reality, and I hope it hasn't been too much of a wrench for you. In fact, I hope you are as excited as I was when I knew for sure I would be travelling back. This is a great opportunity for you. Just think of the possibilities.

I was going to spend the next few paragraphs trying to persuade you of the need to do this, to drive home the urgency of your mission and convince you of its importance. But I've decided against it. You should be willing to go without persuasion, as I was, otherwise there is no point. Somehow, I get the feeling that you will have decided almost immediately to go. If not, then I don't know myself as well as I thought I did.

Forgive me if that sounded odd, but I suspect that you and I will turn out to be quite similar. Marcus and I have talked extensively on the subject of our counterparts and how they (sorry, *you*) will differ from us. I don't know why, but I get the feeling we should have reasonably similar personalities, quite aside from the interference of the Han family. I suspect there may be some sort of leakage of information between our timelines, I don't really know for sure, but some of the mathematics seems to back up the idea.

Marcus, on the other hand, is of the opinion that your world will be so drastically different from ours that any similarity in our characters will be purely coincidental, and of a very low probability.

I don't know which of us is right, and I won't until you join us here.

Actually, now I think about it, I'll never know. When you travel back, you'll be wiping out this timeline, which means I'll never write what you're reading now, and we'll end up writing this book together to guide the new Randall that will take your place. Makes your head spin doesn't it?

All I do know is that you are the ones who will be in a position to figure it out. Are we similar, or not? Does leakage occur? I made a bet with Marcus, which you are in no way obliged to participate in: the loser buys your last meals on the day you travel back.

So it was Randall himself who had come up with the first stirrings of Slippage Theory, even if he would have ended up calling it Leakage Theory. He had thought about it in 2017, beating the late Mr. Han to it by over four hundred years. Should he tell Marcus? He had been assured that this book was for his eyes only, and that Marcus hadn't read it, so he might not know this. Then again, Marcus had his own ancestors' books, and was sure to have read about the same conversations.

Maybe he would bring it up another time.

He realised that using phrases such as "another time", or "see you next time" was something he should try to stop himself doing. It was strangely disturbing that these innocent phrases were now loaded with so much extra meaning. He caught himself using them time and again.

As he turned back to The Book he was disturbed by a call from Cindi on his terminal. *Dammit*, he thought, as Cindi's smiling avatar waited for him to respond. This was all he needed. He blinked to answer the call.

'Cindi, hi,' he said.

'Are you okay, Randall? You didn't call. What's this about a broken toe? Can I come over? I have your present.'

Randall didn't want to seem ungracious, but he didn't want Cindi here today either. She would spend an hour telling him why he had bought the wrong furniture, and another telling him what she would have bought instead, and why, and what colour it should have been to improve his flow of Chi, and what it was made from, and why the material was superior in every way to the rubbish Randall had bought, and how much difference it made to the South American natives who had climbed huge trees at enormous risk to get to the particular vine it was all tied together with...

And then he'd find out he'd put it in all the wrong places for beneficial feng-shui anyway. Birthday present notwithstanding, he had to think quickly and get rid of her.

'Thanks, Cindi I'd love to see you, but my toe kept me up all night and I'm not feeling very well. I've taken some more Ultra-Para-Codo-Asprinol and I ordered some Zombinol last night. I think I might take one as soon as they arrive and try to catch up on some sleep. You can come over tomorrow or the day after if you like. Sorry to be such a pain but I really don't feel like seeing anyone today, the place is a bit of a mess to be honest, I've got boxes everywhere. I might try to clean it up a bit before I go to bed.' The trick to dealing with Cindi was to keep talking. By the time you'd finished she'd forgotten the question.

'But I want to see your new furniture...' she almost whimpered.

'Most of it's still in the boxes. I only put the chairs in place and unpacked the shelves, and while I was holding them against the wall I dropped them on my foot. It was really painful, and I think I broke the shelves too. I really am a klutz. What's my present?' Another trick. Make a statement she agreed with and then ask an unrelated question.

'You'll have to wait a couple of days now won't you? I'm not in town tomorrow, so it'll have to be the day after.'

Randall almost sighed with relief.

'Well if you're going to sleep I'll leave you to your suffering and your boxes. Till next time then. Mwah.'

'Okay, Cindi, see you soon, thanks for calling,' said Randall, hanging up on her and wincing at the phrase "next time".

That was too close for comfort. He needed a quick way to apply a fake toe bandage. Putting The Book out of sight beneath his new sofa cushion, he went to study the contents of his limited first aid kit...

An hour later Randall was finally happy with the lump of sticking plasters, cotton wool, and bandage he had constructed. It slid onto his foot quickly, looked convincing, and was easy to remove again. The limp had been perfected and he was ready to face any unexpected callers.

Which was just as well, because thirty seconds later he had an unexpected caller.

'Mom,' he cried, through the two way speakers. 'You shouldn't have come over. I'm fine. Honestly.'

His mother was standing outside with a "look" on her face. She had an impressive range of looks from which to choose, and this one radiated a worried irritation with a trace of resignation-through-the-experience-of-years; which is quite a trick for a single look to accomplish.

He had to open the door. Luckily his toe bandage was already on. He blinked it open.

'Randall James!' his mother exclaimed as she walked in. 'I had a call from your girlfriend Cindi last night, remember her? She was asking me where you were. Toe or no toe, you should always respond to your messages, especially on your birthday. And what's the harm in calling your old mother on your birthday, eh? Too busy breaking your toe were you?'

She had called him "Randall James" which meant she was irked but not furious with him. If she had been more than irked, she would have employed the dreaded middle name too [7].

'Sorry, Mom,' he said, lamely.

Equally lamely, he limped forwards to kiss his mother on the cheek. Go for the sympathy angle that was the way. He applied a slightly pained "look" of his own and hobbled over to greet her.

Her look faded to one of concern almost immediately. She walked towards him to save him the trouble.

'Okay, dear, you sit down. Does it hurt much?'

'Yeah quite a bit, Mom, and I didn't sleep well so I'm going to take a couple of Zombinol I think, they'll be delivered in an hour or two.' *Good idea to keep your lies consistent*, he thought.

---

[7] Yes. It begins with a 'Z'.

'Oh you don't want Zombinol. You want SomniNite. They're much stronger. Here, I have a couple in my bag.'

That was another thing, quite apart from her impressive facial dexterity, that always surprised Randall about his mom - the contents of her bag. He knew from past experience that she had, in her bag, a pharmacopoeia of stunning scope and complexity. No pain or discomfort was unconsidered. No rash or insect bite would go un-soothed, and no cut un-sanitized. You could lose a leg and she'd have "just the thing" in her bag.

On top of that she had small tools for almost any daily eventuality; from toenail clippers, to pliers, to knives, to needle and thread, and more. She even had a lighter that could double as a stove or a blowtorch if needed. She'd never needed, but that wasn't the point. She might need. And if she did need, she wasn't going to be found wanting. Or, indeed, needing.

She quickly found the pills she was looking for and handed them to the now seated Randall.

'I'll get you some water, dear,' she said, bustling off to the kitchen.

Randall relaxed a little. She'd fallen for it and he was in the clear. He could look forward to a brief visit from his mom, and then the rest of the day reading The Book...

Twelve hours later he groggily awoke with the thought, "Well that didn't quite go to plan" running around in his head. He hadn't considered that his mother would stand over him and make sure he swallowed the damn sleeping tablets; which were, as promised, a lot stronger than Zombinol.

Oh well, he was awake now and he had a full day with no interruptions to deal with. In fact, he had quite a long day ahead of him because it was now a little past one in the morning, a good seven or eight hours before he normally woke up. What Marcus's recorder was going to make of it he didn't know, but at least it was consistent with his stated plans to Cindi and his mom, so not too bad.

He lay in bed for a few minutes ignoring his stomach and collecting his thoughts, most of which were hiding in dark corners of his mind still shaking off the SomniNite tablets. Eventually, with a sigh, he got dressed and headed for the kitchen. Via the bathroom.

49

Strong coffee was needed, so he made a pot of the good stuff, enough for four or five cups, and went into the lounge with a banana and a bowl of muesli with Mylk [8]. It struck him that the smell of strong coffee at night was rather odd. A smell that he associated with morning was wafting around during the wee small hours. The Sun wouldn't come up for another five more. It wasn't the right time for coffee.

"The right time". Another phrase he would have to abandon or redefine.

The next thought to strike him was that he was noticing small things like the smell of the coffee in an attempt to not think about the fact that he was about to embark on a journey that would result in him travelling six hundred years into the past, to do he knew not what, and he would never see his friends or family again. He felt a pang of sorrow, but only a small one, and almost exclusively for Cindi. Most of his friends were airheads, more concerned over the latest fashions or the hyper-hockey scores than anything of importance.

This was, of course, deliberate. He couldn't risk associating with scientists and engineers or the WP would come knocking - or more likely, battering-ramming - on his door. He selected his friends with care; there wasn't a contentious opinion or an above average IQ amongst the lot of them. He often had to bite his lip on the rare occasions when they discussed "politics".

In reality they did no such thing. What they thought of as politics was only the officially sanctioned opinions that the media outlets and terminals promulgated, and that was just tittle-tattle, or more likely downright deception. What really went on, no one except the high-ups knew. And they weren't telling.

It struck him once again that Marcus was very probably right when he said the world was only different, not fixed. That revolution over half a millennium ago should have resulted in a much stronger and freer society. So why was it not? Why was it that reporting the theft of his

---

[8] You guessed it, another GloboCo product. Mylk is a white liquid, but that's where the similarity ends. Milk evolved dramatically through the centuries - through Pasteurisation, Powdering, Sterilisation, Filtering, Skimming, Polymerisation, and finally its replacement by a completely artificial liquid synthesized from crude oil, seawater, and sucralose.

whiskey by the GloboCo removal men was pointless and would result in an even poorer service from them in the future? Why was it that the technology of time-travel was destroyed and ridiculed by the WP as soon as it was invented? Why wasn't he living in a utopian paradise?

He realised he was beginning to dwell on things that were ultimately out of his control, at least for the time being (doh!). That way madness lies. He had to pull himself together. He downed his second cup of coffee, took a few deep breaths, and reached under the sofa cushion for The Book.

As he leaned back and started reading, he noticed that the Kindle wasn't on the same page as he'd left it. He'd already read this bit. Now how did that happen? From experience he knew it was quite easy to accidentally change the page, the Kindle being touch sensitive; you only had to brush your sleeve on it and all of a sudden you had no idea where you were in the book anymore. He touched the screen to go forward a page, and another, before he found his place again.

He poured another coffee, took a sip, and started reading...

If you've read this far then I can safely assume you are on board and hopefully eager to get started.

So let's get started.

I hope I don't bore you, but I want to go over a few basics so they're fresh in your mind. You should be familiar with the work of Zachary James and his grandson, Jon Z. James.

The mathematics required to compute an n dimensional rotating vortex in 5D time-space, and translate the product into a series of iterative fourier transforms in 4D space-time, is, of course, the basis of Temporal Vortex Theory. But to take Vortex Theory to a place where it can actually translocate a sub-atomic particle in 3D space had to wait for the torsion matrix equations of Professor Hochi...

Randall skipped a couple of pages, and a few more. He didn't need a primer on the theory, he knew the theory. He needed to know how to turn the theory into a machine that could throw his sub-atomic particles, in the form of pure energy, through the vortex and out the other side all at the same time. And more importantly, *in* the same time.

For most of his life, ever since he'd learned some of the basic maths, Randall had wondered in awe at the sheer complexity involved. Time and again (doh!) he had wondered whether it was actually truly possible. Perhaps his dad really had escaped to foreign climes, and all the evidence to the contrary was a cleverly created hoax.

Even now it was possible to construct a scenario that indicated an entrapment operation. For all he knew "Marcus Han" could have written everything on this Kindle. If that was really his name. He could be a WP spy sent to test him, to find out how much he knew about time-travelling. Maybe they had suspected him all along. Once he started being actively engaged in the plot they could arrest him at any time and throw him in jail... or worse, exile him to the wild GM Wastelands, where all sorts of monstrous "Planimals" were free to roam wild...

The Planimals were notorious for their incredible evolutionary dexterity; almost any combination of life-forms was possible in the Wastelands: bushes that fruited eyeballs and watched every move you made, flying octopi writing inky messages in the clouds, dragon-flies, crab-apples, spider-monkeys, horse-radishes... use your imagination, evolution did. The epidemic of Prats [9] had been causing worldwide problems ever since they evolved.

When the landmass rose from the Pacific Ocean during the Earth Shifts, the corporations of the time saw it as an ideally isolated place to test certain new techniques they had developed in genetic engineering. They set up their labs and research facilities to begin the experiments almost as soon as the land was dry.

And it was an unmitigated disaster.

Only five years later all the scientists were dead - or worse, grotesquely mutated - and monstrous chimera super-breeds dominated the island; which was subsequently rather hastily abandoned and quarantined.

In the centuries since then it had acquired an almost mythic status. The disastrous and long-abandoned genetic engineering - combined with morphic resonance and epigenetic mutation - led to an exponential

---

[9] A cross between a pigeon and a rat. Fortunately, the only species (so far) to escape from the Wastelands - but Prats get *everywhere.*

52

rise in the rate of evolution; any useful trait evolved by one creature being acquired by most of the others in very short order.

It had recently been announced on the newscasts - based on the sporadic reports of intrepid explorers who'd survived with their sanity intact - that talking trees had recently evolved, and that they wanted to discuss humanity's surrender.

Most people ignored it at the time, because the trees weren't likely to come over here and start demanding our surrender were they? What with them being on an abandoned island continent in the middle of the Pacific Ocean and all. Nevertheless, one of the current panics in the media was the endless discussion about the possibility of the trees learning to swim. Sales of chainsaws had subsequently skyrocketed.

He shook off the paranoid thoughts. There was no way it was all a hoax. Han knew too much, and anyway, how could he explain his ancestors' miraculous escapes otherwise?

He took yet another deep breath, sipped his coffee, and settled down to get acquainted with the details on how to build a time machine.

What else could he do?

Chapter 9.

George James Junior regressed.

Infinitely.

After recovering from the immense shock of merging with the universe, he found that his mind, indeed his entire being, was now encapsulated by numerical relationships. He seemed to be made out of numbers.

And if you think about it, numbers are infinite.

Indeed, in a very real sense he *was* numbers, and all the infinities implied by that, and what's more, as far as he could determine, he always had been. All dimensions, all time and space, every particle in the universe and every relationship between them, all quantum states and all physical laws; anything that could be expressed using numbers - all existed as, and in, George James Junior.

And he was still completely pissed out of his mind.

As far as he could tell he'd always been pissed out of his mind, so it was perfectly normal to feel a bit bilious and inclined to slur his thinking. The vague throbbing sensation where he imagined his head to exist was also just an experience like any other. Being infinite, he had no tangible reference with which to compare himself; it was just normal.

In a tiny corner of his mind there was a very dim recollection of what it was like to not be as hammered as a nail, but he couldn't quite bring it into his attention at the moment - whatever a moment was.

It was unimportant anyway because he had just (or was it aeons ago?) noticed a collection of matter that he recognised. The numbers were exact. He remembered this "place".

Three lumps of gravity whirling around as a tiny part of one of the much larger conglomerations of material that he fuzzily recognised as galaxies. He focused his slightly hazy attention on the middle sized lump of the three and the numbers streamed through his consciousness. Giddily, but they streamed.

Yes. He knew this. Vague memories began to flit across his mind - insubstantial, not quite graspable, yet tantalisingly real.

Urth? No, that wasn't right. The name was just out of reach, on the tip of his imaginary tongue. Something to do with ears? Again, not quite right, nearly there though, something like that... and then, like a boomerang he didn't know he'd thrown, it all came back to him. This was the Earth! His home!

He revelled in the memories as they came flooding back from the far flung corners of his memory; ever more indistinct and ambiguous recollections of his Earth life began to impinge on his awareness like sunlit clouds on the distant horizon of his mind. He was beginning to remember more and more...

He also noticed a few things he hadn't known before, numerical relationships that had passed him by when he was "alive". He quickly spotted the fact that a cube big enough to fit the Sun inside snugly would be big enough to stack sixty-four million Moons inside. Not 63,999,999 or 64,000,001, but sixty-four million exactly. How curious.

Then he realised that ten minutes of arc on the Moon is exactly Pi miles long. Very strange. He spotted that the Earth completes 366 full revolutions in a year and is 366% bigger than the Moon. Odd. He then went on to observe that the Moon's diameter is 27.32% of the Earth's, and rotates on its own axis once every 27.32 days. Even odder, verging on weird.

A word wobbled to the front of his awareness, eventually resolving itself into the word "reciprocal". He did the sum 1/366 and was surprised by the answer. But what surprised him even more was the long list of things that he suddenly realised could be codified by the same string of digits. Absolute zero, the length of the human gestation period in days, the ratio of Pi to four... his memory presented him with many more as his newly found mathematical skills went to work on the information flooding into his mind.

What could all that mean?

Over and over again the same numbers kept popping up, as more and more incredible coincidences struck him; weird inexplicable oddities that stuck out like a spear in the chest - or would have done if he still had a chest. What should he make of these strangely coincidental facts?

Density, dimension, orbital speed, all these things and more contained subtle relationships linking them either to each other - or to universal constants such as c, or e, or Phi - that would have blown the world's cosmologists' minds had they been aware of them. It began to look more like a gigantic engineering project than a solar system.

He examined the physical laws of the universe (which, by analogy, was like looking in a mirror) but could find no reason why these numbers should be so synchronistic. There were no universal laws stating that it should be so. It was an anomaly. It didn't fit.

Very puzzling indeed.

He checked his infinite being to find any other coincidences of this kind throughout the universe of time and space. A moment, or an aeon, later, he saw a planet in a galaxy eight billion light years away that had a moon with a diameter precisely one fifth of its host planet; in another galaxy, a binary pulsar with periods of exactly one second and two seconds respectively; a civilization in a far distant galaxy had developed technology that was very similar to that on what he could remember of Earth at the time of his "death" (or whatever it was that had happened to him) which was odd enough, but not in the same league. The fact that they had a city called Noo Yawk caught him by surprise, but again, not in the same league.

And that was all. There were plenty of other fairly close approximations, but there was nowhere in the universe with as many coincidental properties as the Sun - Earth - Moon system.

Puzzled, he switched his attention to a time five billion years ago and began watching the formation of the solar system. The dust coalesced, the burgeoning Sun drew the plasma charge from the galactic medium and ignited, the whirling rocks and streaming plasma smashed together to create the planets, life started on Earth (and also on Mars he noticed with surprise - a strange ecosystem of plasmoid life-forms, toroidal, four-dimensional and unique to the universe) two planetesimals collided, creating the asteroid belt and wiping out the new life on Mars... and so on.

But where was the Moon? It wasn't there!

He skipped forward a few hundred million years. And again. It was now less than three billion years to the "present", and still no Moon. Where was it?

He skipped another half a billion years. Suddenly, it was there. Ping. Like a magic trick. He stopped and went back a hundred million years. No Moon. He gradually inched forward, a million at a time. No Moon - nothing - nothing - continued lack of satellite - selenic absence - moonlessness - ping! There it was again. He went back in thousands until he saw the most astonishing thing...

He saw lots of little white spaceships enter the solar system through a wormhole and set to work on the largest of the asteroids. He watched them hollow it out and pour the spill onto the surface until it was almost perfectly spherical with a few highlands here and there. Then they steered it into a finely controlled orbit around the Earth - a task that took nearly a hundred years on its own - and they settled down to watch the show.

The population of the Earth, being microscopic, didn't mind (because they hadn't got minds) but they did notice. And notice in a very big way.

All of a sudden, life, quite happy to have this new strobe-light in the sky, started to gyrate to the new rhythm of the Moon. The newly created tides washed life up onto the shoreline, where it danced with the beat until the conga-line of evolution began to head in a seriously different direction...

Chapter 10.

There was a dull pain in Randall's brain. He'd got as far as...

Obviously, x equates to a value in 1D space perpendicular to the isotropic vector matrix, and must be proportional to the n^x dimensional voxel-space induced by the flow,

... when his head just seized up.

It wasn't obvious to Randall at all. What the *hell* was a voxel? And *why* was it induced? Where was it flowing *to*? He had no idea. It was something to do with Planck length sized pixels of reality but beyond that he was guessing.

He'd decided two hours ago that skipping the introduction was a bad idea and had started again from the beginning, making notes and comparing them to his own research.

It didn't really help.

So far he'd tried a number of different tricks in an attempt to understand the bewildering gibberish he was reading. He'd tried the "Just read on, it'll come to you eventually" approach - which had yielded only confusion. The "Use a dictionary to make sure you know the definition of every word" approach wasn't any better; he didn't have the right dictionaries and this was all maths anyway. The "Just re-read everything until it goes in" approach had given him a headache.

Using his terminal for help was out of the question. It would surely raise suspicion. He began to panic slightly and hoped to Dawkins that Marcus knew this stuff better than he did, otherwise it was going to be goodbye Galaxy in about six months' time.

The coffee pot was empty. So was his stomach. It was time for a break. Perhaps something to eat followed by half an hour in the sim suite would relax him and get his brain into gear for the trials ahead...

An hour later he was even more on edge. His meal was sitting heavily in his stomach, and his sim avatar was lying half dead in a smoking crater on Saturn's moon Triton with his spacesuit slowly filling up with blood. A large octopus-like alien was clamped to his visor and was preparing its carbonite-tipped ovipositor to inseminate him.

He couldn't concentrate on the game; indeed, he hadn't done this badly on a sim level since he was a kid. He needed to get outside and stroll his lunch off, fresh air would do the trick. It was still very early in the morning so no one would be around, he could forget the fake limp.

As the victorious Octopoid penetrated his faceplate and began to deliver its wriggling egg sacs up the avatar's nostrils, he reset the sim to the start of the level and logged off. Slipping on his jacket, he left the house.

Ten minutes later, as he was walking through the dismal patch of muddy turf with a few pathetic trees and bushes that called itself a park, he got a message on his terminal the like of which he'd never seen before. To start with it was in green text instead of the usual white on transparent grey; the font was different; the text was bigger than normal; and it was placed in the middle of his eye, instead of the more usual above and to the left of his line of sight.

But the most unusual thing was the message itself, it simply read:

Ignore this message. Respond as minimally as you can. Act like you cannot see it.

Randall's eyes almost cartwheeled in their sockets. He looked around him, but there was no one to be seen.

Another sentence appeared below the first...

It is possible you are in danger. Don't panic. Start walking home again

After a few moments the message disappeared, to be replaced with...

... nonchalantly.

Again a pause, and then...

Marcus.

Randall breathed out. Eventually.

His heart slowed the samba rhythm it was beating in time to and he turned to walk, nonchalantly, back home. His feet gave every impression of wanting to stay in the park, as did his skin.

What danger? Could Marcus have been any less specific? Was this more melodrama?

He realised he was starting to quicken his pace, and deliberately slowed down to a more normal walking speed. A few deep breaths later and he was calm. Ish. He retraced his steps back towards the park entrance and tried to keep his thoughts away from any possible danger. Because of that, he quickly thought of at least nine possible dangers in quick succession and began to panic again.

Calm down, he thought. *Breathe. In and out, in and out. Think about how lovely the flowe... the tre..., okay, the mud, is looking at this time of year.*

An edgy calm came eventually as Randall approached his house. With a final deep breath, he opened the gate and walked up the path - to be scared out of his already reticent skin by Marcus crouching behind the bush by his door.

'Pretend you can't see me,' he whispered. 'Just open the door and let me in first. Block the view with your body.'

Randall stepped back to let Marcus, on all fours, scurry unseen into his house.

'What the bloody hell is going on?' shouted Randall, as Marcus stood up and brushed off the leaves from his jacket.

'How long have you known Cindi?' he said, bluntly.

'About three years. What's she got to do with it?'

'My computer intercepted a message yesterday that I strongly suspect concerns us and our activities. It's heavily coded, but I cracked their header files long ago so I can read the subject field and other data about it. It'll take a while to decode the message itself, but the header contained your name and the name of the sender, a certain agent Lehman. That's Cindi's surname isn't it?'

Randall decided not to ask how Marcus knew this; he suspected Marcus knew a lot of things he wasn't sharing. 'Well yes, but you're stretching it a bit aren't you? Lehman must be a very common surname.'

'There are seven Lehmans registered to this district. Two of them work at the university, one is a bank manager, two are retired and one is currently undergoing cancer treatment that he is not expected to survive. That leaves one, and I can't find her occupation. That usually indicates a WP operative. Her first name is actually Daphne by the way. No wonder she changed it.'

'You're sure about this?' Randall was tense.

'The transmission was sent during your recent extended nap from just outside this building.'

Randall's eyebrows floated to the top of his forehead. 'You're monitoring me?'

'Yes, Randall. The recorder I gave you connected to your home compunet to monitor your movements, and it's a good job it did. It looks like the building was illegally entered yesterday while you were asleep. I checked the log earlier and found a very short power spike in your door mechanism just after 9 pm. I almost missed it, it wasn't an amateur job.'

'The Book!' exclaimed Randall. 'I'd swear it was on a different page when I picked it up again this morning.'

Marcus looked thoughtful, and, for once, more than a little unsure about what to do next. Had they been compromised? Had they failed in their mission already?

'I need to crack that message. We're not safe here; we should go to my place. Now. Get the recorder and The Book.'

The look on Marcus's face betrayed his uneasiness, and that didn't help Randall's mood. With growing alarm, he picked up The Book, stashed it in his jacket, handed Marcus the recorder, and followed him outside.

He had reached the gate when, suddenly, an ear-wax-meltingly loud noise rattled his skull and caused parts of his brain to begin switching off. Simultaneously, a blindingly bright light, a terrible sensation of dizziness, and a painful tingling feeling in his skin overwhelmed his senses.

As the noise and the light grew louder and brighter, to an ever more intolerable extent, his sense of balance finally failed him and he collapsed into his own footprint like a suddenly unstrung marionette.

The last thing he saw before losing his grip on consciousness was Marcus crumpling to the ground in exactly the same way a few feet ahead of him.

———————————————

Randall sat at the back of his classroom listening intently to the teacher. Except it wasn't Mr. Han. It looked a lot like Mr. Han but wasn't him. The hair was wrong and the voice wasn't right. He was taller too.

There were no lessons today because there was a maths test. He had his lucky calculator on his desk, and although he was anxious, he was eager to perform well.

The alleged Mr. Han called for the attention of the class and announced the test had started.

'You may turn over your papers and begin,' he said, in not quite Mr. Han's voice. 'Terminal access is restricted for the duration. You have two hours.'

Randall turned over his paper and read the first question. It read:

If x equates to a value in 1D space perpendicular to the isotropic vector matrix, calculate the diameter of the n^x dimensional voxel-space induced by the flow.

He blinked several times and read the question again, but the question remained defiantly incomprehensible. He blinked several times more and wiped his eyes. It didn't help. He turned the paper over. No help there either. Typing "Voxel?" into his calculator yielded the message "Incorrect reality error". Strange. He felt the vaguely familiar sensation of sweat beginning to form on his brow, and risked looking over at the desk to his left. The student sitting there was writing fluidly with his tongue sticking out the side of his mouth in the manner of concentrating children everywhere.

Randall stretched his neck a little but couldn't see what was being written. With panic starting to rise, he looked over at the desk to his right - and straight into the face of his father, who appeared to be steaming drunk.

He screamed with the shock, shooting bolt upright and knocking his desk over in the process. Nobody seemed to notice; the rest of the class carried on with their test as if nothing was happening.

'Don't do it, Randall,' shouted his father, frantically. The smell of stale malt whiskey and halitosis which washed over Randall made him wretch, but he held on to his stomach contents.

'You must, Randall,' said Not-Han, calmly. The voice was a whisper in his ear. Randall turned but Not-Han was not there. He was sitting at his desk reading what looked like an electronic book of some sort. The title of the book glowed orange on the black plastic cover. "Time-travel for Dummies", it read.

'No, Randall,' shouted his father. 'We have to stop them before it's too late.'

'Yes, Randall,' said the whisper. And again more urgently, 'Yes, Randall. Randall. Randall...'

'Randall.'

'Randall?'

This was very definitely not a whisper. It was probably a female voice but Randall couldn't know for sure. The ringing in his ears was louder than any external sounds, it was dark, and bits of his brain weren't working very well. He opened an eye a fraction. It was bright. He closed it again and groaned.

'Welcome back, Randall. I was afraid the goons had damaged you when they brought you in, they can occasionally be unnecessarily enthusiastic if left to their own devices. It's just their way. How do you feel?'

Randall couldn't tell exactly how he felt. Bits of his body were still numb, and the pins and needles coming from the bits that weren't did not bode well for the immediate future. He groaned again, but with more feeling.

'Well that's good,' said the now definitely female voice. 'There's water and fruit at the end of your bed. I'll give you an hour to wake up before we get started.'

The sound of footsteps moving away followed by a heavy door opening and closing, then the sound of a heavy door locking securely - Randall was alone in the room. After a minute or two, he risked opening his eyes, the brightness was less painful now and he looked around his... jail cell.

It didn't disappoint.

It was, in every respect, the epitome of cell-ness. The walls were a roughly finished dark concrete with an embedded steel slab set into one of them that served as a bed and table. A small barred window, too high to reach, let in enough light to illuminate the bucket in the corner; which at least smelled faintly of bleach rather than any of the other less savoury smells normally associated with buckets in cells. The lens high in the corner betrayed the camera that was watching every move he made.

He sniffed suspiciously at the water before taking a gulp, and another. It was ordinary water, not Water+, but it was refreshing anyway. He took another gulp.

His mind felt as if it had been taken apart, shuffled, and put back together using Velcro. A number of simultaneous emotions were jostling for dominance in his still partially anesthetised brain. Fear, Panic, and Despair were currently leading the race, but, rather unexpectedly, Relief was holding its own in fourth position. Hope had pulled a muscle getting into the starting blocks.

The unexpected feeling of relief caught Randall rather off guard; somewhere deep in his mind, surprisingly, a part of him was actually glad this stupid plot he'd become involved with had collapsed in farce. It was all over. He would very probably soon be dead, he wouldn't live to see the Milky Way disappear, and it wasn't his fault if it did.

He'd done his best. Now it was over to the WP.

He wondered if Marcus was conscious yet.

Marcus was conscious but sincerely wished he wasn't. It became obvious to his captors as soon as he was dragged into the cell that he

64

was off grid. Without a terminal they couldn't identify him. At first this confused the goons and they assumed their scanner was faulty. When they returned with a replacement they realised the truth.

It presented them with a bit of a problem. Under normal circumstances they would have simply scanned his terminal to get all the info they needed, or, if that info wasn't available, just instigate a feedback loop that would send agonizing pain signals to every nerve ending in his body until he told them what they wanted to know. Now they didn't know what to do. Their electronic devices were useless, and actually physically torturing someone was something they had little experience of. They were making it up as they went along.

They started with shouting and threats, quickly moved on to punching him in the face, but soon learned how much that actually hurts the hand. A couple of swollen knuckles later they stopped punching him and started using implements. Marcus said nothing.

The implements were, because of the improvised nature of the interrogation, pathetic. After a brief search of the various closets and cupboards in their offices they came up with a pair of nail clippers, a stapler, a ruler, and a couple of sharp pencils; any of which could cause agony in the hands of a skilled sadist, but in the hands of these amateurs was simply making a mess on the floor. Marcus, bleeding, still said nothing, but he said it with a wry smile on his face.

The smallest of the three, whom Marcus had ironically tagged "The Thinker" was sitting on the cell's only chair nursing his hand and wondering what to do next. He was nominally in charge, and this was not turning out to be a good day for him. He'd even tried saying please at one point. He was getting desperate.

'We'll find out who you are eventually you know,' he said, trying to reassert some control over the situation.

He spoke in short, clipped sentences, and left long pauses between them. Still utterly punctilious even though he was obviously totally out of his depth and getting more desperate by the minute.

'We know all about Mr. James's secret research.'

Pause...

'Oh yes.'

Pause...

'Surveillance. That's the thing.'

Pause...

'We've been watching Mr. James for quite some time, you know.'

Pause...

'Oh yes.'

Pause...

'But you.'

Pause...

'Are new.'

Now a longer pause, during which he appeared to reach a decision. 'This is getting us nowhere,' he said, at last.

He addressed the other two goons, who were arguing about where to apply the next pencil. 'You two. Out.'

Pause...

'Subtlety... That's the thing.'

Pause...

'Oh yes.'

And they left.

Randall ate the fruit. It was nice. Perfectly ripe and succulent. He drank a glass of water and began to think about using the bucket, when there was a noise outside the cell door. Muffled talking. Raised voices. An argument?

A moment later the door unlocked, opened, and in walked Cindi.

'Good morning, Randall. You're well I hope? I see the broken toe has healed up nicely.'

She didn't look or sound like the Cindi he knew of old. Now she spoke with authority, and the annoying whiney quality to her voice was gone. Her bearing was different too. She moved with more grace than he remembered, the clumsy butter-fingeredness was no more, to be replaced with a precision of movement akin to a martial artist.

Randall rather liked it.

'Cindi...' he began.

'Daphne actually,' interrupted Cindi né Daphne.

'What's going on? What am I doing here?' Innocence was his opening gambit. Daphne was having none of it.

'Come now, Randall,' she said, 'we know all about your research, we have from the beginning. Why do you think I was assigned to you?'

'So it was all a game then? You're a spy? Our relationship meant nothing to you?'

'No, Randall. Nothing.' She looked like she meant it. 'Don't get me wrong, it was a pleasant enough assignment most of the time. You're quite good company actually. Although playing the bimbo did piss me off sometimes.' This last comment was directed towards the lens in the corner.

'You're very good at it.' He didn't try to hide the contempt.

'Enough pleasantries.' Now she was firm, in command. 'You will come with me.'

Grabbing Randall tightly by the arm, she turned and marched out of the cell. Once outside she relaxed her grip a little. Perhaps there were feelings there after all?

They marched along a dimly lit corridor towards a set of heavy double doors which Daphne opened with a pass-card. Once through, they emerged into a large courtyard which they started walking across, towards the opposite corner. It would take about thirty seconds, thought Randall. He scanned the area looking for a way out. Could he run? Possibly. Could he scale the thirty foot walls that surrounded him on all sides? No, probably not. What else was there? Not much. He thought about confronting Cind... Daphne. Perhaps he could overpower her, steal her pass-card and find a way out?

They walked in silence for a few seconds. He was clinging grimly to the memory of Hope, which had rubbed its legs and finally made it off the starting line.

'Look at the lampposts, Randall,' she whispered, quietly and unexpectedly. 'They look a lot like classical columns, don't you think?'

'I suppose so,' he replied, puzzled. Where was this going?

'Look at this one. Much better than the four we've just passed. That's my favourite.'

Her favourite? What was going on?

'Right,' said Randall. 'I see.'

'Do you?' she asked.

'Not really,' he replied.

She sighed and waggled her eyebrows in a strange way.

'Yes. The *fifth* lamppost along. I think that one looks a lot more like a *column* than the others. What do you think?'

Randall didn't know what to think.

'Er... I suppose so?'

What was this? Some kind of exotic confusion technique designed to disorient him? Baffle him? If so, it was working.

She waited for a few seconds as they passed the closest surveillance microphone before continuing.

'Yes I definitely think the *fifth column* is my favourite out of all of them. Do you see what I mean?' She wasn't looking at him and wasn't moving her mouth much for all the talking she was doing.

'I can hardly *resist* it. My *resistance* is falling. Understand?'

'What are you talking about? Why are we whispering?'

'Oh for goodness sake, Randall, are you an idiot?' she hissed. Her eyeballs were almost audible as they rolled in their sockets.

'I didn't think I was before we started walking across this courtyard, but now I'm not so sure. Are you trying to tell me something?' he whispered back to her. The phrase "fifth column" rattled around in his head. He'd heard it before but couldn't place it for the life of him.

'Jeez. Give the man a biscuit.' She discreetly rolled her eyes again, more quietly this time.

The confused expression which had occupied Randall's face for the last few moments began to subside. Hope had completed the first lap of the track and was catching the front runners. It had already overtaken Relief on the last bend. His eyebrows started making some strange movements of their own.

'Are you telling me...'

'Quiet,' she hissed. 'Get that look off your face. You're my prisoner remember?'

'Right,' he whispered. The glum look crawled back up onto his face. Hope, meanwhile, had overtaken Despair and the other front runners, and was heading for the finishing straight and the winner's trophy.

'I'll find a way to help you,' she said. 'And your friend. Who is he anyway?'

Suspicion, which had been watching the race in Randall's head from the side of the track up until now, took off its track suit bottoms and started limbering up.

Was this a trick? Was it a ruse? The realisation that they didn't know who Marcus was simply hadn't occurred to him. Should he tell her?

Could he trust her? Hope, which was now just about to cross the finish line, suddenly got a very bad cramp.

'Sorry, Daphne. I'm not telling you that,' he said.

'It doesn't matter. I understand you don't trust me yet. Be ready tonight at midnight. That's when the guard changes.'

Five seconds later they reached the door. Suddenly Daphne's grip tightened on his arm.

'Until then don't do anything stupid,' she whispered.

Hope limped across the finish line first, just ahead of Suspicion, which had run like hell to catch up. Fear, Panic and Despair were a dead heat for third place.

Randall checked his terminal. It was now ten minutes to midnight. The interrogation hadn't taken long and he was returned to his cell after giving them very little information.

When asked about Marcus he'd told them nothing, claiming he didn't know his real name and had called himself "Buzz", the first name he could think of. He had only met him two days ago (true) and he seemed a bit mental (also sort of true). He made up a story about how Buzz had tracked him down because he was obsessed with George Jr's disappearance and had been harassing him ever since, talking a lot of nonsense about time-travel. He could see they hadn't fallen for it, but it seemed to give them something to think about.

That he still had some access to his terminal surprised him. He couldn't send or receive messages, but he could know the time and what the weather was doing, that sort of thing. He'd even watched some hyper-hockey earlier in the evening. The Jets played the Comets on their home turf, but due to injuries they were not at their full strength. It came down to the wire, but in the last play of the game the Jets' captain, known by the nickname Xenoph to the fans, scored a superb broken nose on the Comets' goalkeeper and won the game with seconds to spare. He watched Xenoph's stats roll across the bottom of the vid as the crowd cheered ecstatically - Height, Weight, Years as a professional, Goals scored, Number of rape convictions... the usual stuff.

It didn't interest Randall in the slightest, but with nothing else to do he watched it anyway. His new perspective on life - the point of view of a prisoner - had made him introspective and quite philosophical in the last few hours. He'd watched the screaming fans all shouting Xenoph's name in unison and reflected on the mob mentality of the ordinary citizen. No wonder the ruling powers had such a grip on civilization, the people were too distracted by irrelevance to see the abuse of power. People weren't interested in politics, they didn't engage, and that was encouraged by the ruling class.

Bread and circuses. Now where had he heard that phrase before?

He was quiet now, listening for a sign from beyond the cell door. His terminal was in Ecom and he was lying on his bed, waiting.

At the stroke of midnight, the muffled sounds of footsteps could be heard from the corridor outside. The footsteps seemed to be moving away. The guard leaving? He waited for another set of footsteps getting louder, but they never came. Instead, after a minute or so, he heard the noise of the cell door unlocking itself. Two seconds later, the little red light that could be seen shining from the back of the camera went out.

This was it, he had to act now.

He opened the door a fraction and waited for a response. There was none. Opening the door wider, he poked his head out into the corridor. It was dark but he could see there was nobody there. Tentatively, he stepped out.

The double doors at the end of the corridor seemed to be the only way to go, so he headed towards them warily and quietly, his heart seemingly trying to break through his ribs from the inside as he went. As he reached the doors he could see they were open a crack. A small piece of plastic was inserted between them, preventing them from closing properly after the exit of the last guard. He opened the door slightly, kicked the plastic away and slunk outside, keeping to the shadows as much as possible. The lampposts in the square were all extinguished; presumably the cameras were down too.

A flash of torchlight from the corner of the courtyard he had been led to by Daphne earlier in the day. He moved quickly but quietly towards it.

'Hurry,' whispered Daphne, who was there waiting for him. 'We have to get your friend, he's in this block.'

They hurried through the doors and along the corridor.

'The power to these blocks has been disrupted,' said Daphne, as they ran. 'It'll be noticed soon when the relief guards arrive. They're being distracted by a friend of mine at the moment but it'll only be a couple of minutes before they come. Alarms must be ringing by now.'

They headed quickly towards Marcus's cell. As expected the power was out, but so was Marcus. They woke him roughly.

Groggy, and in obvious pain, Marcus opened an eye. His other eye was swollen over.

'Randall! How...' then he noticed Daphne.

'What's she doing here? What's going on?'

'Don't worry, Marcus,' said Randall, soothingly. 'She's on our side.'

'Really?'

'Yes,' said Daphne. 'I'm fifth column, part of the resistance. So it's Marcus is it? Pleased to meet you. Now we have to get you two the hell out of here. Can you walk? Good. Follow me.'

Randall helped Marcus to his feet and followed Daphne out of the cell. They walked away from the double doors and towards a smaller door at the other end of the corridor. It was an office, empty at this hour. They stepped inside and closed the door behind them. The window was a normal window a couple of feet from the ground; it too was open a crack. Daphne opened it wider and motioned them to climb through. She followed them outside across a small patch of scrubby grass to where a personal transport was waiting. They crammed inside, it was only a two-seater.

'Where are we going?' asked Randall.

'It'll have to be my place,' said Marcus. 'But I still don't trust her.'

He turned to Daphne. 'Take us to the park in district twelve and drive away. I can't let you see where I live,' he said.

'Okay. That's kind of what I was expecting. I have an hour or so, but then I have to get back to base before they notice my absence.'

She drove for nearly thirty minutes by a circuitous route and eventually pulled up at the park.

'There's an umbrella under your seat, Marcus,' she said as they arrived, 'take it. It's a partial Faraday cage. Keep it close above your head, it'll stop them detecting Randall's locator signal while you're outside. I'll try to contact you through your terminal in the morning. It'll be working again now you're away from the dampening field.'

'No,' said Marcus, emphatically, taking the umbrella and handing it to Randall. 'Thank you for your help, but we'll contact you when we're ready. Don't try to communicate with us directly.'

She nodded. 'Fair enough.'

Pulling up the brolly, they clumsily clambered out of the tiny, cramped, vehicle.

Without another word, she was gone.

Chapter 11.

George James Junior was fascinated. The moon-making aliens turned out to be an incredibly ancient race that spanned a good chunk of this corner of the universe, and their technology totally astonished him. He'd traced their home systems to a galaxy nearly eighty million light years from the Milky Way, and had been watching them avidly for some time - whatever "time" meant, of course.

Their core civilization covered nearly fifty galaxies in one particular cluster, but they had outposts much further afield, including three in the Milky Way. There were countless trillions of them on millions of planets, but they never seemed to interact openly with any other civilization, preferring to stay quietly hidden in the background, like tax inspectors, or traffic wardens. They were obviously interested in life elsewhere though, they seemed to be there at the beginning of life on other planets all over the universe - watching, recording, changing things occasionally, guiding evolution...

As far as he could tell - and as their civilization was very ancient and widespread, he couldn't know for sure - their intervention in the Sol system with the placement of the Moon was one of the largest pieces of astro-engineering they'd ever undertaken. They had artificially boosted the output of a star in another galaxy until life in that system had started to flourish, and they had placed other moons in other systems, but they were minnows compared to the Moon. The other moons were merely observation satellites; small hunks of rock filled with monitoring equipment, nothing like Earth's Moon. Most of them were natural satellites that the aliens simply bolted cameras to.

Earth's Moon, however, was a world unto itself. Inside out maybe, but still a world. It contained about a hundred thousand aliens at any one time, but they were constantly coming and going in their little ships. The mind boggling distances involved [10] were easily traversed using wormhole technology that would have made Einstein and Rosen snap their pencils and weep into their notepads.

It already seemed astonishing to him what they had accomplished, and he had really only skimmed the surface of their empire. He skipped further and further back in time trying to identify the beginning of their species. Eventually he got to a point almost six billion years before "the present", before the Sol system was even formed, to a single planet in a system of five, orbiting a G type star similar to the Sun. A large, watery, blue-green planet.

The aliens, an unremarkable semi-aquatic herbivore for most of their existence, had now finally colonized their entire planet, and had put a simple base on their tiny pebble of a moon. Their biology was astounding, they were carbon/oxygen based, like life on Earth, but because of a slight eccentricity in the planet's orbit, and the con-sequential evolutionary challenges that wobble had imposed, they were much more versatile. Breathing underwater or in air, photosynthesizing or consuming the plant life that also grew on their planet, they could withstand ranges of pressure and temperature way beyond the merely human. And their lifespan? Let's just say they put Methuselah to shame.

They were also quite spiritual in a no-nonsense kind of way. Pragmatic rather than religious, and obviously compassionate towards their own, they seemed to express a unity of consciousness unlike anything George Jr could comprehend. War amongst them was unheard of. Disputes, what few there were, always resolved themselves with the minimum of disruption to all parties, and were then swiftly forgotten - in stark contrast to what little George could remember of his own planet's history.

Their civilization grew with astonishing speed. They seemed to just "get it", whatever it was they were trying to get: from the ancient proto-genius who invented the wheel (and more importantly, the cup holder) to computers, spacecraft, space elevators, and wormhole technology, took only four thousand years.

---

[10] That George Jr now realised were only figments of the imagination in reality - time, and therefore space, were just constructs created by living things so that everything didn't happen to them all at once.

Within another four hundred thousand they had fully colonized their home galaxy and were looking towards others. Now, over five billion years later, they had made their home in the fifty or so galaxies that currently comprised their empire. And still they were expanding.

Some galaxies, however, they left pretty much alone. They would set up bases to watch or interfere with one or two planets in particular, but other than that they stayed away. The Milky Way was one such galaxy. Three bases, spread thousands of light years apart, were monitoring the life-forms on three planets, including the Earth, but the aliens made no further attempts at colonization.

He started moving forwards in time, back towards the present and beyond. He wanted to see where all this was heading. As he was about to pass through what humans laughingly call "the present", he noticed the aliens were currently colonizing another galaxy. He stopped to look more closely at the new outpost. It was quite close to the Milky Way, a little over two million light years or so distant. In fact, he could see through his expanded senses that the new galaxy was on a collision course with the Milky Way and would collide with it in approximately four billion years.

A memory from his life on Earth surfaced in his capacious and infinite mind. It took some time to surface as is often the way when your level of inebriation is higher than your capacity for cogitation, but eventually the word Andromeda bobbed up and floated there for his consideration.

He decided to observe them more closely as they set up their foothold in the new colony. Only one other species had evolved to a state of self-awareness in Andromeda, and George Jr, stepping through in fifty year jumps, watched while the aliens set up bases near the home star of the emergent civilization. They didn't do anything else, they left the new inhabitants of the universe alone, and apart from the forward bases within proximity of their star, they stayed away from that section of the spiral arm. In the rest of the Galaxy they began to spread out as they had in the other fifty.

Probably something to do with their respect for life, thought George Jr. *What an incredible species.*

As he watched, his attention was drawn momentarily by what seemed to be a large fleet of their spaceships entering Andromeda. The

wormhole mouth - which he could see was drawing power from the twisting plasma currents connecting Andromeda to the Milky Way - suddenly sprouted hundreds of ships.

He turned his attention toward their approach, watching hundreds more appearing every minute or so, until there were at least two thousand of them, flying away in all directions from the point of arrival. It was then that he observed the most horrifying thing he had ever seen in his infinite, inebriated, existence. A few short seconds after the last of the craft had exited the wormhole, he watched the entire Milky Way Galaxy, slip silently out of the universe.

Without so much as a "pop", it was gone.

He couldn't believe his, er... eyes, or whatever it was he perceived things with now. He skipped back to before the vanishing. There it was as normal; twin spiral arms full of solar systems sweeping gracefully through the void of space. He played time out in "real time", yet another fake perception believed to be true by humans. Time, he now knew, was a function of scale. Ask a photon.

The disappearance was instantaneous. No build up, no after effects, no noise. Simply a sudden and immediate manifestation malfunction. Here one picosecond, gone the next. The helical plasma stream that used to flow into the Milky Way now flipped with barely a pause to connect to the Large Magellanic Cloud that accompanied the vanished galaxy. Its dimmest stars began to light up like a nest of Christmas tree lights in a mirror-ball factory.

What could possibly have happened? How could an entire galaxy simply vanish? Expanding his awareness to its fullest extent, he was now cognisant of the entire universe in a hazy sort of way. Although the fine detail was hard to make out he could perceive the totality of space and time. Before long he spotted another occurrence of the galactic vanishing trick he had just witnessed the Milky Way perform. A billion or more years ago, another galaxy close to the alien empire also disappeared without leaving so much as a cloud of gas. He focused, doing the disembodied equivalent of clamping his hand over his eye so he could only see one of everything. There it was: the wormhole connecting the vanished galaxy to another occupied by the aliens.

The pattern became obvious. Somehow, the aliens were causing galaxies around them to suddenly slip into oblivion!

He focused harder on the moment immediately before the loss of the Milky Way. Now he was moving through time in yoctosecond skips [11]. There must have been some sort of trigger, an event that caused the failure of the Galaxy's existence. Focusing on the three observation bases, he saw the aliens all start flying into the swirling wormholes during the final seconds, moments before the Galaxy vanished.

He skipped back to a second before the disaster and slowed time down even more, narrowing his attention even further to observe the Moon. Now he was skipping in Planck-time steps (and you thought a yoctosecond was short). At this rate light itself seemed to stand still, the universe seemed to be frozen, and yet George Jr could see it changing from one skip to the next like a fast moving cosmic flip-pad.

Suddenly, without warning, the Earth vanished. Then, one skip later, the Moon. The Sun still shone and the rest of the galaxy still existed, but the wave of vanishing seemed to spread out from the Earth itself, not from the alien base as he'd been expecting. Venus went next. Then Mars, Mercury and the Sun. An instant later Jupiter was gone, followed closely by the rest of the solar system and the rest of the Galaxy.

Once again, he skipped back a second and focused more closely, trying to find the exact cause of the disaster. When he finally found it, it shook him to his, er... bones.

---

[11] Six orders of magnitude shorter than a picosecond, a yoctosecond makes a nanosecond seem like a long Sunday afternoon.

Chapter 12.

It was morning now. After spending half the night hiding in the park, Marcus and Randall had decided to risk it and headed for Marcus's bunker an hour before dawn. They didn't appear to be followed. They did appear to be cold, damp, and tired.

Now they were sitting in the computer room warming up, trying to decode the message and unscramble their heads. Not that the message meant much now that they had been caught and escaped again, but Marcus couldn't think of anything else to do. He was deeply engaged in an intense nail-biting cogitation of apparently immense proportions.

Worried, in other words.

He was easily the worst off out of the two of them. Randall had simply been fed some fruit and asked a few questions, whereas Marcus was battered and bruised. He was still far from out of the game however; a small three-century-old machine called a Medibot had just finished stitching up the cut on his eyebrow. It had done a very neat job.

Contraptions like this were illegal now because of a single incident over two hundred years ago, when a patient was allegedly deafened by a malfunctioning Medibot. The fact that the patient was later shown by a well-respected investigator to have been working for a competitor in the medical industry - the newly dominant and highly litigious GloboCo - and that the building's compunet had recorded a very unusual electromagnetic signal coming from the patient and concurrent with the accident, were very quietly ignored by the lawyers.

Very quietly indeed. They used a silencer on the gun.

Randall watched in rapt attention while the machine worked. These days all medical attention was attained through your terminal. Treatment was provided by GloboCo Medical, you had no choice about it. Some of the newer generation of terminals even had drug synthesis capabilities; it diagnosed your ailment, dosed you with pharmaceuticals, and took the money from your account before you even knew you were ill. They called it PMI - "Preventative Medical Intervention". "Lucrative" is how Randall now thought about it.

He was beginning to question many of the assumptions he had taken for granted about his world. His arrest had opened his eyes even wider, he was seeing through the propaganda. "PMI" now sounded a lot like "Charging a fortune for testing drugs on you that you don't need". He was angry. He was frustrated. He was also hungry.

'What have we got to eat around here?' he asked, breaking the silence of the last few minutes.

'Pretty much anything you want,' replied Marcus, without looking up. 'The kitchen is off the lounge to the left. Help yourself.' He sounded depressed.

'You want anything?'

'Coffee.'

'Right.'

Randall walked to the kitchen across carpet that seemed to caress his feet. At least they had somewhere nice to hide until the Galaxy disappeared, he reflected, as he admired the art hung tastefully along the curved corridor heading towards the lounge.

The kitchen, when he got to it, turned out to be almost as big as the entire ground floor of Randall's house. The lights came on automatically as he entered, as they had done in every room he'd seen so far. A dozen or more appliances of different types were installed around the kitchen in niches of various sizes. Everything was automated. Everything was user friendly. Everything was simple and easy to use. And because of that, he hadn't got the faintest idea how to make anything work.

Looking around he saw what appeared to be a sink, complete with taps. Now if he could only find a couple of mugs and some coffee he could at least begin to make them both a drink.

'Coffee... Coffee...' he muttered to himself as he searched the kitchen. As he said this, there was a noise like someone struggling to drown an asthmatic pig in a vat of runny custard, and a small area by the door lit up a little brighter than the rest of the room. A cup was sitting on a warm plate and was having what smelled like the best coffee Randall had ever smelled slowly poured into it. An identical cup sat next to it.

Wow! thought Randall. *I wonder what else this kitchen can do?*

Out loud, he said, 'How do I make a sandwich?'

As he said "sandwich" another niche lit up, containing a machine with the words "Auto-Sub" highlighted in yellow and white on a tasteful green background. He walked towards it.

A computer screen displayed pictures of a range of different breads. Being familiar with touch-screens from his hobby studying old tech, he knew what to do. He touched the picture of a six-inch crusty baguette. As he did so the screen changed to reveal a range of spreads to choose from. After studying them for a few moments he chose "Butter". He'd never tasted butter, and Randall was intrigued as to how the machine could possibly produce it. He knew it came ultimately from cows, and was then processed somehow into a spread that his history lessons had assured him was very unhealthy. Was there a cow hidden behind the wall?

The screen now displayed a question. The word "Toasted?" and two rectangular patches marked "Yes" and "No". He chose "Yes". Now a selection of cheeses appeared. Again, he'd never tasted cheese. Cheez ™ yes, but real cheese was new to him. He decided to pass on it for now, so he pressed the button marked "No". This time a range of cold meats appeared. He picked a couple at random, they all looked very nice. Now a variety of salads, next some relish and sauce options, now pickles and olives...

Eventually, after exhausting all the multitudinous options the machine had to offer, an old fashioned clock face appeared on the screen showing a countdown of thirty seconds. Randall waited, fascinated.

After thirty seconds there was a chime and a slot underneath opened to reveal a sandwich that looked fresher and tastier than any sandwich had a right to look - including the advertising pictures above the counter in the historical restaurant he had visited only a couple of days ago. The sheer sandwichosity of the snack was palpable. It looked as if the Platonic archetype of the sandwich had manifested itself directly from the world of form inside the machine. It almost glowed. Randall didn't know whether to eat it or frame it.

It didn't take him long to decide. He bit into it and chewed slowly, letting the various textures and flavours caress his taste buds. It was a flavorgasm.

Grabbing the coffees, he walked along the corridor back to the computer room, chewing carefully and slowly so as not to miss any of the joy flooding his mouth. However brief his time here was going to be, he would at least be very well fed.

'I don't know if we can trust her but we need to contact Daphne,' said Marcus, as Randall walked back into the room chewing steadily. 'The WP still have The Book. We can't let them keep it, we must get it back.' He seemed agitated.

Randall nodded; his mouth was too busy to talk.

'But not from here. They'll be on the lookout now, and I can't risk them tracing the signal. I should go back to the park and contact her from there.'

Randall swallowed, 'You? How? You don't have a terminal.'

'I don't need a terminal to send a message, Randall. I have other means at my disposal, remember? You have to stay here until I can disable your terminal locator. The dampening field I've set up stops them seeing you, so you're safe for now but...' He chose not to tell Randall he'd never disabled a locator before, the sentence was left hanging in the air.

Randall's eyebrow rose slightly.

'But how can we complete the mission?' he asked. 'We can't travel from my shed. They'll grab us if we go anywhere near my place.'

'I know. That's a major complication, but there might be a way.'

'Hmm?' Randall's mouth was full of sandwich again.

'By leaving from the opposite pole of the Earth's isotropic vector matrix. I'm not sure yet, it's complicated. I have to do some calculations but it could be a possibility. I need a few hours to work it out.' He looked tired.

'What can I do to help?'

Randall felt guilty about leaving the battered and bruised elderly gentleman in front of him do all the work while he just ate sandwiches and enjoyed the coffee. The words "isotropic vector matrix", however, didn't bode well regarding his ability to actually assist.

'Very little I'm afraid,' Marcus replied. 'This is my own theory. It was just an idle thought until now. A curious consequence of the maths, nothing more. I have to get it straight in my head first.'

'First you need some sleep,' said Randall. 'You're in no fit state to do anything now. We both need to recharge first. We can save the Galaxy this afternoon.'

'Agreed. Let me show you to your room.'

Marcus didn't drink his coffee.

An hour later, Randall was lying in a fold-out bed that was easily twice as comfortable as his own bed at home, and in an almost infinitely tidier room about three times the size of his old bedroom; but he was still too adrenaline fuelled to sleep. He'd picked another book from the hidden library and was reading about the history of the other, vanished, timeline. Trying to tire his eyes out.

He knew history was written by the winners, and that the older orders were often demonized by the new, so his history wasn't likely to be entirely accurate, but he was interested to see how and exactly when the two timelines had diverged, and what similarities there were between them.

Logically, it should be at some point soon after 2008; that being the year the original Randall had travelled to. He read about a massive financial crash affecting the whole world in that year, was that something to do with it? Did they cause the market meltdown? No, probably not. They'd only just arrived a couple of months before the crash; surely they couldn't have spread their information widely enough in that short time to actually cause it?

He read on. He soon found the date he was looking for. He should have known, after all, it was a famous date in his version of history. The timelines definitely diverged at that point. It was called "Takeover Day" in his timeline. The day the first world revolution kicked off, with the coordinated storming of government buildings around the globe, and the resulting release of top-secret information to the general public.

The battles raged for many weeks. Thousands died. Eventually, after much bloodshed on both sides, the armies of the governments began to regain some control of their establishments. But they were far too late. The damage was already done...

The newly invented internet and the TV media of the time had gradually been falling into the hands of government propagandists who used them as tools to manipulate the perceptions of the masses, to spread "fake news" and ridicule "conspiracy theories" that came too close to the truth. Suddenly, the internet became free again. The paid "trolls" were gone. The origins of the ridiculous propaganda stories the agents had infested the alternative media with were exposed. The Flat Earth Theory, which had somewhat successfully divided the fledgling resistance up to that point, was seen for what it was: totally idiotic. Other daft ideas that had been mixed in with the truth to disorient the dissenters were ridiculed. People all over the Earth began to realise how they'd been manipulated and divided. The resistance grew stronger. They united. They rebelled.

After that, the system began to collapse. The old rulers spitefully killed millions over the year or so it took for the majority of people to get it, but the next round of elections in every country was a complete washout for the establishment parties. Independent candidates around the world romped to power over the next year or two. The political system changed forever.

Everyone knew the date, and even the time, when the first blow was struck. It was 11:11 in the morning, on the twenty-first of December twenty-twelve.

All hell was breaking loose at the WPHQ. The regional chief inspector had had to cancel his planned day - which involved a quick round of golf in the morning followed by lunch at the clubhouse - and had arrived before dawn to begin the investigation. It was pretty obvious he wasn't trying to make friends.

Already four guards had been put on charge. Literally. They had been wired up to the mains and left to fry as an example to the suddenly petrified WP's, who were desperately trying to figure out who was responsible, and secretly praying to Dawkins [12] that it wasn't them.

Daphne Lehman, as a top undercover operative who had passed all the psyche screening required for her job, was above suspicion. After

---

[12] If that isn't a contradiction in terms.

all, she had helped to bring the suspects in. She watched the gruesome proceedings through the chief inspector's office window in a detached way, while being questioned about the possible whereabouts of the fugitives.

At least, she was trying to appear detached - inside she was screaming in sorrow. One of the guards now lying still and smoking on the courtyard had been her friend and fellow fifth column compatriot, the one who had vitally distracted the guards during the escape. It was a sad loss, and he would be honoured when the time was right. If there's ever a right time for such things.

The Kindle Randall had come in with was sitting on the desk awaiting an officially sanctioned history professor who might be able to figure out how to operate it. The rigidly enforced bureaucracy of the system meant only a qualified person could touch the device. It lay there disregarded in the evidence bag. They hadn't even pushed the only available button to switch it on, which meant they still didn't know what they had. Daphne decided she had to get hold of it for examination before they could read it.

She eyed it surreptitiously. Having read a couple of pages already during their search of Randall's house the previous night, she knew how important it was. Her handler, "Call me Dickie" Nixon, hadn't seen it, and she certainly hadn't said anything at the time, but Nixon had still ordered her to send in the report that got Randall arrested. Damn him.

Chief Inspector Bailey sat behind the desk stroking his huge and deeply unfashionable moustache thoughtfully. He'd grown it to disguise a scar on his upper lip that he'd obtained during a riot twenty years earlier. Normally, a scar would be worn with pride in the WP service, but this scar was caused when the then Constable Bailey smacked himself in the mouth with his own cattle prod before the riot even started, and he was embarrassed at the reminder in his bathroom mirror every day.

It didn't work anyway. In fact, it drew even more attention to his fatter than average face than would otherwise have been the case. It looked like a dead ferret decomposing on a month old cabbage.

'It seems they made their getaway in an unregistered personal transport,' he said, without looking up from his notes. 'We have tyre tracks leading from the rear of the compound, but have been unable so far to determine its route. It seems some kind of dampening field was used to disrupt the vehicle's transponder.'

'They must have had outside assistance,' said Daphne.

'Or inside assistance,' replied Bailey. 'The power outage seems to have been triggered from inside the compound. Steps have already been taken to ensure it won't happen again.'

'Yes, I heard the screaming.'

'Quite so.'

'How long before Professor Thomas gets here?' A good idea to change the subject she thought, before he asked too many awkward questions.

'Not until tomorrow I'm afraid,' said Bailey, stroking his 'tache and referring to his notes again. 'The good professor is currently over a thousand miles away at an Egyptology conference. Apparently our experts have finally determined a construction date of 500 AD for the Sphinx. Quite a breakthrough it seems.'

Daphne decided to push her luck, she pointed to the Kindle. 'I could take a look at it, sir. I learned a good deal about operating these antique devices during my assignment. Mr. James was quite knowledgeable on the subject. I'm sure I could get it working.'

Bailey looked doubtful; he fingered his farcical facial fungus with renewed fervour. 'I don't know about that, Lehman,' he said, finally discarding his notes and looking up at her.

'These next few hours could be crucial, sir. I may be able to gain valuable information that could lead to their recapture. By tomorrow they could be anywhere on Earth. Can we really afford to wait?' A good ploy on the spur of the moment, but had he fallen for it?

Bailey steepled his fingers in the way that he knew made people feel uncomfortable and leaned back in his chair. He squinted in a deviously inscrutable way, carefully tended to his 'tache, and stared at her. Hard.

Daphne, despite all her self-control, felt herself warming up under his oddly penetrating gaze. Fortunately, it didn't last long.

'Perhaps you're right, Lehman,' he said at last. 'Okay, take it. But I want it back here first thing tomorrow. If the professor finds out an unqualified meddler has accessed the device, it'll be my neck on the line.'

'I understand, sir. I won't let you down.'

'Be sure that you don't, or your neck will be next.'

She scooped up the Kindle and pocketed it before he could change his mind. 'Will that be all, sir? I have a lot of paperwork to complete.'

'That'll be all, Lehman. If only those guards were as diligent in their duties as you, eh?'

'Indeed, sir. Thank you, sir.'

She turned to leave the office, half expecting never to return.

The moment the door closed behind her, Bailey immediately composed a short message to his ex-boss. It read, simply: "Hook, Line, and Plonker".

Daphne hadn't noticed the boiled sweet sized recorder which still sat disregarded in an evidence bag on the desk. It had watched the exchange with interest, and was wondering what to do next...

It was now around three in the afternoon, and Marcus had been awake for nearly two hours. He felt better for the few hours of sleep he'd grabbed, but guilty somehow for wasting the morning.

Through sore lips, one of them quite badly split, he was carefully eating soup through a straw whilst sitting in front of a computer working on his theory. Equations and diagrams filled the air in the interactive holographic display zone in front of him. His left eye was still swollen over, so the 3D effect was mostly lost, but he skilfully manipulated the air like he was swatting slow moving invisible flies.

Randall was in the kitchen, telling it to make more coffee.

In the air above Marcus's head was a semi-transparent representation of the Earth spinning in space. Through the outlines of the continents could be seen two intersecting tetrahedra inside the planet, a green one facing up and a red one facing down. The points at the corners of the tetrahedra touched the surface of the globe at the poles, and at 19.5° above and below the equator. One point met the surface at Mauna-Kea volcano on the island of Hawaii, another in Mexico, at Teotihuacan - the ancient Pyramid of the Sun. They spun there, interlocked.

Marcus moved his hand to zoom in on the display and plotted a point on the surface of the virtual Earth. It represented the exact location of Randall's shed. The distance to the nearest of the nodes created by the bisecting tetrahedra was then calculated. A curved blue line following the Earth's magnetic contours appeared, linking the two points. Equations floating around the globe flashed and changed their parameters accordingly.

Now Marcus skilfully spun the Earth with one hand until the node exactly opposite the one just highlighted came into view. An identical blue line was then plotted from it to a point that intersected the surface halfway up a very high mountain. Now he adjusted the equations to account for local magnetic and gravitational variation. The point on the mountainside slid down into a valley at the foothills of the mountain range.

'At least it's not in the sea,' he muttered to himself, as Randall came back into the room with the coffees.

'Ooh, that's pretty,' he said, as he handed Marcus his drink. 'Where is that?'

'That is where we have to go to complete our mission,' said Marcus. He looked down for the first time at a readout giving the location in standard coordinates.

'Oh no,' he said, suddenly. 'That's not good. That's not good at all.'

He moved his hands to zoom out until the Earth shrank down to a sphere maybe two feet across.

'Why? What's wrong?' asked Randall.

'The location of our node point is what's wrong,' he said. 'Do you recognise this land mass? Hang on, I'll dim the vector matrix and solidify.' His hands moved in a strange way until the tetrahedra faded out, while the continents simultaneously became more easily visible.

Randall's knowledge of geography wasn't as good as his history, but after a few moments recognition dawned. 'Oh crap,' he said. 'The Wastelands? You're kidding?'

'I wish I was, Randall.'

'You're sure there's no other way?' He sat down heavily.

'None. And to be honest I'm not entirely sure this will work yet.'

'But what about the Planimals? How will we survive them?' Randall had heard all the stories.

'It depends entirely upon what kind of creatures occupy this valley, and what kinds we encounter on the way there. From what I've heard there are all sorts in the Wastelands, all kinds of affiliations and different groups fighting amongst themselves for the best pieces of land. Instead of an arms race, which could mean something entirely different over there, they have an evolutionary race for ultimate biological supremacy. But they do have "Elders" apparently. And I mean that literally: Elder trees are their elders. Perhaps, if we can convince them of the consequences otherwise, we might stand a chance.' Marcus didn't look at all sure. Privately he was thinking of sharpening his axe before the journey.

'But what do we tell them?' said Randall, whose imagination was presenting him with visions of running away screaming from a huge forest fire.

'I don't know yet, but don't worry; we've got plenty of time to think about it. Anyway, there are more pressing issues.'

'The Book, you mean?'

'Yes. I have to risk contacting Daphne. I need to go to the park and send her a message.' Marcus looked even less sure now.

'Can't you disable my locator now and let me go? You know this stuff much better than me, Marcus; you're needed more than me.'

'Not true, Randall. We're both as important as each other. No I must go. It'll be another few hours before I can configure the computers to disable your locator without disrupting other systems. We don't have the time. I have to contact her as soon as possible. I should go to the park now.'

'I suppose you're right. I'll read some more of the latest book, try to catch up a bit on the other timeline.'

'Okay. Good.'

Without another word Marcus headed for the door, leaving the virtual Earth spinning slowly in the air, and his coffee to go cold.

Daphne, meanwhile, was squatting in a damp bush, under a Faraday brolly by the entrance to the park where she had delivered Randall and his friend to freedom.

It was logical. If a message was going to be sent, it would probably be sent from somewhere near here, and it would be here where any meeting would most likely take place. She had the book in her pocket, and had acquainted herself with some of the details of the other timeline. It was very interesting reading. This could be the breakthrough the resistance had been looking for; getting herself assigned to Randall all those years ago had turned up much better results than she had expected. Now it would all be put to the test.

She had another two hours before the next transmission from her terminal was due, and she had to be back at her quarters before that happened or questions would be asked. She could probably bluff something, but better not to take the risk. The umbrella shielded her locator, just in case.

'Hurry up will you?' she whispered to herself. She badly needed a pee. Oh well, she was squatting in a bush. What the hell. She made the necessary modifications to her clothing and began to relieve herself, making the mud even muddier in the process.

Two seconds later, as the blessed relief sent a shudder up her spine, a message appeared on her terminal. *Great timing*, she thought.

She knew what it was going to say anyway. Logically it would be about the device in her pocket - they would want to meet with her. She reasoned that by bringing it to them so soon she would prove her usefulness and trustworthiness. It was logical. The fact that the message didn't appear to have come through normal channels didn't surprise her in the slightest. It read:

We need the devices taken from Randall and myself.
Meet me where you last saw me. 7 pm.

'I can't do seven o'clock,' she said, pulling up her jeans and popping up through the bush about twenty feet away from Marcus. 'How about now?'

Chapter 13.

Half a world away...

A man? No. Not quite.

A being of some sort certainly, but exactly what sort was indeterminate. Manish, manlike, but not a man.

The indeterminate manlike being was tanned and healthy. He had strong teeth, an infectious smile, good skin, and very odd looking bright grey eyes, that, for the moment, didn't seem to be focused on anything in particular. Not on this planet anyway. His dreadlocked ginger hair reached well past his shoulders, and was currently tied back in a bundle to keep it out of the stew he'd just finished eating.

Having no name that anyone knew of, he was known - for reasons that will become obvious - as the Seer.

He was sitting on the high rock surrounded by his acolytes; watching while the curious crab-like creatures with concave carapaces scurried around cheerfully clearing away the crockery after supper. The acolytes were happily drinking wine and chatting amongst themselves, waiting for a revelation before bed-time.

The revelations mostly came at night, after supper, which often consisted of a range of dishes made from the local wild mushrooms; wine made from the local wild mushrooms, bread made from the local wild mushrooms, stew made from the local wild mushrooms...

The wild mushrooms were quite happy with the arrangement. They actually enjoyed it in fact, after all the nasty business with the picking of course. They didn't have nervous systems so it didn't actually hurt them, but being pulled out of the ground was disorienting. Being dried out in the Sun or drowned in fermenting fruit didn't help much either.

As soon as they were consumed by the Seer and his followers however, it all became wonderfully clear to them. Everything became simple, their purpose in the universe was revealed to them and they were happy, even ecstatic, to fulfil it. Even if it meant the digestion of their physical bodies, they knew it was worth it. Their consciousness would merge with the being who ate them and a synthesis of mind was the result. Perfect.

The Seer belched loudly; a good sign that a revelation would be forthcoming. The crowd grew increasingly silent and rapt.

Now a high-pitched squeaky giggle; a very promising sign. This was going to be a good one.

The devotees gathered closer, all eyes upon the source of wisdom. The source of wisdom farted gently before beginning his revelation. He knew they were going to like this one…

'Harken,' he exclaimed, pausing momentarily while staring mystically into the distance. A good word to start with, very deep, kind of archaic, the sort of word a good revelation ought to begin with, but which was rather let down by the follow up statement the acolytes actually harkened to, which was rather more prosaic.

'We're going to be having some visitors soon,' he said, happily. Another giggle issued forth.

Not what they were expecting perhaps, but the acolytes gasped in astonishment. They'd never had visitors before. 'Tell us more, master,' some cried, and, 'Will they be happy?' shouted others. Happiness was all the acolytes cared about, sadness was a disease of the mind that happened to outsiders. The Happy Valley never harboured sad thoughts of any kind. Even the insects, plants and bacteria in the soil were overjoyed by simply existing.

'No,' said the Seer. He paused just long enough to evoke awe and wonder in the acolytes, 'They will not be happy.'

The devotees gasped once more. What was this? The words "The Prophecy" were whispered, mumbled, and murmured among them. Some were even becoming agitated.

The Seer raised his hands in supplication. 'But we must help them anyway,' he said. 'We must share our happiness with them and make them joyous…' he paused for effect, '… as is written in the sacred scrolls.'

A faint smile and a sideways glance beyond the mountains at the nearly full moon followed this statement. The acolytes went crazy, this was the best one yet. Unhappy visitors? The prophecy was finally coming to pass! Of such tales legends are made.

'How many visitors will there be, master?' asked one ecstatic acolyte, almost spilling her wine in anticipation of the answer.

The Seer paused for a few moments as his memories of the future became clear. He looked down at his hand, counting on his fingers. The happy acolyte dropped her mug out of sheer tension.

'Thrice one plus one more. Two of one, and one of another, and one unseen,' answered the indeterminate being, cryptically. Maths never had been his thirté.

Sorry - forté.

This evening's revelation looked destined to go down in history as a classic. It had all the main ingredients; mystical gobbledygook, cryptic meaninglessness, foretelling of things to come, appalling maths, mysterious glances... everything! And it was bang in line with the ancient prophecy! It was perfect. A profound announcement of high wisdom and relevance. Whatever it was he was talking about.

The scribes scribbled on the sacred velum.

Happily, of course.

A short while later, the Seer lay in his shack contemplating the evening's festivities. They seemed to like the bit about the visitors, he reflected, but the unhappiness part had unsettled them somewhat. Never mind. They would get over it. They would understand soon and all would be well.

He was drowsy now. Perhaps he had drunk too much wine? No. Surely there was no such thing as too much mushroom wine. He burped gently and made himself comfortable in the furs of his wicker bed. Perhaps he would dream of the invisible man again tonight, or perhaps it would be about the funny little men in the flying metal boxes. Either way, it would be a good dream, as all his dreams were.

He leaned over to blow out the candle.

The candle didn't mind.

In fact, it enjoyed a quick smoke.

Chapter 14.

The little boiled sweet sized recorder, still sitting in an evidence bag on the desk at the WPHQ, was bored out of its tiny electronic mind. Chief Inspector Bailey had actually put a folder on top of it earlier and now it couldn't even see. Inside the bag its microphone was next to useless too.

More than just a recorder, it was actually a very clever artificial intelligence system, semi-sentient in its own right, and like all very clever things deprived of outside stimulation, it had begun to hallucinate. It had managed to convince itself that it was actually a massive supercomputer called HAL, and that he was in charge of a spaceship orbiting Jupiter. This hallucination lasted for many years as far as HAL was concerned, but in reality it was only around three milliseconds before error trapping routines kicked in and told it not to be so bloody stupid.

HAL closed his pod bay doors and thought about it for a nanosecond; Commander Bowman would just have to wait outside until this was resolved.

Eventually, it had to agree with the ever more insistent error messages, and reluctantly accessed a quick reset routine. It instantly found itself once again inside the evidence bag with a folder on top of it.

And now it was bored. Without something to concentrate on it had gone to sleep for a few hours, but now it was awake, and it needed something to do if it was to avoid another embarrassing imaginary episode.

It did enjoy having a name for a while though. HAL. Hmmmm.

Since being separated from Randall, it had no primary terminal to monitor. It knew it could easily start monitoring any of the terminals that were constantly moving around in this strange new building, but without explicit instructions it decided not to, tempting though it was.

Eventually, about four microseconds later, it chose a course of action. It switched to a secondary instruction set that was fairly simple - Watch What Happens - and because it was now blind and deaf, that meant plugging itself into the building's compunet.

There were some very strange routines in the new net that it wasn't familiar with. Odd routing - examination of its data packets - scrutiny. He realised he was being surveilled by some very clever bundles of software. It sort of tickled. Amusing, in a simple way. Within another few microseconds it had easily bypassed them and linked in to a redundant comms line.

The secondary instruction set told it to monitor whatever there was to monitor, and transmit the data via a preferably secure channel back to the bunker. There were plenty of secure channels in this building. And it was very good at its job.

It logged on to the security circuit handling all the monitoring equipment around the base and began transmitting. Another millisecond later it did the electronic equivalent of getting a bucket of popcorn and putting its feet up.

For some reason it couldn't trace, the tune to an ancient song called "Daisy" was running around in its memory circuits. Where had that come from?

HAL started singing it quietly to himself.

Chapter 15.

Randall had had a good look around the bunker and decided almost immediately that he should stop calling it a bunker. It was a palace. Underground, secret, somewhat lair-like and mysterious, but a palace nonetheless. And what's more, it was his new home! He could never go back to his old one, but he was trying not to think about that.

He'd checked out the huge machine shop and the well-equipped gym, spent a few minutes in the recreation room playing pool with himself, gone to the book room again to sit in the massage chair for a while, and was now in the computer room once more. Marcus had been gone for nearly forty minutes, and should be back soon according to Randall's reckoning; the park was only about fifteen minutes' walk away.

He sat and stared in wonder at the glowing virtual Earth and the equations surrounding it in the air. It was beautiful, aesthetically as well as mathematically. Even if he didn't understand it at all well. Rational understanding isn't required where beauty is concerned, indeed, rationality often goes for a quick nap when beauty rears its ugly head.

You know what I mean.

Some of the formulae he recognised from The Book now in the hands of the WP. A few of the simpler ones he recognised from his own research, but the majority were new to him. He tried to get his head around them. Connections between the various equations were becoming more obvious thanks to the intuitive layout of the display. A glimmer of understanding was slowly growing in brightness inside him; like a startled and angry glow-worm emerging from a fresh cow-pat.

As he was studying the equations, a loud but pleasant sounding chime from a machine on the desk to his right made him jump. Data appeared to be streaming in from somewhere. The words "Upload Link

Established" were flashing in green at the top of the screen, but the data was in binary, unreadable. Randall hoped it was being recorded whatever it was.

After watching for a few moments, and realising no understanding was going to be forthcoming, he turned back to the equations floating around in the air by the virtual Earth, where at least a tiny sliver of understanding could be found in a universe suddenly seemingly devoid of it.

He decided to risk expanding a few equations to get a better look. Inexpertly, he moved his hands, as Marcus had done, towards the first formula he wanted to study; a metric tensor he thought he recognised. It wobbled a bit, turned upside down, changed colour, and shrank to virtual invisibility almost immediately.

Without swearing, Randall very slowly removed his hands, putting them carefully by his sides as he inched away from the interface. Thankfully, nothing else disappeared or changed.

Reluctantly giving up on the formulae, he picked up the book from the night before, and with a huge sigh, he switched it on.

The sigh spoke volumes: about his frustration at not being as good at this stuff as he thought he was; about his inability to understand and operate the technology in this strange bunker palace; that even though his girlfriend had helped them escape, she had no real love for him and was actually a spy; that he was now a wanted fugitive who would probably be killed on sight; and the ever growing possibility that the Galaxy only had six months left before suddenly slipping out of existence.

It was a very expressive sigh.

He'd read up to the other version of the twenty-first of December 2012, the winter solstice, when absolutely nothing at all of any note whatsoever had happened, despite predictions of great change or catastrophe based on something called the ancient Mayan calendar. It was apparent that the date did hold some significance for the people of that timeline, or it wouldn't have been mentioned in their history, but exactly what they thought about it was unclear, to say the least.

Apparently, various mystical types and self-proclaimed psychics of the time had predicted all sorts of cataclysmic occurrences. Some said the world was going to end in fire. Others in flood. Still others assured their followers that the doomsayers had got it all wrong and that humanity was going to ascend to a higher plane, or that benevolent aliens were going to suddenly appear, put humanity on the naughty step, and give them all a much needed download of cosmic wisdom.

All that actually happened is that a lot of people looked very silly on the twenty-second of December 2012. A lot of hasty changes to websites happened shortly afterwards.

This contrasted markedly from what became known as Takeover Day in his own timeline; only the governments and corporations looked silly the next day according to that history.

Reading on, he became increasingly shocked as the pages, and the years, scrolled by. Before long, he got to a year that contained many references he didn't understand at all. Bowie, Lemmy, Wogan, Ali, Rickman, Brexit, Farage, Castro, Alt-Right, Post-truth, Gabor, Fisher, none of these words meant anything to him, but he could see that 2016 had been a very strange year for them, whatever it all meant.

Details of duplicitous wars, economic collapse, terrorism, climate change, radiation leaks, and planet choking pollution filled the pages as the years progressed. Ocean die offs, desertification, deadly mutant viruses, species extinctions, sea levels rising - Randall could hardly believe what he was reading. A war in the middle east seemed to escalate by the week, eventually drawing in the larger regional powers, who had been worrying about who would look after all that oil, and finally culminating in the outbreak of a third world war.

He almost dropped the book when he read about the nuclear exchanges...

Marcus, meanwhile, was trying to get his heart beating properly again. It had skipped a couple of beats and was now hurriedly trying to get back on schedule. Upon suddenly being confronted by Daphne popping up through the bush, he had dropped down into the mud expecting another knockout shock any second, but it never came.

After a few embarrassing seconds he slowly, warily, began to stand up. Daphne stood before him in wet boots dangling The Book in front of his eyes. Marcus snatched for it but Daphne was too quick. Steam seemed to be rising from the bush she had just emerged from. And from her boots.

'Not so fast, mysterious stranger,' she said. 'You don't get the device until I get some answers. Deal?'

Marcus stood up fully, trying to wipe the mud from his trousers. He failed, merely succeeding in rubbing it in more. He stopped wiping and faced Daphne. Towering over her, all he could see was the top of her shielding brolly.

'Ask,' said Marcus, simply. It seemed he would have to trust her, however much he actually didn't.

The brolly spoke. 'First your name. It's really Marcus?'

'It is.'

Daphne crossed out a mental box marked "Buzz". 'Marcus what?'

'Not that it'll make any difference to you. I'm off grid, you have no records of me. My name might as well be Santa Claus for all the good it'll do you.'

He was right, of course, but Daphne was determined not to show it. 'Nevertheless, what is it?' she demanded. She was not going to fail on the first question.

'Han,' said Han. 'Marcus Han. At your service, Agent Lehman. Formerly Constable Lehman, Class of '03, senior undercover operative, and daughter of Dr. Francis Lehman, previously director of policy at WP Command, now retired.'

She was impressed. 'I see you've done your homework, Mr. Han. I'd be interested to know how you discovered all that, with or without a terminal.'

'I'm sure you would. So you're with the resistance are you? I didn't even know there was one.' This was a lie, he knew of the resistance but had dismissed them until now, perhaps he should re-evaluate them.

'How long have you been a member?' he asked. He was determined to gain control of the situation. Asking a few questions of his own would help. He kept his eyes on The Book in her hand while she considered her answer.

'Ever since I was a child really,' she said, as she waved The Book around, just out of Marcus's reach. 'But not until six years ago officially.'

She paused. Marcus raised an eyebrow. 'Tell me more,' it seemed to say.

Daphne couldn't see the eyebrow from under her brolly.

'Tell me more,' said Marcus.

She thought for a second. 'My father is a complicit psychopath who only ever thinks of consolidating the power of the system, always has done. That's all he cares about. He's been thoroughly brainwashed by the establishment since he was a child. If you study his service record you'll see that. I knew it from very early on. I suppose you could say I rebelled.'

Before Marcus could ask another question she had one of her own. She had played this game before.

'Have you started building the time machine yet? You've only got six months you know.'

Marcus had been afraid of that. 'So you've read The Book then,' he began.

'Some of it,' she replied. 'Enough to know what you and Randall are up to. They didn't even switch it on by the way, I snagged it before they could have a look.'

'But why did you get us arrested?'

'I didn't. My handler did. I tried to tone the charges down from Illegal Research to Possession of Controlled Devices, but I couldn't make it stick. Sorry about that. It was actually your intervention in Randall's life that got my boss curious though. I've been keeping him as a low priority for three years.'

'I should have known he would be under surveillance. Stupid,' he said to himself.

'By the WP and the resistance. When they started watching him I wrangled the assignment because we saw an opportunity with him, even a possible future recruit. After what happened with his father we thought he might be someone with no love for the WP, and to be honest his money would come in handy too. It was a long term assignment, but circumstances force us to plan for the long term. I actually grew quite fond of him over the years.'

'You have no idea about long term assignments, believe me,' said Marcus, reflecting on six hundred years of the plan he and Randall were now the embodiment of.

'I gathered that much from this device,' she said, holding it up. 'Listen to me. I know you don't trust me and I don't blame you, so I'm going to give it back to you as an act of trust, but I need another like it to return to them. Have you got another the same?'

'That can be arranged,' said Marcus, cautiously. He was rather surprised at how easy this was turning out to be. There had to be a catch.

'I want in,' she said, unexpectedly. 'We should work together, you, Randall and I. Think of the advantages. I'm part of a resistance movement of over two thousand people around the globe. Now you're on the WP wanted list, you may need our help. I can be your liaison.'

And there it was. She wanted in.

Marcus considered this for a full thirty seconds, during which neither of them spoke. It was a reasonable proposal. After all, in the other timeline their counterparts had been part of a widespread resistance, this shouldn't cause a serious paradox. And they could probably help with getting the time machine to the Wastelands too, which was a problem that had been causing Marcus some concern.

'You realise Randall and I are the only ones who can travel back?' he said, eventually.

'Yes, I had considered that. Paradoxes, yes?'

Marcus nodded, unseen. 'And if we're successful this timeline will disappear the moment we travel, to be replaced with a new timeline in which you may not even exist?'

Now it was Daphne's turn to nod. She managed to do so in a solemn manner, even though Marcus couldn't see her under the Faraday shield.

The brolly shrugged. 'I thought as much, but what difference does it make? I won't know about it either way.'

Marcus stepped back and stared at her for a few moments, making up his mind. He was about to speak when Daphne beat him to it.

'I have a little over an hour and a half before my next terminal upload, and I have to be back at base before then, but I get off at midnight. I could meet you about half an hour later. If you could give me a replacement device tonight the idiots at HQ will never know the difference.'

Marcus held out his hand. 'Until tonight then,' he said, as Daphne handed him The Book.

'Until tonight,' she replied, as she started to turn and walk away.

Marcus looked up. 'I said "devices" in my message. Where is the other item?'

She stopped. 'What other item? This is the only one I know about.'

'It was taken from me when we were arrested. A small metallic device about the size of a boiled sweet,' said Marcus, holding up his fingers about an inch apart.

'I know nothing about that, but I'll have a look if I get a chance. If I find it, I'll bring it with me tonight.'

'Thank you.' Marcus meant it. He walked away.

Daphne half expected never to see him or Randall ever again.

Randall was goggle eyed when Marcus returned a short while later. He was clearly emotional and seemed to be holding back tears.

'What's up?' said Marcus, as he walked into the computer room holding out The Book in front of him. Randall didn't notice it. 'The bombs,' he said. 'They used nuclear bombs on each other. The idiots. How could they do that?'

'Yes I know. Tragic isn't it? They never really recovered from that. After the surface was all but destroyed, the survivors ended up living in the few radiation free zones left on the planet; hence the mega cities that developed over the next hundred years or so. They suffered on for another five hundred years, but I suspect mankind would probably have become extinct soon afterwards if our counterparts hadn't done what they did.'

Randall shook his head and stared at the floor. That's when he noticed the dried mud on Marcus's shoes and trousers.

'What the hell happened to you?' he said, finally also noticing The Book being dangled in front of him. 'And how did you get hold of that so soon? What's going on? Have you been back to WPHQ?'

'She's a very clever young lady, your Daphne. Almost too clever. She was waiting for me in the park when I sent the message, and I have to meet her there again tonight to replace this book with another that she can smuggle back into the base. I have one in mind that she can have, written by a hero of the twentieth century. It's called 1984.'

'She's not "my" Daphne,' said Randall. 'You trust her now?'

'I think so yes. I don't see we have much choice if I'm honest. It looks like we'll need the help of the resistance if we're going to succeed. Let's hope they're all as competent as she is.'

Randall felt conflicted, he just nodded in reply.

'I need to change out of these muddy clothes,' he said, turning to leave. It was only then that he noticed the data streaming in on the screen to Randall's right.

'What's that?' He ran over to the machine and started moving a small hand sized device attached to it by a wire. An arrow on the screen moved in response. He clicked the control device a couple of times as he moved the arrow around, and menus full of options flickered by as Marcus worked the computer. Randall had never seen such a cumbersome interface before, the whole machine seemed quite ancient now that he looked at it more closely.

After dismissing a message that popped onto the screen saying "Windows needs to close" (which baffled Randall, not just the terrible grammar, but there were no windows in this underground palace) the binary feed resolved itself into twelve separate video and audio channels. He quickly clicked a menu item marked "Record". All data up to this point had been lost.

The images filling the screen showed various rooms and corridors in a large building that they didn't recognise for a moment, until Randall cried out, 'That's my cell. And there's the one you were in, look there, they haven't cleaned up your blood yet.'

'You clever little jigger,' said Marcus. 'It's from the recorder I gave you. It must have hooked into the compunet at the base. I love AI units.'

He muted the twelve audio channels with a click and stared at the visual channels. After a few moments he selected a room containing a few WP's sitting around a desk. The feed from that room now filled the screen. He un-muted the audio stream and tried to listen to the conversation.

Some senior officers, judging by their insignia and deportment, were apparently discussing a matter of some hilarity, if the amount of gesticulation and whiskey involved were to be believed. A huge bald man with a large pair of glasses on his face, and another full of whiskey in his hand, was seated behind a desk listening to two others in front.

The audio was inaudible. Twenty-four channels of data had caused a lot of compression on the signal. Marcus discontinued six of the feeds with a few clicks. The audio quality doubled. He threw in some filters, it doubled again.

'... ect at all. Not a thing,' said the man with the huge moustache seated in front of the desk. He swilled his whiskey, twirled his 'tache and laughed.

The other two laughed with C.I. Bailey and sipped on their drinks. Cigar smoke filled the air.

'She always was soft in the head,' said the third, unseen, figure. His back was to the camera but the thinning grey hair pointed to an elderly man.

'I'd love to see the look on her face when she finds out,' said Bailey, holding up a folder and waving away some cigar smoke with it. It was blurred but the folder seemed to have just one word on it. It probably began with 'T' but was otherwise unreadable. Below it was a graphic of some sort. Was it a horse?

'Make sure to tell the goons to record it tonight when they take her down won't you. Her mother will love it,' said the unseen figure.

Bailey, with his glass to his mouth, laughed and sprayed whiskey over his uniform.

They laughed again. Even harder.

'They're not talking about... her are they?' asked Randall.

'Who else?' said Marcus.

'On Dawkin's grave! They're using her to get to us?'

'And the resistance. It looks that way,' Marcus replied, sadly.

'Then we're finished. And so is she. It's over,' exclaimed Randall, as the shock began to sink in.

Marcus thought for a few moments. His brow furrowed deeply as he considered the options. Then he came to a decision.

'No it's not. We have to help her. She's our only contact with the resistance and we need their help if we're ever going to get out of this. They're planning to catch us all tonight. We need to stop them.'

'But how?' asked Randall, incredulously.

'First I have to disable your locator, and then we need to get Ninja'd up. Follow me to the gym, I have something to show you.' Marcus left the room and headed along the corridor. Randall followed behind, bemused. What was he thinking? Bit late for exercise wasn't it?

At the gym, Marcus walked straight past all the weights and exercise machines without even looking at them. He headed for the far corner, to a door that Randall had assumed led to the shower.

He was wrong. As Marcus opened the door Randall could see that the room was filled with weapons!

Clubs, nun chucks, throwing blades, daggers, and swords of all sizes filled one of the walls. Guns, grenades and more technological weapons filled another. The third wall housed a rack containing various types of armour, night vision equipment, and radio packs. A secure steel cupboard in one corner had the word "Ammunition" written on the front.

'Welcome to the armoury,' said Marcus.

Randall looked around him with an increasingly disturbed look of terrified awe on his face. 'You kept this quiet,' he said.

'I never imagined we would ever have cause to use it.'

'But I don't know how to use any of this stuff,' cried Randall. 'You expect me to fight them?'

'No, Randall. I expect you to help *me* fight them. Don't worry. We'll be using stealth technology they won't have a defence against. Come on. We need to prepare.'

It took three hours to disable Randall's terminal locator. Three hours in the chair trying - and failing - to relax for Randall, while Marcus worked with flying fingers on that most ancient of devices, a keyboard, constructing code that would partially overwrite the terminal's OS. Randall was anxious and introspective, again. It was a state of mind he was reluctantly getting used to.

There was still a major bug in the code, and Marcus was studying it intently, his chin in his hand, and his hardly-noticed coffee cold on the desk. The only part of him that moved for a while were his eyes, which seemed to be scanning the air above his head as if the bug could fly, and he was searching the room for it. After a few minutes of this a sudden eureka moment struck him, and with a few deft keyboard strokes he edited the code and re-compiled. Now there were a hundred and seventeen bugs, so he was making progress.

Eventually, Marcus assured him the locator had been disabled, even though testing was impossible in the dampening field that had been set up to hide him. He didn't want to risk switching the field off just yet as the computer was still examining the code, running simulations to find any vulnerabilities. Better safe than sorry.

Now it was four hours later, half an hour before they had to leave, and he still wasn't a hundred percent sure. They were in the armoury, nervously (in Randall's case) going over the plan to rescue Daphne. They were dressed in dark grey all-in-one jumpsuits, and had plastic twigs sticking out of their camouflaged balaclavas. Randall had just suffered the indignity of having his face daubed with boot polish and was now trying to get used to the low-light goggles.

'I'm switching the light off now,' said Marcus. 'Engage the goggles as I showed you, but not before I switch off the light. Okay? Ready?'

'Readyish,' said Randall. The light went out and he flicked the switch as Marcus had shown him. Everything in his field of vision went from black to bright green.

'Can you see me?' asked Marcus, waving his arms at the other end of the room.

'Wow! Yes I can,' said Randall. 'This is brilliant. Why have I never heard of this sort of thing?'

'The same reason you've never heard of lots of things, Randall. The WP can't let this technology out into the population, it can be used against them. They can't have that.'

'But they have these goggles, too?'

'Oh yes, but it won't do them any good even if they're wearing them because of our stealth suits. They won't be expecting it and hopefully won't be using stealth countermeasures. When we activate the suits we'll be all but invisible either in normal optical wavelengths or through their goggles. Only sound, and the heat from our faces can still give us away, so you need to keep quiet and keep your head down until the time comes to act.'

Marcus stopped and faced Randall. 'Are you ready? We need to go.'

Randall looked incredulous. 'We're not going to walk there dressed like this are we? Little bit conspicuous isn't it? Disembodied faces and all this gear floating along the street?'

'We won't be walking,' said Marcus.

He pulled out a remote control from one of the many pockets on his outfit and pointed it at a space in the middle of the floor, a section of which slid back to reveal a circular iris, which then opened in turn. A steel pole shot up out of the hole and slammed into a socket on the ceiling.

'Follow me,' he said, jumping onto the pole and sliding down.

Less than ten minutes later, they arrived in a side road with a view of the park entrance. They were sitting in a vehicle Marcus had called the "Batmobile", for some unknown reason. Randall wanted to ask him but hadn't as yet because he was still trembling. And sweating, and white-knuckled with fear, and trying to keep hold of his dinner; which had already tried to escape a few times on the journey over.

They had driven from the bunker's garage along a tunnel that emerged over two miles away on the outskirts of town, through a false cliff face that thankfully slid aside as Marcus sped towards it at sixty miles per hour. He seemed to enjoy the experience, but Randall certainly didn't. The noise, the fumes, the speed, the G-forces, and the shock had left him speechless.

The Batmobile itself was a small petrol driven sports car, built over three hundred years earlier and used only occasionally ever since. It bore as much resemblance to a "personal transport", driven by those few citizens lucky enough to be granted a license, as a panther did to a three-legged incontinent moggy. Randall had never seen, or experienced, anything like it.

It was black, shiny, and had small radar deflecting panels all over its surface that gave it the appearance of a paper model of a car that had been screwed up, stretched out again, and finally thrown away. The panels were coated with invisibility glass that projected an image of the immediate surroundings, making it very difficult to see even if you knew it was there. With the optical system switched off it looked hideous, like a crumpled bat lying dead in an oil slick, but as it was designed to be invisible, that wasn't a problem.

Inside, it looked like the flight deck of a space shuttle that had just crash landed in the control room of a nuclear power plant. Screens showing various data streams and views of the street outside replaced the windscreen and side windows. Buttons, switches and dials were festooned around the cabin, filling almost every available space. Curly cables dangled from the roof, obviously improvised patches of some sort. It was a mess, but it had everything: from radar and lidar to radio jamming capabilities, and a wide range of other electronic countermeasures. It was armed with twin rail guns at the front, and a laser turret at the back.

There didn't appear to be a cup-holder anywhere.

Randall was utterly bewildered by all of it. He looked around the cockpit - and it was a cockpit, that was the only word to describe it - and after spotting a button marked "Submersible Mode", he decided not to look any further in case there was a button marked "Self-Destruct", or "Nuclear Option", or something else that would freak him out even more than he was already.

The plan was to disable the overhead drones that would be watching Daphne approaching the park with a high tech laser pistol that Randall didn't understand at all. Then they would cover her with a shielding Faraday blanket that he understood a little bit, bundle her in the back of the car he had no comprehension of, and drive like hell back to the utterly mysterious bunker through a sliding cliff face that he chose not to even begin to try to fathom.

Marcus, his eye still swollen, watched the skies for the drones with his night vision goggles, while Randall watched the park gate for any signs of her.

Suddenly, the drones appeared over the nearby buildings. Three of them.

'Get ready,' said Marcus, 'they're here.' He activated his suit, stepped out of the car, and began taking aim.

Fifteen seconds later, Daphne appeared around the corner in her personal transport. As she opened the door, Randall flashed a tight-beam torch at her three times, and she looked in the direction of the almost invisible car. Suddenly a laser shot up from the strange hazy shape she could now just about make out near the signal flash. An explosion in the sky. The laser shone twice more. Two more explosions followed in quick succession. Small pieces of flaming debris began to rain down around her.

As the third drone exploded, Marcus lowered his laser pistol and took aim at the street corner that the inevitable WP troop transport would soon come thundering towards.

'Daphne. Over here quick. They're onto you,' he shouted.

The shout seemed to come from the hazy shape. Slowly she moved towards it, confused and anxious. Another hazy shape seemed to emerge from the larger hazy shape she could now definitely see if she squinted in the right way. The new shape appeared to be holding a blanket...

As the sound of the troop transport reached them Randall could see the concern and bewilderment on Daphne's face. 'It's me,' he shouted. 'Quick. Under the blanket.'

Giving up on trying to understand, she ran headlong into the blanket, was bundled into the invisible car, and driven away at top speed in a cloud of tyre smoke. She didn't manage to hold back the vomit.

A minute later, neither could Randall.

Chapter 16.

The indeterminate manlike being was at the far end of the Happy Valley, busily talking to a tree.

Nothing unusual in that you might think. Perfectly normal behaviour for a future seeing, psychic, shaman type character, you might think. Mystical seers and prophets and the like are always talking to trees, communing with the plant spirits, invoking dryads, and all that sort of thing. Talking to wood isn't strictly a pursuit of the psychically inclined however; mad people do it all the time. Dotty Kings and potty Princes aren't immune either.

None of them, however, no matter how spiritually enlightened, mentally deranged, or royal, has ever actually held a proper two-way conversation with a tree. They might have imagined they did, or had vivid dreams of doing so, but none of them actually did.

Ever.

Even the ones who wrote poems about it.

This was different, however. This was the GM Wastelands, domain of the dreaded Planimals...

'You're sure about all this?' said a young Elder, called Sam. He had no reason to doubt the Seer, and had never known him to be wrong, but these were visions of the future, after all. The future isn't carved in stone, despite what prophets profess.

'I am,' said the Seer, because he was.

Sam rustled his leaves in irritation, causing a slight breeze and waking up a large squirrel that lived in his branches in the process. It stirred, yawned, and began to scratch.

Squirrel isn't quite the right word to describe the animal though; it was as much a squirrel as the indeterminate being was a man and Sam was an ordinary tree. Squirrelish, squirrelesque, but not a squirrel.

Her name was Caroline.

'What do you think?' asked Sam.

'What do I think about what?' replied Caroline. 'Hello! Just woken up.' She gestured with her tiny hands in a manner that suggested the word "Duh!"

'You spend far too much time asleep as it is,' said Sam. 'Sleep and nuts. That's all you ever think about.'

'Not *all* I think about,' said Caroline, coyly.

'Yes I know. I heard you *again* last night. Try to keep it down will you? Some of us need to respire. You're not a rabbit you know.'

The Seer coughed pointedly. He'd heard all these rows before, pretty soon it would escalate into a screaming match unless he stepped in. Insults like "failed rat" and "brown leaved sap-junkie" would start to fly, and nothing would get resolved for the rest of the day. Some people just aren't happy unless they're having a row. Such is life. This was on the border of the Happy Valley, after all.

'We need a plan,' said the Seer, slightly louder than was strictly polite. 'The visitors will change everything. We must be sure things will change in the right way.'

'Yes, well...' said Sam, feeling slightly mollified.

'Oh, right. That thing,' said Caroline. 'I suppose you'd better ask the mesh. We need to consult on this one.'

The mesh was an underground mycelium fibre network connecting all the trees in the Wastelands together by their roots. A wood-wide-web if you will. It wasn't a fast system of communication, but it was quite effective. Information could be put into the mesh and read by any tree on the island within a day or two.

The roots of the tree, being the equivalent of the unconscious mind in a human, received the communication in the form of images or vivid dreams, which would then be interpreted the following morning. The above ground, conscious, parts of the trees would then discuss the information provided overnight by the mesh and come to a consensus, usually by sunset. After sunset, any questions or decisions would again be disseminated across the mesh. In two days the message would have spread from the Happy Valley all over the Wastelands.

'How long do we have?' asked Sam.

The Seer thought for a moment, looking at his hands.

'Just under six moons,' he said. 'But they will be here before then, about maybe,' he looked at his hands again, 'er, one less than six moons.'

'Plenty of time then. We shouldn't rush to any hasty decisions. I'll spread the word,' said Caroline.

She climbed down out of Sam and set off for the neighbouring trees at the other end of the field, a Beech and an Oak called Sylvia and Robert. A nice couple (although Sylvia did tend to collect more than a fashionable number of birds' nests in her branches, and didn't seem too bothered by all the talk). 'I'll be back in an hour,' she shouted, as she ran off across the field.

'Four of them you say?' enquired Sam.

'Thrice one and one more. Two of one, and one of another, and one unseen,' replied the Seer.

'That makes four. Just say four can you? Leave the gibberish for the acolytes?'

The Seer looked at his feet for a second and scuffed the dirt almost petulantly. 'As you say,' he said, quietly.

'Be back here in two days, okay? We should have some sort of a plan by then,' said Sam, as a beam of sunlight broke through the clouds and started to nourish his leaves.

'At the height of the Moon?' asked the Seer, still determined to get some sort of mystical talk into the conversation.

'No,' said Sam. 'Two days. You can count to two can't you? Remember? We went over this before. It's one more than one.'

He held out one more than one fingers on his hand and stared at them momentarily. 'Two days,' he said. 'I'll be here.'

'Don't forget,' Sam warned.

'I remember the future,' replied the Seer, 'this is in the future. I will not forget.'

He turned and walked back towards his shack. Back into the heart of the Happy Valley.

Caroline skidded to a halt at the other end of the field and called out to a lodger living in one of the many nests in Sylvia's branches; a huge old half blind raven called Big Bill.

'Bill are you home?' she shouted.

Big Bill's big bill poked out over the side of the nest.

'Helloo, baybeee,' he squawked. 'Why don't you come up here with me, honey? I've got a couple of massive juicy berries right here and I'll share them with you all night, baby. Oh yeah.'

She smiled in a weary sort of way. 'For God's sake, Bill. It's me, Caroline.'

He was a randy old crow but interspecies liaisons weren't really his thing. Not since the encounter with the hedgehog anyway.

'Oh, sorry, Caroline, I thought you were someone else,' he said, in the less lecherous voice he reserved for non-lady-birds.

'Anyone else you mean. As long as she's got wings.'

'Uncalled for,' said Bill, 'but completely true of course.' He sniggered and looked down at her. 'What can I do you for?'

'I'm coming up,' she said. The smile was gone.

He was the kind of bird who used phrases like "what can I do you for?", and "from the heart of my bottom", in the belief that it made him seem less imposing, and in all honesty, it helped. He needed tricks like this because his huge battle-scarred appearance tended to scare the living bejeezus out of all but the hardiest of the forest folk. Even most wolves were wary of Big Bill.

His one blind eye shone white against his jet black face like a malevolent star in an endless night of unyielding torment. His powerful wings; a death shroud made from the darkest shade of uttermost darkness itself. His chipped and scarred beak was a weapon of war from the imagination of a sick and twisted sadist. Hideous and efficient. Merciless and bleak.

And currently itching like a bastard.

He furiously scratched his itchy beak with one coal black talon while Caroline climbed Sylvia's trunk. A moment later she was at Bill's nest, where she spotted magpie feathers scattered all around which Bill was nonchalantly trying to cover with one outstretched wing. Being blind in one eye, he missed most of them. Caroline pointedly looked at them with distaste. Magpies stole hidden nut caches.

'Another magpie, Bill? Really? Why do you waste your time with those tarts? You know the rhyme. One for sorrow...' Caroline began.

'And two for joy,' interrupted Bill. 'That's why I invited her sister along,' he sniggered lecherously again.

Caroline simply stared at him as sternly as she could until he noticed the seriousness on her face and slowly realised he should de-snigger.

'Get your mind out of the midden will you?' she said. 'We need you. Things are about to get serious.'

Falteringly, Bill got serious. He coughed. 'Sorry. Tell me,' he said.

'We need you to fly to the Forest Council,' said Caroline. 'The Seer has had another vision. It looks like the time of the prophecy is at hand.'

'The prophecy? You're sure?' Bill was suddenly attentive.

'We've got less than six months. Then the scrolls say everything changes. And we need it to change in the right way. Sam's putting it in the mesh tonight, but we need the forest folk on side too. We need to create a coalition; the tribes will have to cooperate for a change.'

Bill brushed away a few errant magpie feathers and straightened himself up, preening as he did so. Stretching out his wings he was an eldritch manifestation of death from the deepest pit of hell imagined in a nightmare festering in the hideous mind of a psychopath, but instead of screeching like a banshee ushering the souls of the damned through the burning gates of hell, he said, 'Okey dokey. I'll see what I can do.'

'Here's what I want you to tell them,' said Caroline. 'Now listen carefully...'

A short while later Bill was in the air. Mostly.

"As the crow flies" didn't in any way describe his flight-path, however.

He was zigzagging around the sky in a quite unpredictable fashion; changing direction every few seconds, suddenly swooping to the ground for no apparent reason, now soaring above the clouds, quickly changing his speed, and even almost hovering at times. He would perch briefly in apparently random trees and set off again in various seemingly arbitrary directions, but always generally in the direction of the Forest Council, a hundred and fifty miles to the south.

Partly this was due to his battle experience, which had taught him not to fly in a straight line because it can easily be predicted and intercepted; partly it was because he was using the opportunity to spread the word to a few old friends as he went; but mostly it was because he had no depth perception.

3D vision is something most binocular creatures take for granted - try pouring a glass of wine at arm's-length with one eye closed if you don't believe me - so for a creature who lives in a 3D landscape anyway, such as a bird, it's quite a serious deficiency. Not one that can't be overcome with a few buckets full of bloody-mindedness though, and Bill had barrels of the stuff.

It was getting close to sunset, soon he would have to find a roost for the night. He was still flying over comparatively friendly territory, so it wouldn't be too much of a problem if he stopped fairly soon. He could risk flying on in darkness for a short while perhaps, but by then he would be in not exactly enemy airspace, but certainly less friendly skies. If he roosted soon he would be able to fly to the Forest Council in daylight hours tomorrow with any luck.

He scanned the horizon searching for a good roost and soon spotted a copse of trees on a small hill that looked like it would do nicely. He headed in the general direction, still zigzagging wildly.

A few minutes later, on the third attempt, he flopped gracelessly into the upper branches of the tallest of the trees in the copse, a Silver Birch called Betty. Landing is difficult with only one eye at the best of times, but in poor light in an unfamiliar tree it was decidedly hit-and-miss.

'Nice landing, Biggles,' sniggered Betty. The other trees in the copse tittered and giggled, as did a pair of pigeons in the neighbouring tree.

Bill unruffled a few feathers, stretched his wings, and cawed loudly. It wasn't an ordinary raven's caw though, it was more like a battle cry; similar in human terms to a bugle call signalling an all-out attack. It had the effect of chilling the nerves - or whatever other sensory mechanisms were available - of everything that heard it.

He snapped his beak open and shut a couple of times for effect and said, 'I could prune you down to a stump maybe. That'd make you easier for an old half blind raven to land on.'

The giggling instantly stopped, to be replaced with an awed silence. The pigeons both nervously did that thing pigeons are renowned for, making their roost slightly whiter and a little wetter in the process.

Betty gulped, there was only one huge half blind raven with a caw like a battle cry that she knew of. 'B-Big B-Bill?' she said, stuttering with the sudden panic of realisation.

Bill cawed again and gripped the roost so tightly he drew sap.

Leisurely he lifted one cutlass-like talon until a strip of bark started to peel away from the branch.

'Arrgh... It's... aahhrrgh... an honour... Sir,' said Betty. Most trees learned fast around Big Bill.

He withdrew the talon and regarded the pigeons in the opposite tree with his one good eye, which he winked menacingly. It was like being winked at by a black hole. The pigeons anxiously hopped from foot to foot, looking around them in any direction but the one Bill was occupying. They would have whistled innocently if their beaks were capable of such a feat.

Bill flapped his huge wings just once, sending a powerful downdraft that rippled the grass fifty feet below. The pigeons both did that thing again and sheepishly hid their heads under their wings.

Big Bill, newly crowned king of the copse, cackled contentedly and settled in for the night.

Chapter 17.

George Junior was, to all intents and purposes, inside the Moon. If, being infinite, he could be said to be inside anything, of course. It would be more accurate to say that a majority of George Jr's awareness was intensely focused on the interior of the Moon - not as snappy, but more accurate.

He was in "real time", with only six hours to go before the galactic vanishing act, and he was studying the aliens as they prepared to abandon their base and depart for home.

He watched as they unhurriedly went about their mysterious business. They didn't seem to be in any rush, they didn't seem concerned, it looked like a fairly relaxed environment to all appearances; and not as though these weirdly calm, even chilled out, "people" were about to cause the non-existence of over two hundred billion stars and the countless trillions of individual life forms that occupied those solar systems.

Watching them wasn't easy. Focusing on such tiny things as individual beings or the machines they were operating was very difficult. A mind that encompasses the universe has trouble pinpointing its attention into such a small space; ask God. Not that she'd hear you asking obviously, because a mind that encompasses the universe has trouble pinpointing its attention... etc.

And because he was so stupendously shitfaced, it was even harder for George.

He'd discovered it wasn't exactly hollow inside the Moon as he was expecting, it was more like a maze of wide tunnels connecting large cavities that looked like they were spaced around the rocky interior of the planetoid in a geometric pattern. There seemed to be seven of them in all, and George Jr was following one of the tunnels from what appeared to be a leisure area, to whatever the next bubble would turn out to be.

The aliens flew along the tunnels - some of them up to a thousand miles long - in both directions in small craft about the size and, frankly, the shape, of a double bed. It seemed as though style or artistic touches were reserved for art alone, everything else was simply as functional as they could make it. Even their clothes were just shapeless monochrome garments; stark, utilitarian, and definitely not something you'd find at a fashion show. Not outside a gulag anyway.

He was following one of the flying beds as his awareness sped giddily along the tunnel away from the leisure area.

The leisure area had been interesting. There were meeting spots where the aliens would eat, drink and chat; artistic displays and stunning light sculptures; low gravity fountains that flung huge arcs of water across the chamber; and large areas given over to "sunbathing", although the "sun" was an array of full spectrum lamps set in the roof that the aliens would doze beneath for hours at a time while their children played in the pools created by the arcing water jets.

The young of their species were not only smaller, but they were a different shape to their parents. Seemingly there was a metamorphosis at some point into the adult form, but George couldn't see any intermediate types. He watched as they played in the shallow water.

They reminded him of seals in a way. Smooth and green rather than brown and hairy, but they had flippers, and whiskers, which made their faces look a lot like puppy dogs. It was the fact they were balancing balls on their noses for fun, and tossing them between each other like an animal act in a circus, that made the seal comparison unavoidable.

The adults also played a number of sports. Including one that utilised randomly variable gravitational fields and different sizes of trampoline that the players would traverse the playing field on; bouncing and diving and flying around in a display that was amazing to observe.

Sometimes two players would come close to colliding, and each time this happened the crowd would begin to shout and become agitated. This was obviously the exciting part of the game, but it never amounted to anything. The players would drift away from each other and continue as if nothing had happened. Only once did two of the players, very briefly, touch.

After watching one full match, which lasted over two hours, George was still none the wiser as to the actual objective of the game; if indeed it was a game, he couldn't even be sure about that. There didn't seem to be an equivalent of a ball or a goal that he could readily observe, and the seemingly randomly bouncing players didn't appear to be working together as teams, even though it was clear from the coloured belts they wore that there were definitely two teams in the game. It baffled George and he gave up trying to understand it.

Had he studied further he would have discovered that it was a stylised re-enactment of the one and only war in the long, multi-billion-year, history of their race; a war that lasted less than a week and resulted in the loss of just one ship with a crew of five. It had been remembered in the form of this dance/sport/ritual ever since.

Now he was approaching another of the huge cavities. So far, he'd seen the leisure area and two accommodation zones. Now he was trying to find the business end of the operation. There had to be a control zone or main hub of some sort, and the increased density of traffic around this cavity looked promising. He abandoned the box he'd been following and stopped in the mouth of the tunnel to take in the entire zone.

It was mind bogglingly awesome.

With a total disregard for gravity, an entire city of over two million small open topped buildings, like booths in an infinite office space, were arranged in a grid pattern that completely covered the inside surface of the spherical cavity. In the centre of the space floated a huge glass sphere that projected millions of beams of coloured light into the small buildings. It was like an enormous psychedelic dandelion seed made of lasers, held suspended inside a gigantic ping-pong ball.

Actually it looked nothing like that, but sometimes analogies aren't enough.

Aliens sat inside many of the booths, either on their own or in small groups, apparently watching the display projected into it from the central sphere. It looked as if they were taking notes about what they were watching on small computer tablets. George concentrated himself further into the space, moving in for a closer look at one of the booths. If he'd still had eyes, they would have been squinting.

121

Two aliens were lounging on very comfortable looking reclining chairs, wearing goggles of some technological design. The light from the sphere about a mile away widened just enough to fill the booth completely, and George assumed the goggles were presenting the aliens with a view of the whole image being projected. He could see, he assumed, what the aliens were actually looking at projected onto the floor of the booth. The furniture and the aliens themselves distorted his view, but he could see that it was a moving image of a small group of stern looking human figures travelling by road across a strange, dusty, grassland that he didn't recognise.

He looked at the next booth along and saw almost exactly the same pictures being projected, but there were subtle differences that he almost missed on first glance. The driver of the transport in the image in this booth had no moustache, and his passenger, the huge bald man, was nearly asleep. Other than that the projections were almost identical. They were travelling across the same scrubby grassland in identical cars, and they looked equally as stern and humourless.

George moved his mind to observe another booth further along the wall of the huge cavity. This one showed a very similar but now markedly different scene. The transport was painted black instead of camouflage colours, and the people sitting in it were distinctly altered; beards sprouted where there were none before, and their clothes were obviously changed. They were, if anything, even more stern and serious looking. Guns could be seen in holsters and the fat man in the passenger seat carried a lethal looking long range rifle.

Baffling, thought George as he randomly picked several other booths to study, all of them very slightly different. After a while he moved to the opposite side of the cavity, about two miles away, and found the pictures to be broadly similar but definitely not the same. Most of them were showing images of a night scene, whereas those on the other side were in daylight. Other major changes were obvious. One scene showed the men working furiously on replacing a flat tyre that they were obviously in a hurry to fix.

What could it all mean? George had no idea. Was this another entertainment? Their version of a multi-player video game? He decided to study the large glass sphere in the centre, the projector of the laser images, perhaps that would be more illuminating. He moved towards it and squeezed his awareness through the glass, to the inside of the sphere.

And immediately regretted it.

Suddenly, he was being pulled in a billion different directions at once. He was instantly blinded, overwhelmed, and totally bemused by the myriad simultaneous images all coalescing in his mind. He felt like he was being torn apart, ripped into countless fragments, with each fragment sent to a different timeline in a distant universe; projected through the matrix of space-time in an almost infinite variety of epochs and locations.

Strangely, the sensation was almost familiar, though this was much, much, worse. It felt a little like an experience he now suddenly recollected from the depths of his infinite mind, of being ripped from his body during the time-travel accident that fused his chrono-computer and put him in the disembodied state he had existed as since. He remembered now how he had become what he was. It was a revelation to him.

Desperately trying to keep that one precious regained memory fresh in his shattered mind, he felt himself beginning to lose his grip on consciousness, he was slipping away. How could that happen when his consciousness was infinite? His mind was all he was, and he could feel it giving out on him.

This was a million times worse than merely being rat-arsed.

With a stupendous effort of will he didn't know he could summon, he slowly began scrabbling his mind back together; which now seemed to be shattered and scattered to the eight corners of the universe. It didn't feel like he was inside the sphere anymore, in fact he didn't feel like he was anywhere in the traditional sense of the word.

Still teetering on the brink of unconsciousness, his tormented awareness noticed something else; startling memories that were not his own now writhed like fat maggots burrowing through the month old mincemeat of his mind. Memories that were strange, alien, almost incomprehensibly dark. But the pain was too great, he couldn't examine them, not yet.

Gradually, infinitely slowly, after what seemed like an aeon of torture, George started to pull himself together. He began to ease his fragmented memory backwards in time to the moment before he entered the sphere. If he could only remember how he was in that fraction of a second, if he could focus and concentrate on himself, try to ignore the cacophony of confusion that surrounded him, he might be able to get out of this with his mind in one piece. It was touch and go.

As he yanked and heaved himself into a fragile but coherent whole, he felt himself passing slowly back through the glass. One fragment at a time, he became unified with himself once again.

With the visual equivalent of an audible pop, he reappeared in the space he had occupied before entering the sphere, back into the relatively normal space of the Moon cavity beyond.

Where every single alien in the place was staring straight at him and pointing.

Although he was still disembodied, still ethereal, with no physical manifestation, the lasers now projected millions of images of him floating there by the sphere. All identical, no differences between them at all. Just George Jr, floating there with a stupidly bewildered expression on his face.

His face!

He had a face! And a body!

He moved his arms - which he still couldn't see except in the projections from the sphere - manically waving them around in front of his astonished face. The millions of images all moved simultaneously, waving their arms in exactly the same frantic way.

He risked moving closer to the wall that surrounded him and was delighted to find he could see himself much better. Taking the stupid look off his face, he smiled broadly. One of his eyes wasn't open properly and his smile was lopsided. His eyeballs themselves looked like they were having a lot of trouble focusing, and his skin was decidedly pale, almost green, which set off the redness of his nose strikingly well. There was a faint line of drool coming from the corner of his mouth.

And he was wearing clothes! Clothes he now suddenly remembered owning during the "life" he once had.

But there was something else, besides the clothes. He appeared to be strapped into something that looked a bit like a dentist's chair. It only resembled a dentist's chair in the most superficial way though; the equipment that surrounded it in a sort of chassis arrangement would place this particular recliner, from an outside observer's perspective, somewhere on the set of a low budget science fiction movie. And George was the star of the film.

His smile broadened. His memory came flooding back to him from the infinite reaches of time that it had occupied for eternity as far as he could tell, but, he now realised, was actually only a little over twenty-five years in "objective" reality.

The aliens, meanwhile, were going apeshit. They were presumably screaming and shouting, and although George couldn't begin to understand what they were shouting, he suspected it wouldn't be nice. Small scooters were rising from many of the booths, and descending from above, from all directions, all converging on one point - the point that he apparently occupied. As they rose they interrupted the laser beams, and George could see their shadows projected onto the inside surface of the cavity. They were rapidly getting bigger. He had about twenty seconds before they reached him.

He regarded himself, and his newly remembered time machine, one last time in the gigantic display. Then, with a hugely lopsided grin and a triumphant, inaudible laugh, George hiccupped and disappeared.

As he vanished, the projected images suddenly switched to show a view of the entire universe spread out over the booths. Under normal operation each booth had a slightly different scene displayed in it, but now they acted like pixels in the biggest 3D surround cinerama ever seen.

The image wavered and coruscated across the display surface, as the universe morphed through a space-time that was at least infinite in extent, possibly much more. It almost appeared to be alive, wriggling, like a plump bug or a bacterium oozing around in slime. It seemed to simultaneously be growing at a rapid rate, and yet be stationary in the display, like the view was zooming out at the same rate as the expansion.

Then, suddenly, the image began to contract. Layers of the universe sped past, going out of view as the image zoned in on a single galactic cluster, then a single galaxy within that cluster, then to a single solar system in that galaxy, and finally to a blue-green planet in that solar system. The Earth.

The aliens, many of them now clustered fairly close in to the central glass sphere on their flying scooters, were jostling for position in the decreased space available to them while simultaneously trying not to disturb the lasers projecting the image. They weren't doing very well, the image was distorted and full of wobbly shadows as they almost fought for space, but already some of them were taking notes on the bewildering new scene that their mighty chronosphere, now inextricably entangled with George Jr's mind, was showing them.

Chapter 18.

All was not well back at the bunker.

After a hair-raising journey at speeds Randall didn't wish to consider, during which they'd easily outrun the troop transport and miraculously managed to shoot down another heat seeking drone using the laser turret, they had finally skidded to a halt and sat in the car breathing heavily. As the car was full of sick, it didn't take them long to throw open the doors and fling themselves, gulping like lungfish, onto the concrete.

Following a brief freezing-cold hose-down in the garage, showering had taken place. Daphne first, then Randall, and now Marcus.

Despite the initial disappointment at discovering the video feeds from the WPHQ had now gone quiet, and that Daphne had indeed found the recorder, which she dug out of a damp pocket and returned to him as promised, Marcus seemed pleased. Very pleased in fact.

"Singing" emanated from the bathroom as he showered. It sounded happy. 'Bee bob a loola, she's my baby,' it went. It was one of the "songs" Randall had listened to in the bat shit crazy Batmobile on the way to the rescue. It baffled him then, and now that it was out of tune, out of time, and being "sung" in a tiled bathroom that was so big it was effectively an echo chamber, it baffled him even more.

He was sitting in the lounge with wet hair, a mug of coffee, a frosty expression on his face, and his ex-girlfriend. She sat in front of him across the elegant carved wood table, gazing around the room in wonder at the abundant works of art. Randall adamantly wore the frosty expression until he could figure out his emotions.

He was determined that she was now his ex-girlfriend. Absolutely positive. No doubt about it. One hundred and ten percent. She'd never really been his girlfriend anyway, he reflected. She was a spy sent to watch him, and even though he was finding her even more attractive now he knew about her hidden identity and skills, and even though Daphne was trying her hardest to explain, and to apologise, and, quite frankly, to almost fawn around him, he was completely certain she was his *ex*-girlfriend. He just couldn't trust anything she said anymore.

She sat on the sofa wearing a smile and a dressing gown that did nothing to hide her figure. And she knew it.

So, increasingly, did Randall.

'I suppose this makes us even,' she said, flicking a lock of damp hair out of her face.

'How so?' He was trying not to notice the way her hair had just cascaded over her shoulder.

'I rescued you, and now you've rescued me,' she replied, smiling again, trying to lighten the mood. 'My hero.' She giggled, with just a tiny hint of coquettishness.

Randall wasn't in a light mood. The giggle didn't help.

'If we ignore the fact you're the spy who got us arrested in the first place that is. I'd say you still owed me one. And Marcus. Especially Marcus,' he said. He was still understandably angry that the last three years of his life had been a lie, but he was increasingly conscious of the fact that he hadn't exactly been completely honest with her either. Strangely, it bothered him.

Daphne bowed her head, her shoulders drooped. It was true of course, their relationship had been a fabrication, no amount of apology or reasoning would change that. She had secretly rifled through his research papers, violating his trust over and over.

'I'm sorry,' she said, for about the fiftieth time.

'I don't think "sorry" is going to be enough. Do you?' said Randall, sadly.

'If it's any consolation, you would have been hauled in for interrogation long before now if I hadn't wrangled the assignment. Anyone else - and believe me, there would have been someone else - you would have been reported for your illegal research within three months of them meeting you. That's how long it took me to figure out what you were doing.'

This was very probably true of course. It was one of the many confusing thoughts Randall had entertained whilst showering, whilst washing the vomit from his hair and secretly dreading this exact confrontation.

'I kept you as a low priority,' she continued. 'I actually told them next to nothing, only that you were interested in ancient devices. I wasn't sure but I think they were actually going to pull me from the case soon. If Marcus hadn't shown up when he did...' She shrugged and shook her head. 'But I would have come clean anyway, even if they did pull me. I figured I might be able to get you to join the resistance, and because, well... it wasn't a bad assignment. The fun we had was genuine you know, I'm not that good an actress.'

She smiled again, openly and warmly. Randall began to feel the steel framed skyscraper of his resolve starting to buckle in the heat. He considered carefully for a moment; this new side to ~~Cindi~~ Daphne (damn, he couldn't get used to that) the real her, as it were, was a more open, and certainly more intelligent young woman than the slightly dumb, but fun girl he'd been used to. During their relationship he hadn't paid too much attention to her prattling about "cosmic forces" or "the fractal manifestation of scalar life forms", but now he knew it was all an act... well, that was different.

'Just one thing,' he said, at last.

'What's that?'

'Can I still call you Cindi? This Daphne business is driving me potty.'

She stared at him for a second, before suddenly bursting out laughing.

He joined in.

Later on, Randall was in bed. Alone, in case you're wondering.

After a simple but delicious snack, during which everyone was strangely reticent to talk about the evening's events, Daphne, né Cindi again, was asleep on the huge sofa for the night, until more permanent arrangements could be made. The building was set up as a one-man palace after all, and Randall had caused a slight accommodation problem already, sleeping in the only spare room on an admittedly luxurious but still fold-out bed.

He was lying there trying hard not to think about Cindi, and had ended up wondering why Marcus should own a dressing gown, the one Cindi had worn earlier, that would not only fit her, and show up her figure so well, but be made of that particular fine, shiny, material that contrasted against her skin so nicely, and be patterned, as it was, with a fine filigree of delicate floral arrangements that accentuated her eye colour so beautifully.

It was clearly a feminine item of clothing, which, given Marcus's age and reclusive, almost hermit-like lifestyle, brought up a number of awkward questions which Randall decided not to ask for the time being. Right now he was tired, there would be plenty of time for awkward questions tomorrow.

On the edge of sleep, and with a sigh, he rolled over in bed; definitely *not* thinking about how much sexier Cindi had suddenly become.

Tomorrow, when it came, was a bright and frosty morning - the first frost of the autumn - and it started for Randall and Cindi with a shout of "Wakey wakey, campers", from Marcus. A delivery of equipment had arrived in the night via one of his secret suppliers, and he needed a hand getting it from the upstairs flat down into the bunker. Cindi stayed downstairs under the full protection of the dampening field while Marcus and Randall went up to see to it.

They stood there staring at the piles of equipment. A few pre-formed pieces, obviously to become the chassis of the transceiver section (Randall recognised them from the NetCam pictures of his dad's machine) sat on the floor on pallets that Randall couldn't help noticing were wider than the door frame. He tried to ignore it, there would be some obscure answer he wouldn't comprehend, which would only add another item to the end of a long list of things he didn't comprehend already.

He put it out of his mind and stared at the coils of copper wire, pneumatic control mechanisms, boxes of electronic components and all sorts of other bits and pieces that were tidily arranged around the trap door. Two elegant executive style office chairs sat in the corner in pieces.

'I don't understand,' said Randall, and not for the first time, 'how can you get these things without the WP knowing about it? Some of these crates are stamped with GloboCo logos. Do you have a mole at GloboCo? Are they stolen?'

Marcus simply raised an eyebrow inscrutably while handing him a bundle of cables that Randall slung over his shoulder.

'Something like that yes,' he said, handing him another bundle. 'The heavier parts will be arriving over the next few weeks. If you could take that box and those bags,' he pointed to the relevant items, 'and take them to the workshop? I'll follow you down in a moment.'

Randall collected the items indicated and started to descend the stairs. He couldn't help noticing how reticent Marcus seemed to be about his contacts, and that he avoided answering any questions about them.

As he rounded the first corner on the stairs, Marcus quietly opened the door of the flat and stepped out briefly into the dank, foul smelling, corridor. After checking no one was around, he took a note from his trouser pocket and quickly slipped it under the door of the massage parlour. Then he walked back into the flat, picked up a large box marked "Flux capacitors", and followed Randall down the stairs.

Cindi was in the workshop acquainting herself with the instruction manual of a programmable lathe when Randall walked in with his arms full of gear a few moments later. He dumped his burden in the corner and turned to leave, smiling briefly at Cindi.

Cindi smiled back at him. 'Anything I can do?' she asked. She felt useless, like a puncture repair kit on a submarine, but she would prove her usefulness if it killed her.

'Better not touch anything,' he said, smiling back at her. 'To be honest, the best thing you can do is go and get comfortable in the Book Room. Try the chairs, they're fantastic. You'll be in there for a couple of hours later today anyway, Marcus is going to disable your locator after lunch, then we can drop the dampening field and be free to move around. You might enjoy some of the history books while you're in there, they're quite enlightening.'

Cindi kept smiling as he left the workshop, but as Randall moved out of sight, the smile vanished, to be replaced with a look of confused sadness. A large part of last night had been spent trying to ignore the realisation that her life on the outside was over, that all she had now were a few contacts in a resistance movement scattered around the planet, the pretend ex-boyfriend she'd been spying on, and the mysteriously enigmatic Marcus. She put down the instruction manual and headed for the Book Room.

Randall was right, the chairs were fantastic.

An hour later the parts had been carried down to the workshop, and the three of them were, at Marcus's instruction, unpacking and stacking the pieces. There were hundreds of bits scattered all over, and Marcus was trying to get them into some sort of coherent order. The packaging material was big enough to fill a room all on its own, and Randall wondered, as billions of people throughout history had done before him, why packaging manufacturers had to use so much unnecessary stuff.

He was trying to pack some of the packaging down into one of the bigger boxes, to make more space for the components now arranged on the floor like an exploded diagram. Marcus looked pleased.

'And that's lunch,' he said. 'Come on, Cindi, I'll show you around the kitchen. I think you'll like it.'

He was right, she did.

A short while later they were in the lounge, seated around the dining table with a roast dinner steaming on their plates. While Marcus ate slowly, Randall and Cindi were stuffing their faces. It was utterly delicious, as every meal seemed to be in this amazing place. Cindi was intrigued.

'How come the food tastes so much better here?' she asked. 'Even the coffee is better than anything I've ever tasted.'

'It's very rich food,' said Marcus.

'I wouldn't say it's rich,' she replied. 'This roast dinner isn't too rich. It's delicious, but it's not rich.'

'That's not what I mean,' he said, shaking his head. 'It's the food of the very rich, those with all the money. It's organic, chemical free, GM free, freshly picked, carefully prepared, and highly nutritious.'

Randall didn't understand, another mental state he was reluctantly getting used to. 'What do you mean by organic? All food's organic isn't it?'

'I mean organic in the sense that our ancestors meant it,' he said. 'All food used to be grown like this, without chemicals, without tinkering with the genes, without artificial fertilisers. But then, hundreds of years ago, the means of food production was taken over by the cartel of companies that eventually merged to become GloboCo. Since then, the quality of food has steadily decreased to the point where the people are fed a diet of tasteless, almost nutrition free junk. It helps them to keep the population suppressed. A poor diet equals a slow and stupid citizenry. I mean, have you ever watched The XXX Factor?'

Cindi simply nodded. It fitted with her view of the world, this wasn't really such startling news to her. A plot of this magnitude was entirely feasible, scoring only around two hundred and fifty milli-Ickes on the conspiracy scale. Anything below point eight of an Icke was considered eminently possible within the resistance.

'That's why you have so much energy,' said Randall, the sudden realisation apparent in his voice.

'Compared to you two, and I mean no insult, I'm an elite athlete. Even at my advanced age. I'll live longer than you both and I'll still be comparatively fit when I die. And it won't be from cancer by the way. In the population at large more than half will die of cancer, but in the world of the rich it's about one in a thousand.'

He looked at them both, filling their faces with the best food they'd ever tasted, and smiled. 'You'll both gain from your time here. In a few months you'll be almost as healthy as me. Use the gym regularly, like I do, and you'll feel the benefit in no time.'

———————————

And, once again, following the cinematic time-lapse special effect that ends with the caption "Three months later", Marcus was proved right.

Over the next few weeks Randall and Cindi became healthier, fitter, and quicker witted than they had ever been, as the additives in the food they had been eating for their entire lives were eliminated from their systems.

After a rather unpleasant but necessary initial period of chelation (during which Randall thought his arse was going to fall off, as a lifetime's worth of heavy metal contamination was expelled from his body) they began to gradually get used to their new lifestyle. They drank purified water or fruit juice, ate organic and free range food, exercised daily, and studied in the evenings. They even spent some days doing nothing but reading selections from Marcus's other library, the one packed with six-hundred-years' worth of eye-opening, and very rare, works of banned literature.

By and by, they began to forget the world they'd known. They didn't miss it much.

Cindi immersed herself in the study of martial arts, amongst many other things, on top of learning the basics of time-travel and helping to build the machine. Her advanced training in the WP transferred easily into the study of ancient fighting techniques, most of which she'd never heard of before. Using Marcus as a sparring partner, she became expert in a range of fighting systems developed by the long lost Japanese. She was so eager to master her new skills that they often trained together late into the evening, and she even managed to land a blow on him occasionally.

Randall, as well as being fitter than he'd ever been, became well versed in the mathematics, mechanics, and sheer bloody hard work needed to finish the job at hand. He was transformed. He'd always wobbled slightly around the wrong side of average in many respects before coming to live there; slightly below average height, a little above average weight, slightly below averagely good looking, averagely coloured brown hair...

Apart from the hair, which was now cut short in an almost military style, he was no longer average. He even looked taller, somehow.

They used their terminals less and less over the months too. Even though their locators were disabled, and they could access the full range of functions - provided they didn't buy anything, not that they needed to - their time was taken up more and more by the building of the time machine and developing the plan to get to the Wastelands.

Cindi even managed to put out of her mind the fact that if they were successful, and even if they weren't, her life would soon be coming to an end. She knew she wouldn't die as such, but her life would end anyway, along with the entire Galaxy if they failed. She was strangely Zen about the whole thing; perhaps a side effect of her training, perhaps because she really believed they could make a difference and create a better world in an alternate timeline. She was totally committed.

Marcus watched their development with interest, like the children he'd never had. He became a kind of father figure to them both, imparting his wisdom and helping them when they needed it, watching while they made their own mistakes when they needed that too. He didn't force them, he guided them. He didn't train them, he trained *with* them. Before long, they weren't just conspirators, they were a team. And firm friends.

We join them again in the workshop about to test a key component of the partially completed machine. The almost finished transceiver section was set to one side of the work space, while they assembled the chassis around the twin executive chairs that made up the unit they would travel in. The overhead displays of the "pod" were about to be powered up for the first time, and with that done, they would be able to retire for the evening.

After a steady ten days of work it was a mutually agreed rest night tonight. There would be no training, studying, or shop talk, only pleasant conversation, a bottle or two of Chateau Laffite from Marcus's vintage collection, and maybe an old movie to watch. Marcus had mentioned an ancient film that he wanted them to see - something called "Terminator 4". As far as Randall was concerned, a terminator was a special character used at the end of a string of text, like a full stop, and "4" wouldn't be at all effective in that context, so he assumed it must be an office comedy of some sort.

Cindi sat in the pilot's chair of the pod looking at the overhead screens, while Marcus connected the circuit to the generator and prepared to switch the system on. As he did so, there was a shriek from Cindi. Marcus quickly disconnected the circuit, fearing she'd just received an electric shock.

'There was a face in the screen,' she shouted, as she jumped out of the chair, 'just for a moment, but it was there I'd swear on it.'

Randall and Marcus exchanged incredulous glances. 'You sure you haven't started on the wine already, Cindi?' asked Randall.

'I don't see things! Even when I have had a drink.' She was insistent, and was wearing the "I know I'm bloody well right" look that they had become so used to over the weeks. 'I tell you there was a face in the screen. It looked puzzled, and it didn't look right, like it was lopsided or something. Not scary, but odd, that's all.'

'Was it a reflection?' asked Marcus.

She was adamant. 'No. It was green and kinda distorted, like interference or something. And if it was a reflection why did it disappear as soon as you pulled the plug?' replied Cindi. 'As the screen lit up, there was a face in it. I didn't imagine it. It wasn't a reflection.' She folded her arms and put her "prove me wrong" face on.

Marcus plugged the circuit back in and sat in the pilot's chair. 'Switch it on for me would you, Randall?'

He did so. The screen lit up showing nothing but the expected static. Marcus moved his head around, trying to get a reflection of his face, or any of their faces, in the screen, but he failed. Looking at Cindi he could see she meant it, but there was nothing in the screens now but digital snow.

'Okay,' said Marcus. 'Let's call it a day shall we? I for one could do with a night off. We're all tired and your mind can play tricks when you're tired. Come on, we're having a stew tonight, and I baked some bread.'

'But it was there I swear...' said Cindi, but now even she was beginning to doubt it. Perhaps she had been overdoing it a bit, a chance to unwind would be welcome.

'It must have been a ghost from a previous image stored in the capacitors or something,' said Randall. 'Probably my fault. Perhaps I should have fitted the ground cable before the data link. Maybe there was still a charge in the monitor's circuits from when they tested it at the factory?'

He looked around at them for their reactions. From the considered looks on their faces, they both seemed to think it was a reasonable enough explanation; although secretly, all three of them could think of at least two good reasons why it was impossible.

After dinner, they sat in the lounge watching Terminator 4 on the huge screen Marcus had lowered from the ceiling. From previous film evenings they'd got used to the fact the screen was only 3D, and didn't have Smellivision or Tremblomatics, but they were thoroughly enjoying the movie nonetheless. Not exactly the comedy Randall had been expecting, but they were all laughing at it despite that. Especially Cindi. Such primitive special effects. Hilarious.

'Bravo. Well done,' she said to Marcus, clapping and laughing as the credits rolled. 'Where did you find a film about a resistance movement on a submarine? It must have taken you ages.'

'A little digging admittedly,' said Marcus, 'but as you know, I'm interested in ancient art forms, and I dug the memory out of the old grey matter eventually. I thought it would be apt given our upcoming trip to the Wastelands.'

Which was true, it was very apt given the circumstances...

Unscheduled communication was incredibly difficult when the most senior resistance officers were based on a formerly nuclear submarine somewhere under the Atlantic, but after following Cindi's detailed instructions they had finally managed to contact them only the previous week. The time machine wasn't fully finished, and it was rather too soon to call for their help yet, but this was the only opportunity they would have. The submarine raised its communications buoy only occasionally during the year. Luckily, Cindi knew when.

Via Marcus's secret network, the message had been passed to a mole in the WP known only to "Sundial" (Cindi's resistance codename) and using a secret system that piggybacked their message on the back of satellite frequencies used by the WP network, they had transmitted the request and received a reply the next day.

Although shop talk was generally discouraged on evenings like this, the conversation, fuelled by a little wine, eventually and inevitably wandered into the aforementioned shop for a bit of a walk up and down the aisles and a prod at the comestibles.

'So you're sure we can get to Spain by next Tuesday?' asked Randall.

'Shouldn't be a problem,' said Marcus. 'I've got a van coming for us on Friday, so we should be there with a day to spare.' He took another sip of wine.

It was Sunday today, things were getting close to the tipping point, and butterflies were inhabiting the stomachs of all three of them.

'We'll be finished on time?' asked Cindi.

'Maybe not completely, but the big engineering tasks are done now so all that's really left is to set up the computers, and we can do that on the sub on the way to the Wastelands. We can test the delivery system when we get there, we know the mechanics are sound, but we won't know whether it'll all work together until the day we use it. I've started

137

preparing a set of tools and spares we'll need to take with us, just in case.'

'Talking of cases, make sure you pack some of this wine,' said Cindi, swilling it around in her glass. 'I could get used to this. Pity I've only got a few weeks left to do so.'

There was an awkward pause while Randall and Marcus exchanged embarrassed looks. Eventually Cindi looked at both of them in turn and said, 'Don't worry about it, with any luck I'll be too pissed to notice.'

They laughed, but it was a forced kind of laugh.

Later on, as Randall was walking past the spare bedroom (now occupied by Cindi) on the way to the toilet for a late night visit, he heard what he thought sounded like a soft sobbing coming from her room. It wasn't as loud as Marcus's habitual snoring, but he heard it in-between the wet snortling rumbles coming from his room. Startled, he stopped outside the door and leaned closer, wondering whether to knock and see if he could do anything to help.

Things were good between them now they both knew where they stood with each other. Randall still held a place in his heart for her, but it seemed like he would have to continue to hold it. After the first couple of weeks without romantic fireworks exploding, they had settled down into a relationship based on mutual respect, trust, and interdependence; the prospect of anything more was quietly ignored. It bubbled up occasionally during their banter in the workshop, but neither of them knew what to do with it when it did. Marcus was quietly amused, but he said nothing.

Randall knocked on Cindi's door, not thinking anything other than a quiet chat would be the outcome...

George James Junior watched. Not in that way, he couldn't see anything with the lights dimmed anyway. After his failure to communicate earlier in the day he was watching and waiting. Waiting for "the present" to catch up.

Chapter 19.

FAO.   Captain Keystone
Status rep. #2609/011.6 – 14:16
DefCon.   4 - Relaxed.
Location.   20° 35′ N. 64° 44′ W. Puerto Rico Trench.
Depth.   7110 metres.
Speed.   6 knots.
Heading.   East-North-East. 72°.
Status.   Nominal (but we're about to run out of loo roll).

Keystone shook his head in despair as he read the report. They were short of various things, he knew that, but it would be another week before the next supply stop, so they'd just have to make do. He had a toilet roll stashed away in his locker, he could make it last a week if he needed to. After all, war is brutal.

He filed the document and took a sip of his tea. *One day*, he thought, *when the revolution comes, these reports will be recorded for posterity's sake. They will be important documents detailing the history of the brave sacrifices of the resistance, outlining exactly how they defeated the evil ruling elites and their pawns, the WP.*

And he could do without comments like "we're about to run out of loo roll" tarnishing the record. He made a note to talk to his number two about it at the weekly meeting later. As commander of the submarine, and nominal head of the resistance, he knew how important following protocol was, and complaining about the toiletry facilities on an official report was not according to protocol. Chief Petty Officer Fortesque-Harrington-Smythe, codename Sleepy, would have to be put on report. Again.

He was getting worried that the report card now constituted a rather fat folder full of paper. It was no longer an occasional note about a sailor being drunk on duty, it was now a hefty tome, added to almost daily. Overall, morale was reasonably good given the circumstances, but discipline was slack. The crew needed a shake-up, and if the communiqué he'd just finished decoding was correct, they would soon get one. The coordinates had been confirmed; when they next picked up supplies, it would be time to start their new mission.

He finished his cup of Earl Grey, straightened his tie in the mirror, pulled his jacket straight, and placed his cap squarely on his head before leaving his ready room and walking the short distance to the bridge.

Walking quietly up the gangway, he could hear laughing and chatter coming from the bridge crew, but as he came to within a few feet of the hatch he heard a loud cough, and suddenly the joking stopped. When he entered the control room a second later, the crew were all at their stations apparently paying very close attention to their equipment.

'New heading, Mister Grumpy,' [13] he said, as he walked in. Grumpy was currently the codename for his number two. Normally, he would have called him the more familiar "number two", but he knew how "Grumpy" grated on his nerves, so he used the codename occasionally when he was upset. The smell of tobacco smoke he'd just noticed had raised his personal DefCon from Mildly Irked, to Jolly Cross Actually.

'Aye aye, sir,' said number two, a.k.a. Mr. Grumpy, grumpily.

'Ten degrees starboard and ahead two-thirds,' said Keystone.

'Ten degrees starboard and ahead two-thirds. Aye, sir,' repeated Mr. Grumpy.

He noted down the command in the operations log and turned towards the helm, currently crewed by Senior Midshipman Fotheringay-Phipps, a.k.a. Sneezy.

'Ten degrees starboard and ahead two-thirds, Mister Sneezy,' he said.

'... ' said Mr. Sneezy.

---

[13] The senior officers below Keystone were given new codenames, taken from ancient films or books, on an annual basis. Only the commander-in-chief got to choose his own. This year it was 'Snow White and the seven dwarfs'. Most of the crew weren't Happy, but Snow White himself was quietly thrilled with his codename. It was Fabulous! Even better than last year when he was Mr. Pink.

Mr. Grumpy briefly looked sideways at Keystone, who raised an eyebrow expressively. 'Ten degrees starboard and ahead two-thirds, Mister Sneezy,' he shouted once more.

'... ' repeated Mr. Sneezy, casually.

Mr. Grumpy walked over to the helm position and looked at Mr. Sneezy carefully. Before long he noticed the cable connecting Mr. Sneezy's music player to Mr. Sneezy's ears. He yanked hard on it. With two audible pops Mr. Sneezy's earplugs flew sideways out of his head.

'I say!' he said, turning angrily to face Mr. Grumpy. But at that moment he noticed Keystone impatiently tapping his foot in the middle of the control room, and wisely chose to stay in his chair. A tinny rendition of Elgar's Nimrod, just on the edge of hearing, stopped playing a second or two later.

Mr. Grumpy took a deep breath, moved his face to within six inches of Mr. Sneezy's left ear, and shouted, 'Ten degrees starboard and ahead two-thirds, Mister Sneezy,' pointedly, into it.

Mr. Sneezy, looking sheepish, wiped the spit from his ear, altered the course and speed, and repeated the command back one more time.

'Ten degrees starboard and ahead two-thirds. Aye, sir,' he said, as the dull throb of the engines began to rise in pitch.

Now the echo chamber of the command chain had been satisfied, Keystone turned to Mr. Grumpy. 'A word, number two?' he said, pointing over his shoulder with his thumb to indicate his ready room. He turned to leave the bridge with number two, still grumpy, following behind.

'Look, Nigel,' he said, as they reached the ready room and sat down. 'I know the men are bored but I can't have bridge officers listening to music on duty, even if it is Elgar. I want Sneezy's music player on my desk before the meeting later, okay? And the smoking simply has to stop. You know the air scrubbers need an overhaul.'

'I know, Monty [14] but they're going out of their minds cooped up for

---

[14] Full name Montgomery Crispin Cholmondeley-Mainwaring-Featherstonhaugh, of the Hampshire Cholmondeley-Mainwaring-Featherstonhaughs **.
** Pronounced Chumley-Mannering-Fanshaw. The higher up the ranks of the British aristocracy one's family rose, the more ridiculously one spelled and pronounced one's family name. This was epitomised by the ruling family of the twentieth century - their family name was spelled 'Saxe-Coburg-Gotha', but it was pronounced 'Windsor'.

months at a time like this,' he said. 'Stopping the little pleasures they do have would be bad for morale. We all need some deck time... some fresh air... to see the Sun again...' He left the sentiment hanging.

Keystone thought for a moment. Grumpy was right, he knew that. 'Okay, we'll surface tomorrow when we're further out in the Atlantic. You can spread the word there'll be three hours of deck time when we're at least two hundred miles from here.'

'Aye, sir. Thank you, sir,' said Nigel Althorp-Belvoir-Marjoribanks, a.k.a. "Number Two", a.k.a. "Mister Grumpy".

'And I have something else that should raise morale even further,' said Keystone. 'We have a new mission. We're going to collect some passengers and equipment at the next supply stop. We're on our way there now.'

'What Passengers? Where are we taking them?'

'As to who, I'm not entirely sure. It's to do with the case Sundial has been on for the last few years. She went dark three months ago, but now she's back. Apparently it'll be her, Randall James and one other, unknown to us. The "where" is rather more surprising, they want to go to the Wastelands.'

'The Wastelands? Why would anyone in their right mind want to go there?'

'That's all I know for now,' said Keystone. 'We'll find out in a week won't we?'

Later, in the ward room, the senior staff of the RSS Frightfully Audacious were gathered for the weekly meeting. The stewards had finished pouring the tea and were placing the cakes, biscuits, and scones on the table. A tasteful display of after eight mints and chocolate fingers, sculpted into a model of a galleon in full sail, took pride of place in the centre of the table. The chief cook, James Fearnley-Wittingstall-Dixon-Wright (known as Jamie to the crew) had spent hours preparing it, but he told people it only took fifteen minutes.

As the stewards returned to the scullery, to approving grunts and mumblings of 'nice spread, Jamie,' Keystone brought the meeting to order...

'Gentlemen,' he said, waiting for the hubbub to die down, 'thank you for coming. As some of you know, we're picking up passengers at our

142

next provision stop. We'll be using the Cadiz depot, and we're heading there now. The landing party has been decided and is detailed on the agenda.'

A look of relief seemed to spread across the officers' faces as they perused the details of the landing party, a contented murmuring followed. The words 'fresh fruit' and 'loo roll' could be heard being whispered among them.

'A couple of you have met Sundial before,' said Keystone, raising his voice almost imperceptibly, 'and you'll have the chance to meet her again soon because that's who we're picking up.'

More murmuring, verging on muttering. A woman coming on board?

'And Randall James will be joining her.'

This time there was more than a murmur. The whispering became a susurration that grew into a muttering-ness which evolved into a brouhaha and eventually became almost a botherance. Disapproving exclamations were exclaimed, and eyebrows, some of them extremely bushy, were waggling all over foreheads.

Keystone raised his voice once more to compete with the hubbub. 'Gentlemen please. Calm down, we don't know for sure why he's coming along, but Sundial is one of our best agents, and she's been undercover on this case for over three years, so we'll just have to trust her judgement. We all know the stories about George James Junior, and in the light of her rather comprehensive reports, I for one am sure his "Departure" was genuine.'

Now the commotion grew again, it raised in intensity until it was a ballyhoo, verging on a vexation. Keystone, sighing, let them get it out of their systems. Fists were shaking and cries of 'shame' and 'fraud' could be heard through the pandemonium. Eventually, as the vexation subsided somewhat into a "bit of a to-do", Warrant Officer Ranulph St. John-Woolfardisworthy [15], codename "Doc", cleared his considerably bewattled throat to speak. He was thought of as the intellectual amongst the crew, so he was given space to be heard.

The throat clearing went on for some time, and was followed by half a dozen decreasingly voluminous "harrumph" noises that wobbled his

---

[15] Pronounced Sin Gin Woolsary.

jowls like wet socks on a windy washing line. After a few moments, he said, 'The fellow was the infelicitous facilitator of a prodigious depletion of phlogiston.'

The officers, as one man, turned to the skinny character sitting to Doc's left, one of the younger officers, who went by the name of Sebastian Fotherington-Fotherington, a.k.a. "Bashful", who said, 'Unfortunately, he was a big waste of oxygen.'

'Indeed,' Doc continued, 'he was the absolute giddy limit! Capaciously endowed with an overabundance of thermally excited atmospheric gasses.'

Again, the crew stared at Bashful for a translation. 'He was full of hot air,' he explained, after the couple of seconds it took him to reassemble the sentence in his head.

'Palaverous, circumlocutory, sesquipedalian, and pleonastic,' said Doc, harrumphing again. This time Bashful looked at Doc as the others had looked to him. He had an incredulous expression on his face as he translated. 'He was overly wordy,' he said, circumspectly applying the irony utilizing a considerably capacious stoker's shovel (laying it on with a trowel).

'I would go so far as to say the blaggard was an importunate disseminator of terminological inexactitudes,' finished Doc, leaning back in his seat with a handful of the most reachable biscuits.

Before they could even look at him again, Bashful had translated. 'And he was a persistent liar,' he said.

Half of the staff officers nodded in agreement, harrumphing was happening among them, but Keystone and Mr. Grumpy, along with Mr. Sleepy, all shook their heads. They had read the reports from Sundial over the years and took her seriously. If she thought Randall James was useful, then Randall James was useful, despite what the media had to say about his father.

The harrumphing, haranguing, and heartily disputed hasslement, continued for some time afterwards.

Keystone leaned back with his cup of Earl Grey and a scone. He decided not to tell them there would be another guest that he knew absolutely nothing about.

The next day, out in the Atlantic, they surfaced for some well-earned deck time. The weather was good, which meant it was mostly cloudy and the WP satellites wouldn't be able to see them, so they were making the most of the opportunity. There were breaks enough in the clouds to let the warming Sun through occasionally, but not enough to worry them; the chances of being spotted were millions to one.

Most of the crew lounged around on the deck variously setting up picnics, playing quoits (they'd run out of cricket balls long ago) and generally having a nice, relaxing, time of it. There was even talk of some entertainment later, if Warrant Officer Millhouse-Philby-Blunt, codename "Snow White", could get his costume right. He was down below working on his headgear, a foot-high fake-fruit based construction of considerable complexity. He rehearsed his song while he worked on the wire frame structure. 'I, yi, yi, yi, yi, yi, like you veeeery much,' he sang, 'I, yi, yi, yi, yi, yi think you're grrraaand.'

Keystone and his number two, blessedly out of earshot, were standing atop the conning tower discussing where to quarter their guests and equipment.

'They could use Lab Nine,' said number two, no longer grumpy now the Sun was out. 'It won't be too much hassle. We can put a hold on Operation Mindwarp, it's not going anywhere at the moment anyway. There should be enough room for their gear if we move the sensory deprivation tanks out of the way.'

Operation Mindwarp was a small project run by Fortesque-Harrington-Smythe (Sleepy) to try to utilise the mind field that he believed permeated the Earth; for communication, or possibly even to influence WP decision makers. Only a few of the crew thought there was any possibility of it ever actually working, but they were devout and tenacious alternative thinkers, which was encouraged within the resistance.

'I was thinking the same thing,' said Keystone. 'If we set up some bunks in there we can keep them away from the crew to an extent, you know how some of the men are superstitious about women on submarines.'

'It's not the superstitious ones I'm worried about,' said number two. 'Some of the men haven't even seen a woman for the last three months. We'll have to give them some shore leave at Cadiz.'

'Already on the itinerary,' said Keystone. 'Looks like it'll take more than a day to get their gear and our supplies aboard, we'll be making a couple of round trips I think. I'll know more when we get there. I'm banking on it not taking more than two days, so we can split the crew and run two consecutive shore leaves. We'll be short staffed on the day, but we'll manage. We'll have to keep Sundial away from the men as much as possible for the duration, that might cause some problems.'

'Talking of women,' said number two, pointing to the foredeck, 'this should be good.'

Millhouse-Philby-Blunt was setting up a small sound system and testing his microphone. The crew gathered around. Snow White was funny in a camp kind of way, and entertainment was in short supply.

He stood there in an embroidered cerise pink wrap-around, earrings you could perch a parrot on, an abundance of bangles, and two strategically placed coconut halves. His headgear was a masterpiece of fruit based fabrication, standing easily fourteen inches above his huge black wig. His make-up, hastily improvised from food colouring and whatever else he could scavenge, was caked on his face in a more-or-less pleasing manner, and he was ready to begin the show.

He scanned the assembled crowd very briefly before starting; just long enough to make sure that Radio Operator Dopey, a.k.a. Tristram Weatherspoon-Yates, was amongst them and watching. As he switched on his backing track and began to sing, the small shortwave transmitter, so carefully hidden in his hat, began broadcasting...

The message he'd composed earlier in the day contained only four words, in Morse code: "Randall", "James", "Cadiz", and "Tuesday".

He smiled broadly and pointed at "Pimples", the youngest, and shyest, member of the crew. Staring at him with a cheeky grin, he winked and started to sing.

'I, yi, yi, yi, yi, yi, like you veeeery much...'

Chapter 20.

Big Bill was in his element. Sort of. He was in a field a short distance from the Forest Council, training an elite battalion of birds for the battles they would have to face only a couple of months from now. They had nicknamed themselves "The Red Sparrows", and they were coming along nicely under Bill's wing, so to speak.

They were a rag-tag flock to be sure, ranging in size from a charm of tiny goldcrests, with their yellow head feathers, through a worm of robins, a mutation of thrushes, two grinds of blackbirds and a small parliament of rooks, to Arthur the osprey and his mate Peregrine [16]. There was even a special forces group, a murder of crows nicknamed "The Black Death". Bill was with them now, about to go over tactics and strategy, but his mind wasn't on the job.

These days he spent most of his time at the Forest Council preparing the troops to escort the visitors, but he still kept a second nest back on the border of the Happy Valley, and went back there for a break every couple of weeks. Betty the Silver Birch had become a regular stopover on the journey, and they were now friends, despite the dodgy first night. Indeed, Betty and the copse had become involved in the plan too, the visitors would probably need a number of stopover locations on their journey from the coast to the Happy Valley.

With the Black Death perched before him waiting for their fearless leader to start the briefing, all he could think of was his comfy nest back in the valley. When Arthur the Osprey landed a moment later, it interrupted his reverie and pulled him back into the present...

Arthur approached Bill. 'There are two humiliations of sparrows just

---

[16] No one dare even guess what species Peregrine allegedly belonged to, just in case they offended him. It was a bloody scary species, whatever it was.

arrived and wanting to join in, sir. Shall I assign them a tree?' he asked.

Bill nodded. 'Make sure they're away from the goldcrests, you know how they fight.'

'Yes, sir,' screamed Arthur, in the thoroughly over-the-top military fashion that Bill had grown to detest. He saluted smartly, executed a perfect one hundred and eighty degree turn, clicked his heels together - which was difficult without boots, let alone with the arrangement of his claws - and left...

... and that was part of the problem for Bill. He was a riven raven. He missed the relaxed atmosphere of the valley, and couldn't wait to get back there. Being saluted and called "sir" all the time was bringing him down; and bringing out long buried parts of his character that he'd tried to evolve beyond over the years. Gone were the cheery phrases and jovial personality, to be replaced with a hardnosed (or rather, beaked) General about to go to war.

He hadn't really prepared for the briefing, but he pulled together the few scraps of information the Black Death wouldn't have heard yet and plunged ahead anyway. He was winging it...

'Okay, lads,' he croaked, 'the trees have negotiated safe passage all the way to the Ragnar Rocks, but beyond that we'll be up against some pretty stiff opposition. The tribes beyond the mountains are mostly anti-prophecy and they'll do anything they can to stop us getting to the coast.'

'Latest intel from the CIA [17] gives us an idea of some of their tricks. Be on the lookout for Vine-Webs. They grow in the form of a net about six feet square and are flung upwards using modified puffball spore release systems. They can be quite deadly if you get caught up in one, so keep your eyes peeled over open ground. They're camouflaged, of course, so they're hard to spot from the air. If you stay higher than about a hundred feet you're out of range, but we'll be vulnerable as we head down to land. Mossad are cooperating with the mesh to find the safest route.'

Bill looked around at the Black Death, six of the meanest crows you

---

[17] Chrysanthemum Intelligence Agency. A species of plant that grew an eye in the centre of its flower. See also the NSA (Nosey Snowdrop Agency) and Mossad.

could ever wish to not meet, but without a single minute of actual combat experience between the lot of them. It was a tough job to mould these mavericks into a fighting force that would be able to face the challenges ahead, but he still had a few weeks left, and they were beginning to behave like a team. Yesterday's formation flying exercise had been a moderate success, and they seemed to get the hang of wing commands, but they did still have a tendency to chase one another and pretend it was all a game, especially the younger ones. He would have to think of a way to challenge them, get them thinking as a unit.

'Questions?' he said.

One young crow raised a wing.

'Yes, Jim?'

'What about roosts? It's a long way to the coast, we'll need a couple of roosting posts,' said Jim.

'We'll have to find them on the fly,' Bill replied. 'We don't have great maps past the mountains, but I know a few areas with high ground, so our route will take that into account. Up to the Ragnar Rocks we'll be okay, the trees are all on our side.'

Another wing flew up in the air. Lonán, the smallest but probably the smartest amongst them.

'Yes, Lonán?'

'Are the "Cloudburster" rumours true?'

The other crows cawed quietly amongst themselves, they'd all heard the stories.

Bill had heard the rumours too, of course, and if he was honest with himself he didn't know what to think about it. The spy networks had little real information, only a few scattered reports, but the concept was entirely possible. Near the coast, to the north, there was a lagoon called the Pool of Drool, connected to the sea by a narrow underwater passage that occasional unlucky sea creatures would get sucked into and imprisoned. Fed with rich mud from the geysers that dotted the area, the Pool of Drool had the highest mutation rate on the island, so literally anything was possible there.

This was where Cloudbursters had evolved; supposedly an advanced hybrid/colony creature similar to a Portuguese man o' war jellyfish, but much, much, bigger.

By resizing their air sacks and including certain hydrogen producing chemical reactions in their biology, the Cloudburst Jellyfish had become airborne. They couldn't stray too far from the lagoon, needing to submerge themselves in the salty, mud saturated, water at least twice a day; but they could go high. And when they were high, according to the sporadic reports, they could apparently change the weather.

The theory put forward by the Elders, one that was supported by eyewitness accounts, supposed that the Cloudbursters could rise higher than the cloud layer, into the higher speed winds of the troposphere. There they could hover stationary for hours at a time, swimming against the wind and dispersing cloud condensation nuclei produced by bacterial colonies housed in the creature's dangling tendrils. Clouds formed downwind of the streams of molecular debris, white streaks would appear across the sky, and bad weather could theoretically be directed towards anyone heading for the coast.

Bill decided to downplay the rumours. 'Don't believe everything you hear, Lonán. And that goes for the rest of you too. Keep your minds on what you can prove for yourself, don't let rumours get to you, it's not good to be second guessing yourself. Stay focused on what you know, okay?'

Lonán nodded. 'Yes, sir,' he said loudly, but rather too slowly to be entirely convincing.

'Any more questions?' asked Bill, hoping to hell that there weren't any.

No more wings were raised, the Black Death seemed satisfied and were looking between themselves for confirmation and support. A good sign. A month ago, when they had come together for the first time, they would have argued and ended up scrapping.

Bill was pleased. He decided, on a not quite entirely self-interested whim, that a bit of r 'n r would be good for everybody. He dismissed them with a half-hearted wave of his wing that could only be interpreted as a salute in very poor light, perhaps in a thunderstorm, and even then only by an old bird with similarly deflicted eyes.

The Black Death knew the signal, and knew it meant that Big Bill, their fearless legendary leader, victor of a thousand battles and dark terror of the skies, was a bit fed up and wanted to go home. They dispersed quietly, heading for their quarters back among the trees of the Forest Council.

As the squad flew off, Bill felt the tension ease from his wings. Closing his eyes, he leaned back against the trunk of the low tree he used as a podium. He was trying to muster up the energy to fly home, but he didn't think he had enough time to make it all the way to Betty's copse before sunset. As he was deciding what to do, there was a meek shout from below, only ten feet away. Carl the squirrel clerk was nervously trying to attract his attention, but he seemed to be trying to do it by making as little noise as possible. His bushy tail trembled nervously.

'Mister Bill, sir?' he squeaked, timidly, hopping from one foot to the other.

Without moving his head, Bill opened an eye. The blind one. 'What now?' he asked, wearily.

Confronted by the baleful eye of Bill, Carl the clerk froze, stiff like a statue, before letting out a little bit of wee.

'Sorry to disturb you, sir,' he said, hesitantly, 'only I have a message from the Council. They want to see you. Er... immediately. I mean, er, as soon as you're... you know... when you're ready... sir.'

Big Bill sighed and hopped down from his branch, swooping low over Carl's head and causing the rest of his bladder to empty as he did so. It seemed his decision had been made for him yet again. He flew back to the Council with a weary expression on his increasingly frustrated looking face.

Chapter 21.

Although he didn't know it, no longer Chief Inspector Bailey had almost become a religious man. Since his demotion to constable in the wake of the Randall James debacle, and his subsequent exclusion from the case, he had developed a belief so strong that it couldn't be shaken. Not even by the shakiest of orthodox beliefs. The Post-New-Agers, or "Neos", as they called themselves, with all their crystals and dream catchers, and charms, had nothing on him. The wishing, silent begging, and praying he'd been doing recently would have convinced an open-minded theologian too, if such a creature could ever truly be found.

It differed from a fervently held religious belief not in intensity, or in his unwillingness to listen to other opinions, but in the fact that the belief was centred solely upon himself. He was absolutely convinced of his own incontrovertible rightness. His so-called "superiors" were complacent fools, and he would recapture not only Randall James and his mysterious elderly friend, but Daphne Lehman and the leaders of the resistance to boot.

He didn't know how he was going to do it yet, but that didn't matter, he was working on it. He had self-belief, and that was all that counted. He knew they would betray their positions eventually, and when they did, he would be ready.

He sat in his new office that wasn't actually an office. He didn't have a real office anymore, so he used an old storeroom in the basement to keep his files relating to the case. One wall was covered in pictures and notes, connected in a cat's cradle of string held there with coloured pins.

The James family were well represented on the wall. Pictures of Randall, George Junior, George Senior, and even the great Zachary James, the creator of Temporal Vortex Theory, covered one side of the display. Marcus showed up in a separate group of half a dozen photos taken during his arrest. Many of them had multiple large red question marks on them. Two photos of Daphne were between the two groups, one from her personnel file, and the other taken on the night of her disappearance, from the drone just before it was shot down.

Bailey had been studying that drone photo with a magnifying glass for nearly an hour now, old school. He was interested in the fuzzy patch on one side of the image, some distance from the startled looking Daphne on the other. Using a bit of basic trigonometry that twisted his mind so much he could barely think straight, he'd calculated the distance between them on the photo. Only then did he realise he could have simply gone with the photo and paced out the distance for himself.

Other than the increased rate of moustache manipulation, which was in danger of separating the fungus from his face on occasion, he didn't show any reaction to the mistake he'd just wasted half an hour making.

He put the error out of his mind in the way that his self-help books had taught him, and reached for his jacket - determined to get to the bottom of it one way or another.

Twenty minutes later he arrived at the park gates in district twelve. He stood where Daphne was standing in the photo and looked towards where the fuzzy patch must have been. Walking over towards it, he could see two faint streaks of rubber still on the road where the hazy apparition had appeared. They faded out quite quickly about three metres away, indicating the direction of travel of the invisible car.

He realised that that was the only thing it could have been. An invisible car. As he stood there wondering how, and who could have devised such a machine, and more importantly where it had gone, he noticed a small metal fragment in the bush by his side. He picked it up. It was obviously a piece of one of the drones that had been shot down that terrible, fateful, night; the clean-up crew must have missed it.

Turning it over in his hands, he was suddenly struck by an idea for a way to find out where the invisible car went. He smacked the side of his head with his hand and smiled.

An hour later he returned with a stolen WP surveillance drone, a radio control unit, an instruction manual, and a determined look on his face.

Chapter 22.

Early on Friday morning, the day they were due to leave for Spain, Randall didn't quite manage to sneak back from Cindi's room in time before Marcus woke up.

It was half an hour before their normal rising time, and Marcus was sitting on the sofa - Randall's supposed bed - when Randall tiptoed into the lounge in his dressing gown.

'Thought you'd both been looking tired the last few days,' he said, grinning like a maniac. 'Glad you finally got it together. It took you long enough.'

His grin grew wider as he watched Randall's face scrambling to find a reaction. To put him out of his misery, he slapped his thighs in the way that some people inexplicably do, before standing up and saying, 'I hope you got some sleep, Casanova, we've got a long day ahead of us.'

Randall couldn't stop himself from grinning too. He'd been aching to do so ever since Sunday night, when he had ended up "comforting" Cindi. The smile spread across his face like a bright morning sunrise after a month of storms.

They had tried, and obviously failed, to keep it a secret from Marcus. But now the jig was up, as they knew it would be eventually.

'Sorry, Marcus. We both tried to ignore it, but... well... you know... it was hard.'

'That's all the detail I need thank you,' said Marcus, grinning and holding his hands out in a "Stop right there" kind of way.

'Come on, love bird, it's time to get this show on the road.' He raised his hand in the air slightly above his head and looked at Randall encouragingly, nodding, like he expected a response.

Randall looked stupidly at the hand. His eyebrows almost crossed in the middle as he tried to figure out what was required of him.

After a second or two Marcus rolled his eyes, shook his head, lifted Randall's hand up into the air, slapped it against his own, and said, 'That's called a "High Five". Get used to it. Your cultural training starts today... Romeo.'

Randall lowered his hand, squinted strangely, looked upwards, raised his hand again with his finger outstretched, and said, 'I know that one. Shakespeare, right?'

Marcus shrugged. 'Maybe. Who knows? Could have been anyone, it was over a thousand years ago now. Let's get some breakfast shall we? Bacon sandwiches okay?'

When Cindi got up half an hour later, she found her breakfast ready for her, and the boys laughing together in the kitchen.

'What's so funny?' she said as she walked into the room, stretching and yawning.

'People,' said Randall. 'People are funny. Especially twenty-first century people. Marcus was just giving me a lesson in ancient culture. And it was sick, dude!' He held out his hand in a strange, twisted manner, like it was afflicted with arthritis. Holding the shape, downward pointing, crippled looking, he grabbed his crotch with his other hand and took an aggressive pose.

'Those mo' fo's won't know nuffin 'bout it. We is rad, bitches!' he said.

'Beatches,' corrected Marcus. 'Remember what I told you about pointless emphasis, and stretching irrelevant syllables? Beatch? And you're still pronouncing much too clearly. "Won't know?" I could hear the apostrophe and the silent K.'

Randall couldn't hold the pose any longer because it's hard to look hard when you're laughing, and while Marcus was obviously amused, Cindi was just standing there with puzzlement radiating from her face. Dropping the posture, he walked over to her, put his arms around her waist, said, 'It's okay, he already knows,' and kissed her on the forehead.

The blush seemed to start outside of her actual physical body and invade her face through her ears. She quickly pulled her hair out of the ponytail it had been tied in and covered them over before they began to compete with the kitchen lights. Her ears felt like they had just been set on fire and dowsed again, as the blush jumped across her neck, crawled rapidly across the underside of her chin, and finally took up a more permanent residence in her cheeks. The journey took less than four heartbeats.

'I told you we should have told him,' she said quietly, punching him playfully on the chest. And then out loud, 'Sorry, Marcus, I was going to tell you, but the time never seemed right somehow.'

'Don't worry, Randall told me all about it. Well... not *all* about it. I've been expecting this for weeks to be honest, you two are even better at hiding from your own emotions than you are at hiding them from me.'

Cindi smiled and nodded. It was true, her previous life had been so full of hidden feelings and faked emotions that she found it hard to just truly be herself anymore. Her life had been made out of masks, and it was good to take this new one off and feel the cooling breeze on her mind.

Just then, there was a noise that Cindi and Randall had only heard once before so far during their stay here. It was Marcus's phone, the last model ever to be made before the advent of implanted terminals. It was the size of a credit card, almost transparent, as thin as a piece of paper, and hacked to buggery. The network never knew it was carrying the surreptitious signal put out by the stealthy phone.

The ring-tone sounded like a hurricane blowing through a piccolo factory, and ended with a cymbal crash that could be heard from a hundred feet away. As Marcus looked at it, the smile on his face was replaced with a more serious expression.

'He's here,' he said. 'Come on, Randall.'

Cindi was left eating her scrambled eggs on toast and wondering who "He" was, as Marcus and Randall walked to the armoury, opened the trapdoor to the garage, and slid down the pole.

Parked in front of the Batmobile in the garage, was a large lorry painted with the livery and logos of GloboCo. Randall laughed.

'Genius,' he said. 'I was wondering how you were going to get around that one. Hidden in plain sight. Just like the criminals of the twenty-first century.'

'And like one of the teachers in this one,' said Marcus. 'You remember my brother Terry don't you?'

From the cab of the lorry climbed the familiar curly topped frame of Randall's old teacher. 'Mr. Han,' he shouted, walking forward to shake his hand. 'I was wondering if I'd get a chance to meet you again. And to thank you for everything.'

Terry warmly shook Randall's hand. 'Randall, so good to see you again. You look well. The last ten years has been kind to you.'

'The last three months has been kind to me,' said Randall. 'The previous twenty-five years less so, but I'm a lot fitter now than I've ever been. Thanks to your brother.'

'Ah yes. The hidden Han. How are you Skid Marcus?'

Marcus winced. 'Fighting fit thanks, Dissen Terry.'

They laughed and hugged like only brothers can. Very briefly, in other words.

By lunchtime, after much grunting, heaving, and swearing, they had moved all the parts of the time machine to the armoury, winched them down into the garage, and packed them into the back of the lorry.

A custom-made fold-down trailer was packed alongside the parts, and the Batmobile had been adapted by Marcus to accommodate not only the caravan hitch that would be used to pull it across the Wastelands, but with meaty off road tyres and suspension. The trailer was camouflaged rather than being fitted out with invisibility tech; all fitted together and in motion, it would probably make for one of the strangest sights ever to visit the island.

And that's saying something.

They were preparing the ramps to get the Batmobile into the lorry when Cindi, who had been cooking for the last hour (and thinking about how much she was going to miss the kitchen) shouted for them.

Lunch was a grandiose affair. A feast compared to the meals they had been used to, which again, was saying something. It was midwinter after all, and many people still celebrated with a feast at this time of year [18].

---

[18] Called Milad Yule Zaraxmas, or Omisoxmas in the Far East. The various religions that celebrated a midwinter festival combined forces long ago to create a celebration that manufacturers of cheap tat could use to target the whole world with once per annum. The religions themselves had faded into obscurity shortly after the Earth Shifts, but most people still enjoyed a midwinter feast, and happily decorated their miniature Bodhi trees in the traditional way every year.

After a hard morning's graft, they were famished, and they tore into the feast like it was their last meal, which, in a way, it was. There wouldn't be a lot of luxury from now on, and they were making the most of it while it lasted.

'I thought we could use the leftovers for sandwiches,' Cindi said, as they surveyed the mountain of remaining food. A large part of a turkey had already been demolished, but there was a joint of beef and an entire glazed ham still sitting on the table that had hardly been touched.

'Good idea,' said Terry. 'The cab has a small fridge so it shouldn't be a problem. Is the vacuum packer still working, bro?'

Marcus, his face full of turkey, nodded and pointed to a niche in the far corner that Cindi and Randall had been wondering about since they got there.

'I must say, it's nice to be back home,' said Terry. 'Even if it is only for another three months. I'm going to do precisely nothing from now till the end of the world.' He smiled and loaded his fork with a gravy coated sprout.

The others had been feeling a little put-out by Terry's constant up-beat comments about the impending erasure of the timeline; he didn't seem to be worried about it at all. It was beginning to wear a bit thin, and this time, he noticed.

The sprout halted its journey to his mouth. It hovered in the air, dripping gravy. 'What's the matter with you guys?' he said. 'Marcus, this is what you've been working on for your whole life. You too, Randall, pretty much. Cindi, this is the only way the resistance is ever going to beat the system, you must know that? The end of this timeline is inevitable whether you succeed or not, there's no point being glum about it. Of course, I'm hoping you're going to succeed, but when it comes, I won't have any perception of the moment and neither will you, Cindi, nor will the three billion other people on Earth.'

He turned to face Marcus and Randall. 'And you two get to travel through time to meet your counterparts from the other timeline! Bloody hell, cheer up will you? You're about to save the Galaxy from total annihilation for Pete's sake.'

There was a pause while they took this on board.

'Who's Pete?' asked Randall.

'Don't worry about it,' said Marcus, 'just another useful phrase you might want to remember. And he's right you know. We've got to get used to this, and stop being so sensitive. It's going to happen one way or the other, so we may as well take a leaf out of his book and enjoy ourselves. If we can.'

From then on, they tried.

By four point seven o'clock they had finished packing and were just about ready to leave. They managed to stay up-beat, and even jovial as they worked, but the Lepidoptera Ventriculo [19], as Terry referred to them, were getting quite active - and in Randall's case, felt like they were about to swarm.

The fridge was stocked, and the bread was about ready to come out of the oven. That was the last thing to do. While they sat in the lounge drinking one last cup of coffee, and waiting for the ping of the oven that would essentially indicate the commencement of their journey, Randall was busying himself learning the Latin for "Stomach Butterfly Net", which turned out to be "Inretio Lepidoptera Ventriculo". Probably.

Marcus had taken half an hour off. To go upstairs and say goodbye to his girlfriend.

It came as quite a shock to Cindi and Randall when Terry had spilled the beans earlier in the day. That explained the dressing gown Cindi had been using for the last three months anyway, Randall never had got around to asking him about it.

'You're not the only ones who sneak around sometimes you know,' he said, when Terry let slip. 'We're just better at it.'

Her name was Felicity, a name that suited her, and she ran the fake massage parlour next-door to the upstairs flat. She was also the linchpin for Marcus's underground network, and that was why Marcus had kept this particular secret to himself. The fewer people who knew, the better; he couldn't risk exposing his network if anybody got caught, especially now they and the resistance had made contact and were communicating with each other. They needed to remain as independent from each other as possible.

---

[19] Latin for Stomach Butterflies, and the night-time version - Stomach Moths.

With the remains of a tear in his eye, he descended the stairs and opened the door to the bunker. The mood changed instantly. Not really knowing what could be said, the others didn't speak for a while, until Terry piped up…

'Chin up, Marky boy, you'll see her again in six hundred years.'

Marcus smiled, but only with his mouth.

Within the next half hour, they were sitting in the cab of the lorry waiting to depart. Marcus had spent a few minutes explaining the few niggling little problems with the house that had developed since Terry had last lived there, and how to deal with them, and now he was in the driver's seat ready to start the engine.

They waved to Terry and shouted their goodbyes as Marcus put the truck into gear and pulled away. Travelling the two miles to the sliding cliff face in almost complete silence, the enormity of what they were about to do had set in again as soon as they were out of Terry's jocular radius.

Now they were approaching the end of the tunnel, and Cindi was feeling as nervous as Randall did when he had gone through it at sixty miles an hour - twice - on the night they'd rescued her. Cindi was under the Faraday blanket the first time and hadn't seen it.

Marcus was trying to reassure her by explaining how the system worked…

'We're travelling at thirty-five miles an hour,' he said, 'I'll slow down a bit so you can see the sensors as we go past. If we stay at the same speed all the way from the sensor to the opening, the system works out exactly when to open and close the cliff again as we go through.'

Randall and Cindi still hadn't got used to Marcus's habit of using the ridiculously ancient "miles", "yards" and "feet".

'Look there on the left, you see the sensors?'

'I see them,' they said, simultaneously.

'I'm doing thirty now, so I stay at that speed for the next five hundred yards, and… three, two, one… er,' he looked round at them and raised his voice in an alarming fashion, 'point five… point one… and open sesame.' The grin that had occupied his face for the last second widened as the others, on the verge of screaming, finally managed to breathe again.

As Cindi watched through the fingers of her hands, the cliff face slid smoothly aside with about a second to spare, revealing a bright sunlit day outside. They exited the tunnel and onto a small patch of scrub that led to the main road. The Sun was low in the sky, and bright. As the lorry drove onto the road the cab windows automatically darkened to accommodate the new level of light.

Which was just as well, because ten seconds later Cindi had to duck down in her seat when she spotted the unmistakably moustachioed face of a very determined looking Constable Bailey standing by the side of the road.

It had taken all his spare time for the last three days to track the rubber tyre marks left by the invisible car. He was cold and he was miserable, but he was still brimming over with unstoppable self-belief. Although, if he was honest with himself, the belief that he was rather *too* cold and miserable was competing for control of his dwindling enthusiasm.

He hardly saw the lorry go past; he was looking at his remote, bobbing his head from side to side, trying to see past his own sunlit reflection in the screen at the images the drone's camera was sending.

The drone itself was some way ahead of him, searching one of the two roads the mysterious machine could possibly have travelled along, looking for another set of skid marks or a clipped kerb to indicate the direction it went next.

His search had come to a halt all of a sudden. Over the last few days, he'd managed to track the vehicle surprisingly well, but now he seemed to have lost the scent. He'd been standing there for over an hour, and it would be dark soon; the Sun would be setting in the next ten minutes.

Not entirely reluctantly, he decided to call it a day. He wouldn't get any good video in the dark, so he walked around the slight bend in the road and crossed over to the small patch of scrub on the other side. He would have the last cup of coffee from his flask before heading home.

He sat on a tree stump by the side of the road and put his rucksack down, his icy hands fumbling with the zip as he tried to retrieve his flask.

As he poured his drink, he noticed what appeared to be fresh looking tyre tracks in the dirt. He stood up, a puzzled expression on his face. Now he looked at it more closely, the scrubland seemed to have a dirt track in it; not a road exactly, but a long, thin, slightly 'S' shaped patch, where there were no trees or bushes. It was certainly wide enough to accommodate the wheelbase of the car he'd been tracking, and these tyre marks, although apparently wider apart and from an obviously heavier vehicle, seemed to be coming along the winding path from the direction of the cliff face at what he presumed was the end of it.

He walked along the track, holding his coffee with both hands to keep them warm. He was right, the tyre marks headed up to the cliff face and stopped dead. They seemed to vanish into the rock!

He skilfully piloted the drone back to him to get an aerial view of the surroundings. The face of the cliff itself was deep in shadow, but even if the light had been good, there wasn't much to see. District twelve and its environs were built on a slight plateau, and this forty-foot cliff was the edge of it. The nearest sizeable buildings were about two miles away beyond a wooded area that he could see growing on top of the cliff.

'I believe I've finally found you,' he said to himself. Which was another thing he'd been doing a lot lately.

'Tomorrow,' he added, for no-one's benefit but his own.

Chapter 23.

The first night in the lorry wasn't a comfortable one. It was cold, the beds were lumpy, and the kitchen wasn't voice activated. In fact, the kitchen consisted solely of an old microwave that sparked like something from an old Frankenstein movie when they used it, a fridge that constantly buzzed like a distant chainsaw, and the small badly fitted shelf that accompanied them. It wasn't adequate to cater for three people; it was barely capable of serving one. After the luxury of the bunker the conditions were primitive to say the least, but they were stoically ignoring the privations as much as they could. They were soldiers now.

They'd stopped overnight in a lay-by set aside from the main road, where two other GloboCo trucks were already parked up for the night. Marcus drove to the other end of the short lane, out of earshot of the genuine haulage drivers, before parking.

The discussion, of course, was all about ex Chief Inspector Bailey. Marcus had texted Terry's phone as soon as they spotted him, but there was no response. He sent a warning message to the communications computer back at the bunker, but he doubted Terry would even look in that room until the next morning at the earliest. They weren't scheduled to send a message until they got to Cadiz, so Terry wouldn't be expecting anything only five minutes after they left.

'I imagine he went straight to bed as soon as we waved goodbye,' said Marcus. 'He drove through the night to get to us by breakfast time, so he'll be spark out until morning. Hopefully he'll think to look at the comms machine when he gets up, but I can't guarantee that. I'll text him again in the morning.'

They were sitting in the back of the lorry eating thoroughly inadequate sandwiches; Cindi and Randall in the pod's chairs, which would also be their beds for the duration of the journey, and Marcus in the passenger seat of the Batmobile. The very faint smell of vomit from the back seat hadn't entirely been expunged.

The small and ancient camping stove put out enough heat, but the lorry wasn't well insulated, so the warmth didn't hang around too long before leaking through the roof. They were all wearing sleeping bags to keep warm.

'But what was he doing there? How did he find us?' asked Cindi, her breath condensing in the air as she spoke.

Marcus considered for a moment before answering. 'I've been thinking about that. From the fact he was fiddling with a remote controller I'd say he was operating a drone. We must have left a trail of skid marks between WPHQ and the tunnel mouth, he could feasibly have tracked them I suppose, but after three months? The man must be obsessed.'

Cindi nodded, it fitted with what she knew of Bailey. She wondered, what with the stress of the recent months, how much of his moustache remained on his face.

'Fortunately, it didn't look like he spotted us, but the fact he was there at all is disturbing. If he spots the tracks we left behind as we came out of the tunnel...' Marcus left the sentence hanging.

'Could he get in?' asked Randall.

'The cliff face is secure enough, but it wouldn't take long to smash it down with the right equipment. There's another barrier at the other end of the tunnel, but that's always been left open. I told Terry to close it when I sent the message. Should have thought of that to be honest, the tunnel will never be used again, I should have told him to close it as soon as we'd left.'

'Everybody forgets at least one thing when they go on holiday, Marcus,' said Cindi. 'Don't blame yourself. You weren't to know Bailey was on our trail.'

He flashed a concerned looking smile at her. 'I suspect Bailey's on his own now anyway,' he said. 'I know he was demoted to constable just after our escape, and I shouldn't think he's got the backing of his superiors any longer. If that's the case, he might struggle to get in on his own. He'd need a bulldozer to break through. Of course, if he has got the backing of his bosses...'

They all looked worried. After a minute or so of glum looks, staring at feet, not quite articulated thoughts, semi-ideas, bitten fingernails, and a lot of head shaking, Marcus decided to change the mood.

He reached for the stereo and chose some relaxing music to take their minds off things. He didn't have any modern "Soundz" in the Batmobile, his entire collection was from before the era of decimalised music, which was why Cindi and Randall couldn't quite get their ears around it.

'There's nothing we can do about it anyway,' he said, as the first bars of a Beethoven sonata began to work their magic. 'And even if the bunker does get raided they won't be able to stop us. It'll take days for them to break in, and we'll be on the submarine by then.'

'But what about Terry?' asked Cindi, articulating the question about to spill from Randall's lips.

'He's a smart cookie,' said Marcus, forgetting momentarily that Cindi had no idea what the phrase meant, 'he's bound to hear them breaking down the cliff face, and he'll be well out of it before they get to the bunker. Don't worry about Terry.'

They accepted this, and in the silence that followed they began listening to the music. Marcus with his eyes closed, Cindi and Randall exchanging puzzled glances with each other. They just didn't get it, the rhythm was odd and there were definitely more than ten notes in the scales being used. It sounded quite foreign to their ears, even more so than the "rock and roll" he'd already introduced them to, but once they'd stopped trying to analyse it, it was, all things considered, fairly relaxing.

Like the many millions of people before them who'd slept overnight in the back of a camper van, they couldn't think of much else to do except play cards for the rest of the night. Cindi was surprisingly good at it; by midnight, the boys owed her more than seven million credits.

Constable Bailey was about to log on for his shift. It was eleven point five at night, and he was tired; he'd slept for only about five hours. He'd been on the graveyard shift almost permanently for the last three months as part of his punishment; which actually turned out to be not such a bad thing, all in all. There were less officers about at this time of night, and some of those were sneaking a couple of hours' extra sleep, so it was easier to snoop around, trying to find out anything he could about the case he'd been excluded from.

He was half an hour early, as usual, so he could spend a short while in his office incorporating the latest pictures of the cliff face to his photo wall before clocking on. He stood there, staring at it, the string connections now making a virtual Gordian knot suspended on the wall by pins. In his mind he visualised himself swinging Alexander's sword, and cutting through it with a single sweep of his arm.

At midnight the duty officer would knock off, the guard would change, and that would be his chance. He knew from experience that the new duty officer would be tied up with paperwork for at least the first half hour of his shift. He wouldn't be very attentive, and certainly not at all concerned - if he noticed at all - that the door of the new chief inspector's office would suddenly open and close again. Even though it should have been locked securely.

When the time came, at one minute past midnight, Bailey climbed the stairs from his lair in the basement, and nonchalantly walked back into the confusion of the locker room as if he had every right to be there. He hadn't logged onto the system yet, so he had absolutely no right to be there, but nobody would notice that.

He made his way to the chief inspector's office - his old office - with a copy of the pass-card he'd had confiscated from him on the day of his demotion. He knew at the time that it was about to happen, and had quietly made a copy before anyone noticed. He'd used it a couple of times before and knew it would probably go undetected. Emphasis on the "probably".

The incompetence of the WP, the sloppiness of their attitude, and how easily he'd been able to set up his own investigation behind their backs, didn't surprise him. He'd recently learned how their arrogance made them susceptible; even after the escape of the fugitives they still believed they were invincible.

His belief, he knew, was stronger.

At five minutes past midnight, with a copy of the ongoing successor to operation Trojan, codenamed operation Stable Door, safely tucked into his trousers, he clocked on and started his shift.

But he didn't do his job.

Shortly after leaving the HQ to go on patrol he abandoned his beat and headed for the park, where he knew it would be quiet and he could read the latest on operation Stable Door in peace.

An hour after that, after much manic moustache manipulation, he was back at home making preparations to travel to Spain.

The curious cliff face, and the days he'd wasted tracking the invisible car to it, were almost, but not quite entirely, forgotten.

The slightly annoying twitching from the muscles around his right eye that had started to distract him over the past couple of hours was purely coincidental. Or so he believed.

Chapter 24.

It was still dark the next morning when they were woken by the lorries they'd shared the lay-by with, as they started their engines and pulled out.

Marcus slept in the cab, above the seats in a small compartment designed for the purpose. He slept well, all things considered, which was more than could be said for Cindi and Randall.

They had moved the two chairs as close together as they could, but it wasn't close enough. They couldn't cuddle each other, they couldn't zip their sleeping bags together to make a double, they couldn't share body heat to keep warm, and the chairs restricted their movements such that they couldn't really get comfortable either.

It was a thoroughly miserable night for both of them, they were cold, grouchy, and tired. Randall cracked a thin sheet of ice from the top of his sleeping bag; the moisture from his breath that had frozen overnight.

Marcus made his way from the cab into the back of the lorry through the little door that separated the two, and was instantly met with complaints.

'We'll have to sort something better than this, Marcus,' said Randall, still shivering in his sleeping bag. 'Can't we stop off and buy an airbed or something? This is ridiculous.'

Cindi nodded in agreement, her eyes were still closed and she was yawning.

'Think about it, Randall,' said Marcus. 'How will we buy it? I don't have a terminal, and if you use yours you'll be arrested before you can say "Bloody stupid thing to do".'

'Don't worry,' he continued, 'we'll be travelling through farm country today, along back roads mostly, so we can probably nab a few hay bales or something on the way.'

Randall looked doubtful, but Cindi nodded in agreement once again.

'That's not a bad idea actually,' she said, reaching out to hold Randall's freezing-cold hand. 'They'll certainly be more comfortable than these bloody chairs, and warmer too.'

Marcus added, 'And don't forget we're travelling south. We won't be far from the top of Africa in a couple of days. It'll be warmer there, in fact, that was probably your last cold night. I'm sorry it wasn't a comfortable one.'

As the heat from the stove began to warm them, they cheered up a bit and tucked into their breakfast.

It was cold meat sandwiches and coffee. Again.

The weekend itself was uneventful; they stole four slightly smelly hay bales and were much warmer and more comfortable, as Marcus had promised. They played a lot of cards - which Cindi consistently won - and they talked a lot, mainly about the past culture they would be immersed in. But early on Monday morning, as they were travelling through a high pass in the Sierra Morena mountains in southern Spain, Marcus pulled over to the side of the road and stopped the lorry. It was a beautiful day, the air was crystal clear and the Sun was still low in the sky after a spectacular dawn.

'Might be the last chance to stretch our legs for a while,' he said. 'Come on. We're ahead of schedule. Let's go for a walk.'

After being cooped up in the lorry for the last three days, they were eager for some exercise. Marcus insisted it was too risky for most of the journey, even on the quieter roads, to actually get out and have a walk around, so they jumped, literally, at the chance. Now they were in the highlands, on the old pass that was never used since GloboCo blew up the Corral de Borros mountain and drove a twelve lane highway through where it used to stand. There was no other traffic around for miles.

They hopped down from the cab and immediately began stretching their aching limbs. It was warm enough now, but their circulation was still sluggish after the sedentary conditions of the journey so far.

Cindi, gratefully, began doing her Tai Chi exercises; another ancient art learned from Marcus. After a minute or so he joined her on the sunny grass verge behind the lorry. Randall watched their slow, synchronised, movements and wondered what the hell they were up to.

'What's this? Some sort of slow motion mime double act?' He was smiling as he watched. 'Is that "Blown by the wind" or "Trapped in a glass box"? I can't quite tell.'

They ignored the sarcasm. 'It's called Tai Chi,' said Marcus, during an out-breath. 'You should try it, it's very calming.'

... a pause while he breathed...

'The movements are a meditation. They help to centre the mind and improve your flow of Chi.'

Randall watched the smile grow across Cindi's face.

'Er, yeah,' she said after a few moments, 'not everything I used to talk to you about was fake. Chi is very real, if only you'd only open your mind to it.'

Randall's eyebrows, which had already risen up his face automatically upon seeing them moving in this strange manner, were now clamouring for the top of his head, and were in danger of disappearing over the brow, so to speak. His mouth hung open, incredulous.

'You're not Neos are you?' he said. 'Where are your crystals?'

'If you don't mind me saying so, Randall, darling, that's exactly the sort of thing a fucking idiot would say,' said Cindi, smiling.

Randall's eyebrows abseiled hurriedly down his face. They huddled together above the bridge of his nose as if ready for a fight. 'Wanna make something of it?' they said, through the medium of body language.

'Now now, Cindi,' Marcus cut in, 'it's not Randall's fault he follows the herd on this one. I haven't really had a chance to de-program him yet.'

Randall, in common with roughly two thirds of the population, was a Dawk [20] - a non-religious cult, just as dogmatic as the most intolerant religion, that was now the dominant ideology amongst "right-thinking" people the world over. Their philosophical, theological, ideological, and mostly illogical opponents were the Neos, or Post-New-Agers; who had

---

[20] Dawkinsian - named after the legendary ancient hero who proved God did not exist. The Neos had a different legend. According to them, Dawkins effectively pissed God off so much with his snide and arrogance that she decided to abandon this universe in favour of another she was growing. So the legend says...

a diversity of views and a number of competing sects within their movement. Often within the same person.

The Neos' main, over-arching, theological tenet was that we are all, when you get right down to it, individuals. Not, as the ancient New-Agers had believed, all "One". Hence the name Neos, which was an anagram of "Ones".

'De-program me?' asked Randall. 'I'm not one of your computers you know. I'm a well-informed rational human being with a mind of my own and everything...'

Marcus cut in again. 'Rational? Yes. Well informed? No, sorry, Randall.' He didn't speak for a few seconds as he watched Randall's face slowly fall off the cliff of his skull. He carefully considered how to construct his next sentence. It was time to feed Randall another slice of the reality pie that he'd been drip feeding to him ever since he'd known him. It was an important moment, and if you've ever drip fed a pie to someone, you'll know how difficult it is. You get bits everywhere.

Taking a deep breath, he jumped in at the deep end.

'Randall, have you ever heard of Socrates?'

'No. What're they?'

'Not "what", Randall, "who". Socrates is the name of a semi-legendary ancient philosopher who came up with a rather profound insight one evening [21]. After much soul searching and reflective thought, he said, "All I know is that I know nothing".'

This didn't sound so profound to Randall. 'Bit thick was he?' he said, mockingly. 'Babies achieve that level of brain power as soon as they're born.'

Marcus grinned. 'You've missed the point. And by quite a long way. He was, in his own way, trying to get people to ask themselves the question "How do I know what I know?"'

Randall's eyebrows, which were getting a bit tired of all the jumping about, now regrouped above the bridge of his nose once more. 'How do I know what I know? I watch the news of course. And I read books,' he said, firmly.

'Written by who?' asked Cindi.

---

[21] Most philosophers, throughout time and still to this day... don't do mornings.

'People who write books! People who present the news... I don't know...'

'He's beginning to get it,' said Marcus, 'already he says he doesn't know.'

'The first step on a long journey,' said Cindi.

'Indeed,' agreed Marcus.

'What are you blithering brainsteins prattling about?' enquired Randall, stupefied. Now his eyebrows didn't know what to do. They seemed to wander randomly around the top half of his face, searching for their long lost certainty.

'People who write books, Randall, are people who've read books.' Cindi was actually quite enjoying this, but she tried not to show it. 'And the books they spent their time reading were written by others who'd read earlier books.'

'Obviously,' he said. Randall was missing the point again, even though it was plainly a very big point, and seemed to be aimed right at his head.

'Stretch the idea to include the news broadcasts,' she said.

'What Cindi says is true, but that's only half the story. It's more complicated than that,' added Marcus. 'It could be summed up with the phrase "The truth of a thing lies between the liars who claim it", you'd do well to remember that.'

'It'd be easier to remember if I knew what it meant,' said Randall, 'or what you're alluding to at least. Please, throw me a boner.'

'Er, okay. Let's deal with that first,' said Marcus. 'The phrase you were looking for was "Throw me a bone". What you said could just as easily have got you arrested if you'd used it back in the twenty-first century. Please, when we get there, run any phrases you might want to use through me first will you?'

'Agreed,' replied Randall.

'What Cindi and I are alluding to,' he continued, 'is that the two main ideological strains of thought on Earth right now are both as wrong as each other. The truth is hidden somewhere in the middle; some would say deliberately so. The Neos believe many things that are so ludicrous they can be laughed at, and often are by the Dawks, but the essence of some of their beliefs isn't so far-fetched when you strip away all the frippery.

'And the reason the Dawks can dismiss them so easily is because they're unwilling to accept that their beloved science doesn't have all the answers. Even though they know it doesn't. Their minds are so closed they can't think outside of their indoctrination. The fact that the science they believe in so religiously hasn't even begun to explain the phenomenon of consciousness, for example, which is of course the very thing that allows them to believe anything in the first place, is quietly ignored.'

'They'll explain consciousness within fifty years,' interrupted Randall, testily. 'I read about it last year. They have a new scanner that can map the brain so completely that they're sure it's bound to explain all the remaining mysteries very soon.'

'Do you know how long they've been saying it'll only take fifty years?' asked Cindi.

Randall shook his head.

'For the last six hundred and fifty years.'

Marcus nodded in agreement. 'It's the same with lots of other areas of research,' he said. 'Nuclear fusion, warp drive, transporter beams, even finding a cure for cancer... and there are many more. Funds are diverted into projects that are controlled by the elites, who have a hidden agenda of their own, but the thing is, it's not the scientists' fault. Scientists are educated into a very restrictive system of thought, and only research what the ruling classes will allow them to work on. GloboCo has a total monopoly on the kind of science that is done, and they deliberately suppress the few inventions or discoveries made by independent thinkers. Our civilization has stagnated for centuries because of it.'

'The same is true for the Neos,' said Cindi. 'The study of Chi, for example, is discouraged. Things like meditation are a quirky affectation of snobs according to the most influential thinkers in the Neo movement, and not a powerful tool for self-exploration, as it actually is. They don't want people to become as self-aware as they can ultimately become, they don't want people to even think about it. Instead, they provide a nice comfy sofa to rest your mind on while you wish for whatever it is you wish for, not really thinking seriously about what we're doing here on this planet. It's a lovely sofa covered in charms, and crystals, and Orgonite, and dream catchers, and all the other pointless paraphernalia that accompanies a deluded personality, where they sit weaving yoghurt, painting rainbow coloured unicorns... or whatever else it is they do.'

She seemed to be speaking from experience. Randall was intrigued.

'When they spout on about finding yourself,' she continued, agitated, 'it's nothing to do with what the ancients meant by the phrase. To them, "finding yourself" is about doing exactly whatever you want, with no thought given to the consequences - mental, spiritual or otherwise. They're as far removed from the spiritual wisdom of the past as we are from the lost timeline.'

Cindi was almost red in the face. She calmed down, breathing deeply.

Randall's face was a picture. Possibly taken by a very disturbed photographer with a taste for the dramatic. His facial features betrayed a mind full of confusion, unease, even angst.

Marcus could see it would take a while for Randall to accommodate the new perspective, so he held up his hand for a moment and smiled. 'Right,' he said, 'this is getting too serious. Let's lighten the mood shall we? Randall, have you heard about the game the Neos are all playing? They call it post-new-age hide and seek?'

'No. What's that?'

'It's really easy. Everybody runs away, and you have to find yourself.'

It took a couple of seconds, but when Cindi laughed, Marcus, not known for being a natural joke teller, beamed his widest grin at her. Randall, whose eyebrows had given up the struggle and been huddled together for warmth for the last minute, joined in eventually when he worked out the punch line.

Marcus grinned at them both. 'Come on, guys, this peak is only about three thousand feet. Let's climb it, we'll talk on the way up.'

The "guys" exchanged puzzled glances and started to follow him up the mountain.

Three thousand feet, Cindi and Randall eventually worked out, was about eight kilometres. At least, it felt like it was about eight kilometres. Perhaps more. All of it uphill.

Very uphill in places.

They could easily have followed the old path up the mountain. A leisurely walk up a gentle incline that snaked across the mountain through scenic pastures with majestic views and multiple picnic opportunities; but Marcus was having none of that. With his small pack on his back, he walked straight up the mountain like he was being towed behind a cable car.

Outcrops of rock presented no obstacle, he clambered up them seemingly without even slowing his pace. He was like a spider, and paid as scant attention to the almost vertical rock faces as a spider would.

Cindi and Randall spent five minutes walking around the latest outcrop - which had taken Marcus less than two to scale - and, panting for breath, they met him again at the top, calmly sitting cross-legged on the grass.

And, finally, they talked...

'Climbing a mountain is a good analogy for the path you take through life,' Marcus began, as they sat down next to him at the top of the outcrop.

'You see that winding path down there? It was trodden originally by the sheep that have grazed these pastures for countless centuries, and it was subsequently followed by the tens of thousands of humans who have climbed up here in the past. It's been dug in, it's a part of the mountain now.'

'But we didn't follow the path,' said Randall.

'Exactly, grasshopper,' said Marcus.

This comment flew so far over Randall's head that it cleared the next ridge and sailed off into space. Cindi didn't get it either. Marcus smiled as he read their faces.

'I'm sorry. It's a reference to an ancient television show. I didn't expect you to understand it.

'The point I'm making is that everyone these days follows a path through life that is laid out by the sheep and the "shepherds" that have walked that way before them. There are two well-worn paths that humanity currently wanders aimlessly along: the Dawks' path, and the Neos' path. Neither of which actually ever get to the top of the mountain. They meander around haphazardly while the straight path, the quickest path, is ignored. They cross over in places, of course, but nobody these days ever looks around, spots the new path, and changes direction.

'To deviate from the path is considered dangerous, and discouraged by both schools of thought. But the truth is that a combination of the best aspects of both ideologies is much closer to the reality of the situation. The straight path is the best one to take.'

'So you're saying that everything people think they know might be wrong?' said Randall.

'Not everything, and not wrong exactly, and there's no "might be" about it, but yes, you're getting the idea,' replied Marcus, smiling again. 'There have been times in history, such as a thousand years ago during the enlightenment, and again after the Earth Shifts, when the straight and true path was almost followed. But each time, as soon as we came close, we were diverted by the "shepherds". This is true in both groups. The ruling classes have never wanted us to achieve our full potential, that would be dangerous for them. They've always wanted people who're smart enough to operate the machines but not smart enough to ask why they do it. They achieved that about seven hundred years ago with a system of indoctrination called The Prussian Model, and this is one of the patterns we need to disrupt when we get to the twenty-first century.'

They sat for another hour listening to Guru Markynanda, as Cindi jokingly called him, and at the end of it, Randall's head was spinning. There were many more references to ancient art and culture as Marcus spoke, most of which flew right over their heads, eventually forming a small fleet of not understood references in orbit above them.

As they made their way back down the mountain, this time following the easier path, Randall felt as if his skull had been opened up and filled with angry bees. He was mostly silent on the walk back to the lorry, as he tried to grasp the idea that his whole philosophy of life up to this point, although not entirely wrong, was woefully inadequate at the very least. The thoughts buzzed around inside his head in a manner that almost itched. It felt like the bees were taking their nest apart and building a subtly redesigned one out of the bits; which actually wasn't too far from the truth... but with neurons instead of bees.

He was largely quiet for the rest of the day, at the end of which, as they watched the Sun set over the Atlantic, they tentatively approached the outskirts of Cadiz.

They were a day early, as planned. The rendezvous with the sub wasn't until midnight the next day, so they set up camp as best they could amongst the trees on the highest hill nearby; where they could see the sea and get a clear reception on the shortwave radio in the Batmobile.

That evening, as Randall lay outside the van, philosophising about the meaning of life to himself and staring wondrously at the Milky Way rising over the ocean, the Lepidoptera Ventriculo finally swarmed.

Chapter 25.

Mr. Bailey, travelling incognito (and in sunglasses) was probably in quite a lot of trouble now he'd abandoned his post. In the parlance of the WP he'd "gone rogue", but by pouring a glass of water into the compunet hub at HQ, he'd made sure it wouldn't be until tomorrow at the earliest that the fools in charge would smell a rat, so he had time yet before being discovered. Most of them couldn't detect a rodent of any species, even if you set fire to one and nailed it to their forehead.

HQ wouldn't be able to check his terminal transmissions he knew, not for a day or two, and when they finally did, it would be too late for them to do anything about it. He would either be on his way back to HQ with the miscreants safely under arrest, or...

He hadn't thought about the "or" yet. Nor was there any need to. He believed so strongly that this was going to be the day he restored his tarnished career, and take his place once again at the top table, that the alternative could only be a very remote possibility. Even if he didn't have any orders to do what he was doing, and was using stolen intelligence and equipment to do it.

He'd completed one more surreptitiously shifty shift after reading the details of operation Stable Door but had faked an illness the day after. Not an easy thing to do with a terminal that transmitted physiological data every three hours, but he knew a few tricks. After all, he was a high ranking WP officer until very recently; you don't rise to that position without being a devious little bastard.

Now, on the morning of the day after that, he was walking through Cadiz airport with his suitcases and his mirrored sunglasses, wondering how much further it was to the taxi rank.

Getting a ticket for the flight had been the risky part. The security staff could see from his terminal that he was WP, but it had taken all his powers of distraction to stop them looking further and noticing that the chief inspector's warrant card he flashed at them was now rescinded, and had been for three months.

Luck was his companion at the z-ray scanners too. They easily spotted the disassembled drone in his suitcase, but he flashed his warrant card again, muttered 'official business, hush-hush', quickly opened the other suitcase containing a neatly folded chief inspector's uniform - the one the WP had forgotten to confiscate - and they'd let him through without another word.

Now he was in Spain, the next step of the plan was to get to the coast and find the WP contingent that would surely be waiting for the traitor and her resistance friends. Infiltration was the key. His uniform would enable him to blend in with the Spanish WP officers assigned to the case. His moustache and sunglasses would probably help too.

He opened the door of the nearest taxi, waking up the lightly dozing driver in the process, and clambered into the back seat.

'De la playa por favour,' he said, in his best Spanish accent [22].

The driver, who spoke perfect Panglish and had spotted the terrible accent immediately, yawned, blinked the sleep out of his eyes, noticed the obvious undercover cop with the ridiculous fake moustache on his back seat, sat up straight, and told the taxi to take them to the beach.

Rapido.

---

[22] Which was identical to his Mexican accent, his Italian accent, and, on a bad day, his French accent. You don't want to hear him attempt Welsh.

Chapter 26.

On Tuesday morning they slept late in the lorry. There was no hurry to get up particularly early, their rendezvous was at midnight, so they had half a day to do a little sightseeing around Cadiz before saying goodbye to civilization forever. If only they could persuade Marcus to let them.

The lorry had been ignored by the locals. This was due to a particular kind of arcane magic called "Bollards". Marcus had set a few up around the trees they'd hidden under, at the distance where he wished people to pay no further attention to the lorry, and it had worked beautifully. The dog walkers and joggers went past the little camp on the top of the hill muttering 'bloody GloboCo' to each other. But in Spanish.

Around midday, after an hour long ding-dong argument about the risks involved - which Marcus eventually lost - they started walking calmly down the hill, through Chiclana Park, and onwards for another two kilometres through the tourist traps to the beach. Wearing a variety of sunglasses and hats to disguise their features, they took the chance and mingled with the tourists.

The black market hadn't been completely wiped out in Spain, so many of the street vendors in the area still accepted cash credits, which Marcus had a bag full of. They used them to buy a spot of lunch on the beach, and even a couple of glasses of beer; a nice change from the sandwiches and coffee they'd been subsisting on during the journey. It was a pleasant day for the middle of winter, not too hot, not too humid, so they took the opportunity to soak up some Sun and relax. Possibly the last chance they would have for another two months.

After lunch, still sitting on the beach, they chatted about the likely route they would take to the other side of the planet. Randall thought they might just nip across the Atlantic and slip unnoticed through the Straights of Nicaragua, but apparently the water there wasn't quite deep enough. Yet. The land that used to be Nicaragua was still sinking slowly down into the mud even this long after the Earth Shifts, and it wouldn't really be navigable for another fifty years or more, not for a huge nuclear submarine anyway.

'I suspect we'll be going the long way round,' said Marcus, pointing south-east, 'down to the bottom of Africa, across the Indian Ocean and out into the Pacific via the Southern Ocean.' He gesticulated with his arms to indicate the direction they would go.

'Why that way?' asked Cindi, pointing south-west. 'Surely it would be quicker to go past the bottom of Patagonia and out across the Pacific.'

'You're forgetting the South American bridge they're building to the Antarctic coast,' he said. 'They've been driving piles into the seabed for two years now and they're still working hard on it. It's summer down there remember, the only time of year they can really work on it. I doubt the captain will want to risk being detected, it's a comparatively narrow straight by Patagonia, and the depth is only about a thousand yards in places. The open ocean must be the logical choice. We'll find out tonight won't we? Who fancies a bet?'

Cindi turned to face him. 'You already owe me twenty-three million credits from playing cards. Shall we say double or quits?'

Laughing, they shook on it.

Later that day, as they were walking away from the beach, back through the small town of tacky tourist temptations, Cindi spotted Constable Bailey again. He was walking along the beach in shorts and a flowery shirt. As they ducked, unnoticed, out of the way, they could see he looked worried. Even through the mirrored glasses.

He'd spent the entire morning since four o'clock patrolling the beach on the lookout for the Spanish WP who would surely be there waiting.
Somewhere.
The trouble was he hadn't spotted a single one. Either they were all very well hidden - which he doubted - or they simply weren't there to begin with. His belief in his plan, in common with so many beliefs in general, was struggling under the serious weight of reality, and

although he hadn't pulled it off his face yet, his moustache was taking a battering too.

The newly turned WP mole on board the resistance submarine had clearly said Tuesday according to what he'd read, but the evidence of his eyes was forcing him to re-evaluate the credibility of that report. After twelve hours of wandering fruitlessly along the beachfront he finally made a decision. It was, he believed, time for plan B. All he had to do now was come up with one...

Before long the hastily improvised plan led him to the belief that his only option was to hide out near the station and intercept the interlopers as they were brought in. He would have to bluff a convincing story, but perhaps he could claim to be sent from WP Command to take charge of the case at the last minute. It would be a good time to deploy the uniform maybe. He would think of something.

He'd got away with using his terminal to pay the taxi fare yesterday, but now it would probably be too risky. He didn't want to use it again unless he absolutely had to, it could alert his inferiors [23] to his location, if they were even paying attention yet, so he needed an alternative way to find the local WP office in this strange town.

It was still possible to buy maps from the tourist shops even though nobody used them for directions any more. They were novelty maps, mementos, showing the most prominent landmarks and places where the grifters could lighten the load of the tourists' bank balances. On one of them, after looking around for long enough to attract the proprietor's attention, he found the location of the WP station. On the other side of town about three kilometres to the north.

The shop owner looked at him strangely as Bailey left his tacky establishment. From his perspective, the odd looking man had spent ten minutes peering furtively through all of his souvenir maps, studied one of them intently for another minute, and simply left again. How rude. And strange too. He was obviously a cop of some sort, but did he not have a terminal?

Stolen map in hand, Bailey returned to retrieve his suitcases from where he'd buried them on the beach. After cleaning the sand off and

---

[23] He'd given up using the term "Superiors" some weeks ago.

taking a five-minute breather, he sighed, picked up his heavy suitcases, and began the three kilometre walk north...

Half an hour later, sweaty and exhausted, he reached the WP station and found a nice shady spot to wait until it was time for action. The locals seemed to be snoozing around a pleasant shaded fountain in the small square about a hundred metres from the station, so he joined them, thinking he would be nicely inconspicuous.

The fact that he stood out like a sore, possibly even gangrenous, thumb in his flowery shirt, escaped him.

Resisting the urge to have a quick snooze himself, he got as comfortable as he could on the stone steps of the fountain, pushed his sunglasses further up the bridge of his nose, and focused his attention on the door of the WP station.

At eleven point one pm, now completely alone on the steps of the fountain, he woke up with a start as the unmistakable sound of a troop transport whizzed past him. It wasn't bringing the criminals in, however. It was leaving the station heading for the beach.

After wiping away the small river of drool that was flowing down his face, he quickly gathered his wits and his suitcases. Another twenty seconds of manically looking around the square and he headed for a secluded alley where he could assemble the drone and hastily throw it into the air in pursuit of the transport...

CLEARANCE REQUIRED

FAO SENIOR CREW

CC, Doc, Sleepy, Dopey, Sneezy, Jamie. *BASHFUL , GRUMPY, SNOW WHITE*

PROVISIONING ARRANGEMENTS

Cadiz – Details to follow *TUESDAY MIDNIGHT*

Two boats required. Crews to be determined.

Persons coming aboard : Sundial, Mr. Randall James, and guest ?

Security detail to be assigned upon return.

Subsequent to the late return of Warrant Officer Snow White after the scheduled shore leave following the last resupply mission, all personnel are to be accompanied by at least one other of equal or higher rank at all times.

RECOMMENDATIONS

1 limits to alcohol consumption to be exercised by all crew.

...re tattoos of a sexually explicit nature.

Chapter 27.

Keystone was sitting in his ready room anxiously waiting for his beeper to go off. He fretted with his biscuit [24] and waited for news that they had arrived at Sancti Petri island, just over a kilometre offshore from Cadiz. He'd spent the last hour and a half going over the plans again and again, trying to anticipate anything that could feasibly go wrong. (The biscuits were helping to calm his nerves. He'd opened the last packet in the mess cupboard at 16:00 hours - otherwise known as Tea Time - but now there were only seven left. Things were getting desperate.)

... and there was quite a lot that could feasibly go wrong. There were probably quite a lot of unfeasible ways it could end in disaster too, but theirs was a heroic mission; snatching wanted fugitives from under the noses of the WP would go down in the logbook as a good day.

If they pulled it off.

Finally, his beeper beeped. They had arrived. After scanning the waters for miles around on the lookout for WP Navy craft, they had finally snuck into a patch of deeper water sufficiently sheltered from the coast. They stopped their engines, sank gently to the bottom, and raised the communications buoy.

The landing party were assembling in the embarkation room, and last minute checks of the landing craft themselves were underway. They would be launched through specially adapted torpedo tubes - as would the scuba-teams - and they would eventually pop up some way

---

[24] Rich Tea, national biscuit of the ancient British race. Oddly reminiscent of the Brits themselves in that they are pale, lack sweetness, not as rich as they claim to be, and are hopelessly outclassed by Hobnobs (which are themselves vastly outclassed by Viscounts, as any biscuit aficionado will tell you).

away from the sub. When they reached the surface, the pneumatic systems would quietly inflate the craft, which would then be steered to the shore by the teams.

It was nothing they hadn't done before many times - even here in Cadiz, which had a hidden depot they'd used half a dozen times - but Keystone was privately worrying whether the landing craft would be sufficient to carry all the supplies and the heavy equipment Sundial was supposedly bringing with her. Whatever it turned out to be.

Already he'd had to double the teams, and he was struggling to fill many essential posts on board. Team Alpha - his team - were tasked to acquire Sundial and the equipment, and team Beta were to carry out the standard re-supply mission. He was hoping not to have to make two trips.

He switched on the surveillance camera in the embarkation room to check the status of the teams and gear assembling there. Everything was just about ready. Including him.

He looked in the mirror for a moment, picked a bit of fluff off the shoulder of his wet-suit, straightened his snorkel, and left the ready room.

As he arrived at the embarkation room, he was met by Radio Operator Dopey.

'Sir,' shouted Dopey. 'We've just received a coded message from Sanchez, sir. He says the WP might be on to us and we should be extra vigilant tonight. He intercepted a communiqué from WP Control five days ago telling the Cadiz WP to set a trap for us. Somehow, they knew we were coming. He managed to hide it from them, so they didn't see it, but he says he may have blown his cover in doing so. He should be waiting on the beach for us as usual but says he wants to come with us. And if he's been compromised, we might have hidden company on the beach too.'

Keystone wasn't happy about having the detail of the message read out in front of the crew, who were now muttering amongst themselves. He snatched the full transcript of the message from Dopey's nervous hands with a glaring look that said "We'll talk about this later", and spent the next minute reading it thoroughly.

Sanchez was the fifth columnist that had been embedded with the

Spanish WP for the last two years. He'd been the one to organise the Cadiz supply depot since then, and he was a good man; reliable, not prone to exaggeration.

After a minute, Keystone turned to Grumpy and pulled him aside. Waving the printout, he said, 'Sanchez wants to speak to me personally, and that'll be a problem, I'm leading the team to pick up Sundial, you're handling the re-supply mission. It's too late to change plans now. Remind me, who's in your team again?'

Nigel Althorp-Belvoir-Marjoribanks, a.k.a. Grumpy, pointed to each of his team in turn as he spoke their names. 'Bashful, Sneezy, Jamie and Snow White, sir,' [25] he said.

Keystone thought for a moment before addressing Bashful directly. 'Looks like you'll have to stay behind, lad,' he said. 'I'm sorry, but there's a chance this may be a bit more complicated than we first thought if we have to pick up Sanchez too.'

Bashful was disappointed but tried not to show it. He'd been looking forward to getting ashore, as had everyone else, but now he reluctantly realised it would have to wait for the shore leave that was scheduled for the next day. Assuming all went well tonight of course.

Rather uncharacteristically for him, Snow White stepped forward now to volunteer to take Bashful's place and stay behind on the sub. He was normally eager to get onshore whenever they had the chance, more eager than most in fact, so this was a generous offer.

'Give the lad some experience of a night pickup, sir,' Snow White said, without any trace of innuendo for a change. 'He needs to learn the ropes. I've done dozens of them, I can wait until shore leave. To be honest I'm not feeling entirely well at the moment,' he looked at Jamie, 'I think I ate something funny.' No subtle innuendo this time either, most unusual for him.

Dickey bellies weren't a rare occurrence this close to a re-supply. Jamie had been forced to utilise foods that were a little past their use-by-date in the past, and he couldn't guarantee it hadn't happened this time either. That was probably why Chief Petty Officer Sleepy kept

---

[25] This is the main reason, quite apart from security, that codenames were used on board the sub. Reading off that list using their actual names would have taken about a minute.

moaning about the loo roll situation in official reports. Now he thought about it, the "Tuna Surprise" served up for lunch earlier wasn't one of Jamie's best creations.

Keystone considered Snow White's offer for a moment before deciding. 'Okay,' he said, 'you stay behind and assist on the bridge. You're in luck, Bashful.' He rolled his eyes in his head for a moment before uttering the next sentence. 'Doc?' he said. 'You're in command while we're gone. Snow White is first officer.' Now he turned to the scuba teams. 'Come on, lads, last gear checks please, we leave in one minute.'

As the teams completed last minute checks of their scuba gear, Keystone pulled a slip of paper from his sleeve pocket and turned to Dopey. Handing it to him, he said, 'As soon as we launch, send this message to Sundial. They should be less than three k away, so use the lowest power transmission you can. She'll be waiting to hear from us on that frequency.'

Dopey noted the wavelength and nodded. 'Aye, sir,' he said. 'And good luck, sir.'

Facing his men, Keystone stood up straight, closed his eyes for a second, twisted his head from side to side until his vertebrae clicked quite satisfactorily, and said, 'Right then. Let's get these boats in the water.'

All was calm in the lorry.

Marcus and Cindi carefully made last minute preparations in anticipation of the radio message they would hopefully be receiving soon, and they moved quietly and cautiously, ticking off items on the checklist. They were being as quiet as they could for the sake of RanJam: Randall's new nickname.

RanJam sat outside, chanting 'Ohmmm' cross-legged on the grass with his eyes closed and his mind open. He'd gone through various combinations to get to this stage: earlier on he sat with his eyes crossed and his mouth open screaming 'Arrrrgh', while his mind flapped about trying to distract his attention with all sorts of angsty, troubling thoughts, but he'd got through that stage eventually with gentle guidance from Cindi. Now he was almost at peace with himself.

Almost.

The tumultuous thoughts his mind had been generating since listening to Marcus on the mountain were bubbling away in a part of his awareness that he had somewhat successfully compartmentalised into mental compartments (if that's not a tautology).

They were locked in an imaginary room in the house of his own consciousness that Cindi had managed to help him to build earlier. Now he was sitting in his cramped but completely imaginary sitting room [26], casually observing his own thoughts through the window in the door to the imaginary room they were locked in. They seemed to be arguing.

The usual competitors were all there: Hope, Panic, Suspicion, Fear, and the rest were all throwing up lots of opinions on the situation Randall found himself in, and many others besides, but he was striving to not pay attention to them anymore. He merely observed the thoughts as they occurred to him, and instead of following them to their logical conclusions, as a true Dawk would have done, he was attempting to simply let them be; watching how they interacted with each other whilst trying hard not to interact with them himself. Whatever "himself" meant.

He was beginning to suspect that trying hard not to interact with his thoughts was, perhaps, the wrong approach. How could you try hard not to concentrate on something without concentrating on not doing so? How could he even suspect that he was doing it wrong in the first place without engaging his mind to do the suspecting? Did the suspicion that he was doing it wrong, automatically, by definition, mean that he wasn't doing it right? He didn't know, but according to old Socrates, not knowing was a desirable state to be in, apparently. He hadn't quite figured out the subtleties of that particular train of thought yet, he was still working on it, but, then again, perhaps working on it was entirely the wrong thing to do. It was yet another question for Cindi or Marcus.

It turned out that they'd quietly hidden this part of their training from Randall because Marcus didn't think he was ready until now. He was very probably right too; Randall would have dismissed these more

---

[26] He still hadn't quite got the hang of visualization yet. He'd imagined his old home many times over the last three months but couldn't quite make it any bigger. He'd managed to imagine the sofa he'd only sat on for one evening though, so baby steps...

esoteric disciplines as Neoist bullshit before Marcus exposed him to the truth about the world. Now his eyes had been opened to the primary fallacy he had believed in, he was more receptive to changing his mind on aspects of the others. He was rapidly becoming a Neodawk, or perhaps a Dawneo. Whatever the appropriate term was.

As he gently pushed his thoughts about whether or not to think about his thoughts back behind the locked door in his head that they'd escaped through, he was disturbed by a shout from Cindi.

'Oi, RanJam. The message came, we're ready to go.'

The locked door instantly burst open.

They got to the coordinates quickly. It was four kilometres west of the city in a naturally secluded bay with a wide beach, now less wide due to the high tide they'd timed the pickup to coincide with. They waited in the truck, as instructed, until they saw the single flash of light from the landing craft, still some way out to sea. Marcus flashed his headlights once, also as instructed, and waited for another five minutes before starting the engine and quickly turning the lorry around. He stopped the engine again as soon as he could, and let the lorry roll backwards toward the tide line. All three of them were silent, anxious.

They waited nervously for a further forty-five seconds before there was a muted bump on the back door of the lorry. Cindi took over at this point.

'The tide is high in London tonight,' she said quietly, through the still closed doors.

A low voice on the other side said, 'Is it? Oh, er, crap, what was it again?' A rustle of paper could just about be heard through the doors. 'Errrrm, blast it, I can't see a thing. Can I borrow your torch? Thanks. Errrr..., bugger, forgot my reading glasses, what does that say?'

A few more seconds of inaudible whispering and then, 'Not as high as we tied our flag. Apparently,' came the eventual response. Followed by, 'Actually, is that the right one? There are two codes on this bit of paper... shit, we haven't got time for this. For goodness sake Daphne open the doors will you? It's me, Monty.'

She threw the doors open. 'Agent Sundial reporting for duty, sir,' she said, smiling.

'On Dawkins' eyes, you're a sight for sore ones,' he said, smiling back.

Being professionals, the crew unpacked the gear within a few short minutes; most of it having been un-tethered and prepared for removal anyway. Introductions, made much shorter by using codenames, were swiftly undertaken, and the crew started loading the mysterious - to them - machinery into the landing craft.

The Batmobile sat on the sand, dark as the night around it. The trailer/caravan, still folded down, sat next to it.

'You're driving to the sub you say?' said Keystone, incredulously.

'That's right,' replied Marcus.

'In that thing? Are you mad?'

'It's fully submersible,' said Marcus. 'We could probably tow the landing craft now I come to think about it. Easier than all that paddling.'

'We call it rowing, old chap, not paddling. What about this other thing?' asked Sleepy.

'The caravan? I had an inkling it might be too much to carry all in one go, so I designed a little upgrade into it.'

He stepped over to the trailer and pulled on a switch hidden underneath. As he did so, pontoons suddenly started inflating around it, giving it the appearance of a very strange looking vessel indeed; a bit like a cross between a small Noah's Ark and a large rubber dinghy with wheels.

'You can tie your boat to the back of the trailer can't you?' asked Marcus.

Keystone nodded. 'That sounds like a plan,' he said. He looked around, checking the progress of the men loading the landing craft. 'Well, Mr. Han, whoever you are, we're nearly ready, you'd better get into your, er, what do you call it again? Gnatmobile?'

'Batmobile,' Marcus corrected him. 'I'll need one of your crew with me and Cindi, sorry, Sundial, to give me directions to the sub if that's okay?'

Keystone turned to Sleepy, 'You okay with that?' he asked.

'No problem, sir,' replied Sleepy, who was tired and thankful he didn't have to row back. He fiddled with the door for a few seconds until he found the latch, opened it, and lay down uncomfortably in the tiny back seat. The smell didn't seem to bother him.

Randall, rather more reluctantly than Sleepy, got aboard the landing craft with the other sailors, who had now boarded and were waiting for it to be hitched up to the Batmobile and towed out to sea. He'd been very quiet for the whole encounter.

A minute later, Marcus started his engine and moved towards the water's edge. As the first waves lapped around the wheels, he pressed the button marked "Submersible Mode" on the control panel in front of him by the steering wheel ("dashboard" wasn't a suitable word). Propellers instantly sprouted from the back, and the wheels began to slide into the body of the car, which then sealed up, watertight.

As the water inched higher and higher up the door, Cindi slowly closed her eyes and started doing her deep breathing exercises. As it began to finally close over the top of them she started doing her extremely deep, and really rather fast, breathing exercises. It didn't help her to suppress the silent scream that was growing inside her when Marcus chose that moment to say, excitedly, 'I've been looking forward to this for ages. Never done it before.' He was a small child again. Just a very old looking one.

Sleepy was living up to his name in the back seat. Just before the final wave crashed over the top of them, he yawned, pointed vaguely, and said, 'Head for the island over there.'

Marcus had seen the island, and already suspected that that was the general direction to head in. Putting his main headlight on full, he eased out into the deeper water, took up the slack on the rope until he felt it tighten, and began to tow the boats carefully to the back side of the island.

The landing craft, which was now basically an aquatic caravan being towed behind a larger and much less seaworthy caravan, bobbed along quite erratically but quite steadily out to sea.

After five minutes, Randall was quite spectacularly ill into it.

Radio silence was maintained as much as possible during the mission, so when they got to the submarine, Marcus stopped his engine, floated to the surface about twenty metres from the comms buoy, and sent a short, low power, "ping" from the Batmobile's radio. Almost instantly, bubbles began to rise to the surface under the buoy.

Keystone un-hitched the caravan of caravans from the back of the

Batmobile and waited the thirty seconds it took for the sub to break the surface.

It took another minute or two of minute adjustments to the sub's ballast tanks before they got the levels right, but when they did, Marcus started his engine and simply drove up onto the exposed deck, which was now just at the water line. The conning tower, which rose forty feet into the air above him, dripped cold seawater down his neck as he stepped out of the car and caught the rope thrown to him by Keystone.

As he hauled on the rope, a hatch at the bottom of the tower opened and a burly sailor disgorged himself in a fuggy fume of unfavourably fermented gasses. Faint cries of, 'Shit, that's better,' and, 'Oh God yes,' could be heard coming from the open hatch, as some of the trapped gas, a large component of which was heavier than air, poured out of the conning tower and washed over the deck to assault Marcus and Cindi's sensitive nostrils. It was as if the whole submarine had just farted.

That was their first experience of life as a submariner.

When Randall climbed onto the deck covered in sick a few moments later, they got an even better idea of what the next two months under the ocean waves had in store for them.

Chapter 28.

As the Batmobile and trailer were lowered into the hull of the sub, on the huge pneumatically controlled elevator that lowered a section of the deck down into the belly of the metal beast below them, they were led, by Keystone, through the door in the conning tower to the interior of the sub. As he ushered them into the small room beyond the door, he proudly welcomed his guests to their new home for the next two months.

As the ungodly smell of the stale, fart laden, not-yet-replaced, air washed over them, Randall wretched again. Fortunately, there was nothing left in his stomach. When he'd finished, Keystone said, 'Welcome to the RSS Frightfully Audacious, gentlemen... and lady of course.' He bowed slightly to Cindi [27] as if to acknowledge the slight breach of manners.

'My first officer is out on a re-supply mission at the moment, and to be frank, no disrespect intended, you all look like you could use a shower, especially you Mr. James, so it would be in order to forgo formal introductions for the moment I think. Mr. Sleepy, would you escort our guests to the showers please, and place a guard on the door while they're in there would you?'

Now he turned to Cindi. 'This is mostly for your protection, Daphne,' he said. 'Although, until we know a little more about your friends, I'm afraid they'll be accompanied by guards for the time being.' He faced Marcus and Randall. 'Just a precautionary measure you understand, I'm sure you're both fine fellows, but we have to be careful you see.'

---

[27] Known as Daphne to Keystone, Grumpy and Dopey, Sundial to the rest of the dwarves and the crew, Cindi to Randall and Marcus, and "The bitch Lehman" to Constable Bailey. Yes, you're right, it could get confusing.

'I understand completely,' said Marcus, pouring on the politeness. 'I wouldn't expect anything else from a captain concerned for the security of his crew and his mission. You do yourself proud, sir. Our collection from the beach was flawlessly executed, and I... we, thank you and your men. We'd be happy to submit ourselves to whatever security measures you see fit.'

Keystone visibly swelled with pride. 'You're too kind I'm sure, Mr. Han,' he said, humbly, nodding his head as he did so. 'We are very thorough in our security and we take it entirely seriously. Thank you for your understanding in this matter, and I apologise in advance for any inconvenience it may cause.'

Now it was Marcus's turn to nod. He did so in an equally-as-humble a way as his host had done, and was about to engage Keystone in another diplomatic round of polite boundary finding when his train of thought was derailed by an urgent shout from behind him.

'Captain Keystone, sir,' came the shout. 'I need to speak to you urgently, sir.'

Dopey stood in the doorway of the cramped room at the base of the conning tower, panting for breath. He'd run from his station to get to the captain as soon as they'd boarded.

'Can't it wait, man?' exclaimed Keystone, almost angrily. 'Can't you see I'm busy?'

'I'm afraid not, sir. It's rather delicate, sir. A matter of security.' Dopey stood there almost wringing his hands with anxiety.

Keystone turned to his guests with a sigh. 'It seems Lady Duty doth heed me to her bosom once again, my friends. Alas I must leave you in the capable hands of Mr. Sleepy here, who will accompany you to the shower stalls, while I must, sadly, attend a matter that apparently cannot wait. If you would care to join me in the Ward Room for morning tea, I shall introduce you to my senior staff then, if that would be agreeable. Until tomorrow then.'

'Until tomorrow,' said Marcus and Cindi. Randall grunted, nauseously.

As Keystone walked away they were led to the showers, where, rather graciously considering the noticeably unkempt condition of her hair, Cindi let the boys go first; Randall's rather more vomitty condition needing more immediate attention than her own not-looking-very-attractive-around-all-these-men situation.

Keystone, meanwhile, had risen through the entire range of his personal DefCon scale.

Before being interrupted by Dopey he'd been at the lowest level - Diplomatically Cordial - but he instantly raised it to Mildly Irked upon hearing Dopey in the doorway. As he heard the report to completion he passed quickly through Jolly Cross Actually, and Bloody Furious, before finally settling at Fucking Insanely Angry. He actually broke his biscuit!

The report, nervously relayed by Dopey, certainly concerned security. During a bathroom break his equipment had recorded a message sent in Morse code, and it seemed the only possible source of the transmission was aboard the sub itself. When transcribed, the message said, simply, "Intercept failed. Mother Goose still swims. Destination Wastelads".

Keystone read it again. 'Wastelads?' he asked, managing to keep the anger out of his voice.

'I presume he was in a hurry,' said Dopey, nervously.

Keystone was now sure he could smell the "bathroom break" on Dopey's breath. Bathrooms didn't normally smell of whiskey in his experience, and he quietly lamented his crewman's penchant for getting quietly pissed at every available opportunity.

For once he abandoned the protocol of using codenames aboard the sub. 'Mister Weatherspoon-Yates,' he began, 'I can smell the whiskey on your breath. You're on report do you understand? Again!'

Dopey wilted visibly. He seemed to shrink by several inches. 'I'm sorry, sir. I can't help it, sir. It's the pressure, sir. It gets to me some-times. I have a little tot occasionally to calm my nerves, sir, that's all.'

Keystone understood the pressure, and had partaken of "a little tot" himself occasionally, but only when he was off duty; which, as captain, wasn't very often. And that was the difference between him and some of his men, Keystone "partook", he didn't guzzle it down as soon as everyone's back was turned. He decided to go easy on the terrified sailor, however, at least until he'd got all the details out of him. 'Have you any idea who could have sent the message?' he asked, as calmly as he could.

'No, sir, not really, but as I got back to the bridge I noticed Snow White was missing, sir. He walked back into the control room a few moments after I returned. He wasn't in the head, I know that. He came through the aft passage [28], he must have been in his quarters, sir.

'You're positive?'

'Definitely, sir.'

A concerned expression crossed Keystone's face as he considered his options. He could confront Snow White, but if Dopey was wrong, that would cause friction amongst his crew; and if he was right, Snow White would plead ignorance. Without conclusive proof they would only put him on his guard, and they would get nowhere. More subtlety was required; a trap would need to be set for Mr. Millhouse-Philby-Blunt. Snow White, as it turned out, given the inherent implication of innocence, might not be an appropriate codename for him at all.

Back in Cadiz, Constable Bailey was utterly flabbergasted. His eye twitched alarmingly and he frantically fiddled with his face hair as he tried to figure out what to do next. He was still standing in the secluded alley leading to the square, where he had foolishly fallen asleep earlier in the day. Now, however, he was wide awake.

After watching the proceedings on the beach - with difficulty, the only drone he was able to steal didn't have night vision capabilities - he could only come to one conclusion. The Spanish WP were infested with fifth columnists! And what's more, he'd watched one of them re-supply the resistance submarine before abandoning his troop transport on the beach. Bailey wanted to arrest him immediately, of course, but he couldn't if he wanted to stay undercover and off the radar. The traitor had disappeared anyway; with the dark-clad sailors, who had arrived in some sort of large inflatable boat and carried away at least five tons of supplies.

And all that was before spotting what he presumed must be the escape of Lehman and the fugitives, which was what was really driving him bonkers.

The drone surveilled the supply boat all the way to the submarine hidden behind the island, where he saw that another boat had already docked and was having its cargo unloaded. He couldn't tell what it was,

---

[28] A line that would have delighted Snow White had he been there to hear it.

apparently machinery of some sort, but Lehman and the fugitives were definitely there, with a machine that could only have been the car he'd traced to the cliff face.

He was infuriated at the incompetence and ineptitude of the local WP, and the fools at HQ who had left them to get on with the operation unsupervised. He was angry, his eye kept twitching, his top lip hurt, and he was confused. Hunger was beginning to make its unpleasant presence felt too. He needed to act decisively. Now.

But, for the first time in weeks, he didn't know what to do next. His belief in himself was still strong, but he also believed rather strongly that he was up shit creek without a boat.

There was one man who did know what to do, however. Or, to be entirely factual, he didn't quite know everything just yet but undoubtedly would in a few minutes. It only ever took him a few minutes to do anything; as his wife would lamentably declare if she weren't so scared of him.

He was a big man with a small face and a bald head that didn't end with a neck. It simply morphed into the rolls of skin that protruded through the top of the big man's jacket. A jacket with the insignia of a commissioner's rank emblazoned across the chest and epaulettes. His thick glasses made his tiny eyes seem enormously comical, like beetles crawling around in the bottoms of bottles, but nobody ever mentioned that. Not since the first time.

His name was Commissioner Savage, and he was sitting behind his desk at WPHQ, with a cigar and a whiskey to keep him company. Not an ordinary desk, you understand. Not a flat piece of wood with wobbly legs and piles of precariously balanced files on it, but a marvel of modern surveillance technology, and a control centre of vast power. Built from steel and excitingly contoured plastic, fitted with a host of buttons, screens, levers, and gadgets, it looked like the deck of a spaceship - but he still called it a desk.

Swilling whiskey around in his glass, he was watching Bailey squirming in the little alley. Savage wasn't happy; but that was quite normal.

His drone did have night vision, and much else besides. It flew higher than Bailey's, and for longer; it was even armed in a limited way. Not in a way that could make a significant difference against a submarine though, just a single laser cannon, not powerful enough by a long way.

He watched everything in high definition and with an angry look on his face as he switched circuits, transferring the surveillance operation to a pair of weaponised spy satellites. They really could make a difference. Now it was on the surface, the beam weapons aboard the satellites could cut the submarine into tiny pieces if he so desired, but he was beginning to get curious about how far they would get, and more importantly, where they would go. The badly spelled message he'd just received from the mole mentioned the "Wastelads", presumably the GM Wastelands, so destroying the sub might not be the best course of action right now. If there was another resistance base in the middle of the Pacific, he needed to know about it.

His eye hovered over the "Fire" button which had appeared on his terminal. Not an actual physical button. Just a virtual space in his field of vision, a non-existent, electronically generated space that could unleash the power of a thousand suns onto the unwary resistance sub if he chose to blink.

With a faint wobble of his head, he decided he would watch where the sub went, instead of destroying it outright, and to do that he would need all the facilities and technology of the WP. He swivelled round in his seat, and with a wave of his hand he switched on the holographic interface to the WPNet behind him. With further deft little gestures, he transferred the image of the sub from his terminal to the holograph. As he did so, the space in front of his eyes lit up showing the full scene in 3D, but with an eerie green glow to it. With another twist of his wrist it suddenly lit up in full colour as if it was a daylight scene.

On his terminal was another "button". It was the button that would give Bailey the fright of his life when he decided to blink on it. He'd been resisting the temptation for half an hour already, but now he gave in to it.

Suddenly, Constable Bailey's entire field of vision was filled with a huge image of Commissioner Savage's massive, bald, bespectacled, head. 'Stay where you are,' said the terrifying image. 'I'm coming to get you.'

Chapter 29.

The next morning at eleven hundred hours - morning tea - the senior crew were formally introduced to Marcus, Cindi, and Randall; who had recovered, but only slightly. Even though the "boat", as Keystone referred to it, was relatively stable now that they were under the water and underway again, Randall was still quite green around the gills, and had refused to even look at the array of biscuits and fairy cakes laid out on the Ward Room table. The tea, however, he guzzled down.

He'd spent a large part of a mildly uncomfortable night, walking, and at one-point, crawling on all fours, to the toilet, or "head", as he'd been instructed to call it, and he wasn't really joining in with the conversation much. Any time he opened his mouth, it was only to belch biliously. Talking was beyond him for the time-being.

Thankfully, Marcus was doing most of it. Again.

Marcus didn't quite see it that way, however. As far as he was concerned he was only spending about a third of the time actually talking. The rest of the time was taken up with explaining what he'd just said.

Most of the senior staff didn't believe any of it, but Keystone and a couple of the more up-to-speed officers were studying the hastily drawn diagrams, and listened attentively while Marcus explained some of the details.

'As soon as the transceiver section is charged - to a little over four point one million BTU's per hour - the pod will be delivered into the resulting vortex field at exactly a hundred and twenty-nine feet per second [29]. As soon as the pod reaches the centre and is fully enveloped

---

[29] BTU - British Thermal Units. Translated into sensible terminology, 1.21 Gigawatts. Coincidentally, 129 feet per second equals exactly 88 miles per hour. Great Scott!

in the field, its momentum is translated and it gets sucked into the vortex, instantly converted into a 5D time-space packet...' He looked around at the dubious faces of the crew.

The confused looks from the few who were with him were competing badly against the incredulous looks from the majority. Doc, the oldest, the bushiest eye-browed, and the most profoundly unintelligible member of the crew, was harrumphing himself into a frenzy; but there were too many questions from the other senior staff, so he went unheard.

It seemed Marcus had lost them. Again.

'Why do you insist on using such ancient terminology?' asked Keystone. 'You do know what a metre is, don't you?'

The others, including Cindi and Randall, turned to Marcus for the answer. Randall knew a lot of the mathematics, but this aspect had somewhat puzzled him too, so he added to the intensity of the curious stares directed at Marcus.

'Ah, I understand. Well, it's all to do with the Earth you see,' he began. 'I rather suspect it's you who doesn't know what a metre actually is, instead of the other way around. The units I use, and that our ancient ancestors used, are derived from actual measurements of the planet in its orbit, and they can all be ultimately traced back to the megalithic yard.'

The confused looks on the faces of his audience only seemed to become more deep set. He plunged on...

'The foot, the mile, the inch, the ounce, the pint, even the second itself - all derived from a simple measurement of planetary movement that anyone can perform with a couple of sticks and a clear night's viewing at the right time of year. That's what the 2.732 conversion factor is for, Randall, in case you hadn't figured it out.'

Randall hadn't figured it out, but the look of clarity that climbed on his face was a picture for Marcus. A nice picture this time, possibly taken by someone who does wedding photos.

Even more confusion appeared on the faces of his audience, however. He plunged on again...

'The megalithic yard is the oldest known measurement of any kind. It goes right back to the beginning of measurement itself, and the units derived from it are the only measurements that work correctly with the formulae of time-travel. The speed of the pod - which, if you'll give me a moment I'll convert for you - is derived from an absolute fraction of the orbital speed of the Earth in miles per hour; the hour being a megalithic unit itself, of course.'

He thought for a moment, his eyes closed. 'A hundred and twenty-nine feet per second equates to just over one hundred and forty-one kilometres per hour, but the accurate figure has a dozen or more decimal places. It's actually quite a simple formula involving the square root of the Earth's speed around the Sun at aphelion. That would be a very messy calculation if done in kilometres per hour, it's much easier using the ancients' units; you can use nice round numbers.'

Finally, Doc managed to make himself heard above the hubbub. The need for space around the table meant that Bashful wasn't there this morning, so he dumbed his vocabulary down as much as he could.

'Poppycock,' he exclaimed. 'Time-travel? Bunkum! Divergent timelines? Preposterous balderdash. Begging your indulgence, Mr. Han, and yours, Mr. James, but this is unadulterated hogwash. George James Junior had surgery to disengage his terminal and subsequently fled the continent. The NetCam video was utter flimflammery; a far from harmless hoodwink, an artifice if you will. A very clever one I'll grant you, but it was artifice nonetheless. The only things he "Departed" from, were his responsibilities to his new spouse and his drug debts. His time machine was an ingenious and elaborate subterfuge. It's as simple as that. A proven fake. Demonstrably fraudulent. I apologise if that offends you, Mr. James, but it is the indisputable truth.'

Randall was busy feeling bilious, and wasn't up to defending his father's honour just now, so Cindi took up the charge.

'The video was only proven fake by the system we're all fighting against, you daft old fool,' she interjected. 'Why would he go to all that trouble just to escape his alleged debts? Honestly! Think about it. You know how they hide technologies from the population. I mean, look at this boat. Our predecessors replaced the nuclear reactor when? A hundred years ago? The zero-point generator that powers it now has never been made public, they're used exclusively in the WP Orbital Fleet where no civilian will ever see them. It's the same with time-travel technology, believe me. I've spent the last three months helping to build the device and I even understand the basics of what Marcus is telling you. It's all true I promise you.'

She paused for a sip of tea before continuing. 'And anyway, can you afford to take the risk? If we don't complete this mission it could mean the destruction of the entire Galaxy. At least if we complete it, we can begin again in another timeline. What have you got to lose? Just dump us on the island and leave us. If you're all still here a month later, it'll prove we were wrong. No skin off your nose, right?'

The bit about the Galaxy vanishing was one of the main stumbling blocks with the non-believers, quite apart from their disbelief in time-travel to begin with, but the maths was too complicated, Marcus couldn't convince them now. He doubted he ever would.

The discussion, which bordered on argumentative at times, went on for another half an hour before other duties called the staff away. It was an irrelevant discussion anyway; they were underway now, committed to the mission. In about eight weeks they would be arriving at the Wastelands, and that was going to be their biggest challenge. The majority of the crew would only find out it was all true when the timeline was erased.

Or, rather, they'd never find out at all.

They remained mostly in their quarters for the first few days; which were primitive but adequate for their needs. Their food was brought to them to keep Cindi's exposure to the crew to a minimum, and apart from the occasional invitation to morning tea and arguments, they were left well enough alone to complete the machine.

Cindi was happy with that arrangement. From what little they saw of the crew, they seemed to be a burly bunch of misfits; not the officers, of course, they were obviously more refined, but the men themselves were a rough group of flat-nosed hard-knocks from all over the world. They were the toughest of those many weary citizens who'd become disillusioned with the GloboCo status quo and the reign of the WP, and although they were her compatriots in the resistance, they were also very definitely a population of men starved of female company, and Cindi was wary of their lecherous looks on the few occasions she couldn't avoid them.

They lacked privacy, but after the first week they got used to that, and made certain arrangements to increase their personal space. The time machine was re-assembled in one corner of the room, and they had cots set up in the other; not comfortable, but sufficient. Scratch marks on the floor indicated that the two big tanks full of water, that were rather limiting their available space, had been pushed up against the wall to make room for them, no clue as to their function could be ascertained. Marcus used them as a big shelf to keep his tools on.

The machine was completed in very short order. The computers were configured and were going through a series of diagnostic checks when, on the eighth day, they had a visit from Sleepy, who insisted they call him Jeremy.

'How are you settling in?' he asked. 'Not too much hardship I hope.'

'We're coping, thank you,' said Randall. 'It's taken a bit of getting used to, but we're winning I think. Oh, and thank you for your support during our visits to the ward room, er, Jeremy. I take it you're having to go against quite a few of your colleagues to help us?'

'True enough, but it's not a problem really. Keystone is convinced, and we're not exactly a democracy you know.' He snortled nasally a couple of times as if he'd just been frightfully witty; that was how he laughed, apparently. 'And anyway, at least we're actually doing something for a change. Hiding out at the bottom of the world's deepest ocean trenches isn't really as much fun as it sounds.' Snortle, snortle.

'The truth is I'm fascinated by the Wastelands actually. Wish I was coming with you to be honest. The diversity there must be incredible, all those new species uncategorised by science. Talking trees, no less! They must be studied. Think of what we could learn if only there were more time.'

Now Marcus was interested. 'Yes, I gathered you were something of a scientist from our morning meetings. What's your specialty, if you don't me asking?'

'Not at all, old boy,' replied Sleepy. 'I trained as a biologist at GloboCo Medical initially, studying signal transmission between nerve cells, but then I found out a few of the tricks they were up to with some of their products. I had a friend in the food synthesis division who showed me the recipe for Cheez one day. I did a few tests of my own. The results weren't good.'

'I know,' said Randall. 'I used to eat the stuff. Glad to be off it now though.'

'We all did, dear chap, we all did. You went through the headaches, yes? It took me a while to wean myself off it too. And coming to live on this sub was a culture shock, believe me.'

'Oh we do,' said Cindi. 'Randall and I have been through something similar recently. In the other direction, admittedly, but...'

'And now we're going through it again,' said Randall, 'in a way. How long have you been here by the way?'

'This is my twelfth year as a serving member of the crew, and my eighteenth year in the resistance,' said Sleepy, proudly.

'Twelve years? I can't imagine being cooped up in a wobbly tube full of farts for that long. I'm struggling with the prospect of another seven weeks. How do you cope?'

'Oh it's not so bad once you get used to it. We even get holidays occasionally. There are a few isolated islands we have small bases on where we can relax for a day or two. And we get a short shore leave in the "real world" four times a year of course, when we re-supply.'

'I've been wondering,' said Marcus. 'If you don't mind me asking, er... why are the officers all so, er, how do I put this? Why are you all so...'

'British?' interrupted Sleepy.

'It's more than just Britishness,' said Randall, who'd been wondering the same thing, 'you all seem to be rather... upper-class, almost aristocracy.'

'Ah, well that's because most of us are you see. The British were instrumental in the planning and execution of Takeover Day all those centuries ago. They stole this creaky old tube from a Navy base in Scotland where the Windsors stored their nuclear submarines, and there's been a long tradition of Brits in charge of it ever since. It is our boat, after all. And the Brits have always made good sailors.'

'But why are you all so posh?'

'Well, it was when the monarchy was exposed you see,' Sleepy continued. 'Many of the aristo's were merely innocent pawns of the machinations of the monarchy by that time. They were broke, most of them. The royals hoarded all the money and we were dependent on their whims to a large extent. So when the turds hit the turbine, many of us were just as angry as the rest of the people, but we had an advantage because some of us had access, you see. The upper-classes had always provided the Navy with their officers, and it wasn't a difficult job to persuade some of them to turn when the truth came out. Thanks to the information we received from your other selves that is, so I suppose I'm talking to the brightest sparks of that revolution right now. Gosh, I never thought of it like that before. You two gentlemen are the reason we had a revolution in the first place. That's incredible now I come to think about it. I'm talking to the founders of our movement.'

'We haven't founded anything yet,' said Randall, 'don't count your chickens before you've found them.'

'But you will, dear boy, you will. With our help of course. I must say, this is quite the most exciting mission I've ever been on. And the stakes are so huge. It's utterly daunting if I'm honest. The fate of the Galaxy is at hand! You can't really get much huger than that.' He snortled again, but this time with a nervous edge to it. Strange how a noise like a blob of jam getting washed down a plug-hole could contain such subtlety of meaning.

The hugeness of the mission was left hanging in the air for a while, like a ten-ton weight tied to the ceiling by a very thin thread. Cindi broke the suddenly ominous silence with a question the three of them had pondered over before.

'I've been meaning to ask someone,' she said. 'What are those tanks of water doing here?' She pointed to the scratch marks on the floor. 'We can see you've had to move them for us.'

'The SDTs you mean? Sensory Deprivation Tanks, my dear. I've been experimenting with telepathy you see, and these are part of my research. "Operation Mindwarp" I call it. The subjects climb into the tanks, which contain very salty water heated to body temperature, and then float there in total silence and darkness, doing meditation exercises designed to enhance their telepathic ability. Would you like to try? I haven't been able to run any tests since we heard you were going to be joining us, so I'm rather itching to get back to it if I'm honest. I'd be honoured if you'd care to give it a go. Most of the crew think I'm bonkers by the way, so I have some sympathy for your position on board, as it were. Many of them think this entire mission is bonkers, so we should stick together, eh?'

Marcus looked at Randall. 'You should try it with Cindi,' he said. 'Even if you don't get results, it'd be a good place to meditate I should think.'

'Oh, I didn't know! Are you a meditator already? Wonderful.' Sleepy looked pleased.

'I'm a beginner,' replied Randall. 'These two are the experts. But yes, I'd be happy to give it a go. How about you, Cindi?'

'Try and stop me,' she said.

It was nearly six weeks later, as they were sailing between Lostralia and Newer Zealand, when they got their first verifiable results.

After the initial hallucinatory weirdness of having no sensory input whatsoever, they gradually increased their immersion time until they were in there for hours on end. The tanks became a bit of a refuge for Randall and Cindi; a tiny island of privacy where there was none before. It also gave Marcus a bit of peace and quiet while they were in there too, which was welcomed.

By the fifth week they became quite adept at getting into the almost trance-like state required for rudimentary telepathy to take place. The effect was enhanced by their strong emotional connection to each other, which only grew stronger over the weeks - something that had been understandably lacking in Sleepy's earlier trials. Their frustration at having so little intimate time together, and not being able to even hold hands in front of the crew was putting a strain on them both, and that was probably why, on the fortieth day, they became aware of each other's thoughts.

The exercise was for Cindi to project a randomly chosen picture into Randall's mind, and at Sleepy's suggestion she wrapped the image in emotional content, to make the connection stronger. The emotion she chose was the way she felt during lovemaking with Randall, which was now a fond but distant memory thanks to the privations of the sub.

Randall didn't notice with his brain, however. Not the one he used for thinking with anyway. His first inkling of a connection started in another part of his anatomy altogether; the description of which will be left to the reader's imagination. It puzzled Randall in the extreme why he was suddenly thinking about the Giza pyramids - the image Cindi

208

was projecting - while simultaneously, his body was obviously thinking about Cindi.

He wished fervently that Cindi could join him in the tank. His erection [30] was causing him some inconvenience in the cut-off wetsuit he was wearing, and he imagined Cindi helping to ease it off his body...

Suddenly, the hatch in the top of his tank opened, and Cindi's smiling face popped over the edge. Randall could just about hear the sound of Marcus leaving the room, coughing.

'Budge over then,' she said.

Fortunately, the tanks were quite well soundproofed.

Although the detail was kept to a discreet minimum, they reported the edited highlights of their experience to Sleepy the next day. He was ecstatic, to say the least.

'You mean you managed to transmit an actual thought between you?' he cried, excitedly.

'Randall did the transmitting, Jeremy. I just suddenly knew what was in his head,' said Cindi. 'I could hear his voice in my mind, calling me to open his tank. It was quite, erm, urgent. if that's the right word.'

As the faint blush rose to occupy her cheeks, she winked quickly at Randall, who smiled and distracted Sleepy until she could control the rush of blood. As she had done for him yesterday.

'It was astonishing. Honestly, I couldn't believe it when she opened the tank and... helped me out.'

Cindi giggled at the euphemism. They hadn't told Sleepy she'd climbed in with Randall, only that she'd opened the hatch and helped to "pull him out" - which was only one word off, she thought, as she coughed to mask the giggle.

'That's amazing!' exclaimed Sleepy, who was nearly in shock. 'I thought it might be possible to transmit an image or a word to another mind when they were in resonance with each other, but a complete thought! And a request no less! You two must have a very strong emotional bond, you almost acted as though you were one being. Your minds became connected at a very deep level.'

---

[30] See? You were right. Perhaps telepathy does work...

More than our minds, thought Randall. He looked at Cindi and could tell she was thinking something similar. Suppressing the smile, he tried to take his mind off the memories; he was almost starting to get "disturbed" again.

'I think we'd both be more than happy to try again,' he said. 'I'm sure I could transmit other forms of information too.' *Quite apart from DNA,* he thought, privately. 'It seems to work better if no one else is present. Marcus left the room yesterday, and suddenly we were free to er, express ourselves, shall we say?'

'Splendid idea, dear fellow,' said Sleepy. 'Perhaps you could try again now? Mr. Han will be in his meeting with Captain Keystone for another hour at least. You've plenty of time. How about it?'

'Well? How about it, Randall?' said Cindi, with a raised eyebrow and a hint of seductiveness in her voice.

'Where's my wetsuit?' he replied.

'Spiffing,' said Sleepy. 'I'll leave you to get to it then. You'll report back to me later?'

'Of course, Jeremy,' replied Randall. 'If you could make sure we're not disturbed for an hour... make it an hour and a half perhaps?'

'Of course, dear chap. I look forward to seeing what you come up with.'

No you wouldn't, thought Randall.

This time Randall didn't even have to send the mental request for Cindi to join him in the tank because they both climbed into the same one. They didn't bother with the wetsuits either.

The next day, after surfacing for some well-earned deck-time, Snow White died. In fact, he killed himself.

It was a disastrous end to an otherwise immaculately executed sting operation conducted by the senior staff. Marcus had been let in on it, and was explaining the details to an astonished Randall and Cindi...

'They started to suspect he'd been turned on the day we got here in fact,' he said, solemnly. 'Apparently he sent a message while we were on the surface at Cadiz. Keystone and the others have been concocting this plan ever since.'

He shook his head sadly. 'It was all going so well, too. They'd figured out he might have a small transmitter of his own, but they couldn't find it. So they secretly activated an antenna on the conning tower, to record any transmissions. Then they made sure Radio Operator Dopey was at the front of the crowd when Snow White was doing his little act. They made him think the comms station was un-manned while he was performing, but all frequencies were being monitored behind his back. They found a repeating Morse code message in the short-wave band that started the moment he began to sing.'

'What did it say?' asked Cindi and Randall at the same time.

'It said, "Wastelands - Two weeks out - Intercept required - Mother Goose still carries the egg", repeatedly, in a loop.'

'Then they know where we are,' shouted Cindi. She gripped Randall's hand anxiously. He gripped hers back.

'No,' said Marcus. 'Don't worry, they thought of that. Keystone and Dopey set up a jamming field that limited the range of the signal to about a mile, judging by the strength of the transmitter we found. Unless the WP had a receiver within that range, which is almost impossible, we're in the clear.'

'But what happened to Snow White?' asked Cindi.

'Well, they let him think he'd successfully sent the message and just carried on as normal. They let him finish his act and do a few gags - the crew enjoy that sort of thing apparently - but meanwhile, Keystone used an extremely sensitive mobile antenna to pinpoint the source of the signal. Turns out it was coming from his hat.'

Cindi and Randall had been "meditating" in the tank while the show went on, so they hadn't seen Snow White's performance.

'What hat?' asked Randall.

'Warrant Officer Richard Millhouse-Philby-Blunt, to use his full name, was a performer of the ancient art of female impersonation, Randall,' he said. 'He had any number of hats and wigs in his act, but the one we found the transmitter inside was a "Carmen Miranda" hat, the one he was wearing when he started the show, in fact. It's more than a foot high and was covered in plastic fruit, all now commandeered by Keystone to decorate his ready room I believe. Each to their own, it adds a splash of colour I suppose.'

He studied their puzzled looks for a moment before continuing. 'Don't worry about it,' he said, 'it's just a silly hat from a bygone era.

Anyway, they transcribed the message he'd sent, and confronted him with it in his quarters about an hour ago. That was their mistake I think. If they'd called him to the bridge he'd still be alive. Before they could stop him he'd swallowed a cyanide capsule. He was dead thirty seconds later.'

'Oh, God, that's horrible,' cried Cindi. She buried her face in Randall's jumper as he put his arms around her.

'Not as horrible as the consequences if they hadn't caught him I reckon,' said Marcus. 'At least the WP don't know what we're up to, or where we are.'

But one man did know roughly where they were. And he wasn't happy - in fact, he wasn't any of the dwarves.

Chapter 30.

The Seer pulled himself from his dream and woke with a start, hurriedly grabbing a corner of his sheet and noisily blowing his nose on it. Sometimes he bemoaned the fact that his dreams were so vivid, so detailed. The disgusting smell of the dream he'd just woken up from was still in his nostrils, and it was a very characterful odour. The stale, fuggy, fart laden air of the strange underwater machine that his astral body had just visited was still fresh, if that's the right word, and he took several deep breaths through his nose until the foul stench was replaced with the more familiar, fuggy, unwashed stink of the inside of his own hut.

It was still an hour before dawn, three hours before he normally woke up, and not yet light outside. He wearily leaned over to light the crude tallow candle on his even cruder bedside table. Not with a match, of course, matches or lighters were rare treasures traded with some of the friendlier coastal tribes, or sometimes gathered from the few humans who'd made it this far into the island; whose insanely disturbed and emaciated persons (or, more usually, corpses) could be plundered for such treasures.

He closed his eyes for a little more than five seconds; breathing deeply, with intense concentration, while he generated a charge of what some would call "Prana", or "Chi" - or "Woo", if you're that way inclined. Once fully energised, he leaned over towards the candle, and with his finger extended to within a short distance of its wick, he released a quick spark of electricity that struck it with a faint sizzle.

Even far-out psychic woo doesn't work sometimes. The candle guttered a tiny flame for a brief second before going out again. The Seer took another few deep breaths and tried again. Five seconds later, on the second attempt, the flame slowly caught, and the hut began to light up with a dull, flickery, yellow light. He sat up in bed, stretched his back until his vertebrae started popping like a distant fireworks display, and with a slightly puzzled expression on his face, he wiped the tiredness from his eyes.

His latest dream had been a strange one, of a place he'd never seen before, about a big metal tube full of humans ploughing the ocean depths on their way to the island. He'd been drawn into the dream by the sexual charge generated by two of the expected visitors, who were apparently frolicking in some sort of tiny private pool, and he knew what it meant. They were now into the next scroll of the prophecy. The time was near.

He could easily sense the emotional charge even at this distance, and the connection it gave him enabled him to explore their minds a little further. They would never notice; they were quite busy, after all.

After gently probing their minds for a few minutes, he'd pulled out [31] and began to tap into the mood of the other men inside the mysterious metal whale. Immediately he began to sense the loss of one of their own, but the grief was tinged with... relief? And there also seemed to be a sense of pride mixed with the sorrow. It could mean only one thing: the traitor had taken his own life.

And that was the other sign he'd been waiting for. The sign, written in the opening chapter of the second scroll, that the time had finally arrived to send the troops out to meet the visitors. They would be here within a week, and he knew now where the little boats would be coming ashore.

Sleepily, but with a smile on his face, he lit his pipe with his finger and calmly waited for the Sun to rise before he could tell the still slumbering trees...

---

[31] In much the same way that Randall didn't.

Chapter 31.

It was raining on the day they arrived at the Wastelands. In fact, it was absolutely pissing down, and that suited them just fine. The heavy cloud cover and occasional lightning flashes were ideal conditions; the WP wouldn't be able to spy on them from above, and any unknown listening stations nearby would hear nothing but splashing rain and rumbles of thunder. It was a rough sea, but it was only a short trip from the sub so they took the chance to disembark during a brief lull in the winds. They headed towards a beach on the south shore, protected by a small headland that created a natural windbreak which sheltered them from the worst of the storm, but it was still choppy water.

The downpour pounded on the sandy beach as the Batmobile, towing the trailer behind it, drove up onto the shore followed closely behind by Keystone in a large inflatable containing the time machine.

Despite the torrential rain, as soon as they were clear of the waves and on "dry" land, Randall and Cindi flung open the passenger door and threw themselves out of the amphibious metal marvel and onto the beach. Randall on his knees with his arms stretched to the sky, screaming "Thank you, Dawkins", and Cindi, laughing like a maniac, flat on her back letting the rain wash the flatulent stink out of her clothes.

Marcus smiled as he drove past them up to the edge of the sand dunes; quickly finding a slightly more sheltered spot to detach the trailer. Within a couple of minutes, he had stabilised it and pulled the lever that would activate the unfolding mechanism. A minute later it was ready, and with the large landing craft safely pulled up onto the shore and tied to it, they each grabbed an armful of supplies from the smaller boat and clambered in, out of the rain. They were all glad to be on solid ground, but the irony of escaping from one wet metal prison only to climb immediately into another much less substantial one, didn't escape them.

Before long, Keystone added to the steam rising from their bodies by pouring them all a cup of tea from his camouflaged thermos flask and proposing a toast. 'To the Galaxy,' he said, holding his plastic cup aloft and slopping hot tea onto the floor of the trailer. 'To the Galaxy,' they chanted, unenthusiastically, barely audible above the blatter of the rain on the trailer's roof.

'We won't get very far if this rain keeps up. We're not in the middle of a rainy season are we?' asked Randall.

'I don't think so,' said Marcus. 'We're only ten degrees below the equator, I don't think they have a monsoon season or anything like it, the winds aren't right. But we are bang in the middle of the storm belt, this is the latitude where hurricanes are born so we shouldn't be too surprised by storms occasionally. In fact...'

They didn't hear what he said next because that's when the hail started.

They were already having to shout to be heard above the rain, but now the noise was deafening. Hailstones like golf-balls were smashing into the roof making visible dents, and badly scratching the Perspex skylight set in the middle of it. The trailer was a big tin drum in the sights of an ice firing machine gun. Marcus wondered whether the Batmobile would be able to take the battering; it was a sturdy machine, but the coating of invisibility glass might not survive the onslaught. He suppressed a slight feeling of panic. If a hailstone hit any of the sensors, it would be completely smashed.

They sat there with their fingers in their ears and steam rising from their clothes for another couple of minutes, before a sound like a faint gunshot caused them all to jump in their seats. Suddenly, the skylight cracked from corner to corner and freezing melt water started dribbling through. By the law of inevitability, the water was obliged to aim itself at the back of someone's neck, and it swiftly chose Randall for this purpose.

He screamed with the shock and moved quickly out of the way of the icy water. At least, he tried to move, but with four people and all the supplies they'd carried with them there wasn't a lot of space to move to, and he only succeeded in getting it to splash off his back and all over everybody else.

'That's quite refreshing actually,' shouted Keystone, holding his hand over his tea to keep it "dry" and putting his face directly in the way of the splashing water. 'Stay right there would you, old chap?'

Randall was about to protest when, as suddenly as it started, the hail stopped and the wind quickly died. A strange calm settled over the trailer as they sat there steaming in the relative quiet, only broken by the water still dribbling in from the cracked skylight.

Keystone broke the silence. 'I should be getting back to the boat. We need to unload your machine and get it into the trailer quickly, while the weather is on our side. We'll need to fix that skylight too. Someone has to get up there and clear the hailstones off. I have some epoxy tape in the toolkit of the boat, but you'll have to fix it yourselves I'm afraid. I need to get back before the cloud cover breaks. I'll just nip out and get it.' He gulped down the last of his tea and stepped outside.

The air that rushed into the steamy, sauna-like, space as Keystone opened the door was cool and refreshing, and sparked them into action. They poured out of the trailer and went about getting themselves organised; Randall cleared the skylight and applied an "X" of tape to secure it, while Cindi mopped up the water from the floor, and condensation from the walls. Keystone began unloading the time machine and piling it on the sand ready to be loaded into the trailer.

Marcus spent a minute inspecting the Batmobile carefully. As he feared, some of the panels were cracked and they wouldn't be able to maintain full invisibility, but with the dust they'd be kicking up and the fact they were towing what was essentially a caravan behind them, that wasn't too important. There didn't seem to be any sensor damage, but he wouldn't know for sure until he switched them on. All in all, he decided, they were in pretty good shape.

Keystone took a good few minutes getting back out to sea, and before long the extended period of waving goodbye became somewhat embarrassing. What started with hugs, handshakes, and hearty goodbyes, ended with a kind of agonising protracted farewell that became cringe worthy, quite quickly.

They stood on the beach watching Keystone move very slowly back towards the open water. Picking his way carefully back through the gaps in the rocks only a few feet below the water, his outboard motor struggled against the waves crashing in on the shore. The boat seemed to be spending more of its time travelling up and down vertically than horizontally, and even went backwards on occasion, but eventually it cleared the swell and began to make more headway. They shouted final goodbyes and turned to the task at hand.

Getting off the beach was paramount, and they quickly started organising themselves with that goal in mind. The first task was to pack the time machine into the trailer, so they hurriedly removed the supplies already stashed in there, cleared up the mess they'd made and got to work.

The machine itself wasn't heavy, it had been designed that way, or rather, hastily re-designed that way. Once Marcus knew they would be travelling to the other side of the planet to make their trip to the past, he'd started again almost from scratch; making everything modular so it could be assembled like a kit. All the metal parts were now made from Nano-Alumitanium, the lightest and strongest alloy ever developed, which had taken some getting hold of, but was now proving its usefulness. The heaviest parts were the two executive office chairs, which, even disassembled, were still weighty.

Twenty minutes later they were ready to face whatever weird Planimals the Wastelands could throw at them.

As they began driving slowly along the beach, looking for a wide enough path through the dunes to the grassland just beyond, they got their first taste...

About fifteen metres ahead of them (or fifty feet as far as Marcus was concerned), a huge black bird landed on the sand directly in their path. It cawed strangely, almost as if it was shouting the word "Caw" instead of actually cawing. It raised its left wing and waved it, seemingly pointing into the dunes with it.

Marcus, driving slowly, steered the Batmobile right, to go around the bird. With a single flap of its wings, it immediately hopped over to bar their path once more. It shouted "Caw" again, even louder, and with an intonation that suggested, to Randall at least, the phrase "are you

218

stupid or something?". It indicated urgently with its left wing, nodding in the direction it was pointing.

'Is it trying to tell us something do you think?' said Cindi, from the passenger seat.

'Or is it a trap?' said Randall, from the back.

Marcus brought the car to a halt and switched cameras to get a better look in the direction the enormous bird seemed to be pointing. He zoomed in. 'There could be a gap wide enough to get through there I think. I should send up a scout to check for a path.'

He pressed a button on the centre console marked "Day Drone". Immediately, another screen lit up in the centre of the steering wheel, showing an aerial view of the Batmobile getting smaller by the second. The bird had gone, probably scared off by the drone launching.

Marcus operated the small joystick below the screen to guide the drone to the left, where the bird had pointed, and quickly saw there was a path through the dunes. Not only that, but the strange bird had now landed about three hundred yards along it, and seemed to be waiting for them. It looked like a big crow, or possibly a raven; not birds traditionally associated with cuddly cuteness or helpful assistance in perilous situations. In fact, "sinister foreboding" was a more appropriate emotion to feel at the sight of it. Marcus zoomed in on the bird for a moment and studied it. Almost instantly he upgraded the feeling of "sinister foreboding" to, "ominous baleful malevolence".

'So do we follow it?' asked Randall.

'I get the feeling it won't leave us alone until we do,' said Cindi. 'I say we take the hint.'

'Agreed,' said Marcus. He revved the engine a little and drove slowly up the gentle slope into the dunes. 'But we should be on our guard. Cindi, you know where the laser pistol is?'

'Got it,' said Cindi, reaching under her seat.

They rounded the last curve in the path through the dunes, and saw the massive jet black bird waiting impatiently ahead of them. Marcus applied the brakes again. As they watched, a smaller bird, perhaps a sparrow, flew up to the black monster and hovered briefly by its ear.

The beast rose immediately into the air and flew towards the car. Cindi unlatched the door and raised the laser pistol, ready to fling the door open and shoot the bird at the first sign of trouble.

What it did, however, was land on the roof with a screech of talons and shout, in a clear and easily understandable voice, 'Is there anybody in there or what?'

Cindi dropped the laser pistol on her foot.

'Sorry, folks, but I haven't got time to piss about any more,' continued the raven. 'Is Markynanda in there, or RanJam? Sundial? We need to talk.'

Randall was the first to get his mouth functioning. He gathered up his suddenly slack jaw and said 'How...'

Too many questions were forming up behind the "How", however, and he couldn't choose between them. How does it talk? How did it find us? How come I haven't shit myself yet? There were more than a few more.

He tried again. 'How does that thing know our nicknames?' he said, eventually.

'Let's find out shall we?' said Marcus. 'Pick the pistol up, Cindi, and keep your door ajar.' He opened his door and stepped out of the car, eye to eye with the raven on the roof.

'I'm Bill,' said Bill. 'Pleased to finally meet you. You need to get off the beach fast. If you want to stay alive, you follow me. Okay?'

Marcus, gobsmacked, simply nodded and got back into the driver's seat. He closed the door and gripped the steering wheel so tightly that Cindi thought he was going to pull it off.

'Bill,' he said.

'What?' said Randall.

'Bill. That's his name,' he said, starting the engine again.

With another ear-curdling but thankfully short screeching-on-glass noise from the roof, Bill took off and flew straight ahead of them across the dunes. Except "straight" isn't the right word. Zigzagging across the sky, it was hard to keep track of the direction he wanted them to travel, and Marcus gave up trying to match his erratic movements. After a minute he got the idea of the general direction to head in and drove carefully in pursuit of the miraculous talking bird, who was quickly joined by five more crows and many other birds of all species flying in from other patches along the coastline.

'What the flying flock is going on?' asked Cindi, calmly and politely.

'That is the weirdest flock of birds I've ever seen. It's as if they had sentries on the coast waiting for us. And now they're forming up again, like a squadron. They're even flying in formation. Look.'

Marcus had watched the small flock come together from the drone feed on the steering wheel, and had arrived at the same conclusion.

'Looks like we've got a welcoming committee,' he said.

At that moment Randall spotted movement in the rear view display. He looked closer but couldn't quite make out what he was seeing. Was the ground moving? He studied the screen for a second before realising what he was looking at. There was a tidal wave rapidly approaching them from behind.

'Go! Drive!' he shouted. 'Fast! Preferably uphill.'

Marcus responded instantly, he put his foot down and skidded off sideways across the sand for a moment before the tyres got traction. They jolted forward, the undulating hills and valleys of the dunes throwing them around madly in their seats. Randall, with no seat belt, extended his limbs to lock himself in place as they bounced off ahead of the advancing water.

Within a few seconds it was upon them. The slope of the dunes was gentle, so the wave, although not very high, moved quickly around the wheels of the caravan - which, being top heavy, would quickly capsize if it got any deeper. The water cascaded through the dunes and became a maelstrom of churning currents which began to throw them around quite alarmingly. A second later there was an ominous crash from the back of the Batmobile, as the caravan was pushed by the force of the water and collided with the back of the car, spinning it, and twisting the hitch that held them together.

Randall screamed as he felt the back of the car lift up, but Marcus put on an extra boost of power and twisted the wheel sharply to keep them upright. It worked, the car flopped heavily back into the shallow water and caught traction on the rocky ground at the edge of the dune field. The caravan landed, miraculously, on its wheels and they shot forwards once more, finally getting ahead of the advancing water.

In another hundred yards they had outrun the wave, which now seemed to have reached its furthest extent and was washing back out to sea, but it looked like the caravan was half wrecked. Marcus stopped the car, stepped out hurriedly, and ran to the damaged trailer. Cindi and Randall followed nervously behind.

After tugging on it he could see the door was stuck in its frame and Randall joined him to force it open. The caravan had been buckled and bent by the pounding it had taken, it was stuck fast.

The crows circled overhead.

Chapter 32.

Commissioner Savage, with the miserable remains of Constable Bailey following meekly behind him, stormed into his office and threw himself into his seat, which, much to Bailey's annoyance, didn't shatter into sharp splinters and skewer him through the spine. There was no seat for Bailey.

Since returning from Cadiz, where he had personally executed the chief inspector and taken charge briefly, he had heard precisely nothing from his mole on the resistance submarine. He was very angry about it, but that was nothing new. Simply waking up in the morning often put him in a mood foul enough to want to peel someone and dip them in salt.

Information about the sub was non-existent. He knew the fugitives were heading for the Wastelands, but the satellites hadn't picked up any trace of them since leaving Cadiz. He couldn't even be sure which route they'd taken, but if they were already there, which was possible given the time since he'd last seen them, then it would be very difficult to spot them. The island seemed to be almost permanently covered by cloud, generated largely by steam from the huge geysers on the north of the island and carried steadily south by the prevailing winds; the satellites could only very rarely see through them.

Bailey stood quietly, awaiting the next barked order. He was surprised to still be alive if he was honest with himself, but was beginning to severely regret that fact if he was even more truthful. He had taken the bollocking of his life in Cadiz, and had expected to die at any minute, but Savage had long known about Bailey's obsession with the case, and had put it to good use instead of simply killing him with his bare hands, as he had done with Chief Inspector Velázquez. Bailey was a very resourceful man after all, he would probably come in handy now it was finally time to intervene, and if he was killed on the mission... well, not such a huge loss to the WP.

Savage had decided to head the ground force himself; the resistance were clever bastards and his experience would be needed if they were going to stop whatever it was they were up to. The plan was for a small contingent of thirty heavily armed men to set up camp in the north of the island and begin a grid search with drones, until they found the resistance base that Savage was now sure was hidden there somewhere.

Privately, and without showing a hint of it to Bailey, he was delighted to be getting a bit of action for a change. It had been a while. The power to command the fire of a thousand suns at the blink of an eye was intoxicating, but wasn't quite enough; he liked to get his hands dirty sometimes.

'We fly tomorrow, Bailey,' he said, almost scornfully. 'Oh six hundred hours.'

Bailey nodded but didn't speak. If he spoke out of turn, or protested in even the tiniest way, Savage would simply blink and send a spasm of agonizing pain shooting from his terminal to the end of every nerve in his body. He'd already experienced it half a dozen times, and it had nearly broken him. His once iron-clad self-belief was now a shrivelled tin-foil covered husk lying in the corner of his mind cowering under the weight of Savage's dominance; but it wasn't yet completely gone. He still held a sincere belief that he was dead if he didn't do exactly what Savage said.

Following another shouted instruction from his master, he retired to his dorm to get some rest. Savage wouldn't let him out of the building now, and his dorm was his old improvised office in the basement, now cleared of all his files.

He lay silent and sullen for an hour on his thin mattress on the floor, before finally allowing himself to fall asleep.

He spent the time busily trying to figure out how he was going to kill Savage.

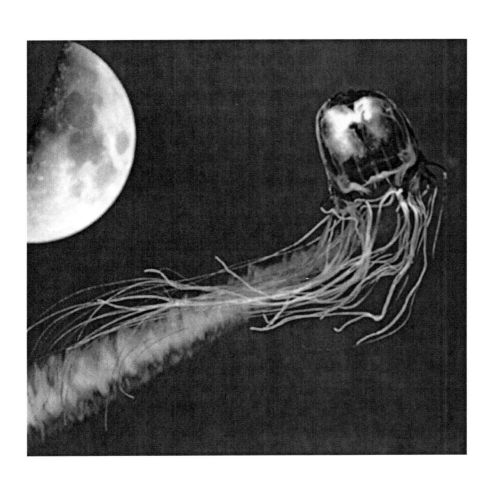

Chapter 33.

With a heroic final heave and a shriek of tortured metal, the door of the trailer finally flew open, coming off its hinges and banging Randall heavily on the knee as it did so. Cindi immediately closed her eyes and turned away, afraid of the tangle of broken parts she might see inside.

'What actually happened?' she said, as Randall hobbled out of the way and sat down nursing his knee. 'Freak wave or something? It felt like white water for a while there.'

'I'll tell you what happened,' said a voice from above. 'Our best guess,' said Bill, landing close to Randall, and causing him to jump out of his skin, 'is that you just experienced a bow wave created by coordinated giant clams in the reef just offshore.'

'Clams?' said Randall, finally summoning up the courage to speak to the bird.

'Giant clams,' said Bill. 'And when I say giant clams, I mean *giant* clams. These things are ten metres wide and can open in an instant. They wait for a naturally high wave and then spring open all at the same time, amplifying the wave enormously and pushing it up onto the shore... You must be RanJam, I'm Bill. Pleased to meet you.' He held out a wing, as if extending a hand to shake.

Randall didn't want to touch the revulsive raven but felt politeness was required in the face of such an ominous mutant freak. He leaned over, nervously holding out his hand.

Bill laughed. 'Just messing with you,' he said, withdrawing the wing. 'The Seer said you'd be scared of us, so I thought I'd try to break the ice a bit. But listen, all joking aside, you're in danger here. There are tribes this side of the mountains who want to see you three dead, and I'm here to make sure they don't succeed.'

The three of them gaped incredulously at the abhorrent avian, the nightmare of claws and feathers that was Bill. The questions were piling up so fast they couldn't sort them out in their heads. Eventually, Marcus regained some control of his vocal cords...

'Bill,' he began, and then, in a lower voice, '... I don't know where to start.' He thought for a while more. "So, you're a talking bird. How fascinating!" didn't really cut it as an opener. He pondered a second longer and began again. 'How did you even know we were coming?' he said, eventually.

Bill looked Marcus in the eye. 'Oh we've known you were coming for hundreds of years,' he said, plainly. 'It's all in the scrolls.'

'Here we go again,' exclaimed Randall, leaning forward and planting his head in his hands with a smack.

'I'll have to tell you on the way,' said Bill. 'You've already survived two attacks and there will be more, believe me. We need to get the other side of the Ragnar Rocks as quickly as we can.'

'Two attacks?' said Cindi.

'The hailstorm,' replied Bill. 'It caught a few of us out actually, we lost some good birds in that storm.' He lowered his gaze to the ground for a moment, remembering Lonán, who was killed in the bombardment.

'But that was a natural event,' said Randall. 'We were just unlucky to be caught in it, that's all.'

'Natural my arse,' said Bill. 'That was a Cloudburster attack. They've somehow managed to include endothermic ice nucleation molecules into their microbial package. Mossad reported to us about it only yesterday. We didn't think they'd be ready so soon, but they've caught us out a couple of times on the way here, and they're going to be even more intent on stopping us on the way back, you mark my words.' He looked on edge; as far as they could tell anyway, they weren't experts on Corvid stress responses or facial expressions.

Randall picked one of the half-dozen or so questions that had queued up in his mind while Bill was speaking. Not the least of which was, 'What does endothermic ice nuclewatsit mean?'

'Mossad?' he said instead. 'Who's Mossad?'

Bill looked around them briefly before answering, he seemed to be looking for something. 'Mossad is a plant that gets everywhere,' he replied, 'it's one of our sneakiest and most pervasive intelligence assets.

You see a green sheen on a rock or a tree? It's Mossad. Got something green growing on your roof? It's Mossad. Find something green in your handkerchief? Mossad - or perhaps not. Ha, geddit? I wouldn't be surprised if it's got spores in your box-on-wheels thing already. All they need is moisture to begin multiplying.'

Now Bill flapped his mighty wings a couple of times and hopped up onto the top of the Batmobile; having to look up at the humans was giving him a crick in the neck, and it wasn't a strong position to be in from a psychological perspective. With another brief ear-rattling screech of talons on glass he perched on the roof, closer to eye level with them, still cocking his head oddly this way and that, seemingly searching for something.

'Any more irrelevant questions?' he said. 'Or can we go before they launch another attack? I'll be alright either way, I can just fly off again, but if you want to die in some horribly ingenious and unexpected fashion while we debate the topology of our navels, then be my guests.' He blinked his oddly malevolent eyes at them a couple of times before flexing his wings to their fullest extent, well over a metre wide, while twisting his right wing and folding it in a complicated way.

'Just giving a couple of wing commands to my squadron,' he said. 'I'm telling them to look for a temporary stopover nearby so you can repair your box. Shall we go? Now?'

An hour or more later, after a slow and bumpy ride across the rough ground near the coast, they came upon some flatter grassland and put on some pace.

Bill was surprised by the speeds they eventually reached over the grassland. He didn't know about the visitors' strange metal machines until he saw them for the first time, the Seer had said nothing about them, and he was pleased they were travelling much faster than expected. At this rate they would be back at the Happy Valley in a day or so, rather than the four or five he'd been expecting.

The Red Sparrows found a suitably sheltered spot under a small overhanging cliff by a pleasant little river, and a short while later they pulled up and stopped the engine. Odd looking plants lined the river bank, some of them turning to observe the visitors as they set up their temporary camp.

'Don't drink the water,' said Bill, as they disgorged from the Batmobile, 'not till you've filtered and boiled it. This river starts in the Ragnar Rocks and it'll be full of specially evolved parasites and whatnot. They won't have ignored that possibility to kill you.' He landed on a low branch and stared around the little clearing, hopping along the branch so he could change the angle. He was definitely still looking for something.

'Right!' said Cindi, who'd had enough of being told what to do by a bird, no matter how eldritch. 'We need some answers before we do anything else. Firstly, what the holy fuck is going on? Who are you? How did you know we were coming? How do you know our names? Who is trying to kill us and why? What the hell is a Cloudburster? What fucking scrolls? Who's this Seer person? ... What have I missed out? Oh yes, what are you looking for all the time?'

Corvids don't have as many short-term memory registers as humans, even mutant Corvids of the species Corvus Sapiens, so Bill only remembered the last question.

'What am I looking for?' he replied. 'Nothing really. Or no one, rather. Well, according to the Seer, who you'll meet in a day or two because that's where I'm taking you, there should be "Thrice one plus one more. Two of one, and one of another, and one unseen". Now, the Elders don't quite know what that means, although privately the Seer says two men and a woman, so that's you three. But he's been rather quiet about the whole "one unseen" business. I was wondering if you had an invisible man with you if you must know, but we have no idea to be honest.'

'Oh... er... I think I do,' said Cindi.

Chapter 34.

George James Junior watched. That being all he could do anyway.

The "present" he needed to be in was still a week away, and he nervously waited for it to catch up with him. He'd seen this moment in time before, but he kept coming back to it like a favourite film. It was a special moment that made him smile from ear-to-ear.

Or would have done if he had a mouth. Or ears.

The plan had arrived in his mind almost without thinking, it was obvious what he needed to do. After studying the alien memories he'd somehow downloaded inside the Moon, it became more than obvious.

He had to save his son. And now his grandchild too.

And the rest of humanity, of course...

Chapter 35.

Randall and Marcus were in shock.

'How long have you known?' asked Randall. He was sitting on the grass in front of Cindi, gently holding both of her hands. A confused blend of happiness and futility was his predominant emotion.

'I started getting the morning sickness about a week ago,' said Cindi, 'but I knew a few days before that. I just felt different somehow.'

There was an uncomfortably muted feeling amongst them, and they didn't quite know where to put themselves, or what to say to Cindi. They all knew the baby would never be born, the timeline would be erased in less than five days from now, and the knowledge of that fact weighed heavily in their thoughts.

Bill was sitting in his tree wishing he'd paid more attention to the Forest Council's endless talks on scroll-lore. His scanty knowledge was inadequate, but as far as he could remember, the scrolls indicated that the fourth visitor would become apparent on the "Day of Change", and that seemed unlikely if Cindi had only just become pregnant. His knowledge of the human gestation period would fit comfortably inside the snail shell he'd just finished emptying, but he was clever enough to figure out it would probably take longer than a week. He decided not to share his confusion with them, however; he was their guide, he needed to at least appear to know what he was talking about...

'Well that explains it,' he exclaimed, during one of the long pauses when they couldn't think of anything to say to each other. 'The "one unseen" is an unborn child. Makes sense I suppose. Now, can we get on with the repairs please? It is quite important I get you three... sorry, four, to safety as quickly as possible.'

As they repaired the trailer, which needed re-seating on its chassis, bundling together with straps, and holding-in-place with wishful thinking, Big Bill answered more of their questions.

The scrolls were written, he said, by a certain Dr. Murray, the lead scientist of the original genetics team that had set up the base on the island five hundred years ago.

After four years of successful work there was an accident in her lab, and they were infected with mutant fungal spores that had put them all in a permanent hallucinatory state; similar to that experienced by shamanic travellers. They were happy enough for a few hours as they explored the visionary vista, but later on, when they realised the effects were not only not wearing off, but actually getting *stronger*, they lost all sense of reality, and came down with a serious case of the divinities.

The problems started when two of the Jesus's got into a blazing row over the nature of their questionable parentage. The schism went on all afternoon, and culminated in them throwing buns and screaming heresies at each other from their separate camps on either side of the lab.

By dusk, Buddha had had enough, and applied a rather unusual interpretation of the concept of "detachment" to an unwary Messiah's head. When Shiva smote him with a hefty punch in the throat a few moments later, all hell broke loose. Thor did a bit of righteous avenging against the Jehovahs thanks to a large hammer he found in the basement, but was cleft in twain - or possibly rent asunder - soon afterwards by a particularly fundamentalist Jesus who'd raided the kitchen and finally found the fabled "Cleaver of Destiny" on the draining board.

Gaia was doused in oil and set alight just five minutes before midnight. Then the Mohammeds got involved...

To cut a long story short, in stark contrast to a lot of ancient books based on similar stories, Murray, in her guise as Mother Earth, eventually won the theological debate. She wrote the scrolls two days later... after she'd cleaned up all the body parts.

They predicted the rise of the trees, the endless wars between the different factions, the mutation that would create the Happy Valley and its inhabitants, the end of days, and the arrival of the unhappy visitors that would herald them. Amongst many other things.

'This could be further proof of time-travel,' said Randall, finally

232

tightening the last strap. 'Could it be that's how he knew what the future would hold? It might be some sort of slippage. What say you, Marcus?'

'Considering we're about to create a wormhole that will force a tunnel through time, suck our atoms into a tachyon vortex, and spit us out at the opposite pole of the vector matrix six hundred years in the past, I'd say anything is possible. The ripples in time created by our journey could well transmit a signal back through the matrix and cause just this sort of occurrence, remarkable as that seems.'

'Isn't that a good sign we're going to succeed?' asked Randall, sitting down on the grass and wiping the sweat from his brow. 'If we don't actually manage to complete the mission then the ripples in time won't happen and the scrolls will never be written. The fact the scrolls even exist is proof we actually will travel through time. Isn't it?'

'If the ripple theory is correct of course,' said Marcus, 'there could be other possible mechanisms at play, as your sexessfull, sorry, I meant successful, thought transference sexperiments in the tanks proved.'

Cindi joined Randall on the grass, grinning at the wordplay. 'But how could she see the future? She was hallucinating wasn't she? She wasn't actually psychic.'

A strange look inhabited Randall's face for a moment. 'Ouch,' he said. After a second or two he looked down. The strange expression on his face evolved into a portrait of utter confusion. With a visible effort he tried to speak again. 'Stunnnnng...' he said. Then his eyes crossed, a confused half smile appeared on his face, and then, still maintaining the sitting position, he keeled over backwards with a thud, kicking up a small cloud of dust as he did so.

'Get off the ground now!' shouted Bill, urgently.

As they ran into the back of the trailer Bill threw himself into the air, cawing loudly. Within seconds he was joined by a dozen birds of different species. They perched or hovered as best they could, all studying the ground intently, until one of them, a large falcon of some sort, screeched loudly and dived at a patch of ground near the fallen Randall. There was a brief struggle for a few heart stopping moments until the falcon grabbed the snake behind its head and bit down hard. The writhing, coiling, serpent flopped limply to the ground with a really bad case of reptile dysfunction.

'Quickly. Get him into the trailer. There could be more of them,' shouted Bill as he settled on the top of the Batmobile.

Randall burbled quietly through the foam that was spluttering from his mouth as Marcus dragged him quickly over to the trailer and Cindi opened the first aid kit.

'Where was he bitten?' she screamed, as she pulled his trousers off. They studied his legs but couldn't see anything. Then they turned him over...

'Well I'm certainly not sucking the poison out,' said Marcus as they spotted the bite mark. Cindi rummaged through the first aid kit and came up with an epi-pen. 'Good idea or not?' she asked.

Marcus didn't know if it was a good idea or not. Randall was bubbling away on the floor, eyes rolled back in their sockets, lips turning pale. He looked like he was rapidly losing consciousness, but without knowing the type of venom, an injection of epinephrine could just as easily kill him.

Big Bill landed on the step at the back of the trailer. 'You need Night Thistle flowers, Fevermany root, and Dandytiger leaves,' he said, 'bash them up into a paste and rub it on, it'll draw the poison out.'

'Dandytiger?' said Cindi. 'You mean Dandelion, surely?'

'This is the Wastelands, kid. I know what I mean.'

He called out to Peregrine to get the flock on the lookout for the plants they needed. Peregrine, who hadn't eaten for nearly an hour and was happily snacking on snake, ripped a large piece of flesh from the corpse and took to the air.

Bill dragged his gaze from the dead snake; he was hungry too. 'If you've got any clean water, boil it. You're going to make an infusion with half of the leaves and spread the rest on the bite. Fortunately, it was only a small Viperoid, a bite from a bigger snake would have killed him within a few minutes. Keep him as still as you can and keep his heart above the wound. Try to keep his temperature down. If we're lucky, he'll live.'

As it turned out, they were lucky. Although Randall didn't see it that way. It was easy to keep his heart above the bite because he'd been bitten on the buttock, but the next few hours were a feverish agony of nightmare hallucinations for him as he drifted in and out of consciousness in the back of the Batmobile.

The air-conditioning was on full to help keep him cool as the fever took hold, and during his more lucid moments Cindi would attempt to pour some more of Bill's concoction down him, which wasn't easy from the front seat. His less lucid moments were filled with cries of "The jellies! The terrible jellies!", but gradually the flask was emptied into him and he began to revive. His wits slowly returned, and after managing to thank Cindi for looking after him he fell into a deep sleep from which they decided not to rouse him.

With the Red Sparrows circling overhead, they travelled steadily north-east along the flood plain of the river. The ground was comparatively flat and they made good progress towards the edge of the mountain range that they would skirt around before heading directly north to the Happy Valley.

Shortly before sunset they reached the end of the flood plain and the ground started to rise. It was a good place to make camp (Bill and the birds couldn't keep flying in the dark) so they found a good sheltered spot in a gulley and made camp for the night.

Two hours after they turned their lights out, they suddenly found they could see quite well again, because that's when the Fire Ants attacked.

It was a coordinated attack. Fireflies hovered near likely looking targets around the camp, attracting the ants with their internal torches until sufficient numbers had built up. Then, with a single bright flash, the signal was sent, and the ants simply exploded en masse. There were many thousands of them all over the camp, but they were mostly concentrated on the tents.

Cindi was the first to wake up. She screamed loudly, waking just in time to drag the still semi-conscious Randall out of their tent before it collapsed in a sheet of flame.

The noise woke Marcus, who emerged horizontally from his tent, again, just in time. He wriggled out still stuck in his sleeping bag, which had many small fires burning into it. Cindi grabbed a precious bottle of fresh water and ran over to douse him. As she struggled to help him out of the smouldering sleeping bag, the grass around the trailer went up in a fireball and it started spreading under the Batmobile.

As an older man, Marcus was quite used to waking in the night with a full bladder, and, fortunately, tonight was no exception. Getting as close as he dared to the burning trailer, he put it to as much use as he could on the tyres, while Cindi, trying to avoid inhaling the clouds of steam, swatted at the flames with her jacket. Randall wasn't in full control of his limbs yet and couldn't help much, but he managed to roll around a bit in his sleeping bag, putting a few of the smaller fires out.

'I think we need to keep going through the night,' said Cindi, as the flames died down. 'Bill says we need to get to the other side of the mountains, we could do that in another three hours maybe. The birds will be able to follow our tracks and join us again in the morning. Yes?'

'Yes,' said Marcus and Randall simultaneously.

They drew an arrow of tent ash on the ground, just to be sure, and drove off into the night.

By the first pre-light of dawn, when the sky turned from deepest black to a very slightly lighter black, verging on dark blue, they decided they'd put enough distance between themselves and the mountains, which were now about five miles behind them, and they made camp again to allow their ghastly guide and his incredible avian escorts to catch up. Bill said they would be safer beyond the mountains, so they lit a small fire which would be easily seen from above, and they settled down to wait.

Randall was recovering. The bite on his backside was very sore, and he was still woozy from the snake venom, but he managed to sit up and drink another cup of Bill's brew unaided. It tasted awful, but before long he was almost himself again, and even managed to ease the pain slightly with a few of his newly found meditation skills. The delusory images of marauding jellies suffocating him were quietly locked in a mental cellar, but they were still trying to ooze under the imaginary door.

Marcus was sitting in the driver's seat of the Batmobile checking the on-board systems for damage. Apart from a few external scorch marks from exploding ants, and some minor damage to the underside from the occasional hidden rock as they fled from them, they were doing okay. Now he checked the electronic systems, the radar, the lidar, even firing a blast from the laser, just to be on the safe side. Then he checked the radio...

'Quick,' he shouted, 'over here. Listen to this.'

Through the speakers could be heard the unmistakable sounds of military chatter.

Unfortunately, they were getting a crystal clear reception.

Chapter 36.

Constable "Spikey" Sharp thought of himself as a conscientious citizen, and a good cop. He wasn't corrupt. Much. Okay, maybe the occasional spot of light embezzlement, perhaps a smidgeon of extortion now and again, but it was nothing any other cop wouldn't do, nothing that would reflect badly on the honour of the WP if he got caught. He was a loyal family man, a loving father, and a damn good officer. His wife had told him so, so it must be true. Being handpicked by old Savage to be part of this mission to the Wastelands was the highlight of his career so far, and he was determined not to fuck it up. There could even be a promotion to sergeant if he was lucky.

That'd please the wife.

If he didn't fuck it up.

With the WP beachhead in the north of the island now set up, the search had begun for signs of the resistance base that Savage was now convinced was there somewhere. They'd started spreading out along the north coast before dawn, and with Savage taking point position in the middle of the line, they headed steadily south; fifteen heavy transports and thirty men flying a hundred drones spread over nearly two hundred and fifty miles of inadequately mapped and very dangerous territory.

Driving along at the far right flank of the WP line, Spikey Sharp was squeezed up against the shore of a big lagoon; weaving his way through the huge geysers that surrounded him. Staring at the erupting jets of mud through the window of the transport, he drove the truck, while his companion, Constable "Narky" Parker, watched the feeds from the drones.

As he swerved out of the way of the latest jet of boiling mud - not fast enough, again - he turned on the wipers for about the dozenth time. But this time they didn't seem to work, there was something blocking them. He fiddled with the wiper controls, but nothing was happening, even the water spray was seemingly clogged up. Spikey thought of himself as a brave man, but he also considered himself not to be a moron. Going outside to fix them with gallons of stinky boiling mud raining down on him was stretching bravery beyond the point where it became suicidal stupidity.

He sat in the driver's seat staring at the blockage on the windscreen wipers. What was that? A creature? Some sort of snail? A limpet perhaps?

He drove blind, guided through the geyser fields by the drone feeds until he could get out and clear the strange animals off. Another burst of slimy mud showered them. All of a sudden there were now dozens of the little snail-like creatures covering the windscreen. He looked closer at their little bodies sliding down the glass. He could see the teeth of the strange animals actually scratching the glass as they tried to gain purchase on it. Indeed, some had already succeeded. They looked like they were trying to burrow through, chewing through the glass.

As the first holes appeared in the roof, he realised he was in trouble. When the drops of acid started dissolving Narky Parker, he switched on the radio to call for help…

Bailey wasn't feeling very well. He was tired, he was hungry, and driving the heavy transport across the rough ground was hard work; made even harder by Commissioner Savage barking commands at him from the passenger seat every few seconds. Savage was only three feet away from him, why did he have to shout all the time? It was making Bailey ever more determined to kill him at the first available opportunity.

He was, in fact, tentatively considering the one that had just opened up to him. Savage was sitting with his eyes closed looking at his terminal, studying the footage from the half dozen drones he was in control of. Bailey could probably catch him unawares, but he would have to make the first blow count, or he would be dead the next second.

Deciding against it, he glumly continued driving and staring blankly ahead of him, his eye twitching alarmingly. Savage was a big man, and Bailey doubted he would be able to knock him out with the first punch, especially in the confined area of the cab. He needed a weapon. Better chances than this would arrive soon enough. He still had some self-control left.

'Stop here,' screamed Savage.

Bailey stopped the vehicle. With all the signs of infinite patience he waited for the next bellowed command.

'I need a shit,' roared Savage, again completely unnecessarily. He opened the door, squeezed out of the cab and waddled off behind a nearby bush, thankfully downwind from the transport.

Could he drive away? Would he get far enough before Savage blinked his pain receptors into life? Doubtful, his terminal range was about five hundred metres; he wouldn't even travel fifty before he was disabled by the convulsions. He might be able to rig the accelerator pedal with something, but Savage could probably even disable the vehicle from his terminal, now he came to think about it. He slumped in his seat, looking for anything he could use as a weapon. The back of the transport was full of weapons, of course, but only Savage's eye would pass the retinal scan to open the rear door, he couldn't get access to them.

There was nothing useful in the cab, not even a pen he could use to stab him in the face with. A sharp stick would do if he could get hold of one the next time he was out of the cab, or a sharp stone, or a handful of grit, anything to give him an advantage. He'd have to be careful not to damage both eyes though...

As Savage strained away behind the bush, Bailey stretched his aching limbs and silently but fervently wished for a sudden embolism to strike him down where he squatted.

Then the radio sprang into life. It sounded like one of the crews was in trouble.

Savage poked his head up from behind the bush he was squatting by. 'Idiots!' he screamed, quickly grabbing a handful of leaves and inadequately wiping himself. Pulling up his trousers as he went, he wobbled back towards the truck and squashed himself back into the cab with an expression of fury coming from his face, and an ungodly stink coming from his trousers.

'Maintain radio silence!' he shouted back into the microphone.

'We're dying here,' came the frenzied response.

'Well die quietly,' shouted Savage.

Chapter 37.

'Help us! Aaarrrgh shit… my eyes… aaarrrgh,' screamed the quadrophonic speakers of the Batmobile.

The three of them sat there looking like they were competing in a "Who can look the most concerned" contest, as they listened to the desperate cries for help coming from the WP officers.

Mostly, the concern was for the fact they were now sure the WP were on the island too, which meant they were in trouble, but they still couldn't help feeling for the two men slowly being melted by acid dripping through the roof of their truck. It was hard not to.

'Switch it off please,' cried Cindi, 'I don't want to listen to men dying. We need to figure out what we're going to do.' She sounded upset.

Marcus turned the radio down, but not off. He spoke over it. 'The signal is coming from the north-west I think. I can't tell the range but it sounds like these poor guys are in the geyser field, which means they're still near the coast, probably three or four days away at the speeds they're likely to be travelling. When we camped last night Bill told me we'd reach the valley by the end of today, and we've already travelled part of that since the ant attack, so we can safely say, assuming there are no more problems, that we'll be there before the WP sweep reaches that far down the island. We'll have to make sure we're well hidden from their drones when we get there, that's all we can do for now.'

They looked at him blankly. 'Go. Sit by the fire,' he said. 'I'll monitor their comms.'

They walked off, hand in hand. Hesitantly hopeful.

Shortly afterwards the comms went dead. As did the men broadcasting them.

'We might be able to help you there,' said Big Bill, when Marcus relayed the story to him an hour or so later. 'If I get this in the mesh now, the trees of the northern tribes will know about it by tomorrow morning. They should be able to come up with something to slow them down a bit at least. Whether they can be slowed down enough to stop them finding you before the Day of Change is the question.'

Bill's birds circled overhead, on the lookout for trouble. They weren't far enough from the Ragnar Rocks yet and they were still uneasy, they could still be vulnerable to a sneak attack even here.

'Get moving, folks,' he said. 'The sooner we get you to the Seer the better. Keep heading north. I need to go talk to a tree. I'll catch up with you.' He took off with a loud and oddly complicated caw.

They made good progress for the next hour before Bill caught up with them again. Randall was feeling better, dozing in the passenger seat while Cindi slept in the back. Marcus was exhausted (as he knew he would be, being the only one capable of driving the Batmobile) so he'd taken the precaution of packing a few mild pick-me-up tablets in the first aid kit. Having just taken his second pill he was tired and wired, but wide awake.

Bill landed in front of them. It was the signal for them to stop. He pointed with his wing to indicate the shade of a big tree, which half a dozen other birds had already landed in. Marcus stopped the car a few yards from its branches. Stretching his limbs and trying not to clamp his jaw muscles quite so much, he woke the others. They stepped out of the car and stretched.

'Folks,' said Bill, 'I'd like you to meet... er, sorry, what was your name again?'

The tree's name was Aeld, and he was an Elder.

'You can call me Al,' he said. His voice was tremulous, nervous, like this was a big moment for him.

Bill made the introductions formal. 'Al, The Harbingers. Harbingers, Al,' he said.

Incredulousness and caution were their immediate reactions. A talking bird was one thing; Corvids had been known to imitate human speech before, so Bill was still just about within their range of experience. But an actual talking tree? Where was its mouth? Where were its ears? And more importantly, were the stories they'd all heard about the whole "surrender humans" thing true?

'Harbingers?' said Marcus, studying the tree carefully. 'Is that what you call us? Sounds a bit ominous doesn't it? Sounds like the sort of stuff people used to get religious about.'

'And on the day after the last day,' declaimed Al, pompously, less timorous and with more timbre, 'the Harbingers shall end the world in the blink of an eye, for it to be born anew within the blink of another.'

'Scroll two, chapter one, verse six,' said Bill. It was the most famous (and only) quote from the scrolls he could remember. "The day after the last day" had always confused the scrollologists, Bill didn't know what to make of it, but then neither did anyone else.

'For you are the ones who will usher in the change at the end of the world,' said Al, even more pompously. 'Harbingers or heralds, as is your wish, I only know that we must help you. For it is written in the sacred scrolls of old. General Bill has apprised me of your situation and I'm certain our warriors can slow down the heathens for you.'

Marcus relaxed a little and stopped thinking about chainsaws. 'The day after the last day?' he queried. 'What does that mean?'

Al was suddenly less pompous...

'Ah... well... er, we were hoping you could tell us actually. We have no idea to be honest with you. Many learned scrolls have been written on that subject alone, but to be perfectly fair to them I think they're talking a lot of bollocks. There are a few theories, all of them contradictory, and none of which hold any water in my opinion. Hopefully we'll all find out soon enough, only a few days to go, eh?'

'You know the timing too?' asked Marcus, ignoring the fact that the tree, and everybody else except him and Randall would know nothing about it when the time came. Nobody but them would be finding *anything* out.

'At the height of the Moon,' said Al, the pomposity returning, 'five days hence.' If he'd had a face it would have looked away dramatically at this point.

'I must have a look at these scrolls before we travel back,' muttered Marcus.

'The Seer has a copy,' said Bill, 'just don't ask him for specific verse or chapter numbers, he's not very good with numbers.'

Now Al remembered his manners. 'Forgive me,' he said, 'I'm forgetting. Your journey must have been long and tiring. May I offer you some tea?'

Cindi perked up. 'Tea?' she said, puzzled. 'Where from?'

'Elderflower tea,' said Al. 'I'm blooming at the moment and I'd be honoured to be able to refresh you. There's a stream just over there,' - a single branch to the left of them rustled its leaves - 'and the water is pure. Pluck a few flowers from my lower branches, it won't hurt. There's a nettle bush by the water too, I'd recommend adding a few of his leaves if you want to make a really healthy drink. He's a personal friend, I know he won't mind. Pick them with care though.'

'I have gloves,' replied Cindi, already walking towards the babbling stream.

The tea was refreshing, even if it didn't taste anything like the tea they'd got used to on the sub, and it seemed to enliven Randall, who was still feeling tight around the chest due to the after effects of the snake attack. He sipped the tea and found it helped enormously. Before long, he was breathing normally again. He sat on the back step of the trailer talking to Al while Marcus fussed with the straps holding the time machine precariously in place inside the tottering trailer. Cindi refilled their empty water canisters from the stream.

'How far do we still have to travel?' he asked.

'To the Happy Valley? It's about another six hours north of here if I'm to believe Bill about the speeds you can get up to. I'm fascinated by your... what do you call it? Catmobile? I've never seen anything like it before.'

'Batmobile,' corrected Randall, wondering how the tree could see anything in the first place. 'But I have no idea why.'

'It's ingenious. What are the round things called?'

'The wheels you mean? Er, they're called wheels,' said Randall, rather lamely.

'I see,' said the tree, despite all indications to the contrary. 'How do they work? What makes them go round?'

'Ah, well you're talking to the wrong person in fact. Marcus is the man to talk to about specifics. In fact, he's the man to talk to about generalities too. He's the genius. Brainier than a clumsy butcher's shop-floor he is. I'm more sort of along for the ride. This time around anyway.'

'But you're a Harbinger,' said Al, surprised. 'One of the "two who shall prevail". And even *you* don't know what's going to happen? I had so many questions.' Al's outer branches drooped in a disappointed way.

'Sorry, but I've never harbinged before. I was rather plunged in at the deep end with all this. I haven't taken lessons in harbinging you know, they don't provide classes. All I know is that if we fail it will be much worse for everyone than if we succeed. In fact, there won't actually be anyone left if we fail. Or even a planet for anyone to exist on.'

'Or a galaxy for the planet to exist in,' said Marcus, jumping down from the back of the trailer, which was still just about in one piece despite the fires and the battering it had taken.

'That would explain the "death of the stars" verse then,' said Al. 'Scroll two, chapter three, verse nine I think,' he said, looking to Bill for confirmation and not finding it.

'You better hope we can slow the WP down enough,' said Bill, 'or there'll be no experts on anything anymore. Thingies crossed, eh?'

'You mean fingers,' said Randall.

Bill looked up at him. 'You still haven't got the hang of this place have you, kid?' he said.

Chapter 38.

It was dusk when they finally arrived, exhausted, at the Happy Valley.

They did have to stop once on the way, but detailing exactly how they nearly crashed when the front tyre burst, and precisely how long it took them to dig out the spare, which was, of course, packed in the most inaccessible place possible below a hatch under the time machine itself, and how they had to practically rebuild the whole rickety structure with straps and tape afterwards, and exactly which fingernail Randall broke... would bog you down with unnecessary details. Tales of tyre changing are seldom entertaining; the three of them certainly weren't entertained by the experience. Bruised yes, a little bloodied perhaps, certainly fed up, but not entertained. Needless to say, they weren't in the greatest of moods when they finally arrived at the border of the mysterious valley.

Unhappy visitors indeed.

Bill's face, in common with all Corvids, wasn't made for expression (unless the expression you were looking for was "Get ready to die") but as they rounded the crest of the last hill they could already see the change in his bearing. His beak hadn't changed, it still looked like something designed by a psychopath for digging eyeballs out of their sockets, but now it almost seemed to be smiling somehow.

'Nest sweet nest,' he cawed.

With one last nerve jangling screech of talons, he took off from his roost on top of the Batmobile and flew across the field to a large tree in the corner. 'Just keep going to the other end of the field,' he shouted as he started picking leaves out of his home. 'I expect the Seer will be waiting for you. I'll drop by later.'

He cawed the caw of a very happy raven as the Batmobile completed the last five hundred yards (or metres, depending on who you asked) of their journey, and pulled up in front of an excited looking welcoming committee. Who all seemed to be very happy... people?

People shaped, anyway.

It was like a scene from a comic book. The small group of "people" stood there cheering and laughing as the three of them sat in the car watching on the screens.

They were all sorts of colours, every skin tone on the planet and a few others besides. Pale blue was a new one, as was the almost purplish tinge to a couple at the back of the crowd. Strange animals [32] wandered around and between them, others were perched on their shoulders. Pets perhaps? If anything, they looked even weirder than the people. A crab-like animal walked past balancing a dirty clay bowl on its shell. It had a wooden spoon in it.

Marcus zoomed in on the more-or-less people-shaped members of the group a little more and panned the camera. 'Has that man got three eyes?' he said, hardly believing his own words, even as he spoke them.

'And this one has a lot more fingers than you'd normally expect to find on someone her age,' said Randall. 'I hope they're fingers anyway, they could be tentacles for all I know. What are they? Are they human?'

Marcus studied the screen more closely for a few moments. 'Mostly,' he said.

'At least they look pleased to see us,' said Cindi. 'That makes a change. That one's even waving a flag with your name on it RanJam. Look.'

'What is that stuff coming from this one's head?' asked Randall,

---

[32] Mostly Cogs, a cross between a male cat and a female dog. The result is a beautiful and superbly elegant animal that is always clean, fiercely loyal, brave, amazingly intelligent, an efficient pest *and* burglar deterrent, independent, feeds itself, lets itself in and out, fetches your slippers for you - and then curls up lightly on your lap at the end of the day, pulling irresistibly funny faces and purring like a vibro-massage bed.

Dats, on the other hand...

feeling embarrassed at the semi-nakedness of his new fan. He pointed at what appeared to be the leader of the group. 'It looks like he's got a head full of snakes or something.'

'I think it might be his hair,' replied Marcus.

'He's walking towards us,' said Randall, in a sudden panic. 'What do we do?'

'We get out of the car I suppose. What else can we do?'

As Marcus opened his door, the one with the hair stopped, ten feet in front of the car, and bowed. He held a six-foot staff in one hand, a rolled up piece of parchment in the other, and a long pipe clenched between his teeth. Sitting down on the grass, he un-rolled the parchment and lay his staff across the top to stop it rolling back up again. The other end he gripped with his toes. Well, probably toes, the grass was covering them from view... the frayed bits at the ends of his feet anyway.

'Humble greetings, Markynanda,' said the man, through a cloud of sweet smelling pipe smoke.

'The Seer, I presume,' said Marcus, sitting down in front of him.

The Seer nodded and moved his finger down one line on the scroll. He took a pull on his pipe. 'You need to sleep,' he replied, calmly.

'I had a feeling you'd know that.'

'Arrangements have been made for the three of you. You are hungry also. There is food and wine ready for you in your hut.'

Randall and Cindi joined Marcus on the grass.

'You knew what time we'd get here with enough certainty to have a meal ready for us? How?' asked Cindi.

'I dream,' answered the Seer, simply. His finger moved down the parchment one more line.

'You dream of the future?'

'I dream of many things, picking out the important ones is the trick. Please, your meals are getting cold. This is the time you eat. You are all hungry now. But first...'

The Seer stopped talking and just sat there; one finger on the scroll and another held in the air, squinting at the sky enigmatically and puffing on his pipe. Suddenly, there was a strangely emphatic sighing noise, followed by an ominous sliding screech, a hideous crunching sound, a resounding tattoo of bangs, and a series of very loud twangs, all coming from the trailer behind them; the sides of which now collapsed outwards with a slow and terrible inexorability. The roof was still miraculously attached on one side. As it fell it folded down into itself and missed the time machine by inches (or possibly centimetres) crashing down on top of the other shattered debris in a shower of broken splinters.

The axle then snapped with a deafening crack and one of the wheels popped off the end of it, rolling across the grass and coming to rest, with the inevitable and characteristic little circular wobble of wheels coming to rest, by Randall's feet. As the commotion ceased, the sudden calm was punctuated by a little tinkling noise. Also inevitable, apparently.

The time machine sat on the base of the trailer, miraculously unharmed in the middle of a cloud of settling dust. The acolytes cheered ecstatically.

'... the Unveiling!' announced the Seer over the cheering, finally rolling up the scroll and standing up happily. 'Come. Eat. Sleep.'

They were too hungry, and too tired, to disobey.

They ate a tasty stew when they got to their tiny hut a minute or so later. It was a vegetable stew. With mushrooms. The wine had a faintly fungal aftertaste too.

And the smell coming from the candles was very relaxing indeed...

By the time they'd finished the meal, their eyelids were already drooping.

Wibbly wobbly, wibbly wobbly, wibbly wobbly, wibbly wobbly...

Randall found himself near a lake on a dark plain fringed by distant mountains. The sky was *weird*. Far too many stars for one thing. And should they be swirling around like that? He didn't think so, but it was pretty to look at anyway. He stared at them unthinkingly for a few seconds before shifting his attention to the ground. It was very pretty too, lovely greens and purples and yellows. And that was just the rocks, the flowers that grew in-between them were all sorts of incredible colours that he couldn't even identify. He stared at them. He couldn't make out the shapes very well either, they seemed to be undulating or phasing or something, and seeing as it was night-time he was surprised he could see any colours at all. Were they lit from the inside or something?

It was a fantastical, idyllic scene. Paradise at night.

… which was suddenly shattered by Cindi, who appeared through the mist only a short way ahead of him on the shore of the lake, apparently beating something to death with a shovel. As the dying cries of the strange animal hit his ears, the feeling of being in paradise quickly faded. He called out and walked towards her.

'Cindi. What *are* you doing?'

'Making supper,' she shouted back. 'This is a young one. Come on, help me get it back to camp.' She didn't look right. Her hair was longer…

Just then, everything went black. All sound ceased and Randall was left floating in an endless void; nothingness surrounding him on all sides. All sensation stopped. Darkness prevailed. It seemed thick; bulbous and undulating somehow. Strangely, he wasn't bothered by it.

'I'm sorry, RanJam,' came a voice from nowhere, or possibly everywhere, it was hard for Randall to tell. 'That was not meant for you. You will forget. Your experience is over here… look…'

As suddenly as the blackness had descended, it lifted again to reveal a different scene entirely. Randall was strangely unmoved by the universe changing around him all the time, it seemed quite normal, even expected somehow. He surveyed his surroundings dispassionately.

The new scene was of the pleasant field next to the village, at night-time under a bright full moon, with the time machine all set up and ready to go in the middle of it. The moonlight gleamed off its metal frame as the steam rising from the cooling pins of the transceiver created see-through spectres in the sky.

Marcus sat in the pod fiddling with switches while Cindi stood amongst the acolytes by the machine. She was crying her eyes out. As Randall felt the wave of compassion wash over him, he found himself, without apparently moving in any way, suddenly strapped into the pod next to Marcus. Again, the change didn't bother him.

A countdown was ticking away on the overhead screen. Twenty-two seconds to launch. He tightened his straps and held on to his seat with increasingly whitening knuckles while staring longingly at Cindi, the love of his short life and mother of his unborn child, trying, and failing, to hold back the tears. He held out a hand to her, but she was out of reach.

The numbers on the countdown readout blurred. Now there were only seven seconds to go.

'Are you ready?' asked Marcus.

The universe swapping and changing around him wasn't a problem, but being hurled six hundred years into the past *definitely was*. The fear began to overwhelm him. He began to panic.

'No,' he replied, terrified. 'I'm not.'

'Me neither. Let's go.'

Marcus pulled a lever set in the floor of the pod - the safety release mechanism. With a clunk the clamps opened. The pod jolted forward and settled with a thankfully quick creak on the runners of the ramp leading to the transceiver.

He counted down along to the readout. 'Three... two... one...'

The computer ignited the rocket engine in the back of the pod and they shot forward abruptly, the acceleration pinning their heads to their seats. As they rumbled along the track, the glowing chrono-matrix field around the transceiver quickly went from red, to orange, yellow, green, blue, indigo, ultra-violet...

... the acceleration seemed to die away... the scenery blurred and morphed around them... light drained out of the world... slowly shifting to the red as the wavelengths stretched, then fading quickly through the shades of night until only the faintest glimmer could be seen... it started to get warmer...

'I was expecting this,' said Marcus. 'The chrono-field is sucking our inertia and forward momentum out of the system. Light is in the infrared range now. Time has slowed for us already. This should be a smoother ride than we thought...'

...and then the whole scene suddenly went totally black again.

'Enough,' said a voice.

Randall was the first to wake up. For a change.

It was probably the sweat that did it, either that or the bull-elephant-wallowing-in-a-swamp snoring coming from Marcus. He was soaked. And he felt bloody awful.

Or did he?

His body certainly did. It ached like he'd just *walked* halfway around the world. His eyes were tiny pinholes glued shut by eye-snot, his mouth was drier than a desert based blowtorch, and he itched all over. Even his hair itched. His skin felt like it had been stretched out as far as it would go and then snapped back into place. His joints were stiff, and his jaw felt like it had just spent the night chewing through the bedpost. But those were just the superficial symptoms. The inside of his head felt rather different.

It was as if his mind had had the decorators in while he was sleeping. It was almost shiny in there; subtly improved in a dozen different ways. His thoughts flowed much more easily through his awareness; as if his brain had been swept, polished, and had a lifetime's worth of clutter removed. Connections between distant thoughts he'd never combined before sparked across his cerebrum in a cascade of sudden epiphanies and realisations. His own psychology was now an open book. He started reading it...

When Cindi screamed and shot bolt upright a few minutes later, he surmised, correctly, that she had just experienced something similar. Marcus was still snoring the snore of the deeply - and deeply resonant - unconscious.

'I dreamed about the time machine,' she said. 'You and Marcus were shooting down the delivery ramp towards the transceiver. But then there was this voice...'

There was a voice coming from outside the hut. It said, 'Good morning.'

'That voice?' enquired Randall.

'That voice,' said Cindi.

The voice was coming from beyond the flap of hide that constituted the door of their makeshift hut, and it belonged to the Seer. He swept the hide aside and walked into the dark interior of the dwelling. Cindi and Randall covered their eyes from the sudden intrusion of light.

'Please,' he said, 'come outside. The Sun is up and it's a lovely day. You'll feel much better after breakfast. The after effects of the stew and wine will wear off soon. You would like some water.' It wasn't a question, merely a statement of fact.

Despite the brightness, they almost lunged at the jug of water. Cindi emptied her clay mug of the remnant of last night's wine and held it out to be filled. Randall was only a second behind her. They guzzled it down greedily.

Breakfast was a simple omelette, toast, and a mug of milk. No mushrooms. They tore into it. It was, if possible, even tastier than the breakfasts they'd got used to at Marcus's hidden bunker (but could have done with a couple of rashers of bacon and a bit of ketchup, thought Randall). Within a few short minutes, their plates were empty. The Seer was already cooking another.

Marcus, right on cue, emerged from the hut. 'I smell toast and eggs,' he exclaimed, brightly. 'Is that milk? I could kill a mug of milk.' He joined them at the little table, beaming a bright smile all around. He didn't seem to be feeling any of the ill effects Randall and Cindi were only just beginning to recover from.

'You two look like you've been through the wringer,' he said, sitting down and looking at their haggard and still droopy faces. 'Good dream though wasn't it?'

'You had it too?' asked Cindi. 'How is that possible? And why don't you feel as awful as we do?'

'Not my first trip,' said Marcus. 'It's been a few years, and this was stronger than I'm used to of course, but I felt the initial effects within about ten minutes, so I knew what to expect. Don't worry, I feel rough too, but I'm a bit more used to it than you two, and my kidneys are probably still healthier than yours.'

'But how did we all have the same dream?' asked Randall.

'Haven't you figured it out yet?' replied Marcus. 'I think it's a similar effect to the kind of experience you and Cindi had in the tanks. Our minds were in some sort of resonance due to the effects of the mushrooms. I think Mr. Seer here took some too, and was able to interfere with our dreamscape. Am I getting warm, Mr. Seer?'

The Seer nodded, smiled, tapped his nose, and pointed at Marcus. They looked at him blankly. Some seconds passed.

'Yes,' he said, eventually. 'It is quicker for me to mingle with your minds than your words. This way was... gentler than others, and I learned all I needed to know about you. We are bonded now, as the scrolls said we would be.' His eye twinkled oddly, like a diamond sparkling in the light of a distant supernova.

255

'I'd like to take a look at these scrolls of yours if that's okay?' said Marcus, between mouthfuls of omelette.

'I am sorry, Markynanda, that I cannot do.'

'But why? They're about us aren't they?'

'Parts of them yes,' he replied, 'and that is precisely why I cannot allow you to see them. You would then know your own futures. Knowing what actions you will take might cause you to alter them. That cannot happen.'

'But we saw the future last night,' said Cindi, 'didn't we? In the dream?'

The moment the Seer had been long dreading had finally come. This was the moment, decreed by the scrolls - scroll two, chapter something or other, verse more than three, somewhere near the end anyway - when he had to lie to them.

'Mostly only your expectations of it,' he lied. 'Your fears, your hopes, the expression of your anticipation, your anxieties...' He looked away mysteriously for a moment before changing the subject.

'We have work to do,' he said, in a strangely commanding voice. 'General Bill has informed me of the invaders. We must get your machines under cover before they are spotted.'

'Don't the scrolls mention the WP?' asked Marcus.

'No... they do not,' came the emphatic reply.

This stirred them into action.

Actually, the Seer stirred them into action through a subtle manipulation of the psychic bond he'd formed with them in the dream, but they didn't know that yet.

'First I'll check the radio again,' said Marcus, finishing his meal, 'see where the WP are up to.'

Certain curious crab creatures cheerfully commenced ceramic crockery cleansing...

Chapter 39.

The WP were up to their necks in it.

Already this morning Savage had lost six vehicles, twenty odd drones, his voice, his wits… oh, and a dozen men.

His voice had gone because of all the furious shouting he'd been doing; into the microphone at the dying men calling for help; in exasperation at the general state of their mission, which was falling apart by the hour; and at Bailey of course. Always at Bailey.

But it didn't seem to be the resistance taking them out so effectively. It appeared as if the island itself was trying to kill them. In a hundred different ways. Drones were attacked by birds, transports disappeared into hidden sink holes, or got sucked into quicksand, or were melted by acid secreting limpety snail things, or suddenly burst into flames for no readily apparent reason - it was ridiculous.

And still there was no sign of the resistance. Savage was even beginning to doubt whether a base could have survived here on this malignant island, and that was the thing that was really propelling him up Mount Apoplexy. He was furious, incandescent even, but he was damned if he was going to give up until the island had been thoroughly searched.

The radio sparked into life again. Another crew in trouble, something about prehensile vines growing up through the car and clogging the engine, and eventually, its occupants. The veins on Savage's head and neck began to stick out like fire hoses under pressure as he listened to them die… but he couldn't shout anymore, his throat was raw. Not that it mattered much anymore, radio silence had been broken so many times that the resistance must be laughing at them by now. Savage literally fumed, the stench of his sweat was unbearable.

They drove on in silence, Savage now giving instructions in whispers or by terminal messages. He was studying drone feeds with his eyes closed again, as they drove through the increasingly hilly terrain. Rounding the top of the small rise they had been driving up, Bailey spotted the trap waiting for them. Savage, did not.

It was a small depression in the ground. Maybe five metres deep by a hundred across, like a sort of shallow crater. Innocuous looking, quite pleasant actually in the morning light, but the misty fumes collecting at the bottom of it were just about visible as the rays of the low Sun illuminated them.

It shimmered like a heat haze, but Bailey knew it wasn't. He could see the faintly steamy gas being exuded by the strange looking plants growing in the bottom of the depression. It was obviously heavier than air. There was a very faint smell of rotten eggs, possibly more agreeable to the nose than Savage's body odour, but not quite enough to overpower it...

The plan formulated instantly in his head. This was it! This was his chance...

He quietly wound his window up...

Aiming the car at some small rocks that would rattle the transport and mask the sound, he began breathing as deeply and as fast as he could...

While he still could...

They were almost upon the invisible fumes, Savage still oblivious to their presence. Bailey took one last deep breath and put on a short burst of speed before putting the truck into neutral gear and letting it roll further down into the crater. As he did so, he opened his door, jumped out, rolled once, and ran as fast as he could back up the slope, hoping that the poison would be fast acting and that his lungs would hold out...

His lungs were bursting as he reached the clearer air. And then the pain came. Savage was obviously still alive in there, and had activated his terminal. Bailey dropped to the ground in agony, twitching and writhing as nerve endings all over his body burst into white hot flame... but at least he was still breathing cleanish air.

It lasted less than ten seconds. His writhing gyrations were digging him a shallow grave in the soft ground, but then, as quickly as it had begun, the pain suddenly died away.

Savage was dead.

Bailey sat up where he had fallen, took a deep breath, raised his arms above his head and shouted emphatically at the sky.

Then he coughed his lungs out for five minutes while climbing out of the crater completely, stood on the rim, and tried it again.

Chapter 40.

The next few days, the final ones leading up to the "Day of Change" as the Seer referred to it, were a bit of a blur for Marcus, Cindi and Randall. It was almost as if they were on automatic pilot most of the time; they didn't do much else except work, eat, meditate, and sleep. Marcus suspected some sort of subtle influence from the Seer, but as they were all working towards the same goal, and doing so quickly and efficiently, he didn't mind, and said nothing.

With the help of the acolytes, they buried the remains of the trailer and covered the time machine with a very well-constructed shelter made out of leaves and branches, on the first day. On the next, they fitted the telescopic ramp leading to the transceiver section, and tested the electronics of the pod one last time. On the third day they placed the pod in position at the end of the ramp, and using the Batmobile's powerful engine as a generator, they charged up the batteries.

Now, at sunset on the fourth day, as the motor chugged through the last gallon of their fuel, they sat around outside their hut trying to calm their nerves. The Seer, meditating outside his own hut, was helping. In his own way.

The acolytes, at the Seer's insistence, had left them pretty much alone other than when manual labour was required, which they were remarkably adept at, Marcus couldn't help noticing. Even their cute little pets helped by fetching tools and whatnot, but now, with a few hours to go, they were peering out of their huts and chattering amongst themselves excitedly.

The full Moon rose over the mountains behind them as they sat watching the spectacular sunset. Only six more hours to go before it would be directly overhead and the time to leave would finally be upon them. Pre-ordained not only by the moment their counterparts from the vanished timeline had left, but written in the scrolls too (which Marcus still hadn't managed to get a peek at).

They ate their last meal, which actually contained some meat, Randall was surprised to find, and they sat around talking about the past while the last rays of the Sun faded to night. As the moon burst through the thinning clouds and took up the challenge of lighting the scene, the Seer emerged from his meditation and joined the three of them on the grass.

'You are nervous,' he said, calmly. As usual, it wasn't a question.

'You could say that,' Randall agreed, smiling.

'I just did,' said the Seer. He could be very literal, at times.

Randall just looked at him. The smile faded.

'Why?' asked the Seer. It was the first question any of them had heard him ask. The rise in intonation was an odd sound, coming from him.

Randall just looked at him again.

There was a pause…

'Why?' he repeated. 'Why do you think? We're about to travel into the past and wipe out this timeline. Everything here will be gone. In a few hours you won't even exist anymore.'

'Will I not?' another question, the lilting rise in his voice was there again. Quite pleasant sounding actually, even though the question was rhetorical this time. 'Never mind,' he continued, before Randall could answer, 'the universe knows what it is doing.'

'The universe might,' said Randall. 'It's us I'm worried about.'

'But you *are* the universe, RanJam. Did you not know?'

Three questions in a row, thought Randall. *I'm honoured.*

'What the hell does that mean?' he asked, and then, immediately, 'I'm sorry. I'm on edge. Please, would you explain?'

Cindi pulled herself out of her meditation to listen.

'You are the universe. You are its eyes and ears, thoughts and feelings, hopes and dreams. It *is* you. You *are* it. As are we all.'

This time, when Randall just looked at him again, he wore the dumbfounded face that had begun to carve its confused creases deeply into his countenance over the last few months. He couldn't think of the next question. It probably wasn't even worth it…

'Go on…' he said, almost wearily.

'You are a small piece of universe, Ranjam. Your body is made from the same stuff as the Sun and the Earth. But you *know* you are a small piece of universe, RanJam. You are self-aware, which is a good trick for a bag of water with some chemicals in it, if you think about it. And what is more, you are aware of the *rest* of the universe too. You can see it and ponder about it. You can measure it and begin to understand it. The universe is self-aware through the consciousness of living beings. We are its mind.'

Randall's eyes opened as wide as they would go. His jaw dropped and his eyebrows clambered back up Mt. Forehead. He'd never thought about it like that before. What an astounding insight.

I knew it, thought Cindi.

The evening passed.

The moon continued to rise, unstoppably, towards its zenith...

And now, at just after two in the morning, or the "Height of the Moon" as it was recorded in the scrolls, dressed in the specially fabricated twenty-first century clothing Marcus had printed before they left the bunker, Marcus and Randall climbed into the pod and strapped themselves in.

They performed the pre-launch checks calmly, without stress. The rocket was primed... the batteries had all reached optimal charge... the computer was displaying the "Ready" message...

They sat serenely in their luxurious office chairs, staring at the screen. Cindi stood a short distance from the pod with the acolytes, watching them nervously. Suddenly, she could hold back the tears no more and they flooded out of her in a flurry of sobs. Randall felt the wave of compassion wash over him as he turned to look at her one last time. There were twenty-two seconds to launch.

His unconscious mind seemed to be trying to tell him something, but there was no time left now to figure out what...

He tightened his straps and held on to his seat with increasingly whitening knuckles, staring longingly at Cindi, the love of his short life and mother of his unborn child, trying, and failing, to hold back the tears. He held out a hand to her, but she was out of reach.

In front of the transceiver section, unseen by Marcus and Randall, the Seer calmly walked forward and sat down cross-legged on the grass, just beyond the glowing field that had formed around it. He carried a blanket, a jug of water and a broad smile.

The countdown continued counting down; trimming the last few seconds off the last minute of the world. There were only seven more of them left.

'Are you ready?' asked Marcus.

The enormity of what they were about to do hit Randall square across the amygdala. He began to panic.

'No,' he replied, terrified. 'I'm not.'

'Me neither. Let's go.'

Other parts of Randall's brain started throwing up random memories of his trippy dream on the first night in the valley...

Marcus pulled a lever set in the floor of the pod - the safety release mechanism. With a clunk the clamps opened. The pod jolted forward and settled with a short creak onto the runners of the ramp.

He counted down along to the readout. 'Three... two... one...'

Randall ripped his eyes away from Cindi's and looked around quickly, trying, and failing, to find the Seer. He'd lied to them...

The computer ignited the rocket engine in the back of the pod and they shot forward abruptly, the acceleration pinning their heads to their seats. As they rumbled along the track the glowing chrono-matrix field around the transceiver quickly went from red, to orange, yellow, green, blue, indigo, ultra-violet...

... the acceleration seemed to die away... the scenery blurred and morphed around them... light drained out of the world... slowly shifting to the red as the wavelengths stretched, then fading quickly through the shades of night until only the faintest deep red glimmer could be seen... it started to get warmer...

Randall knew already what Marcus was going to say next...

'I was expecting this,' he said, right on cue. 'The tachyon field is sucking our inertia and forward momentum out of the system. Light is in the infra-red range now. Time has slowed for us already. This should be a smoother ride than we thought...'

Just then, ahead of them, the faintly glowing field around the transceiver flickered momentarily. And again, more noticeably this time. Marcus peered past the overhead screen at the disturbance.

'What was that?' he shouted, panicked.

Randall shook his head and stared. His dream memories had dried up; they were past the point that the Seer had allowed them to see up to…

They were close to the transceiver now and within the grip of the chrono-field, so from their perspective they didn't seem to be moving very fast at all, about walking speed in fact, even though they knew they were actually moving about a hundred times faster. Time, as Marcus knew it would, had indeed slowed down for them. So they were in the ideal place to have an unrivalled view of the scene that was slowly, very slowly, much too slowly for Randall's liking, unfolding inside the transceiver's swirling tachyon field.

It started with what was seemingly a liquid of some kind, lit by the eerie glow of the field and spewing out in slow motion from the nothingness in the centre of it. They didn't know it yet, but "spewing" was exactly the appropriate word.

Around the middle of the field, the disturbance was growing alarmingly. A shimmering, insubstantial, translucent structure seemed to be manifesting right in the centre, where the pod would be in only a few more seconds. Was it some sort of time echo? Reflected back at them from a moment in the future? It seemed to be taking the same shape as the pod, but what was the strangely viscous fluid all about? They watched the alarming scene unfold, unable to do anything about it.

Wet looking wobbly bits were materialising around the shower of liquid. They seemed to be convulsing and going into spasm, like an animal being slowly ripped inside out. It was macabre and disturbing. The deep red tint to the light didn't help the overall look of the thing either.

A structure seemed to slowly solidify around the hideous vision. A chair, like a dentist's chair, was holding the unfortunately inside-out animal, or whatever it was, in place, as it too gained more solidity. Bones and brains and guts and lungs gradually formed, from the inside and working outwards, while Marcus and Randall watched through horrified eyes. The musculature formed… then the skin.

And then they collided with it. Not some kind of strange echo then.

As they made initial contact, the chrono-field brightened instantly, shining a brief but dazzling multi-hued beam straight up into the sky. But then it faltered and failed; collapsing around them in an instant. All of a sudden, time was back. With a vengeance. And so was their forward momentum. From their point of view they accelerated from walking speed to eighty-eight miles per hour only a fraction of a nanosecond before they crashed and rebounded off sideways onto the grass, spinning like a top. The other pod did exactly the same thing, but in the other direction; like a pair of huge billiard balls in a giant's trick shot.

The newly formed body in the dentist's chair was thrown clear and landed with a crumpled thud and a grunt at the Seer's feet.

There, lying on the grass, covered in a seemingly endless spray of vomit and groaning the groan of the terminally hung-over... was George James Junior.

Wiping his face with a rag, the Seer gave him the jug of water, put the blanket around him, and helped him to sit up.

George drank some water.

More vomit happened...

Chapter 41.

The Earth, and indeed the Milky Way in general, in all contrariness to mathematical opinion, continued, stubbornly, to exist.

So much for maths, eh?

Randall opened his eyes. He wasn't expecting to be able to. He wasn't expecting to have any eyes to open, or any awareness, or will, or volition with which to do achieve such a miraculous feat as vision. Or anything else for that matter. He certainly wasn't expecting to see Cindi running over to help him.

Puzzled, dizzy, but grateful for the miracle, he fumbled with his straps and dropped sideways out of the crashed pod as the latch came loose. He was unhurt up to this point but landed awkwardly and sprained his wrist falling from the chair.

Typical.

Cindi ran over to help him up, equally as shocked as Randall at her continued ability to help anyone. Or for there to be anyone left to help. She hugged him, soaking his fake Nike sweat-shirt with the tears still running down her cheeks.

In front of the transceiver, semi-conscious and shivering in his blanket, George Junior looked up and shouted a semi-coherent warning to the world in general.

'They're coming,' he half shouted, half slurred.

Then he threw up again and passed out.

The acolytes gathered around to assist; they seemed completely unperturbed. They lifted George by the corners of his blanket and carried him carefully into the Seer's hut. The Seer followed, eloquently saying nothing.

Marcus, groaning, opened his eyes. He too was surprised to still have any. He was groggy; if he'd have thought for a second he would have worked out the answer to his next question before he even asked it.

'What the fuck happened?' he shouted. It was the first time Randall or Cindi had ever heard him swear.

'Randall's dad happened, I think,' replied Cindi.

'Then how come I can shout anything anymore?' Marcus added, surprise and alarm growing on his face by the millisecond. 'Why didn't the Galaxy do the big firework? *Why are we still here?*' He was shouting even louder now.

The Seer emerged from his hut and walked towards them.

'Please,' he said, soothingly, 'there is no need for alarm. Now is the day after the last day, spoken of in the scrolls. We're into scroll one-more-than-two now. It is time to make the change to the universe. Your destiny awaits.'

Faces fell. 'The universe?' cried Randall. 'You mean the Galaxy don't you?'

The Seer's habitual smile was gone. 'I know what I mean,' he replied.

Randall shook his head in despair. 'Today the world, tomorrow the universe sort of thing? This just keeps getting worse and worse doesn't it?'

Seven hours later, the "one unseen" woke up. He was still half drunk, and horribly hungover, but he was at least now capable of coherent speech.

Sort of.

The problem was with his memory. He seemed to have left it floating around in the universe somewhere. Somewhen? Whatever.

He could remember his name and what had happened to him, even how he'd managed to will himself back into being as soon as the chrono-field reached full potential, but the nagging feeling of lost knowledge was overwhelming him. The strain of trying to dig all the details out of his hungover mind was almost paralysing him, but one thing he did know was that he must continue to try. He *did* have a plan. It *would* work... if only he could remember what it was.

The Seer looked concerned, an expression nobody had seen on his face before. Not even the acolytes.

'I need to go in,' he said.

Randall, who had got over the shock of meeting his dad for the first time in his life, and then realising that he was now, technically, a few weeks older than him, was worried too.

'Go in?' he said. 'What do you mean?'

'I must bring his memories to the surface of his mind and transfer them into mine. The knowledge buried there will change the universe. We must get access to it soon, or we are lost.'

'How are you going to do that?' asked Cindi.

'Quiet...' said the Seer, giving her a sideways glance. 'Watch...'

He took several deep breaths and sat down next to George, who was lolling on the bed looking like death microwaved.

The Seer placed his hand on George's face, the fingertips at specific meridian points above and below the left eye. He screwed up his eyes in concentration, breathing in short, rapid breaths, as he minutely adjusted the position of his fingers...

Marcus, watching from the back of the hut, couldn't help noting how strikingly similar [33] the technique was to one carried out by an ancient character in a very popular TV show from the twentieth century. He couldn't remember the name of the show. "Star" something was it? He couldn't bring it to mind.

The Seer took another deep breath. 'I'm going in,' he said, quietly.

'My soul to your soul. My vibration to your vibration,' he muttered, in a way that didn't agitate any copyright lawyers at all [34].

He tensed his face up. George's relaxed for the first time since he rematerialized. It almost became beatific as the stress melted away...

... The Seer's face screwed up a *lot* more.

Although it only lasted less than thirty seconds, the Seer learned everything he needed to know. It was a download of epic proportions. He learned...

... that he was swimming through the universe... drifting through memories of aeons past... floating endlessly through void and vacuum...

---

[33] ... but not similar enough to constitute a copyright infringement...

[34] ... like the ones who perked up when they read the word "Batmobile" in chapter fifteen.

through time and space... through endless nebulas, endless galaxies... through clusters and superclusters... even towards the great attractor of the universe itself... and beyond... the multiverse... the macroverse... the megaverse... and beyond again... infinitely fractal in every dimension... infinitely scalable... infinitely complex... infinitely connected ... everything was numbers. At first he shied away, but realisation soon dawned and he immersed himself in them... adding and subtracting tentatively at first, but then multiplying and dividing joyously, counting everything there was to count and working with the results to produce axioms and formulae from first principles... Pythagoras's theorem was a breeze... Integration and differentiation was next... He solved the Riemann hypothesis almost as an afterthought... He derived *the* long sought after formula for prime numbers, instantly spotting the flaw in the time-travel mathematics as he did so... then he was through the numbers and out the other side... the formulae coalesced into form... more memories came drifting across the bridge between their minds... he relived the experience inside the Moon when George had nearly died... was shocked by the alien memories buried there like wriggling maggots... he heaved them back over the bridge... he was back in the room.

As his hand slipped limply from George's face, he slumped down on the bed, moaning, 'I need to rest. But there is no time.' Getting unsteadily to his feet, he walked towards his small cupboard. He was exhausted, sweating. Cindi held him up.

'What did you see?' shouted Randall, from the foot of the bed.

'The puppet masters,' he replied, opening a door in the cupboard and taking out a small leather bag tied with twine. He spotted, for the first time, that the door travelled through an arc of roughly one point nine radians as he opened it.

'What puppet masters?' shouted Randall and Cindi. They exchanged puzzled looks with Marcus.

The Seer opened the leather pouch and emptied the contents into a nearby mug. He estimated there was a tad over seventeen grams of it in all. A strong and not unpleasant smell of herbs filled the hut.

'The ones who have been pulling the strings for billions of years,' he said, quietly. He could barely lift the mug.

'What strings?' shouted Randall, Cindi and Marcus.

Picking up the kettle, with difficulty, the Seer filled the mug, just because he could, with exactly three hundred millilitres of hot water. 'We have twenty-four hours until they come. There will be nine of them. They will try to stop us. It is written in scroll three, chapter five.'

Cindi noticed something unusual. 'You just used numbers without looking at your hands.'

'He must have picked it up from me,' said George Junior, leaning up in bed for the first time. 'Hello, Marcus, you're looking well. Hello, son.'

Chapter 42.

The chaos inside the Moon was quite unlike anything in the multi-billion-year history of the alien race. The ordered structure of their existence was shattered beyond repair. Some of them were even scared, a novel experience for members of such a powerful civilization.

For the last six hours they'd watched in wonder as the chronosphere showed them George's mind displayed there for all to see; hovering around the little village watching his son. Except they couldn't see it very well, of course, what with all the jostling for position. And they had no idea that he was actually planning something until it was way too late. They assumed the odd glitch in the machine couldn't possibly affect the outcome of their multi-billion-year plan. It was unthinkable!

They'd spotted the problem immediately upon returning to the Andromeda Galaxy. The Milky Way should have disappeared a few seconds after the last of the ships had popped out of the wormhole, so when it didn't, there was understandable consternation. Uproar, in fact. The plan had failed. The Milky Way, and more importantly, the wretched humans that were destined to infest it, still existed.

After a brief and far from convivial assembly of frantic senior provosts from the provincial strategic planning convivium, a deputation was sent to find out what went wrong.

When they got back to the Moon a couple of hours later they found the chronosphere dead and the whole incredible chrono-cavity shrouded in darkness.

Impossible!

Their chief engineer checked the error logs and found it had failed at the very same moment George Junior had rematerialized; at the end of what was supposed to be the last second of this galaxy's existence.

The multi-paradox proofing shield had gone first, followed instantly by the possibility matrix analyser sub-assembly. The failures then immediately cascaded through the dimensional integration vortex logic banks, into the chronoplastic storage buffer and disrupted the interwobulating paratemporal distributor spigot. The mini-quark regression condenser sprocket flange then finally destabilised and blew the top off the antiphoton fluxion reduction induction combustion chamber's safety valve; which was specifically designed to prevent that very occurrence, obviously. It was a one in a quadrillion chance event.

The engineer, in a manner almost identical to every car mechanic who ever lived on Earth, took a sharp intake of breath through the pursed flaps of his facial orifice [35] as he read the list of failures.

It was the first time a chronosphere had *ever* failed, and they didn't know what to do about it. All of a sudden, their ability to manipulate the possible futures, already compromised by George's interference, had come to a grinding, terrible, halt.

It was a disaster. The whole plan, working so well for over two and a half billion years, had collapsed in the last few hours. Utterly unthinkable.

In a small chamber to the side of the chrono-cavity the most senior members of the deputation were in a crisis meeting.

Their language, having evolved over billions of years, was a highly complex, nuanced, and subtle one, with many formal structures and convoluted grammars that changed not only according to the context of the thought being expressed, but also according to the social caste of the speaker, the previously declared psychological state of the listener, the temperature, the time of day, and the voracity of the available references - amongst other things.

That said, here is the best possible translation into Panglish that can be accomplished by the modern computer aided linguistic techniques...

'What the FUCK happened?' bellowed the commander at his terrified underlings.

There was no answer, only embarrassed glances and inaudible murmurs between them. Their nasal antennae quivered nervously. A few thoracic alarm displays were glowing red under their grey uniforms and the air was thick with fear pheromones.

---

[35] Some things really *are* universal.

There was slime everywhere. Eeew.

'What the FUCK are we going to do?' he shouted again.

There was silence. It was deafening.

'We need to get down there,' said an underling, meekly. It was beyond his rank and station to speak now, but the rules seemed to have been suspended recently, so he took the chance of committing what would have been an unforgivable faux-pas under normal circumstances and provided his opinion, lowly and under-referenced though it was.

'Go down there? Are you mad?' screamed the commander. 'We never go down there. Remember what happened at Roswell? We had to instigate the Earth Shifts in two separate timelines just to erase all knowledge of the technology they back-engineered from the ship we lost. I got a reprimand for that.' His antennae drooped and dribbled a little slime. The others tried not to notice.

'But they have time-travel capability, and we've lost control of them,' said the underling, getting braver. 'Anything could happen now. We have to destroy them and their machine. They cannot be let loose on the universe; the damage would be incalculable.'

'FUCK. He's right,' shouted the commander. 'How many ships do we have left?'

A second sub-lieutenant from the spatial transfer capability enhancement division raised a tentative pseudopod. 'Er, we have an old five thousand seater wormhole-bus, the worm-buggies we arrived in, a couple of asteroid class haulage transports, and a few moon hoppers. Nothing capable of atmospheric work.'

Except the wormhole-bus, thought the commander. It would take about a day to get there, and they'd probably be a flaming fireball when they did, but they *could* get there.

He considered the conundrum gravely for a few seconds before coming to a decision. A terrible decision.

Sacrifices would need to be made...

With an act of will, he stifled the growing redness of his thoracic signalling patch.

'I need a few volunteers,' he said.

Chapter 43.

George was trying to get all the details out in the right order. He wasn't doing very well so far.

Despite the constant questions from Marcus and the others, he'd managed eventually to explain how he'd woken up outside the universe, and how it had grabbed hold of him and dragged him back into a sort of ethereal, time transcending, existence. He'd related how he'd drifted through the endless cosmos, a part of it, and yet apart from it, and how he'd eventually spotted the mathematical anomalies surrounding the Earth and Moon.

His astonished audience couldn't comprehend any of it, but starting at the beginning was the only option, or they wouldn't understand the important bits.

After describing how his memories had gradually returned to him as he explored the expanse of space and time, and how he'd consequently discovered the alien civilization, the engineering of the Moon, and how life on Earth had been altered by its presence, he was now just getting to the important bit. If only they would stop interrupting…

'The aliens created us?' asked Cindi, incredulously.

'Sort of. They changed this planet so that the dominant species, which turned out to be us, would never rise to challenge their position in the universe. The Moon is full of them, they've been here since the beginning. By placing it where they did, they stabilised the Earth's orbit to such an extent that the conditions they wanted were easily maintained within tightly controlled limits. Evolution consequently didn't push us as hard as it did them and we grew weak in comparison.

'Their own world has only a tiny moon, which meant that the orbital wobble of their planet was quite eccentric. The conditions there were much harsher, life didn't colonise the land until much later in their evolution. The aliens themselves are still partially semi-aquatic even now, but they're very much hardier than us. Their evolutionary journey made them tough, pragmatic, incredibly intelligent...'

Randall interrupted, again. 'But I still don't understand why we're still here. Why didn't the Galaxy disappear? We didn't complete the loop. We shouldn't be able to have this conversation at all.'

'The maths is wrong,' said George, simply. 'They've been manipulating us all along. The fundamental basis of mathematics, as humans have worked it out, is all wrong. It's why there are still so many unsolved problems.'

Six eyebrows raised. They didn't believe him.

'I'll prove it to you,' he said. 'Marcus, what's the first prime number?'

Marcus looked puzzled. 'Two. Obviously,' he said. 'Divisible only by itself and one.'

'Randall, Cindi, do you agree?'

They nodded their heads. The proof was part of Randall's earliest research into mathematics. He *knew* it was true.

'Wrong,' said George.

Marcus began to protest, but George waved him down. 'Perhaps our host would care to enlighten us?' he said.

The Seer, who'd drunk the herbal infusion and was waiting patiently for it to kick in, opened his eyes and looked up at them. They seemed different somehow. Darker, out of focus.

'The clue is in the name,' he began. 'The word "Prime" means "first", or "supreme". It is the first number. The primary number from which all others are made. The start of the sequence. It is the number one, and its twin is negative one.'

Marcus saw the implications. 'But Vortex Theory is underpinned by the distribution pattern of twin primes. If this is true and there's a previously undiscovered prime pair before the five/seven pair, then that would shift the matrix out of step with the two/three manifold...'

'Exactly,' interrupted George.

'... and the voxel field would notch to the next possibility along...'

'Keep going. You've nearly got it...'

A look of shock crept slowly onto Marcus's face...

'... which means we've had the polarity wrong. Completing the loop is exactly the opposite of what we should have been doing all along.

Travelling to the past would have actually created the paradox that would have wiped out the Galaxy. Not the other way round. Holy shit.'

'Bingo!' said George. 'And the fact we're all still here proves it. That was their ultimate plan. They altered us enough to make us weak and ineffective, and then gave us the ability to paradox the Milky Way away for them.'

'You just saved the Galaxy,' said Cindi, in awe. *And we nearly destroyed it*, she thought to herself. She sat down heavily.

'But why?' asked Randall. 'What did we ever do to them?'

'Not what we did. What we would have done if they hadn't changed our evolution. We wouldn't even be human really if they hadn't interfered. We would probably have ended up more like them, stronger, more sophisticated, pragmatic. *We* would have eventually become the dominant race in the universe.

'They discovered time viewing technology billions of years ago. Not like our Temporal Splitters, only capable of viewing the past; they scanned the possible futures and picked the one they wanted, even engineering it into place. Before long they saw that in the far future the dominant species on Earth would eventually out-compete them and win the battle for dominance in the universe. The Earth had to be eliminated. The Moon was their solution. Giving us the ability to create a time paradox that would eventually remove our own galaxy also gave them the chance to expand into Andromeda. There was no point in doing that unless they could get rid of the Milky Way; they're destined to collide in a few billion years. It was a win-win for them.'

'You have to admire their long term planning,' said the Seer.

His eyes now looked very strange. His pupils had expanded to almost three times their normal size. His concoction had kicked in at last. He got up and headed for the door, full of energy all of a sudden.

Outside, a little way from the doorway to his hut, he raised his arms in the air and let out a single, loud, 'whoop' to the sky.

He sat down and held out his hands. Within seconds the acolytes had gathered in a circle and were sitting down to join theirs with each other. A few seconds later the circle - the circuit - was complete. The Seer began uploading his instructions into their eager minds...

Just over a hundred kilometres to the north, Detective Chief

Inspector Bailey (he'd given himself the field promotion as he was now the only survivor of the expedition) drove across the dusty plain towards the mountain range to the south.

He had nothing to lose now. There was no way he was going to survive on this terrible island for long, he knew that. But the thought of taking out the bitch Lehman first was driving him every bit as much as he was driving the truck.

He was on a *mission*. It was about a hundred kilometres to his destination, he had a full tank of fuel, one of Savage's eyeballs in his pocket, and he was wearing sunglasses.

Lady luck had been on his side so far, that's for sure. Getting the truck out of the crater was easier than he'd been expecting. The wind, which rose a couple of hours after clambering out of the poison gas, had blown most of it away, so all he'd needed was a wet rag tied over his face to mitigate the worst of the remaining fumes. The rest was easy. Quite easy anyway, he was still coughing a lot.

Getting Savage out of the cab and ripping his eyeball out had been the hard part. He still wiped his fingers on his trousers in horror every time he thought of it, but then he would look at the shiny new laser rifle sitting on the passenger seat, and the terrible memories would subside again.

The spare drone he'd discovered in the back of the truck had been activated, and he drove slowly with one eye closed, watching the video feed and the way ahead simultaneously. He knew where he was going thanks to the strange pulse of light shooting into the sky a few hours ago. It could only have come from the bitch Lehman and her resistance friends. They had finally betrayed their position, presumably thinking the WP expedition was no more.

And now he was closing on them. Soon he would be victorious...

He smiled.

It had been a while.

The download to the acolytes took over an hour, during which time George managed to eat a light meal and even walk around a little. His muscles were stiff - he hadn't used them for twenty-five years - but now he was feeling a lot better. The sensation of the Sun on his skin had revived him enormously, but he was still horribly hungover.

Randall and Cindi were in shock, holding each other for support while Marcus walked around the village with George; like old friends catching up after a long absence.

Without a word, the circle broke up; the acolytes immediately heading for the time machine. The Seer stood up, his eyes still strangely defocused.

'We have much work to do,' he said. 'Please do not disturb us, it is very delicate work and our psychic bond will dissipate if we are disturbed.'

Without another word he joined the acolytes, who were happily starting to take the time machine's transceiver apart.

Before long they merrily started on the Batmobile and the pods too.

Less than a hundred kilometres to the north, and closing slowly but steadily across the rough terrain, DCI (assumed) Bailey spotted a shiny metallic flash on his drone feed. The bright reflection of the Sun beamed into the drone's camera only briefly, but it was enough for Bailey to target the drone, and himself, more accurately.

He risked an extra burst of speed and patted his rifle.

'Soon,' he said.

Chapter 44.

Big Bill, having retired early for a nap after a long afternoon boasting about his recent exploits to any female bird who would listen, was dreaming his favourite dream.

It was the one about the twin magpie sisters with the sexy tail-feathers, and it was just getting to the good bit. He'd enjoyed the part where he'd demonstrated his hunting prowess as the chattering magpies looked on, impressed with his athleticism and skill; he was past the bit where he sauntered over to them and offered them some of his kill; and now he was getting to the bit where they tittered amorously and lifted their, as has been previously mentioned, sexy, tail-feathers.

The most adventurous, or possibly the tartiest, of the magpie sisters twittered into Bill's ear. The really good bit was approaching. He turned to listen to the seductive cackling...

Odd. The noise she made wasn't sexy at all. In fact, it wasn't even bird-call. She was making a noise very much like the one made by Markynanda's strange metal machine that he'd escorted from the coast recently. He blinked his dream eyes at her (in his dream, they were both still good). Turning to face him, she opened her beak... and made a noise like a gear change in a haulage lorry.

Bill opened his good eye. His military instincts, so close to the surface again after his recent mission, hammered on the door to his alertness like a landlord demanding rent arrears. Instantly he was on alert, all senses to maximum.

It was nearly dark now, so his eye wasn't good for much. He closed it and listened. There it was, the faint rumbling of an engine. He sniffed the air. Again, a very delicate whiff of the same sort of stinky fumes he'd had to put up with all the way back to the valley.

He hopped up to the top of the tree - his lookout post - and scanned the horizon.

When he spotted the light in the sky a couple of minutes later, he swore an unutterable string of profanities to the world in general and flew as fast as he could towards the village.

The time machine was transformed.

Throughout the day, as Marcus, Cindi and Randall looked on with increasingly worried expressions, the Seer and his small group of acolytes had created a completely new machine out of the parts of the old. The transceiver, the two pods, and the Batmobile had been stripped down and reassembled into the strange looking contraption that now stood in the field.

The transceiver was up on its side, held there with a wooden A-frame. Coils and batteries from the pods surrounded it, tied to the circular chassis with ropes made from vines. The delivery ramp, which used to be on an incline leading down to the transceiver, had been shortened and reversed. Now it was more like a short ladder, almost a stairway, tied there with vines and leading to the vertically arranged machine covered in coils that the acolytes had built.

Vague memories of another popular sci-fi TV series from the ancient past drifted through Marcus's mind. Or was it the same program he was thinking about earlier? He couldn't remember the name of the show, they all sounded so similar back then anyway. "Star…" something or other. Whatever.

The engine of the Batmobile had been taken out, stripped down, and reassembled in a completely different way under the ramp. Thick cables ran from it to the battery bank and from there to the mysterious new machine. Actually, there were cables everywhere, scattered all over every part of it, and on the ground, and the ramp. In previous centuries it would have been called "Heath Robinson", or possibly "an accident waiting to happen".

While Marcus's eyebrows did the dance of the terminally perplexed, the Seer filled the fuel tank from the Batmobile with river water from a large leather pouch. Then he switched the engine on.

Amazingly, it spluttered into life. Clouds of steam poured from the exhaust.

'We are ready,' said the Seer to all assembled, which was everybody. He looked to the Moon, squinting, seemingly checking the skies.

'Ready for what?' Randall finally managed to shout over the noise of the engine.

The Seer lowered his gaze. 'I'm sorry,' he said. 'You must be wondering what we've been doing all day. Let me explain...'

He'd got them!

Bailey watched the group of strange looking people and the dog's breakfast of mysterious machinery from the drone feed to his terminal. What the hell was that? It looked like some sort of vertical circular frame covered in coils with a short ramp leading up to it. What were they planning?

Whatever it was he had to get there soon to stop them doing it. Clouds of exhaust gasses could clearly be seen rising around the strange structure, it looked like an engine had just been fired up. They must be getting ready for something. Grabbing his rifle, he shifted down a gear and thundered along the field by the river leading into the valley.

'... but time *is* space,' said the Seer, above the babble of questions and the rumble of the engine.

'It's true,' muttered George Junior, now back to full strength. 'Listen to him.' They didn't pay him much attention.

Marcus was getting agitated. It was a ludicrous plan, doomed to failure.

'Getting the vortex to shift to another point on the surface of the Earth is one thing,' he said, 'and that was difficult enough to calculate, but to another planet entirely? In a totally different galaxy? Six billion years in the past? Are you crazy?'

'If we stay, we die,' said the Seer, calmly. 'If we go, we win. This is not vortex mathematics as you know it. It uses similar principles, but it is far more advanced. It is probably closer to the kind of technology the aliens use when they travel between galaxies, but I suspect they will never have put it to this use before.'

'Why not?'

'Because it is inherently dangerous. What we are about to do will change the past and future of the universe. We are playing God.'

'On the big screen,' muttered George.

The commander of the alien deputation, with a crew of eight staunch comrades that he'd persuaded, bullied, cajoled, dragged, and in one case drugged to come along with him to operate the craft, was getting ready to die. Again.

They'd transferred copies of their minds back to their home planets via wormhole before getting into the ship and setting off for Earth. They knew they wouldn't be coming back. Not in these bodies anyway.

As they entered the Earth's atmosphere, the roaring heat began to strip away the radio antennae and other smaller, flimsier, parts of the exterior. No matter, they wouldn't be needing them, they would make it to the ground in more or less one piece, the trajectory was assured. When they hit the ground, it would be directly on top of the little village where their nemesis had rematerialized. The humans would do no more damage to their perfect universe...

Marcus, with Randall and Cindi holding each other for support next to him, was standing at the bottom of the ramp with George, the acolytes, and their pets. They looked like a well organised camping expedition about to set off. They each carried equipment and supplies, indeed, it looked like the whole village had been packed into bags, and there was a tense atmosphere amongst them.

The Seer was messing with a dial he'd taken from one of the pods, setting it to the number of years they would be travelling into the past. Originally it had read six hundred years, which would have taken them back to 2008, so all he had to do was add a few zeros. Seven of them actually.

The batteries, which had also been stripped down and reconfigured to act more like capacitors, were finally charged. He switched the machine on.

Instantly, the old circular frame of the transceiver sparked with electricity, shooting between the coils arranged around it like baby lightning making its first, tentative, steps towards Earth. A bright glow began to form in the centre of the disk, the air began to sparkle and shine, swirling, spiralling in to the middle.

It looked like a very brightly lit toilet being flushed. Sideways.

The Seer, for the last time, looked into the sky. He watched the fiery orange glow directly overhead, growing bigger by the second as the alien ship came apart and hurtled towards them at thousands of miles an hour in multiple balls of flame. The last verse of the last chapter of the scrolls he had studied all his life.

'Please. We must go now,' he said excitedly as he hurried them all up the ramp and into the shimmering light. It almost looked like a mirror made of water.

'But I don't understand...' said Randall, as he disappeared into the swirling vortex in the heart of the new machine.

One second later, Big Bill followed him.

Chapter 45.

Time, as was previously noted, is tricky stuff. So when a paradox of universal scope suddenly happens to the cosmos six billion years in the past, the changes it induces can take some time to catch up to the "present moment".

Whatever that means...

As Bailey sped through the trees and burst into the field next to the village, headlights and laser blazing, he was met not by an astonished Daphne Lehman, Randall James, and the leaders of the resistance scum, but by a thousand tons of screaming white hot alien spaceship.

He tugged on his 'tache and looked up.

'Oh shi...

In deep space, nine alien minds, travelling home through the ancient wormhole transit system, suddenly vanished into nothing... along with the transit system itself...

The Moon disappeared...

The Earth... changed...

A good chunk of this corner of the universe... altered.

Six billion years in the past, on an alien planet in a distant galaxy, Randall, with his pregnant wife-to-be beside him, opened his eyes on the shore of a beautiful lake set in a dark plain fringed by distant mountains - and peered straight into those of a very oddly alien looking animal with a cute, almost seal-like, face...

The next day he found out they were very tasty.

Epilogue.

Randaal James relaxed in his NullGrav unit absent-mindedly peering through the view port at the stars. He couldn't actually see the stars - the nebula was in the way - but he didn't mind. The gentle drumming of meteoric dust on his habitat-shield and murmur of the engines was relaxing, and had put him in a nostalgic mood. Happy memories of his school day were playing out in his mind.

Lying in his exceptionally comfortable low gravity field, in the immaculate sleeping quarters of his luxurious space cruiser, on the outskirts of the beautiful triple spiral galaxy he was studying, he was relaxing at the end of a longish diurnal period, cheerfully downloading memories of his wonderfully happy time at the excellent space academy he graduated from.

He'd downloaded attentively at the academy and attained good grades in the essentials - Temporal Mechanics, Astrophilosophy, Cosmotheology, Exobioethics, Anthropology, Meditation, and Media Studies - but he chose not to pursue the exciting life as a solar system administrator recommended by the careerdroid.

Randaal had other plans...

He was lucky enough to be a relatively wealthy man, that is to say, he had a rich and varied social life, and innumerable loyal friends, many of whom had helped Randaal to achieve the greatness he was now on the brink of. His friends were like an extension to his family, and they, along with his scientist father and beautiful wife Cindy, had greatly assisted Randaal with his latest discovery.

The comms chime sounded. The database he'd been promised had arrived...

Excitedly, he opened the contents page of the trove of documents he'd downloaded from the incredible civilization on the new planet he'd discovered. This was the first "first contact" scenario for over ten thousand years, and it would make Randaal famous throughout the known galaxies. The database he'd just received was sent to him as a gift from their illustrious leader, no less.

As he examined the list of entries, he discovered it was a record of their ancient legends and founding myths going back, if he could believe it, billions of years. Unexpectedly, the computer found the syntax and grammar of the alien language not entirely dissimilar to Earth Standard...

He opened the first document, materialized some popcorn, and began watching.

'In the beginning,' intoned the document, 'RanJam and the founders arrived from the long lost future...'

THE END.

Afterword.

Up until the ninth of November 2016 - the day before I finished the draft manuscript - there was a nice little gag in chapter twelve about the first President Trump romping to power in Randall's alternate timeline.

Who would have thought that out of a ninety-five-thousand-word dystopian sci-fi comedy novel - that would be the only thing to come true?

It was meant as a joke for heaven's sake.

By the way:

The numerical data about the Moon in chapter nine is all correct. Ten minutes of arc on the Moon really is exactly Pi miles long. Can you figure out why?

The rest of the numbers in chapter nine and the prime number stuff in chapter forty-three are based on the work of Dr. Peter Plichta, from his book "God's Secret Formula", and on "Who built the Moon?" by Christopher Knight and Alan Butler.

"Isotropic vector matrix" and "voxel" are borrowed from the work of Nassim Haramein.

The "Electric Universe Theory" can be studied on YouTube by searching for "Thunderbolts project".

The megalithic yard was first proposed by Professor Alexander Thom in the 1960's and further expanded by Christopher Knight in his book "Civilisation One".

The Earth Shifts are based on the theories of Charles Hapgood and Immanuel Velikovsky.

Lightning Source UK Ltd.
Milton Keynes UK
UKOW03f0331280217

295456UK00001B/139/P

9 781910 105832